Also by Michael McBride

NOVELS

Ancient Enemy
Bloodletting
Fearful Symmetry
Innocents Lost
Predatory Instinct
The Coyote
Vector Borne

NOVELLAS

F9
Remains
Snowblind
The Event

COLLECTIONS

Category V

MICHAEL MCBRIDE

BURIAL GROUND

A NOVEL

FACTOR V MEDIA

For Madison…and your adventures to come

Special Thanks to Jeff Strand, Gene O'Neill, Leigh Haig, Bill Rasmussen, Ann Collette, Shane Staley, Brian Keene, my family, and all of my loyal readers, without whom none of this would be possible.

Beware lest you lose the substance by grasping at the shadow.

— Aesop

Out of the dusk a shadow,
Then, a spark;
Out of the cloud a silence,
Then, a lark;
Out of the heart a rapture,
Then, a pain;
Out of the dead, cold ashes,
Life again.

— John Banister Tabb

The person who runs away exposes himself to that very danger
more than a person who sits quietly.

—Jawaharlal Nehru

Prologue

Andes Mountains
Northern Peru
October 11th
9:26 p.m. PET

The screams were more than he could bear, but they didn't last long. Panicked cries cut short by wet, tearing sounds, and then finally silence, save the patter of raindrops on the muddy ground. From where he crouched in the dark recess of the stone fortification, hidden from the world by a screen of tangled lianas and the sheeting rain, he had listened to them die.

All of them.

The signs had been there, but he and his companions had misinterpreted them, and now it was too late. It was only a matter of time before they found him, and slaughtered him as well.

Hunter Gearhardt donned his rucksack backward, and wrapped his arms around its contents. He'd managed to grab a few items of importance once he'd recognized what was about to happen, and he needed to get them out of the jungle. More bloodshed would follow if he didn't reach civilization. With their inability to access a signal on the satellite phone, there was no other way to deliver the warning. It was all up to him now, and his window of opportunity was closing fast.

His breathing was ragged, too loud in his own ears, his heartbeat a thudding counterpoint. He couldn't hear them out there, but they had attacked so quietly in the first place that the silence was of little comfort. They were still out there, stalking him. There was no time to waste. He needed to put as much distance between himself and his pursuit as possible if he were to stay alive long enough to get down off the mountain. And even then, they knew this region of the cloud forest far better than he did.

He wished he'd had the opportunity to find his pistol, but it would have been useless against their superior numbers. His only hope was to run, to reach the river. From there he could only pray that he would be able to survive the rapids and that they wouldn't be able to track him from the shore. It was a long shot. Unfortunately, it was also his only shot.

Tightening his grip on his backpack, his muscles tensed in anticipation.

Through the curtain of lianas, the rain continued to pour, creating puddles in every imperfection in the earth and eroding through the steep slope ahead, which plummeted nearly vertically into the valley below. If he fell, they would be upon him in a flash. And that was only if he didn't slide over the lip of the limestone cliff and plunge hundreds of feet through the forest canopy to his death.

Hunter drew a deep breath and bolted out into the night. Narrowing his eyes against the sudden assault of raindrops, he focused on the rocky path that led down toward the river. The ancient fortress wall flew past to his left, a crumbling twenty-five foot structure composed of large bricks of chiseled obsidian nearly consumed by the overgrowth of vines, shrubbery, and bromeliads. Every footfall summoned a loud splash he could barely hear over his own frantic breathing. The mud sucked at his boots as though he were running through syrup. He barely managed to stay upright long enough to reach the path, little more than a thin trench between rugged stone faces. The ground in the channel was slick and nearly invisible under the muddy runoff. His feet slipped out from beneath him and he cracked his head on a rock. His momentum and the current carried him downward onto a flat plateau dominated by Brazil nut trees draped with vines and moss.

The roar of the river became audible over the tumult of rain. He was so close—

A crashing sound from the underbrush to his right.

He glanced over as he crawled to his feet and saw nothing but shadows lurking behind the shivering branches.

More crashing uphill to his left.

He wasn't going to make it.

Willing his legs to move faster, he sprinted toward the edge of the forest and the cliff beyond. The waterfall that fired from the mountain upstream was a riot of mist and spray that crashed down upon a series of jagged rocks. Hopefully, there was enough water racing through now thanks to the storm to have raised the level of the river above them. Either way, he'd rather take his chances with broken bones than the hunters that barreled through the jungle, leaving shaking trees in their wake.

They were all around him now and closing fast.

If he could just reach the rock ledge, he could leap down into the river and allow it to whisk him away.

Ten yards.

Through the trees, he could see only fog, but he'd been down here enough times to know that the foaming whitecaps flowed only fifteen feet below. He would then need to navigate a series of waterfalls, and keep from drowning long enough to reach the bottom of the valley and the start of the real trek.

Five yards. Another four strides through the snarl of brush and he could make his leap. Just three more strides and—

Searing pain erupted in his back as he was slammed from behind. Something sharp probed between his ribs to either side of his spine. The mist-shrouded cliff disappeared and he saw only mud rising toward his face. The backpack against his chest broke the brunt of his fall, but his forehead still hammered the ground. He saw only blackness and tasted blood. The weight pounded down on his back, knocking the wind out of him. Something clawed at his shoulders as he slid forward.

The pressure on top of him abated and whatever had stabbed him was yanked out as he rolled over the ledge and tumbled into the fog toward the frigid river, unable even to scream.

Chapter One

I

Pomacochas, Peru
October 14ᵗʰ
8:38 a.m. PET

By the time Wes Merritt caught up with the children, they were giggling and prodding the corpse with sticks.

This certainly wasn't how he had envisioned starting his day.

He had been down on the rickety floating dock on Laguna Pomacochas, loading his 1953 DHC-2 #N68080 seaplane with supplies for a quick jaunt down to the City of Chachapoyas, capital of the Amazonas Province of Peru, when the three boys had raced up the wooden planks and begun chattering at him in Quechua. Far from fluent in the native tongue, he had captured just a handful of words here and there, but the few he understood told him he wouldn't be making the flight that morning. Two words had stood out specifically. The first, *aya*, meant "dead body." And the second, undoubtedly the reason they had come directly to him rather than the policía, was a word that he had been called on more than one occasion himself.

Mithmaq. The Quechua word for stranger.

As Merritt approached the bank of the river and the partially concealed body, he wondered if the children had been mistaken. What little skin he could see was mottled bluish black, and the hair was so thick with mud and scum that it was nearly impossible to determine the color. The Mayu Wañu, or, roughly translated, Resurrection River, rose and fell with the seasons, alternately climbing up the steep slope behind him in the spring into the primary rainforest, where the massive trunks of the kapok trees bore the gray discoloration of the water, and diminishing to a gentle trickle mere inches deep during dry spells. The body was tangled in vegetation, half-buried in the mud on the shore, half-floating in the brown river. Swirling eddies attempted to pry it loose to continue its journey along the rapids into the lagoon, but the earth held it fast.

"*Sayana*," he said in Quechua. Stop.

The boys looked up at him, then slowly backed away, their fun spoiled. One, a shaggy-haired boy of about twelve in a filthy polo shirt and corduroys that were far too short, peeked at Merritt from the corner of his eye and gave the corpse one final poke. All three whirled and sprinted back into the jungle, laughing.

Merritt eased down the slippery bank. The mud swallowed his feet to the ankles and he had to hold the limp yellow ferns to maintain his balance. A quick glance at the ground confirmed the only recent tracks belonged to the barefooted boys. He breathed a sigh of relief. There was a long list of creatures he didn't want to encounter in his current compromised position.

Merritt hauled himself up onto the snarl of branches that shielded the body from the brunt of the current and crouched to inspect the remains. Judging by the broad shoulders and short hair, the corpse belonged to a male, roughly six feet tall, which definitely marked him as a foreigner to this region of northern Peru. The man's shirt and cargo pants had both absorbed so much of the dirty river that it was impossible to tell what color they might once have been. Twin black straps arched around his shoulders. His left leg bobbed on the river, the laces from his boot squirming beneath the surface. His right foot was snared in the branches under Merritt, the bulk of the leg buried in mud. Both arms were pinned somewhere under the body.

Back home in the States, this was when the police would arrive and cordon off the scene so the forensics team could begin the investigation. But he wasn't back home. He was in a different world entirely. A world far less complicated than the one he had left behind, one that had initially welcomed him with overt suspicion, but had eventually introduced him to a culture that had made him its own. And although his white skin would always brand him a *mithmaq* in their midst, no place in the world had ever felt so much like home.

He looked to the sky, a thin channel of cobalt through the lush branches that nearly eclipsed it from either bank. Blue-capped tanagers darted through the canopy in flickers of turquoise and gold, and common woolly monkeys screeched out of sight. The omnipresent cloud of mosquitoes whined around his head, but showed little interest in the waterlogged corpse, which already seethed with black flies.

Merritt had seen more than his share of bodies during his years in the army, and approached this one with almost clinical detachment. That was the whole reason he had run halfway around the world to escape. There was only so much death one could experience before becoming numb to it.

With a sigh, he climbed down from the mound of sticks and rounded the body again.

"This is *so* not cool," he said, leaning over the man and grabbing one of the shoulder straps.

He braced himself and pulled. The body made a slurping sound as he pried it from the mire and dragged it higher onto the bank. Silver shapes darted away through the water, their meal interrupted.

The vile stench of decomposition made him gag, but he choked down his gorge. It wasn't as though this was the first corpse he had ever seen. A flash of his previous life assailed him. *A dark, dry warren of caves. Smoke swirling all around him. Shadowed forms sprawled on the ground and against the rock walls. One of them, a young woman with piercing blue eyes—*

Merritt shook away the memory and willed his heartbeat to slow.

He blew out a long, slow breath, then rolled the corpse onto its back. The angry cloud of flies buzzed its displeasure.

"For the love of God..." he sputtered, and drew his shirt up over his mouth and nose.

The man's face was a mask of mud, alive with wriggling larvae, the abdomen a gaping, macerated maw only partially obscured by the tattered remnants of the shirt. Merritt had obviously dislocated the man's right shoulder when he wrenched it out of the mud. The entire arm hung awkwardly askew, while the left remained wrapped around a rucksack worn backward against his chest, the fingers curled tightly into the fabric as though afraid to release it even in death.

Merritt groaned and knelt above the man's head. He really wished he'd brought his gloves. Cupping his hands, he scooped the mud from the forehead, out of the eye sockets, and from around the nose and mouth. The skin beneath was so bloated it felt like rubber.

Even with the brown smears and discolored flesh, Merritt recognized the man immediately. He had flown him and his entire group into Pomacochas from Chiclayo roughly three weeks ago. So where were the rest of them?

His gaze fell upon the rucksack. If it was still here when the policía arrived, nothing inside would ever be seen again. Corruption was a way of life down here.

Merritt unhooked the man's claw from the fabric, pulled it away from the bag, and set it on the ground. He unlatched the clasp and drew back the flap. At first all he saw was a clump of soggy plants. He moved them aside and blinked in astonishment.

"Son of a bitch."

II

Hospital Nacional Docente Madre Niño San Bartolomé
Lima, Peru
October 15th
9:03 a.m. PET

Eldon Monahan, Consul-general of the United States Consulate in Peru, waited in the small gray chamber, handkerchief over his mouth and nose in preparation for what was to come. At least this time he'd had the foresight to dab it in Vicks VapoRub before leaving the office. He wore a crisp charcoal Turnbull & Asser suit with a navy blue silk tie, and had slicked back his ebon hair with the sweat that beaded his forehead and welled against his furry eyebrows. His piercing hazel eyes absorbed his surroundings. It took all of his concentration to suppress the expression of contempt. Slate gray walls lined with ribbons of rust from the leaky pipes in the ceiling surrounded him on three sides. The fourth was a sheet of dimpled aluminum that featured a single door with a wide horizontal handle, the kind of freezer unit they installed in restaurants. Twin overhead sodium halide fixtures were mounted to the ceiling on retractable armatures. The diffuse beams spotlighted the scuffed, vinyl-tiled floor in front of him.

God, how he hated this part of his job.

A baccalaureate degree in Political Science from Stanford and a doctorate in Politics and International Relations from Oxford, and here he was in the basement of what could only loosely be considered a hospital by American standards, in a backward country half a world away from where he really wanted to be. Paying his dues. Mastering the intricacies of foreign diplomacy. Whatever you wanted to call it, it was still about as far as a man could get from a seat on the Senate floor. Here he was, thirty-six years old and not even an actual ambassador.

The screech of his grinding teeth reminded him of his hypertension, and he tried to focus on something else. Anything else.

The door in the aluminum wall opened outward with a pop and a hiss. Eldon took an involuntary step in reverse. The morgue attendant acknowledged him with a nod as he wheeled the cart into the room and centered it under the lights. A sheet, stained with a Rorschach pattern of mud and bodily dissolution, covered the human form beneath.

"What can you tell me about the body?" Eldon asked in Spanish through the handkerchief.

"The policía dropped it off last night," the attendant said, visibly amused by the Consul-general's squeamishness. He wore a yellow surgical gown and cap, finger-painted with brown bloodstains. "Found him way up north in the Amazonas. Textbook case of drowning, you ask me."

"How do we know he's an American citizen?"

"The pilot who flew him into Pomacochas recognized him."

"But he couldn't identify him?"

"That's all I know. You're supposed to be the man with the answers. Shouldn't your embassy have told you all of this?"

Eldon flushed with resentment.

"Where are his possessions?" Eldon asked.

"What you see is what you get."

Par for the course.

"Let's just get on with this then, shall we?"

With a curt nod, the attendant pulled back the sheet to expose the head and torso of the corpse.

Eldon had to turn away to compose himself, but he couldn't chase the image from his mind. The man's face was frosted from the freezer, his skin tinged blue. Chunks of flesh had been stolen from his cheeks, earlobes, and the tip of his nose. There were still crescents of mud in his ear canals and along his gum-line. He was dramatically swollen from the uptake of water, which caused his epidermis to crack as the deeper tissues froze.

"You don't want to see the parts I left covered," the attendant said. He smirked and clapped Eldon on the shoulder, eliciting a flinch. "Do what you need to do quickly. We don't want him to start to thaw."

Eldon removed the digital camera from the inner pocket of his suit jacket and leaned over the body. Three hurried flashes and he was out the door without another word. He needed fresh air, humid and oppressive though it may be. He ascended the stairs and crossed the lobby through a churning sea of the sick and injured, oblivious to their curses as he shouldered his way toward the front doors. As soon as he was outside, he ducked to his left, cast aside the handkerchief, and vomited into an acacia shrub.

Sometimes he absolutely hated his life.

He wiped his mouth with the back of his hand and headed to where his car idled in the emergency bay. The driver waited outside the open rear door of the black Mercedes-Benz E-Class sedan, and ushered him inside. They drove in silence, save the whoosh of the wind through the open driver's side window. The chauffer repeatedly raised his hand to cover his nose as discreetly as he could.

Wonderful, Eldon thought. He'd obviously brought more than pictures of the corpse with him.

The Mercedes turned through the black, wrought-iron gates of the Consulate. Armed Marines saluted as the car passed and rounded the circular island of rainbow flowers, from which twin poles bearing the American and Peruvian flags rose.

Eldon didn't wait for the driver to come around to open the door. He just wanted to get this over with. As he ascended the concrete stairs beneath the gray marble portico, he focused on the task at hand: upload the digital images into the program that would compare them to the passport photos of all Americans still in Peru, starting with those who had registered their travel plans with the Embassy. Once he had positive identification, he could make his calls, get the body embalmed and on a plane back to the States, and wash his hands of the whole mess.

"Mr. Monahan," the receptionist called in a thick Spanish accent as he strode into the lobby. She pronounced it *Meester* Monahan.

He pretended not to hear her and started up the staircase beside her desk. The middle-aged Peruvian national climbed out from behind her post with the clatter of high heels.

"Mr. Monahan!"

With a frustrated sigh, he turned to face the frumpy woman and raised the question with his eyebrows.

"There's a man waiting for you outside your office."

"I assume he's been properly cleared?"

"Yes, Mr. Monahan."

"Thank you, Mrs. Arguedas."

He ascended to the top floor and headed toward his office at the end of the corridor. A man with shaggy chestnut hair and pale blue eyes sat in one of the chairs outside his office, a filthy backpack clutched to his chest. The armed soldier beside him snapped to attention when he saw Eldon, while the other man rose almost casually from his seat. His discomfort was apparent, yet he seemed less than intimidated by his surroundings. He had broad shoulders and a solid build that suggested he had been shaped more by physical exertion in the real world than by countless hours in the gym.

Eldon extended his hand and introduced himself as he approached. "Consulate-general Monahan."

"Wes Merritt," the man said. He offered his own hand, but retracted it when he noticed how dirty it was.

Eldon was silently grateful. He lowered his hand, gave a polite smile, and gestured for the man to follow him into his inner sanctum. The soldier fell in behind them and took his place beside the closing door.

"How can I be of assistance, Mr. Merritt?" Eldon seated himself in the high-backed leather chair behind his mahogany and brass Royal Louis XV Boulle desk, and made a show of checking his watch.

"Thank you for seeing me, Mr. Monahan. Especially with no notice."

Eldon waved him off, but he would definitely have to discuss such improprieties with Mrs. Arguedas.

Merritt opened the flap of the rucksack and set it on the edge of the pristine desk.

"I wanted to give this to you in person. You know how the authorities are down here…"

Eldon nodded and fought the urge to shove the vile bag off of his eighteenth century antique desk.

"I found this with the body you just visited at the morgue. I need to make sure it reaches the right people back home." Merritt shrugged and rose as if to leave. "You'll make sure it does, Mr. Monahan?"

"Of course. Thank you, Mr. Merritt. I'm sure the decedent's family appreciates your integrity."

Merritt gave a single nod in parting and exited through the polished oak door.

His curiosity piqued, Eldon plucked a handful of tissues from the box on the corner of the desk and walked around to inspect the bag. He gingerly moved aside a tangled nest of dried vines and appraised the contents. His eyes widened in surprise.

He leaned across the desk and pressed the "Speaker" button on his phone.

"Yes, Mr. Monahan?" Mrs. Arguedas answered.

"Please hold my calls."

"Yes, sir."

He disconnected and returned his attention to the rucksack.

Now he really needed to figure out to whom the body in the morgue belonged.

III

Advanced Exploration Associates International, Inc.
Houston, Texas
October 15th
8:47 p.m. CDT

Leonard Gearhardt stood before the wall of windows on the fiftieth floor of Heritage Plaza, hands clasped behind his back, staring out over the sparkling constellations of downtown, the Toyota Center, the theater district, and the distant suburbs beyond. Smoke from the Montecristo No.4 Reserva swirled around his head in much the same manner as the thoughts within. His gray eyes settled somewhere between the reflection of the aging man he had become and the cold black sky. He wore a hand-tailored Italian suit that cost more than most new domestic cars and polished leather shoes crafted from the suffering of some young animal or other. His ghost-white hair was slicked back to perfection and his eyebrows tweezed. Only his callused hands and the wrinkles in his sun-leathered features, which most considered distinguished, marred the illusion of grandeur he paid a fortune to perpetuate. But none of that mattered now. He was already sixty years-old, and felt as though he had aged a lifetime in the last hour alone.

He had been expecting the call for so long that it had almost been a relief when it finally came.

Leo turned away from the window and surveyed his domain through the Cuban haze. He was surrounded by the fruits of his professional labors: a sextant salvaged from the wreckage of the *Neustra Senora de Atocha*; a golden idol of the Mayan god Chac; various coins from the nefarious pirate frigate *Queen Anne's Revenge*; the gilded horn of a narwhal; the porous skull of an ankylosaurus; and paintings and sculptures from myriad expeditions, all encased in Lucite and stationed precisely around the luxuriously appointed office. There were Medieval and Renaissance texts, monographs from centuries past, and handwritten diaries on alarmed shelves. A lifetime of amassed history and riches, but only a single framed picture of the son who had died in pursuit of his father's favor.

Leo had built his empire from his own sweat and blood, from his adventurous spirit and refusal to be cowed by fear. What had begun as a simple salvage operation on the Gulf coast had blossomed into a forward-thinking, diverse corporation with varied interests from exploration and artifact discovery and recovery to management of high-risk extraction sites and implementation of high-tech mining solutions. He had raised entire battalions of sunken warships thousands of feet from oceanic trenches, discovered indigenous ruins on every continent, mined ore and shale from the steepest slopes, and found and named more extinct animals and dinosaurs through fossilized evidence than any other single individual.

The way Leo saw it, he had conquered the world.

And now here he stood amid the trappings of wealth, and all of it was for naught. In just under twenty-four hours, his son's remains would arrive at George Bush Intercontinental Airport, sealed in plastic wrap and boxed in a crate, where the body would be immediately sequestered by the Division of Global Migration and Quarantine under the watchful eye of the CDC. The Consul-general in Lima had been aghast at his insistence that his son's body not be embalmed, that he'd rather delay interment by potentially several days to weeks. There was no way he was going to let some foreign doctor with marginal medical training butcher what was left of his only child. Hunter Gearhardt's body would be autopsied by a real medical examiner and then prepared by a mortician, regardless of the cost.

The image of his son's features pressed beneath cellophane rose unbidden and he slammed his fists down on his desk. Ashes flew and the cigar rolled onto the lacquered wood. He watched the clear coating melt away from the glowing cherry before snubbing it in the ashtray.

Never in his life had he felt so helpless. There was no problem to solve or challenge to overcome. He couldn't step back and brainstorm solutions. His Hunter was dead, and what were his first words? Not an outpouring of remorse or a curse upon the gods who would rob him of the only thing in his life that should have mattered, but "What did he have in his possession?"

He removed a bottle of Macallan 1939 from the bottom desk drawer, poured two-fingers into a glass, and hurled the bottle across the room. A rich amber river ran down the wall to join the shards of forty year-old glass, assailing him with the scents of vanilla toffee, peat and wood smoke, and time.

This small man with his big title, this Eldon Monahan, had listed off his son's belongings like he'd been checking off a grocery list. One Black Diamond Sphynx rucksack; one four-liter MSR Dromedary hydration bladder; one Garmin eTrex Summit HC handheld GPS unit; various items of no appreciable value: possibly collected samples of vegetation, and three four- to six-inch feathers; and, most interestingly of all, two black- and gray-streaked rocks weighing eighteen and twenty-six ounces respectively, and a native headdress of indeterminate origin, cast in pure gold. The Consulate had confiscated the headdress as Peruvian law frowned upon the unlicensed plunder of its heritage, however, Monahan had promised to include multiple photographs with the rest of Hunter's belongings. There had been no mention of the Les Baer 1911 Premium II pistol or the machete Hunter would have been carrying, nor mosquito netting, change of clothes, or food reserves. Hunter hadn't even packed any of his testing supplies, his various rock hammers, satellite phone, or geologic field spectrometer. All indications pointed to a hurried abandonment of camp. His son had taken only what he could quickly pack and what would be of importance when he escaped the jungle and reached civilization.

Hunter was a world-class geologist with the best academic pedigree that money could buy, though he had proudly earned it on scholarships alone. A B.S. in Geology from Texas A&M, and a Ph.D. in Mineral Exploration and Mining Geosciences from the Colorado School of Mines. Throw in the fact that he had spent the last five years reconnoitering some of the harshest unexplored terrain on the planet, and more questions were raised than answers. Something had happened to his son, and he'd move heaven and earth to find out what.

During their final communication via satellite uplink, Hunter had intimated that his party was close to reaching its destination, quite possibly within the next couple of days. Leo had heard the smile in his son's voice, the faint tremble of excitement. He had felt it, too. In that moment, he had been as proud of his son as any father could be, but he had also been his boss. So instead of heaping praise and adoration on Hunter, he had demanded daily reports and detailed his expectations in businesslike fashion.

That had been twelve days ago now, and the last time he would ever speak to his son.

Two black- and gray-streaked rocks.

A native headdress of indeterminate origin, cast in pure gold.

Although it was subtle, he heard his son's posthumous message loud and clear. It was almost as if Hunter had known there was a good chance he might not return to Pomacochas alive, and had brought items only his father would understand. Clues that would stymie a layman, but purvey important information at the same time. The headdress was simultaneously a location marker and a red herring meant to distract whoever found the backpack like a starling with a bit of foil. The real message was in the rocks, the seemingly mundane black and gray chunks of earth. They were stratified layers of volcanic magnetite and quartz, *placers*, streaks that pointed like arrows to their ultimate quarry.

Hunter had found it.

For a heartbreaking moment, Leo's pride eclipsed his sorrow and guilt.

IV

Harris County Medical Examiner's Office
Houston, Texas
October 18th
4:32 p.m. CDT

Despite their indignation that the body had not arrived embalmed, the CDC had cleared Hunter's remains of potentially contagious viral and bacterial agents, infestation, and acute pathological processes in record time, thanks in large measure to Leo's government connections. After taking possession of his son's cleaned and sterilized belongings, he had followed the Medical Examiner's van from the airport, cell phone glued to his ear, calling in every favor he possibly could. By the time he arrived at the Harris County Medical Examiner's Office near the Astrodome, the Chief Medical Examiner had already been informed that he would be observing his son's autopsy. It had cost him a fortune—how quickly the mayor and the good Senator had forgotten how much he'd contributed to their last campaigns—but he had gotten exactly what he wanted, as he had known he would. Now, he stood back toward the rear of the room, staring at his son's lifeless carcass on the cold autopsy table.

He couldn't take his eyes off the body. Whatever had once been his Hunter had long since abandoned that broken vessel, which now only vaguely resembled the child he had known for the past thirty-two years. He couldn't bear the sight of where Hunter's flesh had been chewed away by animals that had had no right to violate its integrity. He wanted to throw himself onto the body, to wrap his arms around the boy he had loved unconditionally and breathe his own life into the young man who still had so much living left to do. A surge of rage rippled through him. Heat suffused his face and his fists curled so tightly that his fingernails bit into his palms.

"Christ. They could have at least rinsed it off for us," the Chief Medical Examiner, Dr. James Prentice, said. His glasses perched almost miraculously on the tip of his bulbous nose, framing brown eyes that didn't appear to blink. The overhead recorder started and stopped with his voice, providing a whirring undertone to his words. "All right. Let's get this show on the road, shall we?"

He took a pair of scissors from the sterile tray beside him and cut twin lines up each pant leg and through Hunter's underwear. His shirt hadn't made the return trip to the States with him. Prentice dropped the tattered fabric in the biohazard waste container for incineration and pulled the retractable hose nozzle out from under the table. With a squeeze of the handle, he sprayed Hunter's face and chest with scalding water. Smears of mud broke apart and dissolved. The runoff traced the contours of his musculature in streams that rolled down the lines of his ribs and into the side gutters of the table. Swirls of brown water turned around the drains. The flesh beneath the grime was a sickly gray and marbled with blue veins and black bruises. There were dozens of insect bite marks.

"Bird mites," Prentice said.

Superficial lacerations bisected Hunter's clavicles and pectorals. Leo could see exposed sections of the lumbar spine through the gaping hole in the abdomen where it appeared that piranhas, or some other small-mouthed, toothy critters, had absolved him of a large measure of his viscera. Apparently they had also feasted upon his manhood. Once Prentice had cleaned his legs, he carefully rolled Hunter's body over. His back, buttocks, thighs, and calves were all livid with blood, cellular fluid, and retained river water.

A quick spray through Hunter's hair and the ME was about to roll him over again when he abruptly paused. Leo noticed several sections where the fluid was beginning to drain in foul, sappy ribbons. Prentice leaned closer and inspected the wounds. There were two large punctures over the lower aspect of the rib cage. He sprayed directly into the holes and clumps of clotted blood and mud washed out.

"Twin dorsal stab wounds, one to either side of the spine," Prentice said. "On the right: entrance between the tenth and eleventh posterior ribs. Visible comminuted fracture of the tenth rib. Inferior displacement of a triangular fragment. Approximate penetration: three inches. On the left: entrance between the seventh and eighth posterior ribs. Oblique fractures of both the superior and inferior ribs without significant displacement. Again, approximate penetration of three inches."

Leo eased forward to better see between the isolation-gowned men. In addition to the Chief ME, there were three other men. He'd only been introduced to one, another medical examiner who had apparently bathed in aftershave before entering the room. Leo had already forgotten his name.

"Both wounds were inflicted by the same weapon as evidenced by the external characteristics of the soft tissue. No telltale indications of a sharpened edge. No "V" pattern from a blade being twisted or widening of the laceration consistent with rapid retraction. Clean incisions through the *latissimus dorsi* and *erector spinae* muscles. The epidermal layer is curled inward with no sign of attempted healing. Superior and lateral sides of the wounds are smooth, the inferior ragged, indicating downward force. No bruising to suggest impact from a hilt or handle. Obviously a rounded implement. Not a knife. Definitely antemortem." He stuck his finger into the wound. "Angled entrance with inferior curvature of roughly thirty degrees. Possibly some kind of hook with a shallow arch."

Leo closed his eyes and struggled to keep from imagining the look on his son's face as someone repeatedly stabbed him in the back with a hook. The doctor's monotonous voice and vivid play-by-play description of his son's injuries faded. He thought about how much pain Hunter must have endured, and it made him sick to his stomach.

The whine of a Stryker saw roused him from his thoughts. Dr. Prentice had finished performing his external inspection and rolled the body onto its back. He had created the Y-incision and reflected the skin from Hunter's chest to expose his sternum and ribs. Prentice used the saw to cut through the lateral sections of the rib cage, and removed the front half as a single unit like the dome of a serving tray to expose the contents of the thoracic cavity.

"The mediastinum is shifted to the right, compressing the right lung against the ribs." The recorder whirred as Prentice poked and prodded with a dull steel implement. "Both lobes of the contralateral lung are contracted and shrunken, a consequence of the tension pneumothorax created by the left dorsal puncture wound."

"Excuse me, Dr. Prentice," the younger man at the head of the table asked. Leo suspected he was a medical student as he hardly looked like he was out of his teens. "If the collapse of the lung was caused by the stab wound, shouldn't it have caused an open pneumothorax, and thus only a mild lateral shift of the esophagus, trachea, and blood vessels?"

"Remember to begin with observation, not speculation. Stick to the known facts. This man's thoracic anatomy reflects a tension pneumothorax, meaning that *no air* entered the pleural space."

"You're suggesting the water provided the necessary seal to hold the wound closed?"

"I'm not suggesting anything. I'm stating the facts as I can clearly see them. We know from the conjunctival petechiae, the fluid in the sinuses, and the water obviously retained in the tissues in the right lung, that his death was due to asphyxiation, specifically by drowning. He had to *breathe* the water for it to reach his sinuses and lungs. Look here." Prentice indicated the left lung. "Note the difference in the color and consistency of the lung tissue. The left lung did not retain water like the right, which indicates it was non-functional prior to the fatal aspiration."

"Then he couldn't have been stabbed more than a few seconds before immersion in the river."

"Correct. Otherwise air would have entered the pleural space and created an open pneumothorax."

Leo had heard more than enough. He turned and stormed out of the room.

Someone had stabbed his son in the back and disposed of his body in the river.

Now it was time to do something about it.

V

Glenwood Cemetery
Houston, Texas
October 21st
10:25 a.m. CDT

Marcus Colton passed like a ghost through the somber gathering, a faceless mourner amid the tearful women and stoic men. The day was gray, the branches on the weeping cypress trees brown. Only the manicured lawn and shrubs provided a background of color for the marble and slate headstones and crypts, most of which were draped with moss. A procession of limousines idled at the bottom of the gentle slope, beyond which he could see the hint of Buffalo Bayou. Somewhere nearby was the final resting place of Howard Hughes.

The funeral director stood at the head of the grave on an elevated platform, hands clasped behind his back, bible on the lectern before him. He was in the middle of reciting the standard speech about eternal souls and lives prematurely extinguished. The polished oak casket hovered over the hidden hole beneath it, enclosed by a cage of red velvet ropes.

A woman sobbed to his right and drew several consolatory pats on the shoulder. In the race for sympathy, she trailed only the man sitting in the front row, a man that he knew needed none.

Colton skirted the periphery of the gathering and vanished behind the branches of a cypress. Gearhardt didn't acknowledge his arrival. He just stared straight ahead through his Serengeti sunglasses, his face stripped of all emotion. Only the clenched muscles in his jaws suggested that he was suffering, and not as a symptom of sorrow.

Colton studied the scene as he waited, memorizing faces and attaching names to those he recognized. His dark hair was cropped military short, his acute gray eyes hidden behind black lenses. His suit matched every other. He looked like anyone else, everyone else. Forgettable.

When the funeral director finally finished speaking, Gearhardt rose and cast what appeared to be a snarl of dead weeds onto the casket, ran his fingers along the smooth grain, and walked away from the gathering. He wound a circuitous route through the maze of ornate headstones and joined Colton beneath the sagging branches.

Colton didn't offer his condolences. Empty platitudes changed nothing. Instead, he waited patiently for his sometimes employer to speak. He had done enough jobs for Gearhardt in the past to know how the man worked. Gearhardt was in charge, but he allowed Colton autonomy over the operation itself. It was a rare combination, and Colton respected him all the more for it. Over the course of the past two decades, they had combined for more than a dozen successful reclamation projects, all of which had gone off without a hitch. There were always complications, but Colton was in the business of providing solutions, none of which came cheap. The mere fact that Gearhardt had called him first spoke volumes about the situation.

"I trust you found my offer satisfactory," Gearhardt said.

"As always." Colton allowed the silence to linger between them, interrupted only by the distant din of voices and the whistle of dove wings.

"You have reservations."

"I'm not exactly sure what you expect from me on this one. On the surface, it's a straight locate-and-excavate job, with maybe a few more bureaucratic hoops to jump through to secure the land lease, but when you factor in your boy's death, I have to wonder if the assignment isn't of a more personal nature."

"Have you ever known me to be sentimental in business matters?"

"No."

"Then give me your assessment."

"The Medical Examiner's report clearly states that Hunter's death was by drowning, and while there were two large puncture wounds in his back, they weren't necessarily dealt with the intent to kill. With easy access to guns and machetes, an assault with a hook seems highly unlikely and reflects none of the traits of a crime of passion. If the men you sent with him had wanted him dead, his body would never have been found. Not in that jungle.

And his associates were well screened. In my opinion, none of them are capable of the kind of treachery you suspect."

"That kind of wealth can alter anyone's behavior patterns."

"True. However, in this case I find it hard to believe. I've thoroughly reviewed their dossiers and see nothing that would imply the potential for subterfuge, let alone violence."

"Then we're in agreement. They're all dead."

Colton nodded slowly. Gearhardt surprised him with his cool reasoning, especially under the circumstances.

"I've been giving this a lot of thought," Gearhardt said. "Initially, given the sheer amount of money we're dealing with here, I suspected some sort of conspiracy. But the more I step back and rationalize the situation, the more I believe that external forces contributed to my son's death, and the probable deaths of the rest of his expedition party."

"What do you propose?"

"I'm not quite sure, which is why I contacted you."

"The location is inherently rife with variables. There are countless species of venomous snakes and insects. That high in the cloud forest, the weather is notoriously unpredictable. They found his body in a seasonal river only after it had receded far enough to strand his body. And then there's the human factor. There are still indigenous tribes hidden in the Andes, isolated groups that might not take too kindly to any unheralded intrusion. And you can't discount the potential involvement of the Peruvian government. If word of your party's destination and what might be hidden there somehow leaked, there could be soldiers crawling all over the site. Then there are diseases we don't even know about yet, and for most we do, there are no inoculations. Any of hundreds of factors could have ultimately contributed to their deaths."

"I understand the overall scenario. I want to know what your gut tells you."

Colton pondered his answer carefully. With so many variables, anything could have happened. The idea of soldiers and natives didn't feel plausible. The Ejército del Perú, the Peruvian Army, would most certainly have mowed them down with automatic weapons and made sure their bodies were never recovered, and with their intimate knowledge of the Amazonas region, the natives would never have allowed the party to reach its goal in the first place if they'd felt threatened. So what *was* he thinking? Disease? Hunter's body had been cleared of viral and bacterial pathogens by the CDC itself. What did that leave? He hated to vocalize the words that came out of his mouth next, but he could see no other response.

"I don't know."

"And that's what troubles me, too."

Colton paused and watched the mourners disperse from the gravesite and pile into the waiting limousines. The sun peeked through the cloud cover, but vanished as quickly as it had appeared.

"I want to show you something," Gearhardt said. He reached into his jacket pocket, removed a folded handkerchief, and held it in his open palm. "These were with my son's possessions. They found them in his backpack."

Colton accepted the proffered handkerchief and felt the weight of its contents, or rather the lack thereof. He unfolded the fabric and studied the objects for a long moment before he looked up to find Gearhardt staring intently at him.

"I don't get it. Are these supposed to mean something to me?"

"I was hoping they would. They definitely meant something to Hunter, and for whatever reason he thought they were important enough to make sure he packed them in his hurry to flee the camp. We're dealing with a vast wilderness consisting of thousands of square miles of the harshest unmapped and unexplored terrain in the world. They're obviously a clue of some kind, but to what? The location? Or something else?"

Colton inspected the objects a while longer, then refolded the handkerchief over them.

"I have to admit, you've piqued my curiosity. However, it remains to be seen if you truly require the kind of dynamic solutions I provide."

Gearhardt nodded, but Colton sensed his hesitation.

"What are you holding back?" Colton asked. He returned the handkerchief, which disappeared into Gearhardt's pocket again.

"I have two stipulations."

"You know that's not how I work."

"Humor me, Marcus."

Colton licked his lips and tilted his face to the slight breeze. The smell of flowers and turned earth washed over him. There was something in the air, something intangible, something that constricted his intestines and fluttered in his stomach. It was a sensation to which he was entirely unaccustomed. He lowered his eyes to meet Gearhardt's and raised an eyebrow.

"I want this entire expedition documented," Gearhardt said. "Camera crews, various experts, the whole nine yards."

"You do remember that your son was stabbed twice in the back, right?"

"How could I forget?"

"If you want me to babysit a bunch of civilians under potentially dangerous conditions, you're going to have to double your offer. I expect four million and a twenty-percent stake."

"Done."

"And your second condition?"

"I'm going with you."

VI

Turlington Hall
University of Florida
Gainesville, Florida
October 22nd
3:03 p.m. EDT

Dr. Samantha Carson leaned back in her desk chair and sighed. Twin stacks of essay tests dominated the blotter in front of her computer monitor. She should have made the exam multiple choice and keyed the Scantron. That way she would have already been done and sitting comfortably on her couch at home with a glass of wine and the new Danielle Steel novel, her guilty pleasure. Instead, she could only stare at the heaps of paper with their scribbled chicken scratch and dread the daunting task ahead.

Normally, she would have already been cruising through them, but the news of Hunter's death had hit her like a truck. Granted, she'd only seen him a handful of times over the past five years, but they'd practically grown up together. While other children had been firmly rooted in their nuclear families and living normal lives, she and Hunter had been toted around the world by their parents like baggage, which wasn't to say their childhoods had been terrible, only…different. They had lived for months at a time in tents and haphazardly assembled Quonset huts in some of the least hospitable locales, playing in jungles rather than on jungle gyms, in the most remote regions of the world rather than in safe little cul-de-sacs. For a long time it had felt normal. It wasn't until she began to develop her own identity and discovered the need for friends and an actual sense of belonging that she realized what she was missing. Hunter had been a brother to her in every way but genetically. It just hadn't been enough for her, and she had jumped at the opportunity to matriculate at one of the most prestigious private prep schools in the country. Hunter had stayed with his parents, but they had always spent holidays and breaks together, and she had looked forward to every minute of it.

And now he was gone.

Sam had promised herself she would make more of an effort to stay in contact, but since her parents passed—her father from esophageal cancer and her mother from the resultant loneliness of a broken heart—she had buried herself in her work and held life at arm's reach. Her professorship was demanding. As co-chair of the paleoanthropology department, she was charged with securing funding and negotiating site leases in addition to the everyday tasks of teaching undergraduate anthropology and graduate-level studies in Indigenous South American Cultures. Throw in the responsibility of being one of the world's foremost experts on the Chachapoya culture, and it was a rigorous schedule that dominated nearly every free second of her time, which forced out all of the things she had originally abandoned the life her parents had given her to pursue. In the end, as the adage goes, she had become just like them, an isolated relic in the modern world doing everything in her power to live in the past.

Sam turned away from her desk and looked out over the commons. Young men and women with their entire lives ahead of them bustled between classes, milled around bike racks, tossed Frisbees and kicked hacky sacks. Here she was, barely thirty-three years-old with a tenured academic post, a leader in her field, and it saddened her that she couldn't identify with any of them.

There was a knock on her office door, followed by the slight squeak of hinges. It was about time her teaching assistant showed up. There were still the next morning's lesson plans to formalize, and she wanted to discuss a couple of changes in the—

"You look just like your mother." She recognized the voice immediately and whirled to face her visitor. "She had those same little freckles under her eyes."

Leo offered an almost paternal smile. He hovered in the doorway for a few seconds before entering the room and closing the door behind him. He gestured to one of the chairs on the opposite side of the desk. "May I?"

Sam could only nod. She hadn't seen this face from her childhood in years, and other than a few more wrinkles around his eyes, he didn't appear to have aged at all. After a moment, she noticed her mouth was hanging open and felt the need to say something.

"I'm so sorry to hear about Hunter. You know how much I loved him."

Leo's smile grew weary. "I had always hoped that you two would end up together. You had so much in common, and you made a good team, you know?"

Sam inclined her head and swallowed the lump in her throat. In a practiced motion, she swept her long, raven-black hair behind her ears and studied this specter from her past through deep blue eyes. She felt like a child in his presence, as though in a heartbeat her skirt and blouse had reverted to dirty jeans and a baggy T-shirt.

The last time she saw Leo was following her mother's funeral. She had just graduated from the University of Pennsylvania with a doctorate in Cognitive Anthropology and Ethnoscience after spending two consecutive summers, and then a full year, excavating the Chachapoya ruins at Kuelap and the Karajia Tombs. Wide-eyed and overflowing with principles, she had lit into him with a ferocious tirade about his practices of raping the sites he discovered, pillaging the heritage of vanished cultures for profit, and stealing natural resources that should rightly belong to the impoverished masses. She had said things she knew she could never take back, and in doing so had tarnished her father's memory as well, but her beliefs hadn't changed one iota in the interim, and she wasn't about to recant.

As if he knew what she was thinking, Leo said, "Perhaps we didn't part on the best of terms last time we spoke, but I hope to make amends. I won't apologize for the life I've led. With your father by my side, we built a financial empire and salvaged lost societies from their own ruins. And we did so by the letter of the law."

"I don't want to have this argument with you again. Not now."

He waved her off. "That's not why I'm here either. Nor am I here just to catch up with an old and dear friend whom I've always thought of as a daughter."

Sam flashed a wan smile. "Who are you calling old?"

Leo returned the smile. This time it was genuine, not forced, though it contained a measure of sadness that she could feel, even from across the desk.

"I've been thinking a lot about my legacy lately," Leo said. His eyes latched onto hers. "I had always thought that Hunter would follow in my footsteps and take the company to a new level. And now there's no one. Certainly not you. No offense." He sighed. "But this isn't about me. Advanced Exploration will persevere, and your father's share—your share—will be there when you decide to claim it."

"I don't need the money, Leo."

He shook his head as though she had made a poor joke. "Indulge an old man and hear me out. All of this thinking about my legacy led me back to Hunter. In the end, I really don't care what people think about me, or if they do at all, but it's important to me that everyone knows that Hunter mattered, that his life made a difference to the world. And that's why I flew all the way out here to talk to you in person."

Sam saw the sincerity in his eyes. But what could he possibly need from her?

"I want to show you something," Leo said. He removed an envelope from his jacket pocket and passed it across the desk. "Go ahead. Open it."

Sam lifted the flap and slid out a small stack of photographs. She tried to maintain her poker face as she flipped through them one at a time.

"Looks like Mochica. Early eighth century possibly. They were a Pre-Inca society that flourished in the Peruvian coastal region. Renowned for their metallurgy and specifically their headdresses." She scrutinized the images of the ornate golden sculpture. The smooth, arched crown was framed with long filigreed feathers that nearly glowed, rather than the traditional Mochica motif of the eight arms of their sea god. The rounded front was lined with pointed teeth and twin jeweled eyes of what she assumed to be chrysocolla, a blue-green quartz found in copper deposits, which would have made the wearer appear to have been looking out through the open jaws of some frightening mythological creature. The Mochica was definitely a warring tribe; however, their rulers were considered gods, and dressed the part. Yet the mask didn't fit the traditional mold. She looked up at Leo, whom she now suspected already knew as much and was holding out on her. Was he testing her? "Where did you find this?"

"It was recovered with Hunter's belongings, several miles northwest of Pomacochas, Peru."

"That's outside the known Mochica range." She paused. "If I didn't know better, I'd say it looks almost Chachapoyan. But they didn't demonstrate such craftsmanship or skill working with metals until after their conquest by the Inca. And that section of the Andes would have been well north of their established territory."

"So what's your professional opinion?"

"I'll need to do some research. Can you give me a little time to think about it?"

"Can you think on a plane?"

VII

United States Consulate
Lima, Peru
October 22nd
4:35 p.m. PET

Eldon nearly fell out of his chair halfway through the article when he saw the dollar amount. He leaned closer to the screen and started reading again from the top. There must have been some crucial information he'd missed. His heartbeat raced and his hands trembled. He skimmed: *Mochica headdress from approximately 700 AD confiscated from London law firm...returned to the National Museum of Peru...estimated value...*and here he paused...

"Two million dollars," he said aloud.

He closed the article and initiated a new search. There were hundreds of nearly identical recounts on as many sites. The words changed, but never the dollar amount. *Two million dollars.*

The Consul-general abruptly rose from his chair and sent it clattering to the floor. The room spun around him as he narrowly averted tripping over his own feet in his rush to the small closet in the corner of his office. He threw open the door, grabbed the wooden crate from the shelf, and staggered back to his desk. Casting aside the lid, he swept out a blizzard of Styrofoam popcorn and removed the headdress. He shoved the box away and gently laid the exquisite sculpture on the antique surface. It wasn't quite as elaborate as the headdress on the monitor, which appeared significantly larger with its curling, stylized octopus arms, nor was the craftsmanship quite as stunning, but it was every bit as beautiful. Say it was worth even half as much as the other. That was still a million dollars. Even through discreet channels he could surely get that amount. A million dollars would go a long way toward buying him a seat in the Senate.

The rational portion of his brain struggled to the forefront. What he was considering was wrong. The headdress rightfully belonged to the people of Peru, which was the whole reason he had confiscated it in the first place. If he were to get caught trying to sell it, not only would he lose his job and his tenuous standing in the world of politics, but he would undoubtedly find himself a long-term guest in the ghastly San Juan de Lurigancho prison. There would be no more dreams of grandeur, only the reality that even the life he now lived would no longer be within his grasp.

But if he managed to get away with it...

He racked his brain. Who all knew about the headdress? The man who had brought it to him, Wes Merritt, had secreted it from the local authorities, and presumably hadn't mentioned it to anyone else out of some overdeveloped sense of integrity. Eldon had been prepared to return it to the Peruvian government himself, but for whatever reason had decided to wait a few days, which had turned into a week. Maybe these thoughts had been brewing all along and his subconscious had caused him to drag his feet. Regardless, the internet search had confirmed what he already suspected. He was sitting on a veritable fortune, and the only person with whom he had shared the existence of the headdress was the dead man's father, who hadn't seemed to care about it in the slightest, and whomever he might have told. Granted, the elder Gearhardt's political connections gave him pause, but his only proof was a handful of photographs, and he hadn't once so much as called since. For all Gearhardt knew, Eldon had already sent the treasure to the government, which certainly wasn't world-renowned for its honesty. It could have disappeared at any level in that chain.

So what was the worst-case scenario? Gearhardt contacts the Peruvians demanding the headdress. If that were going to happen, it would have already come to pass. The only real threat now was time. The longer it remained in his possession, the greater the chances someone might discover it. If he quickly offloaded it, who would ever know? But how was he supposed to contact potential buyers? Surely there was some sort of broker who dealt in merchandise of questionable provenance. Such a person would demand a significant cut, but even if he cleared three-quarters of a million dollars, he could still take a great leap toward making his dreams come true.

He just needed to figure out how to contact a broker and start—

His office door opened inward and he nearly had a heart attack. Eldon scrambled to return the headdress to the crate, but in his earlier hurry had unknowingly knocked it to the floor.

"Relax and have a seat, Mr. Monahan."

Eldon realized he needed to play it cool. Thus far he had done nothing wrong. For all anyone knew, he was readying the headdress for return at this very moment. He could easily justify the delay since so much red tape still needed to be cut.

Straightening his tie, Eldon righted his chair, calmly sat down, and laced his fingers on the desk in front of him beside the golden relic. He faced his visitor with a practiced smile.

"Going to have to get someone to come up and take care of this mess for you," a uniformed Marine said, taking one of the seats on the opposite side of the desk without invitation. He raised a piece of Styrofoam between his pinched fingers and blew it into the air.

Eldon recognized the man as the head of the Consulate's security contingent, though he had never bothered to learn his name. The man wore his crisp dress blues, but had already removed his white cap, which now rested in his lap. He just sat there with a smug expression of secret knowledge on his hard face, and stared impassively through unreadable brown eyes. His dark hair had been shorn to the scalp, and had only begun to stubble. Eldon placed him somewhere in his mid- to late-thirties.

"It's customary to knock," Eldon said. "As Consul-general, I—"

"Should have sent that fancy golden mask to the proper authorities several days ago," the man interrupted. "You don't think we allow just anybody to walk in off the street wanting to drop off a backpack without thoroughly searching it first, do you? Since then, let's just say I've made it a priority to follow through on my commitment to your welfare."

Eldon balked.

The Marine simply smirked and inclined his head toward the clock on the wall. Eldon had completely forgotten about the security camera, especially after repeated assurances that no one would be monitoring his personal space without cause or consent.

"I wanted to do a little research on the object before blindly consigning it to such a corrupt entity," Eldon said. "Until this very moment, I couldn't even be sure it was of Peruvian origin."

The Marine made him nervous, but he still held the power here.

"I would imagine you encountered the same information that I did then."

"And what information is that?"

The man smiled and leaned back in the chair.

"What exactly can I do for you, Corporal…?" Eldon asked.

"First Sergeant. First Sergeant Kelvin Tasker."

"State your business and be on your way, First Sergeant Tasker."

"I just wanted to drop by and share some of my thoughts. You see, I've been thinking about a couple of things over the past few days. Like…where exactly did this headdress come from, and more importantly, if one were to chance upon this location, what else might one find?" Eldon's stomach turned sour. "I also just happened to notice that a gentleman by the name of Gearhardt registered travel plans for ten individuals with our Embassy. I'm thinking he might have grown a wild hair to see if he can do a little searching for himself."

"What do you want from me?"

"Nothing." Tasker rose and pinned his cap under his left arm. "I just wanted to swing by and formally introduce myself." He extended his right hand across the desk.

Eldon eased tentatively out of his chair and grasped the proffered hand. Tasker's palm was coarse, his grip uncomfortably firm.

"Nice to officially meet you, Mr. Monahan," Tasker said. "I trust you'll find that I make a splendid partner."

VIII

California Raptor Center
University of California, Davis
Davis, California
October 23rd
6:30 a.m. PST

This was Galen Russell's favorite time of the day. He still had three hours before his first lecture began, and half an hour alone in the lab before the earliest volunteers arrived. Not that he minded the human interaction, but there was simply something magical about this time alone with his feathered friends. He enjoyed the teaching aspect of his post as chair of the Avian Sciences Department at the University of California, Davis, and liked to think he made a difference in the lives of the next generation, which would have to take up arms in the battle for conservation of the few natural resources left unexploited if there were to be any hope for the hundreds of species teetering on the brink of extinction, but this was his true passion. Birds were the link to the past as well as to the future, their behavior patterns far more complex and intriguing than most even suspected. Their evolutionary adaptations were well ahead of the biological curve, and reflected changes in their habitat more quickly than any other higher order of animal life, thus making them the perfect research subjects for the kind of revolutionary theories postulated by pioneers like Charles Darwin and Ernst Mayr. Galen's professional aspirations were far less ambitious. He merely wanted to know everything about them.

He pulled off the rubber hand-puppet designed to mimic the head and neck of a female California condor and set it in the sink for one of the volunteers to clean and sanitize. It stank of chopped mice, but at least the condor chick had eaten reasonably well this morning. She'd been getting scrawny beneath that mass of white down, and for a while he had feared they were going to lose her. When the hiker who discovered her in the Los Padres National Forest, where she had presumably fallen from her nest high up on a cliff-side, first brought her in, Galen had been sure that death was inevitable, but now she was eating, at least enough to survive, and he felt cautiously optimistic about her prognosis. Unfortunately, the Center wasn't able to rehabilitate all of the birds that were dropped off. Of the more than forty raptors they were currently treating, everything from the smallest hawks to golden eagles to the nearly extinct California condor, perhaps only twenty-some would survive. The odds were often depressing, but at least at the end of the day he could hang his hat on the fact that he had done his part to ensure the proliferation of bloodlines, if not entire species.

In addition to his obligations to the university and the Center, Galen was Executive Officer of the American Ornithologists' Union and served as Chair of the Standing Committee on Conservation for the Raptor Research Foundation. He spread himself too thin and he knew it, but if he didn't do it, who would? It wasn't so long ago that the California condor perched atop the food chain and had a range that covered the entire American Southwest. And now? The encroachment of mankind had driven it to the precipice of eradication. Only one hundred and thirty individuals remained in the wild, and most of those were due to the success of captive breeding efforts spearheaded by the San Diego Zoo. How long would it be before the species was extinct, and would anyone care when it happened?   Galen passed through the incubation room, which was suffused with a red glow from the heat lamps, and the kitchen unit that reeked of worms and raw meat. At the end of a short hallway, he entered his office, a small box no larger than the standard cubicle. He slipped out of his brown corduroy jacket as he walked through the doorway and hung it on the hook behind the door. The half-length mirror affixed to it showed him what he feared it would: a somewhat doughy man in his mid-forties, sandy-blonde hair receding from his forehead and thinning on top, glasses that grew thicker with each passing year, and a slender face with crow's feet framing his sky-blue eyes. After a wasted moment of self-pity, he turned away and slid behind his desk. There were a couple of invoices he needed to check and a memo to write to the membership of the RRF, and then he could formally begin his day. He was already rolling his cuffed sleeves in anticipation when he noticed the objects on his desk, which certainly hadn't been there the night before, as it was a rare occasion when he wasn't the one to turn off the lights on his way out.

He leaned forward and inspected the objects. Three feathers had been precisely laid out on his blotter in a clover formation, the calamuses meeting to form a single point. They were remiges, the stiff contour feathers of the wing suited for flight. The base color was mud brown with an extraordinary green iridescence that shifted as it reflected the overhead light.

"Pretty impressive, aren't they?" a voice asked from the doorway.

Galen flinched at the sound and dropped the feathers to the desktop. There was never anyone in the building for at least another half-hour. He looked up to find a tall, wiry man with short, spiked black hair and an expensive suit appraising him through steel-gray eyes. The man raised an eyebrow.

"You…you shouldn't be back here," Galen stammered. He cleared his throat and tried again with more authority. "This is a restricted area. I'm going to have to ask you to leave or I'll be forced to call the police."

The man merely shrugged, and entered the office.

Galen reached for the phone, but the man's words stopped him short.

"I don't think you can tell me which species those feathers belong to, can you?"

The man was right, but Galen was loath to admit it. They were obviously from a species of raptor, of that much he had no doubt. The brown coloration was an expression of melanin, but he had no idea where the strange green iridescence might have originated. The refraction of light on yellow carotenoid pigments like parrots have, possibly? Raptors didn't showcase the flashy colors of smaller birds, even during mating season. They were predators, which meant the last thing they wanted was for their prey to see them coming. The length of the remiges placed this animal's size at that of a condor, but these definitely weren't from a condor as their feathers were nearly universally black. So what did that mean? Had these feathers been doctored in some fashion, or was he looking at some rare genetic mutation? Maybe a new species entirely?

He looked up at the man, who watched him with a curious expression. What did he know that he hadn't shared? Galen decided to play it cool and buy himself some time with the feathers to do some research. Preferably alone. This guy had no business being in here anyway. Come to think of it, how *had* he entered the building? Galen was certain he had locked the doors behind him when he arrived.

"I'll hold onto these feathers for a couple days and try to match them against one of our databases. Every species of raptor is catalogued in there somewhere."

"You'll find that this one isn't, but I have a hunch you already know as much."

"I can run a mass spectroscopic analysis to determine where they originated. It evaluates the ratio of stable hydrogen ions—"

"They were recovered in the Andes Mountains of Northern Peru."

"Impossible. That's the range of the Andean condor. There's only so much room in any ecological niche for predators and scavengers. And condors definitely aren't the kind to share their niche."

"That's your area of expertise, Dr. Russell. I'm only telling you what I know."

"What I know is that you're about two minutes from being manhandled by campus security." He picked up the handset and dialed.

The man casually crossed the room, sat on the edge of the desk, and depressed the button on the phone to disconnect the call before it even began to ring.

"Perhaps I should have started with an introduction." The man smiled, though he still held his finger in place. "My name is Marcus Colton. I work for Leonard Gearhardt and Advanced Exploration Associates International. These feathers *were* found in the Amazonas Province of Peru just under two weeks ago by Mr. Gearhardt's son. We're putting together an exploration party to locate and excavate the region where we assume the younger Mr. Gearhardt discovered the feathers." He released the button on the phone and the dial tone droned in Galen's ear. "We leave in the morning."

"What does this have to do with me?"

"We don't know precisely where the feathers of this particular species might have been found."

"Why not ask the *younger Mr. Gearhardt?*" Galen immediately regretted his mocking tone.

"Unfortunately, he is no longer with us. He died before he could share this knowledge with anyone."

"That still doesn't answer my question. What do you want from *me?*"

"Dr. Russell, from 1985 through 2001, you worked extensively in the field tracking and studying birds in the wild. Thanks in large measure to your efforts in conservation, nearly a half dozen species of raptors have been placed on the Threatened Animals List and significant portions of their natural habitats declared preserves and conservatories. You understand these creatures: their behavior patterns, their relationships to their environment, their lifecycles. Your knowledge would be invaluable in helping us find the proverbial needle in the haystack. We're looking for one specific location in the middle of a vast section high in the unexplored Peruvian Andes, and being able to identify the natural range of this species will significantly shrink the amount of ground we need cover. You will be very generously compensated for your expertise, but more importantly, when you eventually admit what we both already know, you'll be the first to classify and study this new species. You'll have the opportunity not only to publish potentially revolutionary findings, but you'll also be able to *name* it."

"I can't just up and leave my post. The university—"

"We've already made arrangements with the university to secure your services."

"I haven't worked in the field for close to a decade…"

"It's in your blood, Dr. Russell."

Galen felt himself waffling. The prospect of actually working in the field again was both exciting and mortifying. What if his skills had atrophied? What if he traveled halfway around the world and couldn't help them find what they were looking for? He locked eyes with the man across the desk, whose expression betrayed nothing. If there was a chance of discovering a new species that had somehow existed in complete isolation without being found for thousands of years, then he owed it to himself to take it. Even more exciting was the prospect that this could be a recent evolutionary offshoot of an existing species. If he could somehow identify the environmental factors that had triggered such a change and localize the genetic factors that facilitated it, he could advance evolutionary theories that would surpass anything Darwin had even dreamed of.

"Did I mention there will be a film crew tagging along to document our journey?" Colton asked. "Hence the necessity to involve only the leaders in their respective fields."

Galen ran his fingers through his hair.

Colton smiled like a cat that had finally cornered a mouse.

"I'm going to need time to procure the proper supplies."

"You have until tomorrow morning," Colton said. He reached into the inner breast pocket of his jacket, extracted a blue pamphlet, and tossed it down on the desk.

Galen opened it and examined the contents: roundtrip airline tickets from LAX to Lima, Peru.

"I can't possibly be ready in so little time," he said, but when he looked back up, Colton was already gone.

IX

Advanced Exploration Associates International, Inc.
Houston, Texas
October 23rd
6:49 p.m. CDT

Leo opened the file and perused the images for the thousandth time. They had cost him a pretty penny, and the only life that had mattered to him other than his own. The ultimate price had been so steep that to walk away now would be sheer stupidity. Hunter's posthumous message confirmed that he had found what they had known would be there all along. Now it was simply time to claim it as his own.

Satellite prospecting. That's what he called it. Soon there wouldn't be a single inch of the planet left unexplored, a feat that would be accomplished from thousands of miles away. Maybe the technology wasn't all the way there yet, but soon enough they would not only be able to thoroughly map the entire globe, from the deepest oceanic trenches to the most inaccessible mountaintops, but they would be able to discern the composition of the soil and anything buried beneath it. Then the spoils of the planet would be laid bare for men who specialized in creative solutions and high-risk extractions. Men like Leo, or he had hoped, his son.

The anger flared again and he had to grind his teeth to suppress it. This was not the time for emotions, which were a variable he refused to allow into the equation he now scrutinized. This was business, and business was never personal. Once they safely reached their destination, however…

He returned his attention to the image on the computer screen, which reminded him of viewing some sort of rugged object through a microscope, only slightly out-of-focus to soften and blur the edges. He had purchased the services of NASA's Landsat 7 satellite to survey some of the densest unexplored terrain around the world in hopes of finding something special. The satellite had already proven its worth by locating and detailing indigenous ruins throughout the Americas, even beneath otherwise impregnable forestation and several feet of accumulated soil. Where climate and terrain made aerial reconnaissance impossible, Landsat stepped in and worked miracles. It didn't provide mere satellite photographs. Landsat was equipped with an array of remote sensing devices that could focus on areas as small as a few square miles, with pixel sizes of 30 meters, and generate some of the most detailed images imaginable. All Leo had needed to do was provide exact coordinates—and a boatload of cash—and the brain trust at NASA had been able to program the satellite to change orbit and fly over. Granted, it had taken months to wade through the waiting list and coincide the timing with the ideal weather conditions, but the end result had surpassed even his wildest expectations.

He had specifically requested three different types of remote sensing. The standard imaging provided a topographical lay of the land, a generic map of sorts. The multispectral imaging created a precise, color-coded picture based on the absorptive and reflective properties of the minerals in the rocks, soil, and vegetation. And the sonar signals constructed the physical aspects and contours of the ground and upper strata of the soil. Their combined data allowed for the creation of a digital elevation model, a three-dimensional representation of the zone of interest right down to the phosphorous soil beneath a grove of Brazil nut trees.

Unfortunately, his geographical guess hadn't been as accurate as he would have liked.

The map covered a secluded area of roughly twenty-five square miles of steep mountains and sheer canyons separated by close to five thousand nearly vertical feet of lush tropical forest. A blotchy haze eclipsed a good portion of the detail from the cloud cover that clung to the higher ground essentially year round, part of the reason so much of this region remained uncharted. A rainbow of pixellated color dotted the screen, concentrated in some areas and diffused in others. The sides of the grid featured wedge-shaped dead zones, a consequence of the Landsat's scan line correction system malfunction in 2003, where the satellite was unable to accurately rectify the geographical data. On the very edge of one such anomaly was a bright splash of white that reflected a distinct mineral concentration near the summit of a ten thousand-foot peak.

The mineral signature was unmistakable, but the size of the lode was indeterminate thanks to the unfortunate cropping.

This was the reason he had sent his son to his death.

"You should probably get some sleep," Colton said. Leo had been so absorbed in thought that he hadn't heard the man enter his office. "We have a long day ahead of us tomorrow."

Leo nodded, but he knew there would be no rest for him tonight. He'd barely slept since he lost contact with Hunter weeks ago anyway.

"I trust all of the pieces are in place," Leo said.

Colton eased into the chair across from him. "As you requested. Dr. Russell's flight will arrive in Lima shortly after ours." He paused. "He's only going to slow us down. He's gone soft as a marshmallow. Are you completely sure he's the best choice?"

"I need to know the significance of the feathers. Hunter wouldn't have packed them, especially if he were abandoning camp under duress, if they didn't have some meaning. I'll carry Russell across the entire Andes range on my back if I have to. If anyone can discover their importance, it's him."

"And this documentary crew? You know how I feel about it. Are you sure toting them along is a good idea?"

"Advanced Explorations owns the principle interest in Four Winds Productions for this very reason. I want everything recorded. This will be Hunter's memorial. And also our cover story. We don't want to draw more attention to ourselves than necessary, especially considering we're potentially dealing with tens of millions of dollars here. Everything needs to be done by the book, and it needs to be documented."

Colton shrugged, but the tight line of his lips betrayed his disapproval.

"I've hand-selected the four men who will be working as our excavation labor," Colton said, changing the subject. "They are all exceptionally well-qualified for their designated tasks." He smirked. "I only hope they can dig, too."

"What about the details of Hunter's death?"

"Other than my guys, no one has any reason to believe it was anything other than an accident."

Leo leaned back and sighed wearily.

"And none of them suspect the true purpose of this expedition?"

"You mean the gold ore?"

"Recovering the gold is a foregone conclusion. We only need to formalize the logistics."

Leo rose from his chair and turned his back on Colton. He could feel the man's stare burning into his back as he surveyed his realm, watching as the distant city lights twinkled into being and the shadow of the coming night settled over the land.

"I intend to find out who's responsible for my son's death," Leo said in the tired voice of an old man. "And then I'm going to kill him."

Chapter Two

I

Pomacochas, Peru
October 25th
3:26 a.m. PET

Merritt knifed down through the wispy clouds that would shroud Laguna Pomacochas until the morning sun burned them off. The night was a solid black, save the flashers on his wings, which diffused into the mist, pale haloes of light that barely penetrated the cabin. He had made this run to and from Chiclayo so many times that he could have done it blindfolded, only this time he was thankful for even the wan glow so he could study his passengers. They weren't his normal fare. They obviously weren't tourists, nor were they locals. Usually, a flight like this in such an old plane, which rocked and swayed and made popping sounds as though rivets snapped with every hint of turbulence, had his passengers constantly fidgeting with their flimsy lap belts and turning green around the gills, but this group appeared unfazed. This definitely wasn't their first sojourn into the South American wilds.

"We're going to circle around the lake before landing on the water and taxiing to that pier you can vaguely make out through the clouds on the western shore by the town proper." He spoke into the microphone, though only the woman in the copilot's chair was wearing cans. The other six sat in the seats behind them, faces alternately hidden and revealed by shadows. With the roar of the engines and the shriek of wind-shear, they wouldn't have been able to hear him even if he shouted at the top of his lungs.

The woman leaned forward so she could see past him through his window. He dipped the wing to give her a better view. Like the others, she looked as though she had spent the past twenty hours in transit, yet when she saw the darkened silhouette of the City of Pomacochas rising up the slope beyond the pier, she lit up. A few stray strands of jet-black hair had slipped out from beneath her headset. She brushed them aside and stared through him with the most exotic eyes he had ever seen.

"First time in Peru?" he asked.

She smiled as though he had asked her the most asinine question ever.

"Not even close."

"First time in Pomacochas then?"

"From the air."

He banked the seaplane around the eastern shore and started his rapid descent. The clouds rose away from them to expose the placid lake, a sheet of fresh tar against the asphalt darkness. The plane's lights reflected back up at them like submerged jewels.

The other plane, carrying the remaining members of the group, including a film crew, and the lion's share of their supplies, dropped from the mist behind him.

For whatever reason, the man who had booked his services on behalf of Advanced Exploration Associates International had specifically requested him. Merritt liked to think that it was because his reputation preceded him, but he was by no means a stupid man. This all went back to the body he had found by the river. He *had* looked in the man's backpack after all. He'd seen the golden headdress. He should have known it was only a matter of time before word leaked and the treasure hunters descended like vultures.

Merritt felt the heat of the woman's stare and glanced over to find her scrutinizing him.

"So you were the one who found Hunter," she said.

He hadn't learned the man's name—it was better that way—but he hadn't stumbled upon so many corpses that he didn't know exactly who she was talking about.

"I should have known," he said.

"Known what?"

"I didn't initially peg you guys as *huaqueros*. I guess I'm losing my touch."

"We are *not* grave robbers. I'm a paleoanthropologist, for God's sake. The man you found was a good friend of mine, a good person."

"Who just happened to have a priceless artifact stashed in his backpack."

"How dare you judge him. Any of us for that matter. Who do you think you are?"

"I'm a man who flies a plane, honey. That's all. I like to keep things simple."

"You've done an excellent job. I don't think I've met anyone simpler than you."

"Ouch," he said, and watched as she huffed, crossed her arms over her chest, and turned to look out the opposite window.

Merritt laughed inwardly. The girl had spunk. No doubt about it. She radiated an inner strength, almost a sense of self-possession, which made her positively glow.

Sure, he had been with more than his share of beautiful women in his life, and there had even been one or two back home who had shown long-term potential. The problem was that none of them had ever really challenged him in any meaningful way. They had all lacked that mythical spark, that element of passion beyond the physical that inspired a man to follow his heart to the ends of the earth rather than face a single moment without her. But since coming to Peru years ago, any relationship at all sounded like more trouble than it was worth. Of course, for the right woman, he could probably be coaxed into giving it a whirl.

As he prepared for landing, he glanced back at the rest of the party in the mirror to his right. The two men directly behind him met his stare, or had they been watching him the whole while? Every time he looked back, there they were, studying him in the mirror even as he appraised them. A white-haired man in his late-fifties or so, and another man perhaps ten years Merritt's senior with eyes of stone, a military man if he'd ever seen one, and he'd seen far more than his share.

There was definitely something going on here, something brewing beneath the surface. He sensed a hint of danger that he hadn't felt in a long time, an unwelcome sensation he would have gladly lived his entire life without ever encountering again. His heart beat faster, and his palms grew damp on the controls. In the span of a blink, he was there again, on the other side of the planet in an eternity of sand and rock formations that he was certain mimicked the landscape of hell.

Smoke billowing from the mouth of the stone orifice. Footprints in the sand, some bare, some sandaled. The mechanical echo of his own rapid breathing inside the constrictive rebreathing mask. The barrel of his Heckler & Koch HK416 assault rifle swinging in front of him, barely visible through the swirling dust and smoke. Piles of rock in his path; gravel raining from the sandstone roof. The earthen walls scored black. The bodies...flames lapping at their clothing and hair...dark skin caked with soot and ash...and the young woman, her wide eyes shot with blood, one hand still at her swollen throat, deep lacerations from where she had torn through her skin with her own fingernails...

The pontoons touched the lake with the sound of thunder and water fired up against the underside of the fuselage and wings. He throttled down and coasted toward the pier, desperate for a breath of fresh air.

II

Hotel Spatuletail
Pomacochas, Peru
6:12 a.m.

Colton spread the maps out on the table before him. They had rented two adjoining rooms in what passed for a hotel in the middle of the Amazon basin, a converted Spanish hacienda that hadn't seen so much as a paint job since the conquistadors defeated the Inca with Christianity and smallpox. It was little more than a square of decomposing adobe enclosing a central courtyard with wild greenery attempting to claim the obligatory fountain, itself a cracked-tile basin brimming with slimy rainwater that smelled of flatus. But it didn't matter. They were only going to be here for a single night, after which the rooms would serve as storage for their boxes and the packing materials they wouldn't be lugging into the mountains. The sooner the better, he thought. He was no stranger to the type of accommodations one must endure in such remote locales, but the walls were alive with small green and brown lizards and several enormous black spiders had made themselves at home inside the mosquito netting over the beds. He expected that kind of hospitality from the jungle, not the hotel.

He had already formalized their route into the mountains, but there were still any number of variables for which he couldn't account. The maps couldn't predict the depth of the bodies of water or the speed of the current any more than they allowed them to find trails through the dense forestation. For the most part, experience suggested they should be able to follow certain aspects of the topography, but that still remained to be seen. Regardless, they had a starting point, and somewhere in the southern portion of this twenty-five square mile grid was their final destination.

The first thing they needed to do was inspect the area where Hunter had washed up along the Mayu Wañu. The medical examiner had estimated that his body had been in the water for somewhere in the neighborhood of seventy-two hours. He had, of course, qualified that assertion with the caveat that he hadn't been able to examine the remains quickly enough as the body had been delayed by the process of identification and the ultimately unnecessary quarantine. However, a detailed inspection of the river and its current, coupled with an educated guess as to its level at the time, ought to help him narrow down the range where Hunter must have entered the water. The boats had already been reserved, and the guides would be ready to lead them up the river before sunrise tomorrow.

But there was still one element that didn't sit well with him.

The sharp scent of guarana coffee preceded Gearhardt into the room. He carried a Styrofoam cup in each hand, and set one down in front of Colton.

"Here's what passes for coffee down here," Gearhardt said. He sat in the chair beside Colton. "It has the consistency of syrup and tastes like they burned it, which I didn't think was even physically possible."

"The guarana bean has four times as much caffeine as the coffee bean. They even use it in soft drinks."

"That doesn't make it taste any better."

"Get some cream and sugar then."

"And just when do you think I became a woman?"

Colton looked up from the digital elevation reconstruction to find Gearhardt smirking at him. This was good. It was the first time Gearhardt had made any attempt at levity since he had first called. Colton didn't blame the guy, but single-mindedness in a situation like this impaired the ability to adapt and recognize options and alternative solutions. And besides, he didn't much care for the idea of having to drag his old friend's corpse down out of the Andes.

"What did you think of the pilot?" Gearhardt asked.

"Merritt? Or should I say the former James Merritt Westlake? I read his dossier, same as you. Went AWOL from the 160th Special Operations Aviation Regiment during his second tour in Afghanistan in 2002. Just up and vanished in the middle of the night. Somehow, he managed to get out of the Middle East, and ended up here, piloting that flying heap of junk. In times of war, going absent without leave equates to desertion, an offense just shy of treason. If the Army were to somehow learn his whereabouts, they'd have him cuffed and on a plane stateside in a matter of hours. And now he reappears with your son's remains and a priceless headdress that could have financed a comfortable retirement down here where no one could ever find him. He took a huge risk sticking his neck out like that. Just walking into the Consulate where they could have challenged his fake identification and arrested him on the spot took serious balls."

"That's not what I asked, and you know it."

Colton sighed. "I don't trust any man who doesn't try to fence the headdress, or at least melt it down and sell it, under the circumstances. It goes against human nature. No one would have known, let alone caught him. Not unless he had his eye on the bigger score, and even then he'd be stupid to turn in the artifact. In my opinion, this makes him unpredictable. But to answer your question, no, I don't think he had anything to do with your son's death. I do, however, think he knows more than he's letting on."

"And this unpredictability? How does it factor into the equation?"

"It could not be a factor at all. He could climb back in his plane, take off, and we'd never hear from him again. Or..." Colton paused. "Once we turn our backs on him, we could find that we've made a terrible mistake. He was in special ops after all, and I've learned not to trust a military man."

"You were a military man."

Colton smirked. "You're the one who has to trust *me*."

"So what do you suggest?"

"How much do you think it would take to convince Mr. Merritt to willingly join our expedition without having to threaten him with his past? Keep your friends close and your enemies closer, and all that."

"What if he proves...unpredictable along the way?"

Colton smiled and nodded toward the doorway to the adjacent room, through which he could see two of the four men he had personally selected as their "dig crew" leaning against the far wall, taking advantage of the downtime while they could.

"We're prepared for every contingency," Colton said. "There's absolutely nothing we can't handle."

III

Laguna Pomacochas
Pomacochas, Peru
6:25 a.m.

Sam sat on the blonde sands of the shore and watched the sun rise across the rolling blue lake. The crescent ball of celestial fire seemed to set the gentle waves ablaze in a stunning showcase of oranges and yellows. She had nearly forgotten how beautiful this area of the world truly was. The smell of dew and exotic blossoms rather than exhaust and pavement; birdsong and the lapping of waves versus the grumble of traffic and airplanes; the crisp blue sky unfettered by the haze of pollution. She almost imagined she could see the thin rays radiating from the sun. Had it really been two years since she'd been here last? The bustle and demands of the university had swept her away, but it almost felt as though her heart had been here the entire time and now suddenly she was again whole, at peace with herself and the universe. She wished she could sit in this very spot forever, but there was a part of her that was raring to strike off into the mountains, where somewhere, hidden for centuries, lay the virgin ruins of the ancient civilization that had spawned the unique headdress, itself an amalgamous anomaly of cultural hybridization that should by no means even exist. The mystery of its origin was thrilling. Just thinking about it caused her heart to race.

She took a sip of the steaming guarana bean coffee and savored its bitter tang. This was one of the few perks of modern society she was going to miss in the weeks ahead. Boiling a handful of grounds over a fire served its purpose, but it just wasn't the same. Not by a long shot.

Draining the last of the brew, she rose from the sand and mounted the pier, accompanied by the hollow *clump* of her footsteps on the weathered planks. The two pilots were at the far end, unloading the gear from the cargo holds with less care than she would have liked. Some of those boxes contained sensitive electronic equipment: a ground-penetrating radar unit, a portable magnetometer, digging and grading utensils, cameras, sound gear, and a host of other goods they could never replace so many thousands of miles from home.

The dark-skinned pilot dropped a large duffel bag that made a crashing sound.

"Careful!" she shouted.

He looked up at her, shrugged, and muttered something under his breath. Her Spanish was a little rusty, but she recognized that he hadn't been apologizing. He turned away and went back to piling their belongings in an ugly heap that threatened to topple into the lake.

"If any of that stuff is broken—"

"You can take it out of my check," the other pilot said.

"That equipment is worth more than you make in a year."

"You'd be surprised what I make." The man offered a lopsided grin before resuming his task. "You could always help, you know."

"Sure. I'll do your job and then you can do mine. Think you can handle that?"

"So far all I've seen you doing is sitting on your duff drinking coffee. It might be rough, but I think I can swing it."

He was exasperating. She resisted the urge to stomp her feet in frustration and turned away. "Just try to be more careful," she called back over her shoulder.

If anything was broken, she'd do more than take it out of his check. She'd take it right out of his hide, and she'd revel in every second of it. Who did this guy think he was anyway? He was a pilot in the heart of the Amazonas Province, a washout who obviously couldn't cut the job back home in the States. And why was she allowing him to get to her anyway?

She glanced back only to find him still watching her with an amused expression. With considerable effort, she suppressed the urge to storm back down the pier and let him have a piece of her mind, and walked up the dirt road toward the hotel, where the others were already establishing a base of operations from which to launch their expedition.

An iron gate, flaking with rust, barred the thin walkway that separated the guest wing from the owner's abode. With a squeal of hinges, she opened it inward and passed into the courtyard. A flock of startled saffron finches exploded from the nests they'd chiseled into the building itself and swirled around the enclave. A rain of yellow and orange feathers and droplets of feces filled the air. She stayed safely beneath the overhang until she reached the first room, rapped a couple times with her knuckles, and entered.

Leo and the man who never left his side—Marcus Colton, if she remembered correctly—were still sitting at the small square table, poring over the stack of maps and conversing in hushed tones. Fat lot of good those fancy satellite maps would do them. The jungle grew and changed in unpredictable ways every single day, and it would determine their course, not the other way around. This region of the Western Andes had remained uncharted for a reason. No man was going to impose his will on the refined chaos that was the tropical cloud forest.

The flimsy door between the two rooms stood ajar. Beyond, the documentary director and her cameraman, neither of whom looked as though they'd been out of film school for more than a couple years, shared an animated conversation over steaming mugs and a platter of scrambled eggs dotted with red and green peppers. The four large men Leo had hired to carry their heavier equipment and act as her excavation crew lounged against the wall, seemingly reserving their energy for the journey ahead. They certainly weren't the graduate students with which she was accustomed to working. All four were in their late-twenties and appeared somehow hardened. In their hurry to catch the connecting flight from Lima to Chiclayo she had only been introduced in passing, but she believed she remembered their names. Nate Webber was the man on the end, shorter than the others, yet by no means small. He stood perhaps five-ten and had Hispanic dark eyes and skin, yet his shaggy hair was sun-lightened to a streaked auburn. Tad Morton sat beside him. He was taller and wirier, and reminded her of a farmboy with his sandy hair and freckles, but his brown eyes were sharp and always moving. Then there was Aaron Sorenson, a hulking, stereotypical Swede who could have passed for Dolph Lundgren from a distance, and Devin Rippeth, who immediately made her uncomfortable. His leathery skin was pock-scarred, his eyes a cold shade of blue. His head was shaved bald, but he had thick black eyebrows and a gruff goatee. What looked like the tail of a dragon curled around his neck from the tattoo beneath the collar of his T-shirt.

Knowing Leo, these men had been hired for more than their digging skills, but she wasn't about to complain. They needed to be prepared for anything. There were no hospitals or police in the unforgiving wilderness.

The final member of their party was conspicuously absent. She peered around one final time before slipping back out into the courtyard. He sat on the edge of the fountain, cold cup of coffee at his feet, his attention focused on his lap. She hadn't seen him when she originally entered, perhaps because he was sitting stone-still, the only movement his hands turning something over and over between them.

He looked up as she approached and gave her a weak smile, then returned his attention to his hands in his lap. As the only other academic here, she figured she should make an effort to get to know him. A cursory internet search had yielded a dozen articles and citations from the late-Eighties and early-Nineties. She'd been surprised to learn how similar their fields were, despite the subject matter. She had always pictured ornithologists as glorified hobbyists crouching in bushes with binoculars around their necks, but when it came right down to it, they were both scientists tracking the evolution of species over time.

"What's that?" she asked with a nod to the object in his hands. She sat down beside him on the lip of the tiled fountain.

He steadied it and held it up. It was a brown feather roughly the length of her palm with the faintest hint of green toward the end.

"I don't know. There are more than ten thousand species of birds in the world, just under a third of them in South America alone. Nearly every one of them is in one database or other, but this feather doesn't belong to any of them." He chuckled softly to himself. "That's the most exciting thing about it. Somewhere up there is a species that no one else has ever studied before, and I intend to be the first."

IV

9:08 a.m.

Merritt sat on the pontoon beneath the wing of his plane and dangled his bare feet into the lake. He fought the initial reflex to recoil his legs from the shock of the cold water, and finished the last of his guava juice, wishing it had been coffee. God, how he missed the stuff. Not a single day passed that he didn't question his decision to give it up, but at least he was sleeping better now, rather than lying awake for hours, a victim of his waking nightmares. It was a small sacrifice, however. Life was good again for the most part. Uncomplicated. Just how he liked it.

The military had granted him the opportunity to spread his wings. Unfortunately, it had also sharpened his talons and trained him to use them however and whenever it saw fit.

A bare-chested native rowed his dugout into the middle of the lagoon, a dark silhouette against the reflection of the rising sun on the waves. The diminutive man stood, gathered a fishing net from the heap at the back of the boat, and tossed it out onto the water. After a moment, the man sat back down and rowed farther away, the net's buoys bobbing in his wake. Merritt almost wished he could be like that man, but he did need just a little more excitement after all. For all intents and purposes, the flying provided just that. The speed. The heights. The battles against the volatile tropical elements and the rush of alighting on nothing more substantial than water. There was a part of him, the same part that had driven him to enlist in the Army and then pushed him into special ops, that longed for adventure and danger, but he still wasn't able to forgive that aspect of his persona. It had sent him careening through the gates of hell, and it had taken every last ounce of his strength to claw his way back out.

He closed his eyes and let the sun warm his face. It hadn't always been like that. He remembered all of the hours he had spent dusting crops with his father back home in Iowa, learning to fly in his old man's lap, rocketing so low over the fields that his props clipped the grain. Like his father before him, he was never happier than when he was in the sky, where nothing could touch him and he controlled his own destiny. The problem was that that life was too simple. He could see how it wore down a man in his father's eyes, like those of a dog tethered in a yard by the highway, watching all the cars speed past on the way to destinations it would never know. And it would have killed him just a little bit every day.

He heard footsteps on the pier, but paid them no mind. As far as he was concerned, his job was done. He'd unloaded every last bag and box from his cargo hold. They could sit on the end of the dock until the Second Coming for all he cared. It wasn't his responsibility to play bellboy, or pack mule for that matter. They could drag their weary asses down here and carry that stuff for themselves.

"Mr. Merritt," a voice said from behind him.

Merritt shook his head and enjoyed the gentle roll of the waves a heartbeat longer. He really wasn't in the mood for this.

"Look," he said, lifting his feet out of the lake. He rose, walked down the length of the pontoon, and hauled himself up onto the weathered planks to face the silver-haired man who had been sitting behind him on the flight, the one whose eyes had never left his reflection in the mirror. "I unload the stuff as a courtesy. Beyond that, you're on your own."

The man offered an amused smile and extended his right hand. Merritt simply looked at it for a second before matching the man's stare and shaking his hand.

"My name is Leonard Gearhardt." The handshake lasted a beat too long, and Merritt had to slide his hand out of the older man's strong grip. "I wanted to thank you for what you did for my son."

Merritt should have suspected it. He was going to have to be much more careful. The lackadaisical life had dulled his instincts. Now that he knew, he could see the familial resemblance in the brows and eyes, the set of the broad jaw.

"I didn't do anything for your son, Mr. Gearhardt. There was nothing I *could* do."

"You made sure that his remains reached the proper authorities, and flew across the country to hand-deliver his belongings to the American Consulate." Gearhardt paused. "You could easily have made what was inside that bag disappear and no one would have been the wiser."

"And what kind of person would that make me?"

"A very wealthy one, Mr. Merritt. I can only assume you looked inside the rucksack. How easy would it have been to just slip out one little thing for yourself?"

Merritt felt his face flush with anger and his fingers automatically curled into fists. If there was one thing he'd learned in life, it was that either a man had honor or he didn't. It was a choice one had to make. There was no such thing as situational integrity. One bad choice invariably led to another, and the next thing one knew, he was sighting an innocent down the barrel of an assault rifle. Damn the consequences. He was never going down that road again.

"Are you suggesting that I stole something from a dead man? I'm not the criminal here. I wasn't the one looting the ruins, the very heritage of these people. I may be a lot of things, but I am *not* a thief."

Gearhardt flashed a disarming smile that might have had the desired effect under other circumstances, but Merritt already had his quills up. Maybe his character and loyalty were often suspect, but never his integrity. Never.

"That isn't what I meant to imply at all, Mr. Merritt. I was simply pointing out that had any other man on the planet found that bag, he would have taken the headdress, if not all of the contents, for himself. You're an uncommon man. And I just wanted to personally thank you for it."

Merritt softened subtly, but he could sense the other shoe hovering overhead, and he had run out of patience waiting for it to drop.

"Let's get this over with. What do you really want?"

"I want you to show me where you found my son's body. I need to see it." There was a barely noticeable shift in the man's posture, a sagging of his shoulders. "Please."

Merritt saw just a glimpse of the man's true pain before the stoic, businesslike demeanor returned. His anger softened in the face of such anguish. He knew the soul-deep sorrow of losing friends and family, but he could only imagine the sheer torment of having to bury a child.

"My son was my world, Mr. Merritt. I'll pay you whatever you want. Money is of no consequence right now. I just need to find out what happened to my boy."

"Of course," Merritt said. "I'll help in any way that I can."

"Name your price, Mr. Merritt."

Merritt smiled. "I wouldn't mind another cup of guava juice."

Gearhardt looked quizzically at him for a moment, and then laughed. He clapped Merritt on the shoulder and gently turned him toward the shore.

"I suppose you should put on your shoes while I track down some *guava juice*. From what I understand, we have a bit of a hike ahead of us."

V

11:10 a.m.

Leo's heartbeat accelerated at the sound of the river ahead, an almost mocking chuckle. Until this very moment, he had felt as though he were walking through a dream, his movements sluggish, his mind shrouded in fog, disconnected. There had been no sensation in his legs, and yet they had somehow propelled him down the muddy path through the jungle. Passing from the dirt roads, through the meadows, and into the suffocating prehistoric forest had been like journeying back through time. He felt small and insignificant, while the mounting burden he bore grew larger with each step. Somewhere through the oppressive jungle of broad, vine-draped ceiba and Brazil nut trees with their buttressed roots and impregnable canopies was where his son's remains had been discovered, facedown in the mud, rotting even as the piranhas feasted on his viscera.

He wanted to cry, to release the anguish from inside if only for a time, but the tears refused to flow. Perhaps it was the years of repressing his feelings in order to build his empire, or maybe it was the rage burning in his chest that prevented the display of emotion. Either way, someone had killed his Hunter, and even now the murderer was still out there, possibly in this very forest. And unlike his son, the killer was still alive.

But his days were now numbered. This Leo vowed. Even if it cost him his life, whoever had slain his son would know true suffering.

Poison dart frogs chirruped out of sight and invisible creatures scampered through the branches. Mosquitoes swarmed around him, drawing blood as quickly as he could swat them, their frenetic humming punctuated by the occasional chirp or squawk of a bird and the clap of wings.

Merritt pushed through a screen of branches, and abruptly, stepped out onto the lip of a sloppy trench, at the bottom of which flowed a dirty brown river. Sunlight shined between the interlocking branches in shifting kaleidoscopic patterns that lent the impression of motion to the muddy ground. The pilot slid down the slick slope, using the limp vegetation that clung to it for leverage until he reached the edge of the water. Leo joined him a moment later, hands and boots caked with muck, cheeks smeared brown from smacking the mosquitoes, whose numbers were reinforced at the river's edge.

Merritt looked back at him with an genuine empathy, but said nothing. He merely turned and advanced upstream toward a tangle of branches reminiscent of a beaver dam to the side of a gentle bend.

"He was right here," Merritt said in little more than a whisper. He gestured to the ground, where Leo could still see a vague human outline filled with standing water. The earth surrounding it was choppy with hundreds of footprints.

Leo crouched beside it and ran a finger along the contours of the impression left by Hunter's head. He raised his stare to the west, where, through the wavering gaps in the branches, he could barely discern the jagged line of the green Andes, their peaks hidden by clouds.

A single tear eroded through the mud on his cheek.

He lowered his gaze and scoured the bank, but found only what he expected. Nothing. Flashes of silver caught his eye from the murky water, and then they were gone.

"Are you okay?" Merritt asked just quietly enough that the others couldn't hear.

Leo nodded and rose again, smearing away the tear. He studied the pilot's face, searching for answers. When he found none, he looked past him to the edge of the forest where Colton and Sam waited. Colton at least had the decency to turn his attention elsewhere, but Sam stared directly at them, tears shimmering on her cheeks. He had to look away before his fading strength abandoned him entirely.

There was a splash on the opposite side of the river as an unnoticed black caiman plunged into the river from the swath of sun where it had been basking. Leo watched for the crown of the skull and the bubble-eyes to break the surface, but they never did. At least not that he could see. He took a few cautious steps away from the water and positioned himself to make eye contact with Merritt.

"I'm willing to offer you fifty thousand dollars to join our expedition."

"Me?" Merritt's face reflected shock for a beat before he again composed himself. "Why would you possibly want me?"

"Make it a hundred grand." Leo scrutinized the man's reaction, watching for an unconscious tell. "For roughly one month's work."

Merritt's gaze flicked uphill, then returned.

"I'm a pilot, Mr. Gearhardt. My place is in the sky. What good would I be to you in the jungle?"

"You have certain training that could prove advantageous, Mr. Merritt. I would imagine those particular skills will be even handier in the wilderness than in the air. And for someone looking to stay lost, there's no better place than the jungle."

"You've been checking up on me?" There was a flash of fury in Merritt's eyes. He quickly regained control and feigned nonchalance. The subtle threat had been received.

"You were the one who discovered my son's body."

"So you assume that I had something to do with his death?" Again, Merritt's eyes ticked toward the jungle, then back. Leo discreetly glanced in the same direction, but saw only Sam. "You're out of your mind. It's awful what happened to your son, but the poor guy drowned. Like you said, *I* found the body. Trust me, your son was in the water long before I arrived."

"Hunter was a very strong swimmer, Mr. Merritt."

"Which makes you wonder if it's possible he ran into some other kind of trouble up there." Merritt furrowed his brow. "And you suspect I might know something about it."

"I don't know what I think." Leo shook his head. "The bottom line is we still haven't received word from the rest of Hunter's party. For all we know, they could have met the same fate up there in the mountains. Enough time has passed that they should have returned to Pomacochas if they were physically able to."

"Then why in the world do you want to go up there?" Merritt glanced at Sam again. Not at the forest. Not at Colton. But directly at Samantha. "If you're thinking of hiring me as some sort of protection, then whoever you had digging into my past didn't do his job. I'm obviously not who you think I am."

Leo let it drop. His message had been delivered. The silence was pregnant with tension until he broke it with a sigh.

"Mr. Merritt, something happened to my only child and his group somewhere up there." Leo inclined his head toward the Andes. "And I was the one who potentially sent them to their deaths. I am ultimately responsible for their lives. I need to learn what happened to them. For all I know, there may still be men alive up there. Communications gear broken. Starving. Lost in the cloud forest. If that's the case, then it's my responsibility to bring them out."

Merritt narrowed his eyes and appraised him.

"I understand. But if you suspect foul play, you shouldn't have brought civilians." His gaze lingered on Sam for emphasis.

So Merritt was interested in Sam, was he? Leo steadied his poker face. He had him now. If Merritt had nothing to do with Hunter's death, then he might prove a valuable asset. And if he had? Well, hundreds of men vanished in the jungle every year.

"These 'civilians' are here to help us find our destination. Only they have the necessary knowledge to find exactly what we're looking for in a range of nearly twenty-five square miles of practically vertical primary forest."

"You didn't share your suspicions with them, did you?"

Leo allowed the question to hang in the air between them.

"You would willingly subject these people to possible danger without forewarning them first?" Merritt flushed with anger. Then, suddenly, a puzzled expression crossed his face. "What else is up there? What aren't you telling me?"

Leo masked his surprise. The man had made the connection so quickly. Perhaps too quickly. Had he recognized the gold vein placers among Hunter's belongings? Was it possible that he too knew more than he was letting on?

"So are you coming with us or not?" Leo asked.

Merritt sighed. When he looked up toward the dark-haired woman crouching at the base of an epiphyte-addled kapok tree, Leo had his answer.

VI

2:36 p.m.

"Now pan left and sweep up the hillside," Dahlia Warner said from behind him where she knelt on the dock. "Make sure you get that little market and the church across the street."

Jay Sizemore did as he was directed. The shot of the street and the Spanish-style buildings against the backdrop of the lush rainforest may not have been exciting, but it was an improvement over the ten minutes of footage he had filmed of the nearly naked fishermen just sitting in their boats out in the middle of the lake. He felt the constant need to wash his hands for fear of contracting some disease or other. He looked forward to heading out into the jungle. Granted, everything would be dirty and covered with fungus and moss, but it was supposed to be. For whatever bizarre reason, that made all the difference in the world.

Jay rose from where he crouched and walked down the center of the road leading away from the dock. Dahlia's goal was to shoot this documentary in a way that made it feel like a first-person exploration, as though the viewer were actually a participant in the expedition. She had delusions of the film appearing on IMAX screens across the country in wide, panoramic splendor, and who knew? If they indeed discovered ancient ruins filled with priceless relics that had remained hidden for a millennium, she just might be right. And if she was, he could only imagine the fame and financial rewards that would come. Perhaps even a little golden statue or two.

Gravel crunched underfoot. Mosquitoes hummed and flies buzzed. The din of voices drifted down the street. None of these sounds would reach their final version, of course, as they would be replaced by voiceover or music of some kind. For whatever reason, the score from the Indiana Jones movies played on a continuous loop in his mind.

A ramshackle cantina clouded by cigarette smoke and desperation passed to his left, their humble accommodations to his right. A hairy monkey scrabbled up the side of the shack beyond and disappeared over the roof. For a brief moment, Jay thought he saw the silhouette of a man in the shadows between the buildings, and then it was gone. He watched from the peripheral range of the viewfinder as he passed, but saw only an empty alley filled with garbage and rusted appliances. Apparently, the natives were both curious and camera-shy.

A burro stood in front of the market, saddle bags brimming with round green lucuma fruit. It raised its tail and dropped a pile of manure for the eager flies, which gleefully abandoned the rack of cured meats upon which they'd been crawling. An elderly woman wearing a traditional oversize sweater and skirt made from alpaca wool seized the opportunity to peruse the selection in their absence. Across the street, the church, which reminded him of the little missions scattered throughout Southern California and Mexico with its sloping tiled roof, terraced bell towers, pedimented gables, and fortified *quadrángulo*, stood vacant. He had heard the bell's Call to Mass not so long ago, and wondered how much it would cost to convince the priest to make it ring again for the camera, or would even the request be considered sacrilegious?

There was a shift in the shadows beside the church. For a heartbeat, he thought he saw a human form peel apart from the darkness. He stepped to his right to get a better view, but saw nothing between him and the *quadrángulo* wall. Probably just another monkey or a skittish child. Nothing to get worked up about.

"Zoom down the street and then up to the mountains," Dahlia said. "Focus on the clouds covering the peaks, and then fade out."

Jay did as instructed, then lowered the camera. When he turned to Dahlia, she was positively beaming.

"You realize we're about to make history, don't you?" she asked.

Her enthusiasm was contagious. He couldn't help but return her smile.

"I believe you've mentioned that once or twice."

"I mean, no one has ever documented the discovery of ancient ruins like we're about to."

"Technically, the ruins have already been discovered."

"You don't know that for sure. Mr. Gearhardt's son could have not found them at all. There's no verifiable proof."

"If that's the case, then there might not be any ruins up there at all."

"When did you become such a pessimist?"

"Where have you been? I've always been the voice of reason in the sea of unbridled optimism. Even back in film school."

"Way back then, huh? What was that, three years ago now?"

"I already feel like I've been paying the student loans forever."

"Well, this ought to put an end to that nonsense," Dahlia said, and gave him a wink that weakened his knees.

He'd been crazy about her for more years than he cared to admit. Unfortunately, he knew nothing would ever come of it, so he would have to settle for proximity and hope that like a mold or a fungus, he would eventually grow on her. He wasn't a bad looking guy by anyone's definition. He just wasn't in the same league as Dahlia. From the right angle, he imagined he looked a little like Kurt Cobain with dark hair, while in reality, he was probably more reminiscent of a long-haired Gary Sinise in *Forrest Gump*. Dahlia, on the other hand, had all of the magical qualities that would have served her every bit as well in front of the camera as behind it. It wasn't just the Jaime Pressly hair or the Claudia Schiffer eyes, the Jennifer Aniston body or the Denise Richards lips. It was everything about her: the way she moved, the way she projected herself, her boundless confidence. The way she elevated his skills to her level whenever she was around.

Perhaps the formation of Four Winds Productions had been a marriage of convenience at first, but it had become a true partnership. Granted, his father owned the rundown sound studio they'd been able to renovate with only a small bank loan and charged only nominal rent, and his uncle had known a guy at Paramount who had sold them the used equipment for a song and dance, but she had brought the ambition and the will to succeed that he often lacked. Now if only she could see him as a partner in more than the financial sense.

"So are you just going to stand there, or are we going to get in on this strategy session and figure out what the plan is from here?" Dahlia asked. She smirked, slipped her arm under his, and led him back down the street toward their hotel.

Jay glanced back over his shoulder at the church. He was certain he could feel the weight of unseen eyes watching him from just out of sight.

VII

4:19 p.m.

First Sergeant Kelvin Tasker called for another beer in Spanish and adjusted his sweaty flannel shirt to ensure the sidearm in the hostler beneath his left armpit remained invisible. There was only one other patron in the dark cantina, a downtrodden local who guarded his bottle of Pisco Soldeica Huaco with both arms and never once looked away from it, as though the clear fluid held the secrets of life itself. An uneven scatter of scuffed tables and unmatched chairs covered the sticky wood-plank floors, upon which only a few rays of sunlight shined through the twin windows covered with faded promotional posters. Tasker sat in the rear corner with the doors to the kitchen and the rear exit to his left, the main entrance diagonally across the room to his right. The shadows surrounding him momentarily peeled back at the snap of his lighter, then swallowed him again, save the glowing cherry of his Ducal cigarette. Whatever had crept closer along the wall under the cover of darkness scurried back toward the ceiling with a series of clacking sounds.

The bartender set Tasker's Malta Polar on the table in front of him with a slosh of fluid. Tasker dismissed him with a fifty nuevo sol note that not only covered the beer, but his continued privacy as well. Thus far, there hadn't even been a sideways glance from behind the warped maple bar. That was one thing about the people down here. They knew how to mind their own business.

Tasker allowed the world around him to vanish while he focused on the chatter from the wireless receiver in his right ear and watched the entrance carefully. They had placed the audio surveillance microphones and transmitters inside the walls of the hacienda, in the deepest reaches of the finch nests. The voices were somewhat muffled, but the words were clear enough. He eavesdropped while they detailed their plans and made pointless conversation about things that didn't concern him. The different types of birds they would encounter; the social hierarchy of the Chachapoya people pre- and post-Inca conquest; the various kinds of structures they should expect to find; the species of plants and animals to avoid; and myriad ways to repel insects. It wasn't until a female voice, that of Dr. Samantha Carson, began detailing the types of artifacts they might stumble upon that he paid close attention. Apparently, the headdress was a cultural anomaly, but that didn't change the fact that it existed. And where there was one, surely there were a dozen more just like it. He had been able to secure a buyer for the first in a matter of hours, a Korean businessman who had offered seven figures for it and asked if he could ascertain any more artifacts of similar quality. Through his newfound international channels, he expected this venture to bring in somewhere between ten and twenty million dollars, and he fully intended to keep half for himself. After all, he had come up with the plan and was responsible for its implementation. He was the one out here risking his neck. Monahan should consider himself fortunate that he had even been offered a cut, but when it came right down to it, Tasker needed him. For the time being anyway. The office of the Consul-general provided a measure of legitimacy, and would help facilitate a speedy exodus from Peru when the job was complete.

Monahan also gave him a scapegoat should anything go wrong. He was certain that nothing would—he had planned this too meticulously—but one must be prepared for every eventuality.

Tasker committed the eavesdropped details to memory, and simultaneously plotted his course. He had already reserved the boats that would take him and his men upriver under an alias, and a little extra cash had ensured that no one would witness their departure. It was amazing how much more the dollar was worth here than back home.

He drew a long swill from his beer, feigned wiping his mouth with the back of his hand, and whispered into the microphone in his watch. Four voices acknowledged through the earpiece.

The two men who had been monitoring the hotel from hidden locations on the street would now fall back to their rendezvous point, where the others would already be waiting with their supplies packed and ready. These were four of his best and most trustworthy men. Four *Marines*. They would follow his orders to the letter, and every bit as importantly, they would follow their bank accounts. Their careers would soon be over, and either they would be living life large in the Cayman Islands, or they would be facing a court marshal and prison time. That in itself was motivation enough should millions of dollars not fit the bill. It was a calculated risk they were taking, but a risk nonetheless. Besides, what did they have to lose? Appointment to a consulate in a backwater country was certainly not the fast-track to advancement. He had already been in his post for three years, and largely forgotten by the powers that be. They wouldn't even think about him until he disappeared, but then they would definitely think about him a lot.

He imagined the expression on his commanding officer's face when he heard the news and had to stifle a laugh. Captain Patterson was simply going to explode, and if they were unable to track down and extradite Tasker, the responsibility would fall squarely on the old blowhard's shoulders.

There was just one more thing he needed to do before he vacated his post in the cantina and met up with his team.

He removed the prepaid cell phone from his pocket and dialed the only number programmed into memory. The calls could never be traced back to him, but unknown to the recipient, when the shit hit the fan, they would point like an accusatory finger at the man on the other end.

"Now isn't a good time," Monahan answered. He had proved a hesitant accomplice at first, but any man could be swayed with the right number of dollar signs. Too bad he would never get a chance to spend his share.

"Just wanted to let you know that everything is right on schedule."

"You're responsible for the details," Monahan snapped. Man, he whined like a little girl. "Meanwhile, I'm the one back here trying to conduct business as usual with half of my regular security contingent on 'vacation.'"

"You'll live. Just keep thinking about what you're going to do with all that money."

This statement was met with silence, beneath which Tasker imagined he heard the gears in the Consul-general's brain grinding.

"I'll be in touch again soon," Tasker said, and terminated the connection.

His only regret was that he wouldn't be around to watch Monahan as he was cuffed and led out of the Consulate in tears.

Chapter Three

I

Galen was thankful it was still dark. He didn't want to see the size of the cloud of mosquitoes that swarmed around the long, slender aluminum boat. The humming was so loud it nearly drowned out the putter of the outboard motor as they chugged slowly upriver from the weathered shack where they had procured their transportation. The guide assigned to Galen's boat, a native named Naldo who spoke Quechua and a seemingly random smattering of Spanish and English words, stood at the bow with a long pole to help navigate the unseen rocks and snarls of debris, while one of their party, a man he knew only as Sorenson and with whom he had never shared more than a nod in passing, manned the Evinrude. Naldo wore a dirty white Henley missing several buttons and a pair of brown corduroys so old they lacked nearly all texture. He balanced on the prow with filthy, bare feet, humming tunelessly.

Frogs and insects raised a ruckus from the forest around them, while the drowsy cries of birds and monkeys echoed hauntingly. Something splashed near the bank to his right, but with the fading moon and stars eclipsed by the canopy overhanging the river, all he could see were shadows. He could barely discern the silhouette of the lead boat ahead. It's grumbling motor left a thin trail of diesel smoke that settled over the river like a fog in the stagnant air. His generous benefactor and his henchman, as Galen had come to think of Colton—though he would never speak as much aloud—rode at the front behind their guide, a man named Santos, who wore only a pair of cutoff jeans. His thick black braid trailed down his back between bony shoulder blades that bracketed his knobby spine. Galen hadn't been able to tell in the moonlight if the man had been wrinkled by age or by too much time in the sun. Truthfully, he hadn't paid much attention to their guides at all. He could blame it on the darkness and his inability to clearly see them, but he knew it was a consequence of his nerves, which were strung as tightly as high-voltage wires.

Behind Leo and Colton sat Dr. Carson, Samantha, whose head turned on a swivel. She was in her element out here, so full of excitement that she nearly glowed. Not for the first time, he envied her passion, and wondered if she were similarly passionate in other ways. At her back, a mound of supplies had been roped to the frame of the craft. Rippeth lounged in the stern, maneuvering the outboard motor with such practiced ease that it appeared to be an extension of his arm. What little light pierced the canopy reflected from the man's freshly shaved scalp.

The men behind Galen made him uncomfortable. He was going to have to try to barge his way onto the lead boat the first chance he got. He still couldn't figure out why their pilot, whose knees seemed hell bent on bruising Galen's kidneys, had come along with them. It wasn't as though they were going to encounter any rogue aircraft in the middle of the Andes. And Webber certainly wasn't any graduate student or research assistant. He had the air of a brawler, but the quiet temperament of a fisherman, a dichotomy that could only have been spawned in the service. Perhaps it was simply the way the man rode with his rifle in his lap that caused Galen's unease, or maybe it was the fact that Webber patted down the mound of roped supplies behind him as though to ensure that something hidden remained that way.

The third boat was piled high with the majority of the scientific gear between the pole-wielding guide, a kid named Kemen who didn't even look old enough to shave, and Morton, who manned the motor. The documentary crew was squashed between them. Dahlia wore a khaki vest with snaps that glinted from the countless pockets and matching shorts, her hair tucked up beneath a Dodgers ball cap. She pointed excitedly to either side of the river for Jay, who followed her direction with his camera. His long-sleeved thermal top was already damp with sweat, despite the removal of the flannel shirt that was now tied around his waist. As it bore the bulk of their supplies, the trailing boat moved more sluggishly in the current, and required extra time to change direction to follow in the wake of the first two.

Even in the relatively placid river and with the engines cranked to a fierce whine, they couldn't have been moving at more than five miles an hour in the straightaways, and a fraction of that around the bends. The plan was to take the river as far into the mountains as they could before striking off on foot, unless they saw something in the jungle to necessitate premature disembarkation, specifically, any sign of Hunter's passage. In an ideal world, Gearhardt's son would have left signs to indicate his trail, carvings or flags on prominent trees, but under the assumed circumstances, they couldn't count on being so fortunate. And that was one thing none of them seemed to want to talk about. Leo's son had *drowned* up in the mountains ahead, and none of them knew why or how. What in the name of God were they doing following in his footsteps at all?

But deep down, Galen knew why. The nature of Hunter's discoveries was far too amazing to leave unexplored, which was why even now, despite the cramp of fear in his gut, he could hardly contain his anticipation. Somewhere in the vast uncharted cloud forest was a species of raptor that had never been documented, perhaps one that no man had ever even seen.

Galen slapped his neck and readjusted the mosquito netting that covered his head and shoulders to keep those pesky stingers at bay. The last thing he wanted was some bizarre tropical disease.

As they rounded a bend in the brown river, he caught a glimpse of the mountains, which rose straight ahead in sheer, jagged cliffs, their upper reaches invisible beneath a mass of clouds. That was where they were going, straight up into those clouds. And somewhere up there, protected from human intervention for millennia, was the ornithological discovery of a lifetime.

A contented smile had barely graced his lips when he heard the thrashing of leaves above him. Before he could even look up, he felt raindrops on his shoulders and arms. The air became water, and the surface of the river appeared to boil. It had been too long since his days in the field. He had forgotten how quickly these tropical storms descended.

Galen tried to remember where the pack with his poncho was loaded, but in the span of seconds, it no longer mattered.

II

8:56 a.m.

When they had come under siege by rain without the slightest warning, Sam had been prepared. Her shoulders and hair were still damp beneath her slicker, but at least she wasn't soaked to the bone like some of her other companions, who hunkered down in their seats in their rain gear or under tarps. Only their guides appeared unaffected. Santos still stood at the bow in only his cutoff jeans, a sheet of water covering his bare skin, poling them around hidden obstacles as the river grew more tumultuous. At least the rain had brought a respite from the assault of the mosquitoes. No longer did animals chatter from the dense canopy. Even the birds had ceased their relentless chirping to bed down in whatever dry alcoves they could find.

These storms were unpredictable. Sometimes they lasted just a few minutes, while other times it could pour for weeks on end. There was no way of knowing until it simply ceased as suddenly as it started. It had only been raining for four hours now, but already it felt like an eternity.

Sam occupied herself by watching the bank slowly disappear to either side as the river rose. The runoff carved channels through the mud and whole sections of earth fell away from the forest, exposing roots and rocks, which tumbled into the water. Branches and trunks raced toward them from ahead and banged against the aluminum hull. Progress slowed as the current grew stronger. The motors had begun to whine and issue a darker black smoke that reeked of burnt oil. They would only be able to go so much farther before they would have to rest the engines.

The stream that had once only been twenty feet wide was now closer to thirty, and flowed thick with muck. At a guess, they had traveled maybe twelve miles, which put them halfway to their first checkpoint, a deep valley beyond the easternmost row of mountains where the river was fed by countless waterfalls that had eroded into the sheer slopes from the higher country. They wouldn't be able to take the boats any farther than that. According to their maps, there was a thin gap that led to the southwest into a perpendicular canyon. That had been the start of Hunter's original route, and assuming they didn't stumble upon any sign of him before they reached it, that was where theirs would begin as well.

It was now just a matter of getting there.

A large gray trunk with wild roots like the tentacles of an octopus slammed into the side of the boat, and for a heartbeat she feared they would capsize. She locked her feet under the bench and gripped the sides so she would be better prepared for the next collision. A glance over the side showed her a dent the size of a satellite dish. And they hadn't even seen the tree, which had fired up from beneath the water like a torpedo from a submarine.

They couldn't afford to lose any of the equipment, let alone their lives. They had to get out of the river before it was too late.

Colton must have recognized the danger as well. He leaned forward and shouted into Leo's ear, but she couldn't make out his words over the roar of the rapids. Leo in turn stood and yelled at Santos, who looked back with a placating smile. He gave a single nod and pointed upriver toward a section of the bank that was several feet lower than the rest. It looked like there might be just enough room to drag the boats out of the water and into the high weeds, but the slope was slick with mud. Scaling it without the weight of their craft would be hard enough. Maybe they could tether the boats to the enormous kapok trees. Unfortunately, that would leave them at the mercy of the projectiles cruising downstream.

Santos guided the boat to the edge of the slope, beached the prow, and leapt out into the mud. He grabbed the coil of rope attached to the frame and scampered up the sloppy incline on all fours with simian agility. At the top, he wrapped the thick cord around a wide gray trunk and signaled for them to disembark.

Sam followed Leo and Colton to the front of the boat, and dropped down into the mire behind them. With none of Santos's finesse, she slipped and scrabbled and clawed her way up onto solid ground. By the time she caught up with the others, there wasn't a single inch of her that wasn't coated with brown sludge.

The remaining craft puttered over behind the first, their guides poling like gondoliers to keep them up against the bank until the lead boat was dragged out of the water.

Sam joined the others on the opposite side of the tree and helped pull on the rope. The boat was a lot heavier than it looked, but with the leverage and relatively solid footing, they were able to drag it up into the weeds under the broad arms of the kapok. Thirty exhausting minutes later, all three boats were crammed into the tiny clearing. They stood shivering as a group beneath the dripping canopy, which only served to mildly attenuate the deluge.

"Check this out," Dahlia said. She leaned closer to a heliconia shrub, and gently peeled back a cluster of broad-leaved branches. "Jay? Do you still have the camera handy? I want a shot of this."

Sam crowded closer with the others while the cameraman separated and headed back toward the boats. It was a phasmid, a walking stick insect, a long-legged, slender-bodied bug that perfectly mimicked the stem upon which it stood. She had to smile at the memory of the first time she had seen such a creature, and the hundreds of others with similar strange and wondrous adaptations they would encounter along the way. She envied these first-timers. There was truly something special about the instances when one's eyes were opened to the magic of the Amazon basin.

"Such an amazing evolutionary marvel," Dahlia said. "To think that somehow through the ages this insect's entire body changed shape to replicate its natural environment. And look how slowly and stiffly it moves, almost like the branch itself in a gentle breeze."

"Wait until you see some of the epiphytes," Sam said. "The world's largest flower grows from the rafflesia epiphyte, and blooms for only three days a year. It has the most beautiful maroon and yellow flower, but releases the most horrible stench to attract flies for pollination. And there are butterflies you have to see to believe."

"And hoatzin hatchlings are born with two claws on the end of each wing that allow them to climb around in the canopy until they're able to fly," Galen said. "The spatuletail hummingbird has two long tail feathers that end in large turquoise discs that it has developed the ability to control independently."

"Jay!" Dahlia called.

"I'm coming, I'm coming." Jay held the camera in one hand and his backpack in the other. He tried to swing it up over his shoulder at the same time that a section of the bank fell away from his foot. There one moment, gone the next, Jay slid down toward the raging river.

Sam ran to the edge and fell to her knees. Jay had managed to stop himself halfway down, his legs buried in the mud nearly to the knees. With one hand he clung to a tangle of roots, while he reached toward the water with his other, where his backpack rested in the trench carved by the hulls of the boats, inches from being washed away by the current. Branches and whole tree trunks raced downstream. One particularly dark trunk with thick, ridged bark even appeared to be heading straight toward the bag as Jay finally took hold of the shoulder strap.

"Leave it!" Sam screamed.

"I've got it," he said. The expression on his face was that of embarrassment, not concern. He shook his head as if silently chastising himself, and began to drag himself upward.

"Let it go! Hurry! Get up here!" Sam grabbed his wrist and pulled as hard as she could.

Two of the men dove to her side and seized Jay by the forearm and elbow right as the trunk reached the river's edge and exploded out of the water in a blur of wide jaws and sharp teeth.

The caiman snapped down on the backpack and nearly yanked the cameraman out of their grasp. It shook its head violently from side to side and jerked away. There was a flash of its yellowish belly, and then it disappeared with a splash, dragging its prize to the bottom of the river where it could pin it against the soft bed and wait for it to drown before consuming it.

Fortunately, all the beast had stolen was the backpack, and Sam was able to help Jay up over the lip. He fell to all fours and retched. His face had gone a deathly shade of pale and one of his boots belonged to the mud for the time being, but at least he was alive.

"Are you all right?" Merritt asked from her right. He and Sorenson had been the ones to rush to her aid.

"Jesus Christ," Jay said, rubbing his hand as though to confirm it was still there. "I saw it coming the whole time. I thought it was just a tree trunk."

"You have to be more careful," Sam snapped. "Out here, nothing is ever what it seems."

III

2:28 p.m.

They ate and lounged at the edge of the rainforest until the torrent waned to a patter. The river had risen nearly to the banks, but the amount of debris had diminished substantially. Large branches and broken trunks still sped downstream, although in nowhere near the same numbers as before, and the current had slowed just enough to provide suitable notice to dodge them. There were sections where the limbs had tangled to form impromptu barricades, which were fairly easily skirted. All in all, they had only lost two and a half hours, and were again making excellent time. Barring any further delays, they should reach their point of debarkation shortly after nightfall.

And from there the real trek would begin.

Merritt hunkered down in the boat with his poncho over his head, using the man in front of him as a screen from the brunt of the rain, now more of a blowing mist then an actual storm. At first, listening to the birdman naming every species of avian that poked its beak out of the trees had amused him, but over the last three hours it had grown monotonous, and he currently enjoyed fantasies of casting the man over the side in hopes he might have the opportunity to identify the various species of crocodilians and carnivorous fish. Merritt shifted in his seat to get some feeling back into his rear end. His knees bumped the birdman's back, silencing his Latin recitation between genus and species. He couldn't hide his grin.

What was he doing here anyway? He had allowed himself to be bullied and bought, neither of which sat well with him. While the old man hadn't come right out and said that he would go directly to the Army with news of his whereabouts, the threat had certainly been implied. There was more to it than that, though. He had lied. The money would be a godsend and would buy him several more years of anonymity, but that wasn't the true reason he had agreed to come along either, if he were being completely honest with himself.

He peered over the birdman's shoulder toward the lead boat. His eyes immediately settled on Sam's back. She turned to look at the forest and he studied her profile. What was it about her? It wasn't as though she had shown any interest in him. In fact, quite the opposite. She hadn't missed an opportunity to be condescending, and her personality was really quite maddening, but there was simply something about her…something more than just her outward beauty that drew him inexorably to her. Of course, he could justify his presence here in any number of ways, but truth be told, he was here because he had sensed the aura of danger surrounding them. He imagined rolling over the body he had found by the river, only instead of Gearhardt's son's face, he saw Sam's, her wide blue eyes reminiscent of another pair already scarred into his soul, and quickly chased the image away. He couldn't allow that to happen to her. That was the reason he now sat in this boat, shivering and stinking like a wet dog, listening to the litany of scientific names for random birds, staring at a woman whose skin crawled at the thought of him.

And he couldn't have been more content.

Perhaps he would find his decision a poor one, yet for the first time in years, he felt like himself again. Even the sensation of the cool rain on his skin was invigorating.

He shifted again and prodded his right knee into the birdman's kidney. Just for fun.

Sam turned around and caught him looking. He offered a guilty smile and averted his gaze. Even soaked to the bone and wrapped in an unflattering poncho, she was positively stunning.

He tilted his face to the sky and reveled in the caress of the elements. The clouds had settled into the upper canopy and clung to the leaves like smoke…*billowing from the mouth of the dark tunnel. The red rock blackened in the aftermath of the explosion. They enter the charnel cloud single file. The man in front of him is swallowed by the smoke, and a moment later, so is he. Detail resolves from the murk. Bodies. Everywhere. His breathing grows rapid, echoing inside his mask, but it still isn't enough to drown out the sounds of wailing and sobbing. Cooked skin, split away from weeping burns. Flames burning from charcoaled skin.*

The pitiful screams of the dying.

Then the gunfire.

A crawling man, crying and shaking. The barrel of an automatic rifle against his temple. An explosion of blood and gray matter. The thump of the body against the stone floor.

A woman. Lying on her back. Bleeding. Burning. She opens her startlingly blue eyes and whimpers. Extends a trembling hand through the smoke. Beseeching help, relief from the pain, compassion. She finds only the smoldering steel eye of darkness thrust into her face.

A gloved hand grabs the rifle and jerks it aside. Before he can question whose hand has stayed the woman's execution, he feels the heat in his palm, and sights down the barrel of his Heckler & Koch HK416 at the surprised face of his friend and brother behind the plastic shield of the rebreathing mask.

The man's eyes widen behind the dim reflection of flames.

"There!" the birdman said. He pointed up at a high branch where an ugly bald bird perched. The sagging pink skin on its head reminded Merritt of an old man's, the body too large and fat with slick black feathers. It had a white ring around its neck and a floppy fin of flesh between its eyes. A swarm of flies buzzed around the mangled remains of what once might have been a capybara on the shore below it. "*Vultur gryphus.* The Andean condor."

The condor spread its wings as wide as a grown man's embrace and dropped to the ground. Wings still fanned, it half-walked, half-hopped toward the carcass. Its movements were fascinating. It raised the first toe of each foot high, bearing its weight on its outer digits, and held its neck and stiff tail feathers parallel to the ground. When it reached the remains, it flapped its wings to stir the flies and speared the meat with its sharp beak. It was a hideous sight. The bird ducked in, ripped away straps of dead flesh, and raised its head to choke them down its gullet.

There was one thing for which to be thankful, Merritt supposed. At least if something happened to them in the jungle, they would be long gone before having to confront such a horrible monster up close and personally.

IV

8:38 p.m.

They raced the darkness. The setting sun had cast long shadows from the steep peaks over the river hours ago, but the ambient light that diffused through the canopy had provided a wan twilight aura. Now, even that was fading, and the night had begun to close in around them. With its descent, the forest had come to life with screeching, cawing, and howling, as dark forms knifed through the branches and darted between the trees. They had even heard the husky growl of a jaguar and glimpsed a flash of its golden fur from time to time as it mirrored their progress from the bank before it eventually lost interest. The sky continued to drizzle, yet the insects appeared unaffected, their numbers swelling in anticipation of their evening meal. Leather-winged bats shot out of the darkness, whistling between the passengers in the boats and just over their heads before vanishing back into the trees. The river had taken on a pale gray cast, and would soon be as black as the night.

The motors had been throttled down to give the guides extra time to maneuver around the obstacles in their way, yet still the resounding thuds of the hulls bouncing from unseen boulders echoed around them. Prudence suggested they should make camp for the night and finish the remaining leg in the morning, but they were so close now. Too close to simply give up.

The overgrowth of trees no longer merely towered over them. Instead, the forest rose above them, ascending the steep mountains to either side in tangles of vegetation that seemed to cling to the slopes by sheer will alone. Vertical basalt cliffs, formed by distinct volcanic columns and smoothed by eons of running water, crowded the river before finally relenting and falling away as they passed through the first wave of the Andes.

Leo felt the journey in a spiritual sense. His son was all around him here, as though his soul were preserved by the very jungle itself. He could feel the same excitement, the same sense of anticipation Hunter must have experienced, the same awe at the majesty of his surroundings and the secrets they kept. He had been in dozens of locations similar to this one over the course of a life spent in pursuit of both natural and manmade treasure. This time was different, though. This time it was intimately personal, not just because he was following in the footsteps that had led his son to a premature grave, but because he knew this would be his final expedition. In losing his son, he had lost a part of himself as well. Where once his lust for adventure had resided, there was now only rage. The life that had given him so much through the years had in the end stolen back more than it had ever offered, leaving the scales tipped in cruel life's favor. He was here to restore the balance.

Sheer limestone embankments pressed in from either side, narrowing the river by half and increasing the speed of the current. The outboards wailed and the bow rose and fell roughly on the choppy waves. For the first time, Santos had to hop down from his perch. He used his pole to keep the boat from slamming into the rock walls, which showed a watermark of discoloration a full five feet above its current level. Roots and lianas trailed down the smooth stone like so many serpents, their shifting shadows imitating movement.

After several minutes, during which Leo feared they might capsize, the cliffs fell aside and opened into a deep valley reminiscent of a volcanic crater. Lush green mountains rose on all sides and reached up into the clouds. Streams cascaded down their faces, alternately hidden behind dense vegetation and then revealed in series of waterfalls that stepped down from the mist and thundered into the lake onto which they now motored. It was as though they had passed into an Eden of sorts, a great bowl of virgin rainforest surrounding a seasonal lake perhaps two hundred yards wide, fed by streams from what appeared to be the entire Andes range.

The sight was positively breathtaking.

They skirted ceiba trees that grew miraculously from the middle of the lake on unseen crests of land on their way to the southwestern shore, where a dense fog was trapped in the thin passage separating two steep mountains. Groves of ceibas interspersed with the dominant Brazil nut behemoths encroached all the way to the edge of the water, and down the slope to where only their leafy canopies remained above the surface. Branches scraped against the underside of the hull as Santos again stood and steered them toward dry land. A riot of birds exploded from the trees with a near deafening cacophony of cries, black bodies against the night sky, swirling overhead before alighting deeper in the valley. A shimmer of scales traced a squiggle across the water and vanished into the night. The cough of a jaguar echoed in the distance.

Killing the motors, they slid silently to the muddy shore. Santos hopped down into the shallows with a splash and dragged the bow up onto solid ground. Leo rose and jumped out onto the earth for the first time in hours. His legs wobbled and the ground seemed to shift beneath his feet. He walked into the trees as his body adjusted, and found a little privacy behind the tented roots of a tree. With a prolonged sigh, he relieved the pressure in his bladder and was just about to rejoin the others when something on the trunk caught his eye. A series of marks scarred the gray wood. Not marks, but letters, and they appeared to have been recently carved. Leo traced the sap-crusted edges in the darkness. There were three rows: two letters on the top, two numbers in the middle, and two more letters on the bottom.

HG
10/7
SW

He flattened his palm over the carvings. A tentative smile spread across his lips and tears welled against his lashes.

Hunter Gearhardt had passed through here on October 7th on his way to the southwest.

Just under three weeks ago, his son had stood in this very spot, preparing to head out into the great unknown, wide-eyed and naïve. Had he sensed somewhere, deep down, that he wouldn't be making the return trip?

Leo was inclined to think so, for with each passing mile, the feelings of impending doom intensified and he couldn't help but worry that he wouldn't be leaving this jungle alive, either.

V

11:28 p.m.

The fire had dwindled to smoldering coals. Colton had thrown a pile of waxy green leaves onto the embers to create a thick cloud of smoke that would hold the bloodthirsty insects at bay for a little while, if only long enough for the others to fall asleep inside their tents beneath the lower canopy. Rain still fell as a mist and dripped in swollen droplets from the tips of the leaves, creating a sound like invisible creatures scampering across the detritus. The others needed to rest while they could. The journey ahead would be perilous and physically demanding. Colton would have been more than happy to join them were it not for the tingling sensation in his gut. He trusted it implicitly in the way an arthritic trusts his aching joints to predict an imminent storm, and right now it felt as though an electrical current had formed a circuit in his bowels.

His men must have sensed it, too. They prowled the darkness with feigned curiosity, but Colton knew they were looking for something. The same thing he was. It was gratifying to know that they felt it as well. However, the validation was also unnerving.

They had grown a tail.

He had first noticed it earlier in the morning. There were many variables within a man's control, even in the rainforest, but he could never influence or predict nature's response to his intrusion. There had been one bend in particular where their boats had startled a flock of red-masked parakeets to flight. The green and crimson birds had swirled overhead until all three boats had passed before finally returning to their roosts. Roughly two hours later, he had witnessed the same flock rise from the canopy, mere dots through the wavering branches against the pale gray sky in the distance. Later in the day he had seen that same ugly black condor take to the skies far behind them. It had circled the meal it had already claimed for some time before dropping back down out of sight. And every now and then, like the spectral mooning of the wind across a Scottish moor, he could have sworn he heard the faint echo of an outboard motor.

Someone was definitely following them, but who? And why? This wasn't a frequently traveled waterway. Its seasonal nature and the unpredictability of its rise and fall made it dangerous. Floods could rush down the mountains from the high country with a ferocity that could swamp a boat and drown all aboard. Conversely, the river could also peter to a trickle that would mire even a shallow dugout and potentially leave it stranded for months. It could always be more explorers like themselves, but he hadn't seen anyone in town who fit the bill. Then again, they hadn't kept their profile as low as he had recommended while in the city. Between the roving camera crew and the simple influx of white faces, they had surely drawn enough attention to have half of the population following them out of suspicion. Colton tended to think otherwise, though. He couldn't trust that no one had learned about the relic in Hunter's possession. Antiquities of questionable provenance fetched huge money on the black market, and there were men who were willing to do anything to get their hands on them. If word had leaked that there were artifacts crafted in solid gold at an unspecified location in these mountains, then the hills could already be crawling with murderous bandits. Or worse, if someone had recognized the implications of the rocks Hunter found, they could be dealing with a different kind of pirate entirely. Relics were small game, but a gold mine with a yield in the tens of millions was the big time. Entire expedition parties had been slaughtered for less.

Or maybe he was just being paranoid.

One glance at the other men only confirmed that if that were the case, it was contagious.

If anyone had learned of Hunter's discoveries, then someone must have blabbed. Merritt had found the body and could easily have shared the information. Based on his background and his shady history, it was possible that he had the knowledge to recognize the significance of the placers and the kind of brass clankers it took to stand before them and lie right to their faces. Was he in collusion with those that followed them? Then there was the Consulate. There could be potential leaks anywhere in that building. It was a cog in the capitalistic machine that was the United States after all. And, of course, there was the Peruvian government, which could have sent entire military contingents into the rainforest to search for more treasure.

He needed to take a step back and evaluate the situation objectively. The Ejército del Perú could be safely eliminated, as its soldiers weren't the kind of men with the requisite patience to follow from a distance. They would have descended upon them with all guns blazing and dragged them by their hair through the jungle to secure the prize. So what did that leave? Again, his thoughts returned to Merritt. The pilot was the wild card, the element of unpredictability. If he were responsible for their stealthy pursuit and proved to be a snake in their midst, then Colton would take great pleasure in slitting his throat.

Rippeth sidled up to him and spoke so that only he could hear.

"We could head back downriver while it's still dark and flush them out."

Colton admired the man's directness. In cases like this, however, patience was more than a virtue. It was a weapon.

"Not yet. Let them think we don't know they're there. They'll eventually grow overconfident. When they make their move, we'll be ready." Colton followed the man's gaze to the channel leading into the valley. Whoever was following them would eventually have to pass through there. "Besides, I need some time to figure out if we have a mole in our ranks."

Rippeth nodded, but kept his hand within easy reach of the sidearm tucked into the back of his pants.

"You and your men take shifts watching the camp," Colton said. "If anyone so much as attempts to breach the perimeter, I'll pay you fifty grand a head."

"Just the head?" Rippeth asked through a smirk. A strange light twinkled behind his eyes.

Colton clapped him on the shoulder and strolled back over to the fire. The humming of the giant mosquitoes had swelled to a whine. He threw more leaves onto the coals to reinforce the smoke.

Smiling, he turned back toward the lake.

Let their followers come, for they would soon learn that in the jungle, the roles of predator and prey were easily enough reversed.

VI

October 27th

2:58 a.m.

Tasker crouched at the base of a moss-covered stone formation shaped like a sinking ocean liner, concealed by the masses of shrubbery and the enormous prehistoric trees on the crest of the southeastern rim of the bowl-shaped valley. He brought the night vision scopes to his eyes and again surveyed the camp. Where once there had been five men patrolling the perimeter of the oblong circle of tents, nearly concealed by the wide arms of the Brazil nut trees, there were now only two. They feigned nonchalance, but Tasker knew better. These men were professionals with military training. It was obvious from their posture, their stride, and the angles they maintained to one another while surveying the forest. The arrogance that radiated from them. These were men whose egos were bolstered by skill and experience. Their impudence would be their undoing.

The shift change at precisely two a.m. had been rigid, and the discussions more involved than a simple verbal exchange in passing. They had obviously sensed they were being tailed, and thus stood at heightened awareness. Tasker had planned for this contingency, of course. He had never expected to be able to follow them upriver without betraying their presence, not while maintaining the necessary proximity to keep from being shaken. It was all part of the game. As long as their quarry continued to look over their shoulders, they wouldn't be focused on what was *ahead*.

His right hand in this operation, Corporal Terrence McMasters, appeared as a faint shadow among shadows to the southwest of the camp exactly as he had been instructed. The soldier was flat on his belly in a snarl of vegetation, visible only for a split-second by the whites of his eyes before he again closed them. He was within feet of the stacks of supplies unloaded from the boats. Less than a minute later, he was gone, his assignment complete.

Tasker lowered the lenses and crawled back around the stone abutment until he was safely on the other side of the mountain before standing. The rain drew lines through the mud he had smeared over his face and hair, and which still clung to his fatigues. It reeked of sulfur and decay, but in addition to making him nearly invisible against the ground and the night, it held the mosquitoes at bay.

He half-slid, half-scrabbled down the wet slope, silently skirting massive trees and jagged boulders, and slipping through tangles of shrubbery like a ghost. Even he didn't see the three men guarding their boats until he was right on top of them. He both confirmed the success of the mission and dismissed them with a nod. Making no more sound than the falling rain, the men, specters as intangible as mist, eased their boat out of the undergrowth and into the river. They pushed away from the bank and drifted into the fog that clung to the rapids, and then they were gone.

Tasker vanished into the recently vacated blind and waited for McMasters. Two hours from now, before the first rays of the rising sun highlighted the cloud cover, they would rendezvous with the rest of the unit several miles to the east. Then the waiting would begin.

He withdrew the handheld tracking device from inside his filthy jacket and shielded the display with his hand before turning it on. A small blue beacon radiated in concentric rings at the center of the grid. Everything was going according to plan. He switched off the unit and returned it to his jacket.

Half an hour later, McMasters emerged from the forest, and together they lowered their craft into the water. With a shove, they floated away from the shore and gained momentum as they were carried downriver.

Soon enough, their tracking would begin in earnest. For now, they had plenty of time to relax and let their prey expend all of their energy hacking through the forest and creating their path for them. Then all they would have to do was overwhelm them once they found the rest of the relics.

It was now only a matter of time before they were multimillionaires.

Tasker couldn't help but smile in the darkness.

No one would ever find the bodies. There were countless places to dispose of the remains, and just as many creatures that would be happy to expedite the process of decomposition.

There was just one more thing he had to do before the hunt officially commenced.

VII

4:06 a.m.

The ringing phone roused Eldon from a sound slumber. His eyes were still too blurred by sleep to clearly read the clock. All he knew was that it was late enough that there had better be a really good explanation for waking him.

He snatched the phone from the headboard after the third ring and answered in his most irritated tone.

"Monahan."

"Good morning, Mr. Consul-general."

He immediately recognized the voice, and was suddenly wide awake.

"How did you get this number?"

"You insult me, Eldon."

"Why are you calling me? Especially here? If anything happens, you know how quickly it will be traced."

"Which is exactly why I'm calling. To remind you that we're in this together. I'm not the only one taking a risk here, am I *Consul-general*?"

Eldon's heart beat so hard and fast that he could barely breathe, let alone formulate a reply. This had gone beyond threat to implication. If their plan spiraled out of control, he would no longer have the luxury of deniability. How had he allowed this to happen? He could have somehow maintained the upper hand, or he could have simply walked away. But he would have still been a third-rate diplomat in a Third World country, and the prospect of that future was even more frightening than the consequences of a liaison with the devil.

"Don't tell me the sound of my sweet voice has lulled you back to sleep," Tasker said.

"No," Eldon whispered.

"Good." He could hear the smile in Tasker's voice. "Now here's what I need you to do..."

Eldon held his breath while Tasker detailed what he realized would be the end of his career in politics. The room began to spin around him and the floor tilted on an unseen fulcrum. There'd be no opportunity to return to the States to vie for a seat in the Senate. He'd be lucky if he ever had the chance to return to America again, luckier still if he managed to stay out of prison.

Life as he knew it had come to an end.

Something broke inside of him and he started to cry.

"You're pathetic," Tasker said. "Suck it up and do exactly as I told you," he added, before disconnecting.

Eldon buried his face in his trembling hands. His shoulders shook as he sobbed. He would be unable to return to sleep tonight, if ever.

There was no immediate need to climb out of bed and do what Tasker asked, but he feared that even from hundreds of miles away, Tasker would know, and the consequences would be dire. The man was a snake without a conscience. Though Eldon had been wrong to trust him to uphold his end of their original deal, he completely trusted that the man would follow through on this most recent threat.

Rising, he passed through his bedroom and stepped out onto the hardwood floor in the hallway of the old hacienda that had housed countless Consul-generals before him. Until now, he had never paused to wonder what had become of those who had never reached the ambassador's mansion. A short staircase led him down to the recessed living quarters. As he had been instructed, he weaved through the maze of leather couches and chairs in the darkness until he reached the wet bar at the back of the room, and walked around behind it. He shoved aside a row of champagne bottles on the bottom shelf to reveal a rectangular white box standing on end. It looked like the kind department stores used to wrap sweaters, only larger.

Collapsing onto his rear end, he pulled the box down into his lap. It took several minutes to muster the courage to open it. The headdress fit snugly inside, polished to a high shine that reflected the moonlight from the window behind him. As Tasker had promised, an envelope rested over the jeweled eyes of the relic. Eldon fumbled it open and held the small stack of photographs in hands that shook so badly he could hardly see the pictures clearly.

They were snapshots from the surveillance camera in his office. In the first, he sat at his desk with the headdress in his left hand, lovingly tracing the contours of the precious stones with his right. In the next, he accepted the golden artifact from the dirty pilot. And there were more. All of them showed him in various poses with what the Peruvian government would undoubtedly consider a national treasure. Each bore a time and date stamp. If he had a change of heart and attempted to renege on his side of the bargain, copies would be sent to a dozen different Peruvian and American agencies. Too much time had passed for them to forgive him outright. The Peruvians would undoubtedly love nothing more than to make an example of him and give Uncle Sam a political black eye in the process.

He suddenly realized the true depths of Tasker's deviousness. What if the man had never intended to cut him in on the profits? What if Eldon's only purpose was to serve as a smokescreen for the operation? The black market connections were Tasker's. When he found the relics, they would be in his possession. There were no guarantees that he would ever come back for Eldon. All he had was Tasker's word, the word of a blackmailer who even now was stalking an unknowing expedition into the mountains where he intended to kill them.

His only option was to go through with it, even assuming Tasker had no intention of honoring their partnership.

What were his alternatives? Slip off in the middle of the night and go into hiding, his life ruined? He'd sooner kill himself than live like that.

There would soon be questions regarding the whereabouts of the marines, questions he would be unable to answer without incriminating himself. And in this envelope was the rope they would use to hang him.

Worse still, if Tasker was as evil as Eldon now believed, what would prevent the man from returning to Lima to tie off his loose ends?

But the greatest injustice was still to come. Tasker had arranged for him to make the handoff to the representatives for the Asian buyer. They would see him, and ultimately be able to identify him should their underhanded deal be uncovered. His fingerprints would be all over the transaction.

Eldon was damned if he did, damned if he didn't.

Damned.

Chapter Four

I

Merritt had passed the point of exhaustion long ago, and they'd only been on the move for five hours. Again he found himself asking what in the name of God he was doing here. He could have been back at his plane, preparing to head anywhere in the world he wanted to go. Instead, here he was, lugging nearly everything he owned in the pack on his back, while the ever-present cloud of mosquitoes made a human pincushion out of him. He had long since abandoned the worry of vector-borne diseases, and now feared he might not have enough blood in his body to simultaneously feed the humming masses and sustain his life. And the more he sweated with the exertion, the more insects he seemed to draw to him. His shirt was already drenched, and rivulets traced the line of his spine to his waistband and rolled down his legs. He could even smell himself over the stench of the rotting detritus. Worst of all was the claustrophobia caused by the low ceiling of branches that admitted precious little sunlight and airflow, and closed in from either side as though constricting. Ever since Afghanistan, the sensation of an impending panic attack was never far behind. His heart raced, his fingertips tingled, and he suddenly couldn't draw enough air. He had to pause to focus on regulating his heartbeat and breathing, and used the momentary respite to steal a glance back over his shoulder at the rest of the party.

The birdman, with the fancy net over his Panama Jack hat and head, appeared blissfully unaware as he continued to annoy Merritt from behind with his need to bludgeon them with his knowledge of every avian species they passed. The other men had fallen a dozen paces behind. They conversed in whispers, which only served to make Merritt nervous. It wasn't the subject of their conversation that worried him as much as the grim expressions on their faces. He was going to have to keep a closer eye on them. Sam remained toward the front, where she walked behind the birdman. She looked frustratingly comfortable in her tank top with her flannel shirt tied around her cargo shorts, and somehow had found the eye of the mosquito tornado. She neither swatted nor slapped, and had developed only a thin sheen of sweat on her brow.

The documentary crew chattered excitedly as they filmed everyone and everything. Merritt made sure to keep his back to them. He had thought the risk had ended when the caiman stole their camera, but he should have known they would have brought several in case of such an eventuality. They had to have nearly twenty-four hours of footage already, and must have catalogued every species of animal and tree they encountered. He tried to ignore them and, in turn, hoped they would return the favor. The last thing he wanted was for his face to appear on the silver screen.

Gearhardt's son's path had remained relatively clear at first; however the deeper they pressed into the jungle, the more the vines and branches encroached. Merritt was taking his turn swinging the machete, which had looked easy enough when the others were wielding it in the morning. The reality was entirely different. The weapon was far heavier than he had imagined, and the muscles required to slash it with enough force to part the sea of foliage weren't the kind he exercised on a regular basis. Both shoulders burned and his arms had begun to tremble. Maybe it was a guy thing, or perhaps the unwillingness to show weakness in front of the men who thought they had him by the short-and-curlies, but he wasn't about to be the one to call for a reprieve. So he continued to swing, refusing to think about his aching appendages, or about how few miles they had actually traveled, or about what the men in the rear were plotting.

With a ferocious hack, a mess of branches crashed down around his feet, and a flood of light flowed onto the path. After so long traveling in relative darkness, the sunlight was blinding. Merritt shielded his eyes and stepped warily into the clearing. It was a light gap, an area where one of the massive kapok trees had fallen and taken a cluster of smaller trees with it, allowing the sun to reach ground unaccustomed to its golden touch. The four-foot-wide trunk sprawled diagonally across the gap, pinning broken trunks and shrubs under limbs that sagged with dying leaves. Saplings that would otherwise have withered and died in the shadows now stood taller than Merritt. Scampering sounds raced away from their approach and a flock of birds, black against the sudden suffusion of light, took to wing.

The oppressive humidity relented for a few precious seconds as a gentle breeze reached the forest floor. Merritt enjoyed the sensation while his eyes adjusted before starting forward. With all of the abrupt changes at once, he didn't immediately notice the stench.

"Ugh," he groaned. "What the hell is that?"

"You mean *was*," Sam said. She slipped past him and approached the fallen tree. Some kind of film glistened on her forehead and cheeks.

Merritt caught up with her and had to ask, "What's all over your face?"

"A combination of ground up lemon verbena and pennyroyal leaves," she said. The tone in her voice suggested she thought the answer self-evident. He waited for her to elaborate, but she turned back to the tree and scaled the smooth bark.

"So you're going to make me ask, huh? Why did you smear plant sludge all over your face?"

"And arms and legs." He could tell she was enjoying this. "Isn't it obvious?"

"I guess not." He mounted the tree and crawled over behind her. Santos and Naldo scurried past him and dropped down into a cluster of ferns. "Enlighten me."

"Have you seen any mosquitoes on me?"

Merritt hopped down into the weeds. Something fast and green slithered away from his feet. A buzzing sound drew his attention to the far side of the clearing, where a black cloud roiled behind a gnarled ceiba trunk.

"So are you going to hook me up with some of that magic concoction of yours or what?"

"I already told you which flowers to look for. *Verbena triphylla*, lemon verbena, has lancet-shaped leaves with little purple and white flowers, and *Mentha pulegium*, pennyroyal, looks like a mint plant with columns of purple dandelion flowers. Surely even you can figure it out from there."

He grabbed her by the elbow and turned her around to face him. "Why are you riding me so hard? What did I ever do to you?"

"You called me a grave robber and attempted to tarnish the memory of a dear friend," she snapped. Her face flushed. "I'm one of the world's foremost experts on Chachapoya culture, and I've undoubtedly spent more time in the jungles of Peru than you. I've helped excavate two of the most fascinating and scientifically important ruins, which draw thousands of tourists every year and help stimulate the local economy. Every artifact I discovered at those sites is now displayed in the Chachapoya Museum in Leymebamba. Every single one of them. And you have the nerve to call me a grave robber?"

Merritt released her arm and took a step in reverse.

"I'm sorry," he said with a shrug. "I obviously misjudged you, but can you blame me? No sooner do I give the headdress to the Consulate than you guys show up with all your digging gear. Like you, I tend to get a little defensive when it comes to defiling the heritage of the people of this country."

A faint smile crossed her lips, but it vanished as quickly as it appeared.

It was a start.

"What do you say?" Merritt asked. "Can we start again from scratch?"

He proffered his hand. Her eyes met his. Even the touch of her skin and the weak reciprocal shake made his heart race. With a curt nod, she released his hand and turned back to where Santos and Naldo now stood, appraising the angry swarm of black flies.

Santos muttered something in Quechua as they approached. He kissed his fingertips and made the sign of the cross, then backed slowly away. He had paled considerably. Naldo aped the older man's movements and headed back toward the trail.

"*Supay*," he gasped, and nearly bowled right through Merritt in his hurry.

Merritt was unfamiliar with the word, but Sam wasn't.

"Demon," she translated. A crinkle formed in her forehead between her brows.

"What's that supposed to mean?" Merritt asked, but a moment later he had his answer. Were it not for the tufts of golden fur hanging from the branches of the ceiba and scattered through the ferns, the animal would have been unidentifiable. Broken and disarticulated bones littered the ground, the white calcium stained brown with blood. The flies fought for space on the vegetation, which was crusted with what looked like rust. With the exception of the knots of tendons on the ends of the long bones, there wasn't a single scrap of flesh to be seen. It looked like the animal had struck the ground at high velocity like a meteorite, spreading its remains in a shotgun-pattern that covered close to thirty feet, at the end of which were the shattered bones of the skull.

"What could have done this to a jaguar?" Sam asked.

"Probably poachers," the birdman said from behind them. "And this is all that's left after the scavengers were finished with the carcass." He stooped, plucked a feather from a clump of grasses, and studied it for a moment before he stuffed it into his backpack.

"I didn't see any even remotely fresh tracks," Merritt said. "Those vines we were hacking through would have taken weeks to obscure the path, and this mess can't be more than a couple days old."

"They could have come from another direction."

"Then they would have had to have been natives since we're thirty-some miles into the heart of the rainforest and that river is the only way in or out of this valley from the east. And I don't see natives being this careless or destructive. They would have carefully skinned the animal and utilized every inch of it, right down to the bones."

"And most native South American cultures revere, if not outright worship, the jaguar," Sam added.

"Well then, you tell me," the birdman said, puffing out his chest and focusing on Merritt. "With your vast knowledge of the animals of the Amazon and the cultures of the hidden tribes, what happened to this jaguar?"

Merritt crouched beside the broken remnants of the skull. Teeth surrounded the fragments of the mandible. A hairy black spider scuttled out of one of the eye sockets where it had funneled a web. He heard the crunch of footsteps as the rest of their group arrived. Brushing aside a cascade of fern fronds, he exposed the round cap of the animal's cranium.

"I have absolutely no idea," Merritt said. He held up the crown of bone. A ragged hole had been punched squarely through the middle, from which lightning-bolt factures radiated to the very edges. "But I can't imagine it was a pleasant way to die."

II

10:50 a.m.

Dahlia could tell something interesting was transpiring in the clearing ahead. She and Jay had been trailing in the rear with the freckled farmboy Morton, the dark-skinned Webber with the sun-bleached hair, and their youthful guide, Kemen, allowing the others to forge a path through the jungle while she and her cameraman waited like vultures for anything intriguing to pop up. They were definitely going to need it. So far, all they had was some boring footage of the town, the river, and a bunch of trees and animals.

She skirted around Morton and Webber, who carried the large crate containing the ground-penetrating radar and magnetometer units between them on long wooden poles that rested on their shoulders, to get a better view of the gathering at the far end of the light gap. The way everyone had rushed through the opening reinforced her belief that there was something out there worthy of documentation.

"Jay," she said, turning to her cameraman. He had paled significantly and was soggy with sweat and the last of the rain, which apparently had abated sometime while they were beneath the dripping canopy. "Start filming as you exit the path. I want to record everything as if we're walking into the clearing and seeing whatever's out there for the first time."

"Isn't that exactly what we're doing?"

"Don't be a smartass. Just get that camera rolling."

She stepped to the side of the beaten path and waited for Jay to pass her. He held the digital recorder in front of him and studied the four-inch monitor. Somehow, he managed to mind his feet and the image at the same time. She had to give him credit. The automatic stabilization system would prevent the recording from bouncing violently with each step *Blair Witçh*-style, but it would be useless if he tripped and fell.

Dahlia watched over his shoulder as he traversed the path, ascended the toppled trunk, and dropped again to the ground. The crowd ahead had begun to disperse, and was now spread over a span of roughly twenty feet, at the end of which several crouched amid the ferns, inspecting something on the ground. Whatever they had found held them enrapt. Her heart raced. It took every last ounce of restraint to keep from commanding Jay to run ahead. This was the perfect opportunity to build dramatic tension. If the viewer felt even half of the anticipation that she currently experienced, their film would truly be something special.

"I want to see it like they did when they discovered whatever's down there," she said. "Stick to the path until you can clearly tell what's going on, then go over to where those guys are kneeling."

Jay followed her direction perfectly. By the time he broke off to the right, she had an unobstructed view of what had attracted so much attention. Between the roaring buzz of the swirling flies, the curls of desiccated skin and fur, and the wash of blood and broken bones, it reminded her more of news footage from Serbia than anything she had expected to find in the jungle. The sheer ferocity with which the animal had been slaughtered was frightening, beyond even the aftermath of the attack of a great white shark. What could possibly be responsible for such carnage?

"Are you getting this?" she asked. Her voice trembled with excitement.

"Hard to miss."

Jay slowed his pace and angled the camera in such a way that if she craned her neck, she could see the monitor too. Part of her had expected the scene not to translate through the lens, but if anything, the camera and the level of the zoom served to amplify the atrocity.

When they finally caught up with the others, Merritt was holding up a fractured section of the cranium.

"Give me a tight zoom on that part of the skull. Make sure to get the hole."

Merritt noticed the camera in his face, dropped the bone, and backed hurriedly away.

Camera shy, Dahlia thought. Now that she truly pondered it, she didn't have any footage of the man's face at all. Only his back and shoulders as he rode in the boat ahead of theirs or hacked through the jungle. Interesting. She made a mental note to test his reaction to the lens the next chance she got. There was definitely something strange about his response, but not nearly as strange as what had happened here. The jaguar hadn't simply been killed. It had been obliterated.

"Cut," Dahlia said. Jay stretched his back and rolled his head on his neck. "Let's get one more shot looking straight down this mess from the edge of the tree line. Zoom in past the remains, and then zoom out as fast as you can. It looks like the animal was torn apart while it was running. I want to see if we can replicate the effect on film."

She turned and headed toward the wall of foliage, listening to the crackle of Jay's tread on the detritus to ensure he was following, the only sound other than the muffled voices and the static buzz of black flies. She paused. That in itself was noteworthy. Where was the dissonance of the calling birds, the screeching monkeys, and the croaking frogs? It was as though nearly all other life had vacated this region of the rainforest.

After just a few short minutes in the blazing tropical sun, she felt the cold emanating from the shadows beyond the trees. Hackles stippled her triceps and crept up her spine as she turned her back on the watchful jungle.

"Stay right there," Jay said. He had nearly reached her, but now stood in place, ever-so-slowly raising the camera in her direction. "Don't move."

The way he said it made her want to scream and run back to join the others, yet the sudden onset of fear rooted her to the ground.

"What is it?" she whispered. Every muscle in her body grew taut. Her heartbeat thumped in her ears.

"Just don't move. You're going to have to see this to believe it."

Jay approached her slowly, but without trepidation. She noted he focused the camera past her and above her left shoulder. Her stale breath finally escaped and she started to relax.

"For the love of God, Jay, tell me what you—"

"Shh! Hold still. Just another few seconds and…aw, man."

He lowered the camera and walked toward her, grinning.

"What the hell is wrong with you?" She punched him in the shoulder. "You scared me half to death."

"Believe me. You'll thank me when you see this."

He stood at her side and positioned the camera's screen so they could both see it. Sensing she was still wound as tight as a spring, he offered a crooked smile and nudged her with his hip. "Relax already." He rewound the scene and played it back at normal speed.

Dahlia saw herself against the gnarled green backdrop of the forest. The pastel blossoms of bromeliads poked out from where they were rooted to the branches and trunks. She heard the scuffle of feet and then Jay spoke. On the small screen, her body tensed and the blood drained from her face.

Jay chuckled, and she pinched his arm.

"Ow! Just watch, would you?"

Over her smaller self's shoulder, Dahlia saw twin dots of an almost turquoise color, and below them, a jagged slash of white. It looked like the face of some terrible predator: slanted eyes and a savage snarl against an olive-green face.

And then the face collapsed in upon itself.

The camera zoomed past her shoulder and focused on it. When the face folded open again, she recognized it for what it truly was. One turquoise eye encircled by a black ring dominated each forewing, while each hindwing featured half of the sharp-toothed mouth. Thin ebon veins mottled the wings in such a way as to create the impression of scales.

The massive butterfly closed its wings together to reveal its gray thorax and legs against a plant that reminded her of aloe, then opened them again and took to the air, flapping away into the shadows.

"You could have told me it was just a damn butterfly."

"Your reaction was far more entertaining," Jay said. "And it wasn't *just* a damn butterfly. Didn't you see it? That thing had a freaking face on its wings. Have you ever seen anything like it? How cool would it be if we just recorded it on film for the first time ever?"

She had to admit he had a point.

Jay started to pull the camera away. She noticed movement on the monitor and grabbed his wrist.

"Wait."

"What?"

"Rewind that last bit."

He held up the screen and rewound to the point where the butterfly fluttered back out of the jungle.

"Now play it back at half speed," she said.

The wings opened and closed, flashing the face of evolution and then nothing, face and then nothing. There was a moment when the forest was perfectly still, and then she saw it. A silhouette shifting through the shadows.

"Pause it."

The image was slightly pixellated, but she could still clearly see the distinct outline of a man with the faint reflection of the sunlight on his eyes and on teeth that had been filed to points.

Jay allowed the film to run, and the man vanished into the darkness again.

III

11:15 a.m.

"What do you make of it?" Leo asked.

They had left the light gap and the terrible stench behind them in favor of pushing deeper into the jungle. Morton now took his turn chopping through the overgrowth while the massive Swede Sorenson and the tattooed Rippeth carried the delicate sensing equipment between them. Webber hung back with Colton and him as they discussed the implications of the video in whispers. Dahlia had gathered them all around and shown them the recording mere feet from the remains of the jaguar. While the appearance of what they assumed to be a native hadn't caused panic to descend upon the group, they weren't far from it. Everything about the man had been unnaturally dark, save the sharp teeth. The fact that he had been able to encroach to within ten yards of their position without betraying his presence was unnerving. How many more of them were out there at this very moment, stalking them unseen from the shadows without so much as the sound of crinkling leaves? Had the man been responsible for the carnage in the clearing? It seemed impossible that even a group of men could have been capable of doing such a thing to so ferocious a creature, and if they had, what did that mean for Leo and his party?

"I'm not exactly sure," Colton said. "If there's more than one of them out there, as I suspect, they could have already attacked us ten times over. My guess is they're just curious for now, however, I can't rule out an ambush down the road. As far as whether or not they're responsible for what happened to that jaguar, I tend to think not. I can't see even an experienced hunting party being able to bring down the animal in that fashion. The way the carcass was spread out across the field suggests it was overcome while running at a high rate of speed and torn apart even before its momentum died, which is beyond the physical capabilities of any number of men without a pair of Gatling guns."

"So you think it was shot?" Leo asked. "If the natives have the kind of firepower to—"

"I didn't say that. A barrage of large-caliber rounds would have shredded the whole area."

"What about the hole in the skull?"

"It was too large to have been inflicted by a bullet. Besides, there would have been carbon scoring around the wound, and I doubt the bone would have been fractured in such a manner. My guess is those fissures were the result of an inordinate amount of pressure on the skull by whatever punctured it."

"Punctured?" Leo asked. He and Colton shared a knowing glance. In his mind he saw the twin wounds on the bare back of his son's body on the autopsy table. "You don't think—?"

"I don't think anything at this point. As far as I'm concerned, we have no choice but to reserve judgment until we have enough information."

"But if we're in agreement that the jaguar wasn't shot, and that no amount of men could have killed it like that, then what could have?"

Colton was silent for a long moment, during which the only sounds were the whine of mosquitoes and the crackle of their footsteps.

"Honestly," he finally said, "I can't figure out exactly how the animal was killed. I'm sure we could dream up a thousand plausible scenarios, but operating under a faulty assumption can be deadly. Let's keep an open mind. For now, we need to continue moving, cautiously, and keep an eye out for these men—"

"*Supay*," Santos interrupted. The diminutive man had obviously been eavesdropping. He stopped in front of them, face ashen, eyes wide. The darkness under the canopy had necessitated he don an alpaca-wool sweater, yet he still walked barefoot across the mat of dead sticks and leaves. "Is *legendario supay* in *selva. Necesitamos dar vuelta detrás.*"

"There are no demons in this jungle, and we are not turning back," Leo said. This needed to be nipped in the bud right now before the guide spooked the entire party. He looked to Colton, who gave a hesitant nod to Morton. The freckled man parted his khaki vest to reveal the SIG556 automatic pistol under his left arm. Santos's stare darted to it, then back to Leo. He returned to the path and scurried ahead to join his fellow guides, for the time dissuaded from spouting his superstitious nonsense.

"That's going to cost us," Colton said. "First chance they get, they're going to bolt."

"Let them. They served their purpose and got us up the river. They don't know this area of the jungle any better than we do. Why should we hang on to guides who can't guide anymore?"

"That's not the point. If we end up confronting these natives, having darker-skinned men fluent in Quechua would be helpful. Even if the natives don't speak Quechua, the sound of the language ought to be much closer to theirs than English."

"Sam speaks Quechua."

"She's a white *woman*. Most native cultures still see women as inferior. The mere idea of her speaking directly to them could be seen as provocation."

"Would you rather I let talk of demons undermine the entire expedition?"

"No," Colton said. "You did what you had to do. I'm just sorry it had to be done in the first place."

The conversation lagged for several minutes before Sam dropped back to join them. She wore an expression of extreme concentration.

"I've been thinking about the man in the jungle," she said. "I would guess he's a member of some offshoot of the Chachapoya tribe. The shape of his eyes was almost Caucasian, and he was significantly taller than most indigenous Peruvians. Those were the trademarks of the Chachapoya people. Some historical accounts even referred to them as 'white.' Or I could totally be off-base. Without being able to see his clothes or the structure of his facial bones—or anything for that matter—I can only speculate. But here's what I *know*. We can't be very far from the rest of his tribe. They must have a village within walking distance, and I'd be surprised if it's more than a day or two out."

"It could be in any number of directions," Colton said. "We could be heading in the complete opposite direction."

"Which would make the village somewhere near the mouth of the river where we camped last night. That's always a possibility, but I'm not inclined to think so. Granted, very few people travel that river. I just don't see any indigenous tribe staying so close to civilization. To remain autonomous, they would need a less accessible region, and one not visible from the air. That means they're ensconced in either a heavily-forested section of the jungle, or like their ancestors, they've built their village on the steep face of a tree-covered mountain. I favor the latter."

"Then it could be anywhere," Leo said. "Hell, with as thick as this jungle is, we could be walking past it right now for all we know."

"True," Sam said. "All I'm saying is that we need to be prepared for the possibility that we might stumble right into it, or come close enough that we could invite aggression."

"Or we could be walking away from it, and soon enough our company will grow weary of watching us do nothing and return to report back to their elders or whatever," Colton said.

"You could be absolutely right. I still think we should have a plan in place should we encounter the village, though. They may not ordinarily be hostile, but a bunch of strangers—especially *white* strangers—wandering into their midst could startle them to action."

"Who's to say they wouldn't welcome us with open arms?"

"Is that a chance you're willing to take?" Sam asked, looking first at Leo, then at Colton, emphasizing the question with her raised eyebrows.

"We're prepared for anything that comes our way," Colton said.

"We'd better be," Sam said. She glanced back over her shoulder into the dark jungle. "Can't you feel it? Something's wrong. The rainforest is too still, too quiet. There's something out there. Something's going to happen and all of the animals know better than to be around when it does."

IV

10:07 p.m.

The sun had nearly set by the time they reached a suitable spot to pitch camp, although under the nearly impenetrable canopy, darkness had settled over them long before. Had there been enough light to continue stumbling through the snarls of shrubbery and vines, even at a snail's pace, they would have gladly done so. An uneasy pall had descended over the lot of them. They could all feel it. Merritt was out of his element here, but even he had quickly recognized it, and once he had, the feeling became impossible to shake. The entire tropical rainforest had grown silent. No longer did strikingly-colored birds dart from tree to tree. No monkeys cavorted in the upper reaches of the branches. Even the occasional white-tailed deer failed to bound across their path. Eyelash vipers still dangled like vines from above them, and tegus and whiptails still popped up from time to time, though in nowhere near the same numbers. Only the mosquitoes and flies appeared unfazed, their ranks swelling with each passing mile.

Merritt was not one to be swayed by superstition, despite the genuine fear he could see in the eyes of their guides, but he trusted his instincts. And right now they were telling him that something definitely was not right.

They had found another light gap, though this one was only a fraction of the size of the last. The tree that created it must have fallen quite some time ago. The saplings were already taller than he was. Soon enough, they would close off the welcome view of the waxing moon and constellations. There was a small section where the trees had been hacked away to make room for a campfire. The trunk of a ceiba tree had been carved with Hunter's initials and the date that Leo had last spoken to him, which meant that they were only a few days away from their ultimate destination.

Merritt wondered if Gearhardt's son had felt a similar preternatural disquiet when he camped here.

Gearhardt and Colton sat apart from the others, conspiring in whispers. They scrutinized their maps, compared their current position to the GPS data on the handheld unit, and plotted the course ahead. Their four associates patrolled the overgrown perimeter, no longer maintaining the charade of being simply the hired excavation help. They didn't carry their weapons out in the open, but neither did they allow their hands to stray far from their holsters. He had seen one of the automatic pistols they carried. They weren't the kind one could pick up at a sporting goods store. SIG Sauer only dealt such heavy artillery to law enforcement agencies and the military. Considering he was armed with nothing more threatening than a Swiss Army knife, he drew a measure of comfort from the fact that someone had his back, even if he didn't trust them in the slightest. There was definitely more to the situation than any of them was willing to admit. Merritt sensed there were ulterior motives in play here. He had a pretty good grasp on the force driving Leo, but what was in it for Colton and his men beyond a simple paycheck? There had to be something else up there in those peaks, more than just the missing members of Hunter's party. What had that expedition originally been dispatched to find?

The wind shifted directions and assaulted him with smoke from the fire. He coughed and scooted down the fallen log toward the fresh air. Twenty-four hours ago, he would have reveled in the smoke, regardless of how badly it burned in his chest, but now that he had smeared Sam's concoction over every uncovered inch of his skin, he no longer had anything to fear from the mosquitoes. He smelled like he'd rolled in his grandmother's herb garden and the tackiness on his flesh took some getting used to, yet it was a small price to pay for a respite from the pain.

The birdman sat beside him, twirling a feather by the quill. All of his concentration was focused on the feather and his lips moved along with his unvoiced thoughts. His brow furrowed and he gnawed unconsciously on the inside of his lower lip. The campfire reflected from his glasses.

"Aren't you going to name the species for me?" Merritt asked.

Galen obviously didn't pick up on the sarcasm.

"I wish I could," he whispered, still turning it over and over as though the answer could be ascertained from motion.

"I was beginning to think you knew everything there was to know about every bird in the rainforest."

"No chance of that. I could probably identify just about every genera, and half of the thousands of species. Except this one. And raptors are my specialty."

"What makes this one so unique then?" Merrit asked. Not that he was genuinely intrigued, but he figured the opportunity to razz the birdman might momentarily amuse him.

"Everything about it. The background color, the strange iridescence. Even the calamus has an unusual tapered shape. There are no downy barbs, and one would expect to see a small amount of skin surrounding the proximal umbilicus where the feather plugs into the wing, but in this case, there isn't any."

"All feathers look alike to me. Some are obviously longer and more colorful than others. I don't understand why you're beating yourself up over this. It's just a feather after all."

"Just a feather? I found this near the remains of the jaguar. It's from the exact same species as the feathers that were in Hunter Gearhardt's possession when he died. This bird had been standing precisely where I stood, and I'm still no closer to identifying it than I was when we left."

"I'm sure you'll get it," Merritt said. He rose and clapped the man on the shoulder. The pudgy little guy was getting himself way too worked up. It was starting to make Merritt uncomfortable.

He walked away from the fire and toward his tent. The exhaustion set in with a dull ache that he could feel all the way into his bones. Perhaps it was time to call it a day. He'd just slip off behind a tree, drain his bladder, and pass out for a few hours until they roused him before sunrise to put him to work again.

On the other side of a tree with roots that formed a skeletal teepee around the trunk, he unzipped and sighed. Fluid trickled through the leaves. He leaned his head back and looked up toward the night sky. A single star twinkled through a tiny gap between the rustling branches. Something skittered over his right shoe. He flinched and hosed down his left shin in his hurry to flick it away.

"Son of a—" he started, but his words died when he caught a hint of movement through the trees.

He could clearly see the silhouette of a man against the foliage.

Merritt held perfectly still while he weighed his options. If the man had wanted to kill him, he'd be dead already. So what did that mean? He slowly zipped up his pants and continued to face straight ahead while he monitored the shadow from the corner of his eye. Was it the same native Jay had captured on film earlier? If so, and they had nothing to fear from this silent watcher, then perhaps the time had come to make contact.

Cautiously, he turned until he faced the man, raised his hand in greeting, and took a step toward the silhouette.

The man retreated deeper into the darkness. Merritt caught the faint reflection of firelight from the whites of two narrowed eyes.

"I'm not going to hurt you," Merritt said. He walked forward, both hands where they could be easily seen.

Another step and he was nearly close enough to reach out and grab the man, who shrunk back into a cluster of shrubs. The outline of a bow protruded from behind the man's right shoulder like the broken wing of an angel. He could barely discern the feathered ends of the arrows in the quiver over the opposite shoulder.

In one swift motion, the native sprinted toward the jungle to Merritt's right.

Instinctively, Merritt lunged for the man, but only managed to grab a handful of wool from his skirt.

A rustle of leaves and a few soft footsteps on the detritus, and the native was gone, a ghost vanishing into the ether.

No, definitely not a ghost.

Merritt brushed the wiry wool from his right palm and walked toward the clump of saplings through which the man had disappeared. His left foot kicked something on the ground. With one final glance at the jungle, he stooped, picked up the object, and headed back toward the campfire.

As he neared, he studied what appeared to be a leather satchel cinched closed by a drawstring. He opened it and fished around in the contents until his fingers settled over something hard and metallic.

He stepped from the forest into the firelight and held up what looked like a miniature pickaxe. One end was sharp, the other blunted.

A rock hammer.

He caught Leo's stare from where the older man sat on a log by the flames in time to see the expression of pain wash over his face.

V

10:32 p.m.

Colton turned the satchel over and over in his lap. It was the dried stomach of some large animal, easily identifiable by the telltale horn shape and the coarse rugae lining the inside. He couldn't bear to look at Leo, who stared helplessly between the small hammer and the shadowed wilderness, where the hired crew tromped through the underbrush in search of tracks they would never find. Dahlia and Jay followed them in hopes of capturing the native on film, which saved him the trouble of having to run them off for attempting to memorialize Leo's suffering. There were probably consolatory words that should be said, but he didn't know any of them. Instead, he scrutinized the remaining contents of the native's bag. There were several arrowheads, dried lengths of jerked meat, and two irregular clumps of what he had at first erroneously believed to be clods of mud. He broke one open and inspected it more closely. At the center of the sphere was a small chunk of something metallic. It was an amalgam of some sort, part reddish and flaking, the remainder a smoky gray. The outer portion that had been packed around the odd core was composed of clay that had been mixed with metal shavings. He brought it closer to the fire. The flecks glinted of silver and copper.

"Well, what do you know?" he said out loud.

"What is it?" Galen asked from behind him. Colton didn't realize he had drawn an audience.

"See this outer layer? Those metal shavings are copper and magnesium." He pinched off some of the clay and carefully set it on one of the branches in the fire. After a moment, a fierce greenish-white glare enveloped the clay like a birthing star. It faded quickly to nothing again. "And this chunk of metal in the center? The red portion is iron oxide, more commonly known as rust. The grayish part is aluminum. Together they form an incendiary compound called thermite." He crumbled off a section and threw it into the flames.

"Nothing happened," Galen said after a long moment.

"Right. That's because the temperature required for the auto-ignition of thermite is higher than the fire can generate alone. But throw in the magnesium as a fuse…"

He wadded up the ball again and dropped it into the fire.

It smoked and smoldered before the magnesium flare blazed again. A heartbeat later, the thermite ignited with a brilliant expulsion of light and heat. The logs in the campfire incinerated and the blinding glow eclipsed the flames.

Galen stumbled backward and fell onto his rear end with a gasp.

Colton chuckled and moved away from the fire. His shins already ached from the searing heat.

Powdered rust and aluminum combined to form a flash powder that burned extremely hot and fast. He had never experimented with them in this rock-like form. Was it created through come sort of metallic precipitation process?

"You could have at least warned me," Galen said. He picked himself up and dusted off his backside.

Colton smirked.

The thermite continued to burn.

They were dealing with some very smart natives. And while that in itself didn't trouble him, something else did. Why in the world did an aboriginal tribe in the middle of nowhere need incendiary devices?

VI

10:44 p.m.

Once the intense heat and flames had diminished enough to comfortably approach, Leo had taken a seat on the fallen trunk by the fire. He clung to the rock hammer as though his life depended on it. Whatever semblance of control he had once maintained over his emotions was now gone. Tears rolled down his cheeks and his hands trembled, yet he refused to allow this development to break him. Instead, he poured all of his sorrow and pain into a burbling cauldron of rage. He squeezed the miniature hammer so hard his knuckles cracked. He had finally discovered what happened to his son. Rather than this newfound knowledge allowing for even a small measure of closure, it widened the chasm that had been torn inside of him.

"Are you one hundred percent sure it's Hunter's?" Colton asked. The tone of his voice expressed not doubt, but the solemn need for confirmation. They both knew the ramifications of such verification.

"Estwing Supreme Light Weight Rock Pick. Customized leather grip. I bought him an entire set as a graduation gift when he finished his doctorate," Leo said. "I even had them engraved with his initials."

He tilted the sharp hammer so that Colton could see the HSG in flowery script.

Colton rose without another word and struck off away from the camp toward where his men combed the surrounding area. Flashlights strobed between trees and diffused into the impregnable snarls of shrubs and vines as they searched for the painted native.

They were never going to find him. Not until he wanted to be found.

The man knew this jungle far better than any of them and had spent his entire life avoiding detection. At the same time, Leo was certain that he wouldn't run either. He was a specter capable of hiding in their midst, and he was still somewhere out there.

Watching.

His thoughts returned to his son. What happened during Hunter's final days before his body was dumped in the river?

He had to piece together that seventy-two hour span, during which Hunter had obviously reached his quarry, as evidenced by the placers in his rucksack.

And it all started with this hammer.

During his last satellite communication, Hunter had made no mention of natives, nor had he so much as hinted that he suspected his party was being followed, which meant that the natives had shown themselves for the first time after that fateful call and before the next was scheduled the following evening. That left a twenty-four-hour window of opportunity for ambush, and another forty-eight that would prove to be the final two days of his son's life. The only variable he could rule out with any sort of certainty was that Hunter's terminal wounds had not been inflicted by arrows based on the ME's assessment that the object with which he'd been stabbed had been hooked.

He heard one of the men holler to the others from somewhere out of sight, but when no further shouting or gunfire ensued, he returned his gaze to the orphaned rock pick.

"They didn't kill him," Sam said. Leo hadn't heard her approach. She stood to the side of the fire with an empathetic expression on her drawn face, and gestured to the trunk beside him. "Do you mind?"

Leo shook his head and she eased onto the log beside him. Had she been anyone else, he would have told her to leave him alone, but she was his link to the past, and in many ways an extension of the memories of his son. He cherished the years he had spent in pursuit of fortune and adventure with this grown woman's deceased father, the best friend he had ever had. He missed the challenge, the camaraderie, the feeling of belonging to a family. Ever since his wife left him and his son went off to college, he had felt an emptiness that couldn't be filled, only ignored by throwing himself into the conquest of the business world. And now, here he was again, no wife, no son, sitting with the adult version of the pigtailed child from a better time, who undoubtedly despised him nearly as much as he despised himself.

"How can you be so sure?" Leo asked.

"Because he drowned," Sam said. "At least that's what you told me…"

Leo looked quickly at her from the corner of his eye. She had turned to face him so she could scrutinize his reaction. It had been a test, and he had failed miserably. He shook his head and inwardly chastised himself.

"What haven't you told me?" she asked in little more than a whisper. "How did Hunter really die?"

"He drowned, Sam. Just like I said."

"You're lying."

Leo shifted so that he faced her. She reminded him so much of her mother, but at the same time, her father's inquisitive spark shined behind her eyes like the lamp in a police interrogation room. And if she were anything like her old man, she wasn't going to let this drop without some small concession. At least for now.

"He *did* drown, Sam. Two medical examiners worked the autopsy, and I made sure I was standing right there to watch it. That's the God's honest truth. But you know as well as I do that Hunter was an excellent swimmer. You two grew up in jungles just like this one, swimming in rivers and lakes filled with any number of things that could probably have killed you on any given day. I just can't seem to swallow the idea of accidental drowning. Can you?"

Sam looked away and didn't answer. Perhaps she feared wounding an old man who had lost his only child, or maybe a part of her had suspected as much all along. He hadn't been forced to divulge the truth, but had given her something to think about until he eventually had to come clean about the stab wounds. She would hate him when that time came, but she probably already did anyway.

"Do you want to know what I think?" Sam finally asked after a long moment of silence.

Leo nodded. He could see the camera crew hovering on the far side of the campfire, presumably waiting for him to set down the hammer long enough for them to film it. While he admired their tenacity, and had brought them along specifically for this purpose, he had the urge to bludgeon them both with it.

"I don't think the natives intend to harm us," Sam said. "They've undoubtedly had ample opportunity to do so already.

And Merritt said the man he saw had a bow and arrows. They could have easily picked us off from the cover of the trees a hundred times over, especially considering how accurate they would have to be in order to survive out here for so long." She paused. "I do, however, think that the man made sure he was seen. They've followed us this far without us noticing. They could have continued like that for a long time. He wanted Merritt to see him, to see his weapon. I believe it was a message of sorts."

"A message? What was he trying to purvey? That if we don't turn back they'll shoot us?"

"Perhaps, but they've already had infinite chances to do so already. If they wanted us dead, they never would have betrayed their presence."

Her theory made sense, yet it did little to calm the turmoil inside of him. True, any marksman of the caliber she suggested could easily have sniped them from a distance, invisible in the forest. The problem remained that these people had come in direct contact with his son, and now he was dead.

"Hey," Merritt called from the edge of the forest. He jogged over to where they sat. "Have either of you seen our guides? No one can remember seeing them since shortly after nightfall. And I can't find my backpack either."

VII

11:02 p.m.

They had slowly worked their way to the periphery of the camp, remaining just within earshot, where they had waited patiently until their chance had finally come. Something had distracted the group near the fire, drawing everyone's attention, even the men who scoured the wilderness with their automatic weapons. Santos had sensed that there would be no better opportunity, and they had sprinted away through the jungle until they had traveled far enough to safely return to the path.

Only the faintest hint of moonlight permeated the canopy, but it didn't matter. They ran as fast as their tired bodies would allow, tripping and falling, only to rise and run again. Their knees and elbows bled freely through abrasions thick with dirt, and their panting breaths were the only audible sounds over their slapping, barefooted tread.

Kemen cried out. He stumbled and collapsed yet again. Santos and Naldo slowed only long enough to drag him back to his feet and jerk him forward.

Santos knew that once the men discovered they were gone, the search would commence, but only for a short while, and the hunt would be contained to the immediate area surrounding the camp. No one would stray this far to the northeast for fear of giving up hard-earned ground or sacrificing sleep. He and his friends were in the clear now, but they weren't about to slow for anything in the world.

Damn the money. The half they'd received in advance was more than enough to cover the cost of their time and gas. Besides, Santos knew now that their fare would not be returning to Pomacochas to pay the balance. As long as he and his friends escaped with their lives, that would be more than compensation enough.

While he had forgotten the tales his grandmother had spun in his youth, they had returned in startling clarity upon first sight of the jaguar's savaged carcass. He had thought the old woman mad.

Her stories of winged demons in the mountains of her ancestors had always seemed designed to scare him. Even then, though, he had understood that as ridiculous as they had sounded, she had believed them. And after witnessing the carnage in that field, now so did he. There wasn't a man or animal in the entire Andes range that could run down an adult jaguar, overcome it, and tear it to shreds. Perhaps he didn't subscribe to the legend of winged demons, but there was definitely something in the jungle that he didn't want to encounter, especially in the dark.

His companions had felt it too, and the agreement to abandon their party had been struck without reservation.

The youth tripped again. This time when he landed, the shoulder strap of his backpack ripped. Its weight slammed into the back of his head and hammered his face against the ground. Kemen moaned and tried to roll over, his pitiful cries muffled by the loam. Santos stopped to help him. It was then that he noticed how fancy the backpack was. Crouching in the forest, awash with darkness, and running in the lead with the boy at his heels, he hadn't even seen it.

Now they were in real trouble.

"What is wrong with you?" Santos asked in Spanish. He wanted to strike Kemen for his foolishness, but the urge was superseded by the need to keep moving. "You should not have taken this. Now they will definitely come after us."

"Mine was falling apart," Kemen sobbed. He rolled over and blood poured from his nostrils. His nose must have broken when his face struck the earth.

"We leave it," Santos said. "When they find it, they will call off the search."

He wrenched the functional strap off of the boy's shoulder, unfastened the top flap, and dumped the contents onto the ground. Kemen's threadbare canvas satchel was buried in a pile of clothes, notebooks, dehydrated rations, and foil-backed punch-cards of medications and water purification tablets. There was also a brand new digital camera. He held it up and shook his head. The desire to beat some sense into the youth with it was overwhelming.

"This? A camera? You risk our lives so you can steal a camera?"

Tears streamed from Kemen's eyes and he blubbered something unintelligible.

"We are wasting time," Naldo said. He had to double over to catch enough breath to continue. "The forest is still too quiet. We can not afford to delay here any longer."

Santos felt the man's trembling hand on his arm and realized the truth of his words. He dropped the camera onto the clothes, grabbed Kemen's pack, and threw it down onto the boy's chest.

"Get up. We must continue. With or without you."

He turned and sprinted after Naldo, who was already twenty paces ahead on the path, a silhouette against the shadows. Either Kemen followed them or they would leave him. The boy had jeopardized their flight for a stolen camera that would only bring a handful of nuevo sol. What in the name of God had he been—?

With a crash of breaking branches, a dark shape knifed across the path ahead, and just like that, Naldo was gone.

A scream erupted from the trees off to the left, but only for a split-second before it was cut short. It trailed into a wet gurgle that was swallowed by thrashing sounds from the underbrush. The bushes shook violently.

Abruptly, the noises ceased and the branches shivered back into place.

"What was that?" Kemen cried from behind him.

Santos held up a palm to silence the boy, who only continued to sob. He could hear nothing else. The jungle was still, the night unfettered by even the soft whoosh of a breeze. He drew a deep breath and sifted through the myriad scents: soggy earth, rotting kapok fruits, palm buds and cacao pods, and something else...the almost metallic smell of raw meat, which grew stronger with each passing second.

"Santos..." Kemen whined.

A single crackle of dead leaves to his left and Santos threw himself into a jerunga shrub to his right. He crawled toward the trunk of a massive tree framed by wooden liana vines, slipped between them, and huddled against the base of the trunk.

"Santo—!"

Another crash from the brush, but this time there was no scream. The crunching sounds grew louder, building to a ferocious crescendo, before dying as quickly as they had begun.

Santos closed his hands over his mouth to mute the sounds of his breathing. It was a futile effort. The jungle was so silent that he could still clearly hear his frantic respirations. He pressed backward until the bark bit into the bare flesh on his back. His eyes darted from side to side. He could see only darkness beyond the wooden bars of his prison.

A hawk-like shriek pierced the night from the far side of the path. A heartbeat later it was answered by another, this time from the opposite direction.

He held his breath and waited.

The only sound was the rapid thud of his pulse in his temples.

Craning his ear toward the path, he listened for even the subtle crinkle of footsteps on wet leaves.

A faint breeze caressed his cheek, bringing with it the intensified scent of bloody flesh.

Santos turned toward the source.

He didn't even have time to scream.

VIII

11:33 p.m.

"You have to see this," McMasters said.

The words snapped Tasker from his slumber. He was instantly awake.

"What is it?" he asked, donning his camouflaged jacket and slipping out through the seam in the mosquito netting over his hammock.

McMasters had already climbed out of the tent and into a small gap they had created between their tents, over which a blind of leafy branches had been constructed. Tasker followed, and found the other four men bickering in whispers. They wouldn't have roused him if it hadn't been important.

Their muddy faces were stained by the weak blue glow of the beacon on the monitor of the tracking device. McMasters looked up at him as he sat, then passed him the handheld unit.

"At twenty-two twenty-three, the beacon began to move at a rate of somewhere in the neighborhood of five miles an hour."

"Why would they break camp in the middle of the night?" Tasker asked, thinking aloud.

"We're not sure, but here's the kicker. They weren't traveling deeper into the jungle. They were heading straight back toward us."

"What do you mean 'were'?"

"The beacon's movement subsided at exactly twenty-three fifteen," McMasters said. "And it hasn't moved since."

"Not at all?"

"No, sir."

"That doesn't make any sense." Tasker paused while he tried to work it out in his head. His men had surely been trying to do the same, and when they hadn't reached a consensus, the only alternative they had seen was to wake him. "What could have spurred flight in the middle of the night, and why would they have stopped so abruptly? They sacrificed nearly half a day's progress."

And then it hit him.

The sudden and rapid movement. The stasis of the beacon for almost an hour now.

"Saddle up men," he said. "We break camp in fifteen minutes. Full night vision. We're running hot."

There was a moment of hesitation.

"They've discovered the tracking device," Tasker snapped. He shot a glance at McMasters, who seethed under the accusation. "Once they found it, they relocated it as quickly as possible, hoping to throw us off their scent. They're probably already moving out while we're wasting our time sitting here debating it."

Tasker looked at each of his men in turn. McMasters, Telford, Reubens, and Jones: four identical dark-eyed, mud-crusted interchangeable grunts. How dare they not immediately respond to a direct order.

"Move!" he snapped. "Now!"

This time the men leapt up from where they sat. Within ten minutes, all supplies were packed and all gear stowed. They hit the path in double-time with the awkward lenses strapped tightly across their foreheads. The darkness brightened in subtle shades of green and gray. Snaking roots cast uneven shadows across the path, making the ground appear to rise and fall in waves. Severed vines dangled to either side from where they'd been hacked away during the previous day.

McMasters fell back from the lead when the trail widened and spoke softly so that only Tasker could hear.

"What are the rules of engagement?"

"You are not to directly engage the targets until I give the order. We need them to lead us to the prize first. For now, this is old fashioned recon. We wait and watch. And once they've led us to the treasure, we wipe them off the face of the planet."

McMasters gave a sharp nod and jogged back to the point.

Tasker was furious that their surveillance had been discovered. He had thought McMasters the most skilled of his men, but apparently he had been wrong. Their prey had found the tracking device within twenty-four hours of its placement, which was entirely unacceptable. Now, like rabbits, they were running. As always though, Tasker was prepared for this contingency. The night vision goggles would still allow them to track their quarry, and they would be able to do so under the cover of night.

Everything would still go according to plan. All this setback had cost them was sleep. Still, they were better rested and in better shape than those they pursued, who had barely slept either of the past two nights, and had surely exhausted themselves creating this path that he and his men could now traverse at more than ten times the speed with which it had been forged. They would reach the location of the tracking device shortly after sunrise, and by the time the sun set again, they would be within striking distance.

Movement from his right caught his eye. For a fraction of a second he could have sworn he'd seen the blur of a running man off in the jungle. It must have only been an illusion created by the random alignment of branches and leaves. They were professional soldiers. They would have known if anyone had even tried to get within a hundred yards of them.

He returned his focus to the path ahead, and the fortune that awaited them.

Chapter Five

I

Andes Mountains, Peru
October 28th
7:19 a.m. PET

The backpack was crumpled in the middle of the path amid the mess of its dumped contents. Crimson dots spotlighted the jumble from the thin beams of the rising sun that managed to reach through the interwoven branches. The world around them hummed as though with an electrical current. Mosquitoes swarmed over the bushes to either side of the path in greater numbers than he had ever seen in one location in his life. They covered the leaves and filled the air in roiling clouds.

He knelt beside the overturned rucksack. His men surrounded him, automatic rifles pointed into the infested jungle at the four points of the compass. The tracking device was still in the bottom of the outer left pouch where McMasters had pinned it into the lining by the single metal prong. It showed no signs of tampering or manipulation. He moved on to the former contents of the bag, and sifted through long- and short-sleeved shirts, jeans, cargo pants, socks, boxers, and a host of other personal items: toothbrush and toothpaste, eye drops, a small medical kit, and prescriptions for Ambien, BuSpar, and Xanax. The foil punch-cards intrigued him. A sleep aid, an anti-psychotic, and an anti-anxiety/anti-depressant. Whoever the bag belonged to appeared to be a real nut job. He turned over a windbreaker and a spider the size of his hand raised its forelegs at him.

"Christ." He drew his hunting knife and impaled the creature through the thorax, pinning it to the earth. While its legs squirmed and twitched, he evaluated the sections of soil beneath it and between the proliferation of roots and weeds. There. Two distinct sets of footprints, both bare. Interesting.

Tasker yanked the blade from the spider's back, wiped it on his fatigues, and shoved it back into its sheath. He stood again and surveyed the chaos as a whole. Several feet to the west of the path, the groundcover was flattened and uprooted. Beyond were more partial footprints, spaced far enough apart to confirm what they already knew. The men had been running. The one carrying the pack must have tripped and fallen, spilling everything out of his backpack. So why hadn't he repacked his belongings and continued onward? Even an expensive digital camera remained facedown in the dirt.

He turned his attention to the swirling masses of mosquitoes. Now he needed to determine what happened to the men whose footprints terminated right here.

The smell of violated flesh and spilled blood reminded him of the scent of the bodies he had pulled out of the rubble in the aftermath of a market bombing in Baghdad during Desert Storm. It was all around him, which made it impossible to pinpoint the source. Fortunately, he didn't have to look very far. He pushed through a spear-leafed bush tangled with vines that reached the ground from the branches of the ceiba tree above it, and immediately saw the remains through the swarming insects and the carpet of them on the ground. The bones were shattered and spread out over an area ten feet square. A disarticulated foot rested closest to him, skin black, capped with the severed tendons that attached to the stub of the ankle. There was a portion of a knee here, a section of spine there. A broken ribcage crawling with bloated black flies and mosquitoes alike. He skirted the carnage until he reached what was left of the cranium. The crown had been broken to leave just the bowl of the occipital portion of the skull, which was alive with bugs feeding on the residual vessels in the membranous lining. The upper row of teeth was still attached, minus the four in the very front. The conglomeration of bones that formed the bridge of the nose and the orbits was splintered and fragmented. Tatters of clothing were draped over the surrounding branches like garlands. He looked up to see flies fighting over the droplets of blood that had dried on the undersides of the broad leaves in the lower canopy.

Tasker whistled in admiration. Whoever attacked this man had absolutely obliterated him.

Crouching, he studied the mud despite the protests of the startled insects. There wasn't a single discernible human footprint, only a handful of faint impressions that barely compressed the earth. They resembled the imprints of a camel's hooves, only much lighter and with a wider splay. Whoever did this had done an exceptional job of covering their tracks.

"There's another one over here," Telford called from somewhere off to his right.

Tasker rose and fought his way through the snarls of vegetation. Telford hovered over what was left of the body, nervously swinging his rifle from side to side as he watched the forest. The area was similarly littered with bones and ripped clothing.

"This ain't right, man," Telford said. "I can't think of anything that could have possibly done this. Anything."

Beads of sweat drew lines through the mask of mud on Telford's face. The whites of his eyes stood out like beacons. He freed one hand from the weapon and pulled the golden cross out from beneath his shirt so that it dangled over his fatigues.

"Grow some balls, soldier. This is neither the time nor the place for cowardice."

Telford opened his mouth to object, but thought better of it. The expression on his face spoke volumes, though.

"I found a third," Reubens shouted from behind them and across the path.

Tasker quickly appraised the ground. There were more prints like the ones he had discovered at the first site, but still no human, or even feline, tracks.

He burst from the jungle, crossed the path, and shoved deeper into the forest, following a series of broken branches and torn vines until he came upon Reubens and McMasters, who stood near the base of a tree with wild, angled roots, several of which had been broken. The ground behind them was carved with eight parallel marks in sets of four. He guessed the man had been hiding in the cage of roots before whoever attacked him broke through and dragged him out into the open while his fingers carved uselessly at the earth. The rest of the scene was the same as the previous two: a scattering of bones in no decipherable pattern, congealing blood over the entire area upon which nearly every insect in the country had been attracted to feast.

Tasker glanced at his watch. 7:31 a.m.. All of this had happened just over eight hours ago. Even more disturbing was the prospect that whoever had attacked with such speed and savagery could still be nearby even now.

The dour expressions on the faces of his comrades reflected the fact that they were probably considering that notion as well.

There was nothing more for them to do or see here. They needed to keep moving. His preliminary assessment had been wrong. These men hadn't discovered the tracking device in the backpack, nor had they been trying to relocate it to throw off their pursuit. If he had to wager a guess, Tasker would have said these men were fleeing from something, attempting to return to their boats and civilization. But what had they seen that could have startled them so badly that they had felt it necessary to run away in the middle of the night?

Tasker had a flash of memory, of what he thought might have been a man in the forest beside him several hours ago. Perhaps he had dismissed the notion too quickly, but could any number of men have done...this?

He didn't have to order his troops to move out. By the time he turned back toward the path, they had already fallen in behind him. Their breathing grew rapid, and he could almost smell their fear even over the reek of death.

When they reached the overturned backpack, Jones and Telford were waiting. Telford rubbed his golden cross between his thumb and forefinger. He took a deep breath and faced Tasker. He was unable to hold eye contact. His gaze darted from one side of the forest to the other like a cornered mouse.

"With all due respect, First Sergeant Tasker," he blurted, voice quavering, "I will be relinquishing my rank and returning to Pomacochas."

Telford stood there, chest puffed out, shaking in his boots.

"With all due respect, *Lance Corporal*," Tasker said. "I can't allow you to do that." He paced a circle around the terrified man, who suddenly looked like a scared little boy playing soldier in his backyard. "You do remember that our little sojourn here wasn't exactly sanctioned, don't you?"

Telford swallowed hard. His Adam's apple rose and fell, but he could only muster a meek nod.

"So you see," Tasker continued, "if we were to allow you to tuck tail and run, you could put the rest of us in a rather untenable position, and for what? Hmm?" He paced another slow circle around the man. "Or maybe I'm being too hard on you. You won't talk to anyone, will you?"

"N-no, sir."

"I don't know if I believe you, Lance Corporal."

"You have my word, sir. I won't tell a soul."

"There's only one way to guarantee that," Tasker said. He rounded Telford until he was directly behind him. In one fluid motion, he pulled his knife from its sheath, reached around the front of Telford's neck, and yanked the blade to the side.

Telford sputtered and coughed blood. Grasping at his open throat, he wavered in place for a long moment before collapsing to the ground. Blood gurgled in his lacerated trachea.

Tasker leaned over Telford's prone form, wiped the blade on the already bloody jacket, and returned it to his hip.

"Do the rest of you have any reservations about pressing on?" Tasker asked, looking each man directly in the eyes in turn.

"No, sir," they said in unison.

"Good. Then dump this garbage where no one will find it and let's get a move on."

II

11:13 a.m.

Galen walked in the center of the pack, thankful for the armed men both leading and trailing the group, though he was increasingly aware of the proximity of the jungle to either side. At best, he could see perhaps ten feet into the foliage, and only half that far the majority of the time. The events of the previous night had unnerved him. Their guides vanishing in the middle of the night would have been traumatic enough without the appearance of the native with Hunter's rock hammer. He didn't care what Sam said: he perceived the appearance of the painted man as a genuine threat.

Reaching into the inner pocket of his khaki vest, he stroked the smooth, slender feather.

There was still a mysterious, unclassified raptor out there in the wilds, he reassured himself, and he was going to be the first one in the world to study it, regardless of the consequences. Of course, he not so secretly hoped there wouldn't be any. His nerves were just getting the best of him. After nearly a decade's absence from field work, he had been anxious from the start. Throw in all of the strange happenings and the presence of guns all around him, and who in his right mind wouldn't be on the verge of tasting his bile? He just needed to find a way to relax a little, take the edge off.

He un-shouldered his pack and rummaged through the contents while he walked. There it was. The small hydro-bladder he'd had the foresight to fill with as much vodka as it would hold before they left civilization. Just a nip would dull the stress nicely. Here was one thing to be thankful for. At least it wasn't his backpack that had been stolen from the campsite.

Merritt hiked directly ahead of him, encumbered only by the clothes on his back. Everything the man had brought with him was gone, and they all knew they would never recover any of it.

Good thing the thief hadn't looked in *his* pack, Galen thought. He had just dropped a good chunk of cash on a brand new, state-of-the-art—

"No, no," Galen whimpered. He rifled through his backpack. When he still couldn't find it, he dropped to his knees and dumped the contents. He scattered everything across the ground and rummaged through the piles. It wasn't there. "My camera. Has anyone seen my camera?"

"So it wasn't just me," Merritt said. Galen looked up to see an almost smug expression on the man's face. He could have punched him right in the nose. "They got you too, huh?"

"This isn't at all funny," Galen said, stuffing his belongings back into his pack. "I spent three thousand dollars on that camera. I need the best technology money can buy for when we find the raptor."

"Relax, Dr. Russell," Colton said. "We have plenty of technologically advanced equipment to properly document anything we encounter." He inclined his head toward the film crew. Jay held up his camera to illustrate the point.

"That's not the point. It was *my* camera, and they stole it. *My* camera."

"You'll be fully reimbursed for your loss, Dr. Russell."

"You'd better believe I'll be reimbursed. I wasn't the one who brought those thieves into our midst. I wasn't the one who was supposed to be guarding—"

"Dr. Russell," Leo snapped.

Galen fell silent.

Leo's face turned red with fury and his eyes narrowed to slits. "I take full responsibility for what happened and will personally reimburse you for the camera." His expression softened. "Now, unless you want to turn back and walk for another week to buy a new one, I suggest we keep moving. We're within a couple days of our destination, and I, for one, am anxious to see what awaits us."

Galen nodded and shouldered his pack again.

Merritt clapped him on the back. "At least you still have a change of clothes." He smiled and fell back in line ahead of Galen.

The pilot looked exhausted. His eyes were bloodshot and set deeply into dark sockets. Galen wondered if Merritt had slept at all over the last few days as he began to walk once more, grumbling under his breath.

They'd been hiking all morning without anything resembling an actual break. The sun hadn't even reached its zenith and it already felt like a sauna under the smothering canopy. He had accidentally ripped the mosquito netting for his hat and was now forced to use Samantha's sticky concoction. The mixture of lemon verbena and pennyroyal made his skin itch, yet still the mosquitoes found a way through his defenses. His legs ached. His back ached. He was tired and thirsty, and since dawn he had only seen five species of birds, all of them flocking so high in the upper branches that he had only caught occasional glimpses and heard their distant calls. Every tree was identical to the last, and he was tired of having to make sure that every vine didn't have eyes and fangs before brushing it aside. Five hours had passed, and they had stumbled upon nothing more exciting than—

Galen barely stopped in time to keep from running into Merritt's back. The entire group stood still. Ahead, he saw Rippeth holding up his fist, the signal to halt.

"Shh!" Morton hissed into his ear from behind.

He held his breath and waited.

No one moved.

What the hell was going on?

III

11:53 a.m.

The moment Rippeth gave the signal, Merritt's old instincts reawakened. Adrenaline surged through his veins and his senses grew hypersensitive. He became one with the jungle, his body attuned to the very heartbeat of the Earth. He could feel even the slightest movement of one leaf rubbing against another, the sudden onset of tension radiating from his companions. Every sound was amplified. He heard their breathing, the nervous shuffle of their feet on the detritus, the patter of condensation dripping to the forest floor, and the soft rustle of movement from beyond the edge of sight.

He leaned forward and whispered into Sam's ear.

"Get ready."

An eternal moment of silence passed, and still no one moved. His muscles tightened like springs, preparing to release their potential.

When Rippeth lowered his fist and lunged away from the path, Merritt was already in motion. He grabbed Sam around the waist and dove into the underbrush. She landed on top of him with a startled squeak. He rolled her over so that their faces were mere inches apart, her wide eyes staring directly into his. She opened her mouth to speak, but he pressed his forefinger to her lips to silence her. He leaned forward until their cheeks touched, removed his finger, and whispered directly into her ear.

"Stay down."

Her breath tickled the fine hairs on his ear and raised the goosebumps along his arms when she spoke.

"Did you see anything?"

He drew his face away just far enough that she could see him shake his head in response. Her eyes held his for several rapid breaths.

"We need to sit up a little so we can see," he whispered, their lips nearly brushing. "Be prepared to run as fast as you can."

She nodded and he helped position her so that she crouched directly in front of him. He could see the path over her shoulder through the branches. She shifted to the right for a better view. He took her hand, ready to haul her to her feet at the first hint of trouble. Her fingers trembled as she tightened her grip. He leaned forward against her to provide a measure of physical reassurance.

Together they studied the end of the path twenty yards away where it appeared to open into a clearing.

Something was definitely out there. All he could see were the shifting shadows of the ceiba trees, but he could sense it, moving invisibly through the darkness.

IV

11:56 a.m.

"What do you see?" Dahlia whispered. Her breath on the fine hairs of his ear gave him goosebumps.

"Nothing yet." Jay zoomed the camera down the path and into the small light gap beyond. It reminded him of the last one, only he couldn't see the fallen tree that had created it. There were other subtle differences. There were no clusters of saplings, and the wild grasses and ferns were much shorter, almost as though they'd been trimmed.

Still, none of the others had emerged from hiding. He could see their backs and occasional profiles through the foliage. Most of them appeared to be every bit as confused as he was.

And then he saw it. A large, dark shape lumbered into view. Its head swiveled nervously on top of a long, slender neck that stood perfectly erect from its impossibly wooly body. Four spindle-thin legs hardly appeared capable of bearing its weight.

"You've got to be kidding me," Jay said. Shaking his head, he rose from behind the flowering orchid bush and lowered the camera. "It's just one of those freaking llama-looking things."

Colton leaned out across the path and waved for him to get back down.

Forget that. The bush was crawling with brown ants with pincers so big they could hardly lift their heads. He wasn't about to willingly climb back in there and provide them with lunch at his expense. No way. If none of the others were brave enough to approach this terrifying alpaca, then he was just going to have to—

"Get down!" Dahlia whispered. She jerked on his pant leg. It was only then that he noticed the black form standing perfectly still past the animal.

"Aw, crap."

He dropped and scooted into the ant-covered leaves. Before he was even situated, he had the camera up and rolling. He zoomed past the fuzzy gray and black creature and onto the shadowed apparition. The camera focused on a man at the edge of the forest, just shy of the point where the sunlight forced back the shade. He was painted black from head to toe. No wonder Jay hadn't initially seen him. Of course, if he could see the man, then surely he had already seen them as well. If that was the case, then why was he still just standing there?

The man hovered at the fringe of the jungle for several long minutes while they all waited silently. Why didn't they just keep going? Jay wondered. They outnumbered and outgunned the man. Surely they were just being overly cautious, but still, it was always possible that the native was friendly and posed no threat. What in the world were they waiting for?

Finally, the painted man stepped out into the sunlight and approached the alpaca. He grabbed the braided rope hanging from the animal's neck, gave a sharp tug, and guided it toward the wall of foliage.

Raindrops pattered on the leaves above him as a gentle rain began to fall.

The man paused and looked up into the sky. He acknowledged the sudden onset of rain with a nod, and then continued into the dark forest. A moment later, he was gone.

"Did you get that?" Dahlia whispered.

"You mean that guy standing there doing nothing? Oh yeah, I got it. Fat lot of good it will do us though."

Slowly, Rippeth rose in the lead and eased out into the clearing. He scoured the light gap down the sight of his pistol, then finally gave a wave to indicate they were safe to leave their hiding spots.

Leo and Colton hesitantly eased to their feet ahead. Jay did the same. He still didn't understand the need for such overt prudence, but he followed the others at a snail's pace out into the open.

"He brought the alpaca down here to graze," Sam said.

Jay looked down. His initial assessment had been mostly correct. The weeds hadn't been trimmed, but grazed down to nubs in sections.

"Why did we all have to hide?" he asked. "I mean, there was only one of him and there are ten of us. What could he possibly have done?"

"We could easily have frightened him," Colton said impatiently. "Then the next thing you know, we have natives crawling all over us. They know we're here. When they're ready, they'll either come to us on their own terms, or just continue to hide and follow us from a distance until we've passed out of their territory."

Jay nodded. It made sense, but it didn't exactly make for a good documentary. He wasn't rooting for an attack by a tribe of bow-and-arrow-wielding savages by any means, but they needed some element of drama and danger to make the film really sing.

While the others discussed how long they should wait before continuing along the path to keep from spooking the lone man with the alpaca, Jay raised the camera and wandered the perimeter of the light gap, hoping to encounter something remotely interesting. There were stumps where trees had been cleared, and about a million hoof prints in the damp earth, but it was otherwise unremarkable.

Raindrops tapped his shoulders and drained in cool lines through his hair, down his neck, and along his spine. It felt wonderful after so many hours of being sticky with sweat from the humidity. As long as this didn't turn into another tropical deluge, he'd be happy if the storm never stopped.

He panned along the edge of the jungle one final time, and was just about to stop recording when something caught his eye. At first, he thought it was another one of those strange butterflies, but it appeared to hover in the shadows at the base of a tree trunk without flapping its wings. He zoomed in and stumbled backward in surprise. Another painted man crouched in the darkness, unmoving, watching Jay even as he filmed him. A sharp-toothed grin slashed the man's face, and then he vanished.

"Hey," Jay called without turning. "There's another one out there."

He panned the camera from left to right, but there was no sign of the native.

The forest had fallen quiet, save the soft sound of rain dripping from the higher reaches onto the groundcover.

"Are you sure?" Colton asked.

"Of course I'm sure. I have him on film. He was right over there." Jay pointed vaguely off to his right, and turned to face the direction from which they had come. A blur of black streaked between two trees. "There's another."

The rest of the group closed in around him, their conversation forgotten.

There was more movement off to his left. He whirled in time to see another shadow vanish into the brush.

"They're all around us," Jay said.

"Stay calm," Colton whispered. He placed a steadying hand on Jay's shoulder. "Everyone form a tight line. We're too exposed here. We need to get out of the open."

Rippeth resumed the point, flanked by Colton. Morton brought up the rear, walking backward, while Sorenson and Webber slipped into the middle of the group with the poles that supported the crate on their shoulders, ready to drop it and go for their weapons at a moment's notice. Together they advanced into the unnatural twilight beneath the trees. No one spoke. The tension mounted.

Jay kept the camera to his eye, but moved it to either side of the path too fast for the aperture to reconcile. He saw motion in every shadow, and felt the weight of unseen eyes.

Why didn't they just attack?

And then it hit him.

They were being herded, driven like cattle, but toward what?

V

12:43 p.m.

During the half-hour after leaving the clearing, they had walked in an unnerving silence. Sam tried not to think about her encounter with Merritt in the bushes, although she was acutely aware of the lingering sensation of his warm breath on her lips. Best to just keep him behind her and focus on what lay ahead, which proved easier said than done. The natives had never come right out and shown themselves, yet they made their presence continually felt in sporadic glimpses of dark forms moving through the shadows and the snapping of twigs when she knew good and well that these men could move through the forest without making a sound. What exactly were they doing? Sam and the others were being ushered toward something, or were they instead being driven away? It wasn't until they arrived at an impasse that she had her answer.

A great wall rose thirty feet above their heads. It was covered so densely with blooming vines that she had to sweep them aside to reveal the construct formed of three-foot cubes of chiseled limestone. The abutment reached up into the canopy where it blended into the branches and leaves, and extended as far as they could see in either direction. Her heart skipped a beat. It was a fortification, but what was on the other side that needed protection?

Dozens of moss-covered stone columns capped with charred iron grates stood sentry every twenty-five feet or so.

"Over here," Rippeth called. He had opened a curtain of vines to expose a dark gap in the wall.

Merritt stepped up beside him, and together they pulled away the vegetation to uncover a rectangular opening. It was roughly six feet tall and three feet wide. A doorway.

"What now?" Galen asked. His face had paled to a chalky white.

The rustling sound from the bushes behind them made the decision for them.

Rippeth held a finger to his lips for all of them to see, then raised his pistol and walked slowly out of sight. Sorenson followed, face grim, gun raised. After a brief hesitation, the rest fell in behind them, leaving Morton and Webber to defend their rear.

Sam trailed closely behind Leo through the veil of vines on the opposite side of the wall, and emerged into shadows beside a large stone that appeared to fit into the gap through which they had just passed. It was attached to a system of pulleys and primitive wooden gears.

She drew a sharp intake of breath. It felt as though she had stepped through some invisible temporal barrier into the past. All of her professional life had been spent chasing history, and here she stood face-to-face with it in all its glory.

"It's amazing," she whispered, looking this way and that, absorbing every minute detail in hopes of committing it to memory.

Dahlia and Jay funneled in behind her. Sam heard the director whisper for her cameraman to stay at her hip, to record her reactions and get footage of everything she so much as looked at. The recorder started to purr and she forgot all about them in her excitement.

So much of her work was composed of guesswork predicated upon supposition. Her job was to piece together the lives of people who were no longer around to tell their own tales, and now she had the opportunity to evaluate just how right, and wrong, she had been. She forgot all about the fact that she was being herded into the fortified city.

It reminded her of the Chachapoya fortress at Kuelap, but with an undeniable Inca influence. The central path upon which they crossed into the city was several feet lower than everything else around it. Circular huts crafted from the same rock as the fortifications had been built upon elevated stone platforms and surrounded by cornices, with a single opening for a door facing the main walkway. While maybe only six feet tall and twelve feet in diameter, their conical, thatch roofs rose just as high as the fortress walls into the overhanging trees, where they tapered to sharp points. The faces of curious men, women, and children peered out from the shadowed openings before quickly ducking back out of sight. Massive kapok trees grew between the familial dwellings, their branches laced tightly overhead, except where they were pruned so as not to violate the integrity of the odd roofs. No vines or lianas dangled from the trees, yet entire colonies of epiphytes and bromeliads bloomed from the moss-covered trunks and branches in beautifully orchestrated shades of pastel yellows, purples, pinks, and blues.

The stones that lined the walkways and the borders between the structures were carved with decorative friezes, crafted with intricate zigzag and rhomboid patterns and sculpted designs. Here she truly recognized the Inca influence. There were depictions of serpentine, feline, and avian gods, especially one that appeared to be a combination of all three; faces of men in elaborate headdresses; and a series of images that appeared to tell the story of moving from one village to the next. And all of the designs were filigreed with gold.

Sam turned to her left at the sound of running water. A thin stream, channeled by low, smooth blocks, bisected the path perpendicular to the one they traversed. There had to be a spring somewhere ahead that pumped the water down the gentle slope, and somewhere out of sight was surely a mechanism of reclaiming it.

Stone domiciles passed to either side, perhaps twenty in total, before the path opened into a wide circular courtyard roughly forty feet across. Thick-trunked trees grew from the flat stone terrace at regular intervals. The lower branches had been trimmed back to the trunks to encourage proliferation in the upper reaches. Monkeys screeched above and green parrots with red rings around their eyes cawed and darted just overhead. The tree in the center had a thinner trunk than all of the others and broad, eleven-fingered leaves that folded open like hands. Sam recognized it as a cecropia tree, a sophisticated evolutionary anomaly that fostered a symbiotic relationship with a colony of cecropia ants. The ants helped the tree by defending it from herbivorous insects and mammals, while the stems and branches were riddled with hollow passages that provided a suitable home for the colony, and food in the form of glycogen that grew from the Müllerian bodies on the undersides of the leaves. One species was contingent upon the other to survive.

To her right were two circular stone stages separated by a short staircase, at the top of which was a much larger rectangular building with six trapezoidal doorways. The upper walls were designed with a step-fret frieze, while the remainder featured a mosaic of multicolored quadrangular stones. They were carved with more historical images, many depicting a god with the face of a snake, the eyes of the jaguar, and a receding crown of feathers. Sam imagined the domicile served as a palace of sorts for the ruling family, in front of which various rituals were performed.

Jay stepped in front of her to get a better view through the lens, then ducked back in line.

"Talk to me, Sam," Leo whispered into her ear. "You're the expert. What are we looking at here?"

Sam was still trying to decide. She had definitely formulated a theory, but she didn't want to be rash. She needed to be certain before she said the words out loud.

Leo's eyes locked on hers. His question wasn't one that required a simple answer. There was another question lurking beneath the one he had vocalized. He wanted to know if they were going to have to fight their way out of the village. What could she say? She was piecing it together as fast as she possibly could, and she was every bit as overwhelmed as the rest of them.

She averted her gaze and stared past Leo. Through the maze of tree trunks she could see several tall stone tiers ascending the steep slope of the mountain that served as the rear fortification. At the top of each retaining wall grew green tufts of plants, one of which she could readily identify. Maize. It was only then that she knew beyond any shadow of doubt who this lost tribe was.

"They're Chachapoya," she said, again meeting Leo's eyes. "We had thought that after the conquest by the Inca and then the Spanish occupation that their bloodlines had been diluted into the general population. But this tribe must have somehow eluded capture by leaving the traditional tribal boundaries of the Utcubamba and Marañón Rivers." She became more and more animated as she spoke. "All of the buildings and the layout of the village are Chachapoyan, but the artwork on the friezes and the main building are Incan. And do you see that terraced garden over there? You'll find the exact same thing at both Kuelap and Machu Picchu. These people fled here nearly five hundred years ago to elude the conquistadors. They've survived in complete isolation for longer than the United States has even existed."

Leo narrowed his eyes. "Both the Inca and Chachapoya were warring tribes."

"And they could have already killed us if that was their intention."

"We need to know right now if things are going to get ugly."

There was movement to her left. Sam whirled and saw three black-painted faces leaning around the trunks of the kapoks. Each man held a bow with an arrow notched, pointed directly at them. She glanced to her right in time to see more scrabble up onto the stone platforms to cover them from above.

"Just keep moving," Colton whispered from ahead of them.

Across the twin stages, in one of the middle dark openings of the large dwelling, the shape of a man took form from the shadows. He lingered in the darkness a moment longer before stepping out onto the stone platform and into the light.

"My God," Sam gasped.

VI

1:05 p.m.

"Here," Colton whispered. He reached around Merritt from behind and pressed something against his belly.

Merritt knew the object by feel, and tucked the pistol under his waistband.

He didn't like this. Not one bit. They had been herded into the city walls, and now they were sitting ducks, far too exposed as they slowly walked through the central courtyard. He hadn't fired a weapon in half a decade, but that didn't worry him nearly as much as how quickly the skills and the ability to kill without reservation would undoubtedly come back to him.

From the edge of his peripheral vision, he watched the natives take their posts behind the trees to his left, while they simultaneously assumed the higher ground to his right. His fist found the grip on the pistol too easily and his index finger caressed the trigger like an old lover.

What were they waiting for?

With his free hand, he pulled Dahlia behind him so that he was between her and the natives. Her blonde hair stood out like a bull's eye.

His heart pounded. Not with fear, but in anticipation.

The man who had emerged from inside the stone building strode to the edge of the platform and surveyed them as though they were no more significant than a line of ants marching through his kingdom.

He stood a full seven feet tall with the ornate golden headdress, from which both real and filigreed feathers stood like the rays of the sun to frame the crown that covered the man's forehead and brow. It reminded Merritt of the one he had discovered in Hunter's rucksack, only instead of golden teeth along the front rim, these appeared to be made of bone. The wrinkles on the man's face placed him somewhere in his fifties to sixties, yet his body was as muscular and toned as that of a man half his age. He bared his teeth as he watched them pass, showcasing brown triangles that knitted together like the fearsome jaws of a shark. Worse still was the fact that even beneath the thick application of black paint, the scars covering the man's body were clearly visible. Long, straight scars transected his chest and abdomen, and curved around his shoulders and biceps. His legs had been carved in numerous directions to create divots in the flesh where the scars intersected. Even his face had been slashed in such a way that it appeared cooked. His right eye was lower than his left, and the cheek beneath was thinner, the bones more prominent, as though a large section of meat had been torn away. He wore only a gray skirt woven from alpaca wool, from which hundreds of dark feathers hung to his knees. There were even feathers in his hair and hanging by leather straps from the wide holes in his ears.

Upon closer scrutiny, Merritt could tell that the other natives on the circular stages to either side of the stone staircase were similarly scarred, though to nowhere near the same degree.

He imagined some rite of passage ceremony like a bris, only instead of being circumcised, these boys were cut to within an inch of their lives. What kind of monsters were they dealing with here? Any tribe willing to torture its own members would surely be willing to do far worse to them.

The man, whom Merritt could only assume was some sort of leader or chief, inspected them like livestock, as though he were accustomed to the sight of strangers walking through his village. He bellowed something Merritt couldn't understand in a deep, thunderous voice.

As one, all of the natives lowered their bows. The arrows remained notched, but at least they were no longer an immediate threat.

Merritt looked back at Sam. A puzzled expression crinkled her pale face. When he turned back to the building, he saw only the silhouette of the man disappearing into the dark doorway.

"What just happened?" Merritt whispered.

"Just keep walking," Colton said, picking up the pace. He caught up with Rippeth at the front of the line and the two men spoke in hushed tones.

Merritt noticed he had unconsciously fingered the safety off on the weapon, and clicked it back on again. As much as the feel of the cold steel in his hand repulsed him, he couldn't bring himself to release it. He drew reassurance from its familiar power.

They walk in formation through a small village in the sand. He adjusts his grip on the Heckler & Koch HK416 clasped in his hands. Terrified faces peer out from behind boarded windows in whitewashed buildings scored by sand and smoke. The horrible silence. He fears the attack will come at any moment, from anywhere and everywhere, and the knowledge of what they will do to these people, what they have already done...

The path forked at the edge of the central courtyard. One branch veered to the right toward a series of staircases that ascended the sheer slope to where topless women tended to flourishing crops in stone-walled gardens. They weren't slathered with paint like the men, and had far lighter skin than Merritt would have expected, only a few shades darker than his own. The women stopped and watched them as they reached the intersection, and resumed their tasks when Rippeth led them down the path to the left, which descended toward the outer fortification.

Painted men continued to parallel their progress from the shadows. They darted from behind one tree to the next, weapons at the ready.

Ahead, a lone figure stood before an identical contraption of pulleys and gears to the one they had seen upon entering the village. The large stone that served as the door was still fitted in place. An alpaca grazed at the base of an agave plant beside the path. It was the same man they had encountered in the light gap. He gripped the handles of the gears and looked to the other natives as if seeking permission.

"You'd better open that gate," Rippeth said. "Now."

He raised his pistol and pointed it at the native's chest.

The man quickly recoiled.

An arrow sang through the air.

Rippeth cursed and his weapon fell from his grasp. He grabbed his right hand by the wrist. Half of the arrow protruded from either side of the base of his thumb. Blood flowed freely from the wound. Cradling the hand to his chest, he dropped to one knee and reclaimed his weapon in his other hand. He pointed it toward the trees, where now all of the natives had their bows raised.

"No!" Sam shouted.

She shoved through Merritt and the others until she reached Rippeth, and stood between him and his assailants.

"What are you doing?" Rippeth asked. He tried to sight down the barrel around her, but she moved from side to side to block his shot. "Get out of the way!"

"When you raised your gun, they perceived it as an act of aggression," she said. "They could have killed you, but they didn't."

"That doesn't change the fact that they shot me!"

"In the hand. It could just as easily have been through the neck."

Merritt studied her. She could have been killed stepping between the trained soldier and his target. He had seen it in the man's eyes.

"Everyone lower your weapons," Sam called without breaking eye contact with Rippeth.

"You're out of your mind," Rippeth said.

"Would you just lower your gun before you get us all killed!"

With obvious reluctance, Rippeth slowly allowed his pistol to fall to his side.

"Thank you."

Sam turned to face the native who again stood at the gears. He glanced to his armed companions, then unlatched the handle and cranked the wheel of the contraption. With the grinding sound of stone on stone, the massive slab inched backward from the wall to reveal the dark passage.

They passed through cascading streams of vines and shadows to find themselves in the jungle. Again there was the grinding sound as the stone slid back into place, sealing them outside the village.

"You should have let me shoot them," Rippeth said. His lips pursed over his clenched teeth as he yanked the arrow out of the back of his hand and cast it into the forest.

Sam said nothing, and instead shed her backpack, opened the flap, and removed a long-sleeved shirt. She ripped it at the seam and tipped her chin toward Rippeth's bloody hand.

He appraised her for some time before holding it out.

She wrapped the wound twice around and then tied the fabric tight. Rippeth flexed his fingers into a fist, but the thumb didn't respond.

"I'm sorry," she said. "That's going to have to do for now."

Rippeth whirled and stormed away from her down the earthen path.

The others followed in silence. Merritt had to jog to catch up with Sam.

"What did he say back there?" he asked.

"That I should have let him kill them."

"No. Back there in the village. The man with all of the scars and the headdress. I saw the look on your face when he spoke. You understood him, didn't you?"

Sam looked off into the forest as she whispered to him.

"It was a dialect of Quechua I've never heard before, so I can't be completely sure."

"Okay. So what do you think he might have said?"

She turned to face him and their eyes locked.

"It sounded like he said something to the effect of 'Let them pass. They are dead already.'"

VII

1:32 p.m.

Sam hung back toward the rear of the group. Her thoughts were a blur. She had seen so much, too much. It was sensory overload on a scale she'd never experienced before. She could spend a lifetime cataloguing and studying just what she'd been able to see from the central path leading through the village. What else could be stored inside the buildings? What other surprises lurked just out of sight? All of the answers she had sought during the course of her education and career were somewhere within those city walls, which were now falling rapidly behind her. Not only could she unravel the mystery of the disappearance of an entire culture half a millennium ago, but she could hear it told in the words of the people themselves. How had they managed to stay hidden for so long in an age when technology had shrunk the globe to the size of a pebble and laid bare so many of its secrets? They couldn't be more than forty-five miles from Pomacochas, and yet it might as well be a thousand.

She wished she could turn around and head back to the village, if only to memorize the history told through the carvings on the stone walls. There was so much they didn't know about the Chachapoya. No one was even sure what language they had spoken. Some speculated Aymara like so many Andean tribes, while others believed they spoke Quechua, especially following their defeat at the hands of the Inca. And now she had incontrovertible proof that they did indeed speak a variant of Quechua, but at the moment there wasn't a blasted thing she could do about it.

The Chachapoya were an enigma. Even that name wasn't what the tribe had called itself, but rather what it had been called by others. The name was most likely a corruption of the Quechua words *sacha* and *puya*, or "people of the clouds." They were known as ferocious warriors who lived high in the mountains under the cover of cloud forests where they thrived as a sovereign nation until falling to the Inca under the rule of Tupac Inca

Yupanqui in roughly 1475. Within a hundred years, the Spanish arrived and began their systematic conquest of the entire continent, bringing with them their Christian God and a host of European diseases. One of the few historical documents that even mentioned the Chachapoya was in the written account of Pedro Ciezo de León, who described them as "the whitest and most handsome" of all of the natives he had encountered.

So who were these people who were markedly taller than the average Peruvian Indians, nearly as pale as Caucasians, and lived in such secrecy? She had spent nearly the last decade trying to figure out just that. The first Chachapoyan ruins had been discovered at Kuelap more than a century and a half ago, and now here she was, a quarter-mile from the answers to all of her questions, and all she had to do was ask. Instead, they were traveling in the opposite direction. She wanted to scream.

Why didn't she just turn around and return to the fortress?

Unfortunately, she already knew why. She needed to earn their trust before they would welcome her and share the mystery of their heritage, and banging on the stone walls and demanding admittance wasn't the way to do it. There would be plenty of time over the coming years to break down the barriers. That is, if they let her. An entire colony didn't survive in isolation for so long without going to great lengths to preserve its anonymity…

She stopped walking abruptly and Merritt bumped into her from behind. Her features crinkled as she followed that line of thought.

There was no doubt in her mind that these people wished to remain concealed from the rest of the world. So why had they allowed her group to walk freely through their village? The tribe had to realize that once they returned to civilization, they would report their discoveries. Unless…

Let them pass. They are dead already.

Unless they were certain that Sam and her companions would never be leaving these mountains.

A chill crawled up her spine. She wrapped her arms around her chest to combat the sudden onset of shivers. What awaited them down the path ahead?

"Look over there," Galen called from around the bend in front of her. "Back behind those trees."

Sam followed the sound of his voice to where the others had gathered around him at the side of the path, where a thinner branch diverged into the dense rainforest. At first she didn't see anything, but after taking several steps deeper into the jungle, the structure resolved from the trees. The stone walls were just like those that surrounded the village, only nowhere near as intimidating. They were only fifteen feet tall, and covered with vines and lianas. Soil had been mounded over the roof of the structure to support a thriving crown of flowering shrubbery.

She wasn't even within twenty feet of the building when a stick snapped underfoot, and the screaming began.

Sam ran toward the front of the construct. From the other side of the wall she heard horrible cries and the sounds of a struggle. They weren't human screams, but she had no idea what kind of animal could make such awful noises. She brushed aside the vines in search of the entrance, and found that the stone cubes weren't fitted snugly together like those that composed the fortifications. Between the sides of each were six-inch-wide gaps, through which she could see only swatches of the dim interior. Columns of light shined down to the inner, straw-lined floor from holes in the earthen roof. They swirled with dust raised by a stampede of dark bodies. She smelled dry grain and manure, but it wasn't until a snuffling snout pressed into the gap in front of her that she understood.

"It's a barn." She tentatively reached through the gap and allowed the alpaca to nuzzle her fingertips with its wet nose.

"Why would they keep them closed up like this?" Galen asked. "Surely an outdoor pen would serve the same purpose. And the animals would be able to graze in the sunlight."

"You've heard of veal, haven't you?" Merritt asked.

"Galen's right," Sam said. "Why wouldn't they just fence off this area? Nearly all of the indigenous ruins in Peru have alpacas grazing everywhere. They actually live there. Why would these animals need to be caged like this?"

The screaming died down and the dust started to settle. She could see dozens of the wooly beasts through the crevice. Most of them were clustered together in the middle of the large room in a maze of support columns. The interior space was reasonably large, perhaps a hundred square yards, but it wasn't nearly large enough to accommodate so many animals. It was inhumane to keep them like this when they could be roaming the jungle with little chance of wandering off. It didn't make sense. Were the Chachapoya worried that the alpacas would escape and return to their native highlands, or were they keeping them in there for their own protection? Why else would they possibly need to enclose them behind the same kind of walls they had used to build their fortress? And by that same logic, why weren't the animals within the fortifications with the village where there were groves of trees and fields of crops?

She thought of the man she had seen with the lone alpaca. Had he taken it out of this very pen in order to allow it to stretch its legs and graze?

And why had the alpacas reacted as they had at the sound of her approach?

She withdrew her arm from the hole, and in doing so noticed that the edges of the stones around it weren't smooth and even. They were carved with notches as though poorly chiseled, or deliberately scraped with sharp objects.

"There's a gate over here," Dahlia said.

Sam walked along the face of the structure to where the blonde woman held back the curtain of vines so Jay could film the interior. A foul gust that reeked of dust and feces passed through an iron grate that was moored by iron rungs to stones set into the earth. Through the slots she could see a short stone corridor that branched at a ninety-degree angle to the right to prohibit visibility directly into the chamber. Was there another gate at the far end of it? Why else wouldn't the alpacas have approached the gate if she was right and the man came here to take them out for exercise?

The rock edges around the gate had been carved as well, and all of the rust had been scraped from the iron rails. Some even appeared to have been scored down to the virgin metal that had only recently been exposed to the elements.

Galen crouched beside her and sifted through the dirt. He pulled out a filthy brown feather. He blew off the dust and spun it between his fingers by the quill. Sam only now noticed that there were feathers all over the ground. They blended perfectly into the mat of dead leaves and sticks. Galen tucked the feather into the breast pocket of his khaki cargo vest, looked up at the sky, and then back to the ground.

He shook his head and furrowed his brow.

"What is it?" Sam asked.

Galen seemed to puzzle over her question before finally speaking.

"The walls make sense, but why would they need to build a roof over the animals?"

"To protect them from above," Jay said, retreating from the bars to capture better footage of the entire building.

"Possibly," Galen said. "But if that were the case, then why wouldn't they have done the same thing for their village?"

"You think it's possible that they're shielding their livestock from some sort of birds?" Sam asked.

Galen just chewed on the inside of his lip as he appraised the structure.

"I'm beginning to wonder...," he finally said.

Sam followed his gaze to the threshold, where the stone edges had been chiseled away.

It almost looked as though the rock had been carved in an effort to pry the iron gate loose.

VIII

6:36 p.m.

Leo didn't care if Sam believed that the tribe wasn't hostile. The more he thought about it, the more it made sense. The natives had killed his son. They had allowed Hunter to reach his destination, and then they had stalked and murdered him. When he ultimately found the source of the placers and concluded that his son's party hadn't mutinied against him, he would have all of the proof he needed. And then he could return to the village and let them know how he felt about the cowardly act of stabbing a man in the back.

He glanced back at Sorenson and Webber, who ferried the crate affixed to long wooden dowels on their shoulders.

Oh yes, he would show these natives exactly how he felt.

Darkness descended upon the forest. The heat began to dissipate by degree, which only served to amplify the humidity, and welcome more mosquitoes to the ranks swarming around them. They were still more than an hour from the formal time listed for the setting of the sun, but the high mountains bathed them in premature shadows. Soon they would need to pitch camp for the night if they were to rest up for the final push during the coming day. He had compared the maps to their current position on the GPS unit. Tomorrow they would reach their goal, he could feel it.

Leo's heart raced at the prospect. Within twenty-four hours, he would learn the answers to the questions that plagued him about his son's death.

Twenty-four hours and he'd finally be able to determine what he needed to do about it.

Few vines eclipsed the trail and the branches were easily enough shoved aside, which allowed them to advance at a rapid pace. Unlike the path leading into the jungle from the river, this one appeared frequently used. Rippeth scouted ahead, often disappearing entirely. He held his gun in his left hand, and cradled his bloody right against his gut. The man had barely spoken since leaving the fortified city. Flames burned behind his eyes. He was

obviously itching to extract a measure of revenge, and soon
enough Leo would give him the opportunity.

A glimmer of red sparkled through the branches of the trees. It
grew brighter and brighter until they pressed through the final
stand of trees and stepped out onto the bank of a small lake, upon
which the reflected brilliance of the setting sun shimmered. The
water was still and crystalline. A startled school of fish darted from
the shallows, leaving a cloud of silt in their wake.

"It's beautiful," Galen said.

Leo nodded his agreement. It truly was a breathtaking sight.
The lake was circular, and perhaps a hundred yards across.
Waterfowl appeared as dark dots in the very center. The jungle
encroached to the edge of the water on all sides. Sheer, tree-
covered mountains rose up into the low-lying clouds ahead and to
both sides, forming a bowl to cradle the lake.

"This is their *pacarisca*," Sam said. "The Chachapoya always
built their villages near one. It's generally a lake or river,
sometimes a mountaintop. They regard it as their point of origin,
the sacred place where their souls—for lack of a better term—were
born. Somewhere nearby we'll find their *chullpa*, their tribal burial
site. The dead are always interred close to the metaphorical point
where their lives began, the completion of the circle of life, if you
will."

Leo wondered what Hunter must have thought when he came
upon this incredible sight. Had he camped here as well before
beginning what might have been the last day of his life?

Rippeth emerged from the forest twenty yards up the bank,
strode directly to Colton, and whispered something into his ear.
Leo watched Colton closely. His old friend's stare darted to the
point where Rippeth had appeared, and then back.

Leo sauntered over to join them, but by then they were already
done speaking.

"Why don't you guys start setting up the tents," Leo said, and,
without a backward glance, joined Colton as he walked northwest
along the muddy bank, which was choppy with alpaca hoof prints.

Rippeth vanished into the trees, with Leo and Colton directly
behind him. They followed the shivering bushes that trailed
Rippeth deeper into the jungle. The smell hit them first, the awful
stench of decomposing flesh. Leo had to cup his hand over his

mouth and nose until he adapted to it. Another dozen paces and the sound of buzzing flies reached them.

"Jesus," Leo gasped as they stumbled into a circular clearing. The largest kapok tree he had ever seen stood in the center. Its trunk was so wide that even if all three of them joined hands, they wouldn't be able to encircle it. All of the shrubs and undergrowth had been torn out to expose the rich loam in a fifteen foot radius around the behemoth. The massive branches formed a leafy roof five feet over their heads. Lianas coiled in serpentine fashion around the trunk. The smooth gray bark looked as though it had been assaulted by an angry group of ax-wielding lumberjacks. There were cuts and gouges from the ground clear up to the first row of branches. Amber sap bled down the surface like wax on a candlestick. Several ropes had been tied around the tree, their frayed ends dangling toward the dirt.

Bones were scattered everywhere throughout the clearing. Some were still tacky with rust-colored blood, while others had yellowed with age and started to deteriorate. Bloodstains decorated everything in arcs and spatters, upon which the flies swarmed like seething black scabs.

"I told you it was a mess," Rippeth said to Colton, who had crouched to inspect the remains.

Leo didn't have to study the bones to recognize to which species they had once belonged. Wiry wool clung to the surrounding bushes, against which it had been blown into small drifts at the edges of the clearing.

A light flashed from his left. Colton had turned on his penlight and now used it to scrutinize the sloppy earth. It was growing darker by the minute as the lingering residue of the sun faded from the sky.

Colton shoved aside a pile of broken bones and inspected the mud. His beam fell upon a clear set of tracks in a V-shape that appeared to have been made by some sort of deer, only the impressions didn't have the sharply defined edges to delineate them as hooves.

Leo turned his attention again to the tree. Designs had been carved into the bark at the level of the lower canopy. The sun, the moon, and stars of various shapes and sizes were framed by twin zigzagging lines.

"They brought them out here and tied them to the tree," Colton said. He stood, approached the end of one of the tattered ropes, and pulled it taut. At his feet lay the cracked remains of a camelid skull. He lifted it and held it up for them to see. The occipital bone had been broken away from the hollow hole where the brain had once been, and the elongated snout had been snapped in half so that only the worn rear molars remained. He tossed it aside and pointed his light at the dirt, which had obviously been scuffed and gouged by alpaca hooves.

"Why would they do that?" Rippeth asked. He kicked a femur that shattered into chunks of calcium.

"They were sacrifices. But to what?" Colton turned in a slow circle. Leo noticed the man had drawn his pistol. This was the first time he had seen Colton act in a manner that was anything other than calm and collected, which unnerved him even more than all of the death surrounding him.

"Jaguars?"

"No," Leo said. "Remember the jaguar carcass we found in the light gap? This looks like it was done by the same animals. Jaguars don't hunt in packs like lions. They're territorial, and they don't slaughter their own kind."

"They could have done this to those alpacas though."

"This isn't the work of jaguars," Colton said. "We're dealing with something else entirely."

"What do you propose then?"

"I haven't got a clue." Colton bent over and held up a trio of dark feathers. "But we do know that the buzzards had their way with the leftovers as well."

"So we can assume that the natives have been bringing the alpacas out here from that stone pen as part of some sort of sacrificial ritual, where they tether them to this tree—"

"*Waka*," Sam said from where she'd been watching them from behind a stand of ferns. She stepped out into the open. "The tree is a *waka*, a sacred object the Chachapoya believe holds great power, but they didn't perform any kind of sacrifice here. Life was the most valuable commodity to these people. They respected and revered it like few others. Animals served an important function in their everyday lives and in the way they perceived the world around them. They weren't sacrificing them." She stooped and picked up a sharply-fractured rib. The broken end appeared serrated. "They were feeding them to something."

IX

10:45 p.m.

Merritt stood at the edge of the placid lake, basking in its serenity. The moon was nearly full now, and reflected from the surface of the water amid a smattering of white stars. A gentle breeze rustled the leaves on the trees and stirred the whining cloud of mosquitoes. All of the others were asleep in their tents, minus Morton and Sorenson, who patrolled the perimeter of camp. The men were definitely more alert than they had been during the previous night, and reacted to the slightest sound or any shift in the shadows. He couldn't fault them for it, not after seeing the alpaca remains in that clearing. Had they not already burned through the last of the daylight and their waning energy, they would have pressed on, if only to distance themselves from the carnage. The decision had been made to rest while they could with their guards standing at heightened awareness, and get the hell out of there at the first hint of the rising sun.

As far as Merritt was concerned, dawn couldn't come soon enough. Not because he was terrified that whatever had slaughtered the alpacas would steal into their camp while they were dozing, but because even though he was physically exhausted, he couldn't force his brain to shut down long enough to fall asleep. This was now his second night without his medication, and already the dreams had returned with a vengeance. They were right there waiting for him every time he so much as blinked. The combination of the drugs and the excision of caffeine from his diet had held them at bay for so long now that he couldn't remember how he had ever dealt with them on his own. So many years had passed that he would have expected the nightmares to have lost some of their power over him. Instead, the years of suppressing them only seemed to have magnified their urgency and intensity. He had only been able to lie on his back under the mosquito netting, which positively crawled with little black bodies of all ilk, for so long before he had needed to escape the humming and buzzing, and the images that assaulted him.

He turned away from the lake and returned to the bonfire in the center of the circle of tents. With a scorched stick, he stoked the blaze until it was several feet tall, then threw on more logs from the pile. Rich ebon smoke plumed from the wood until it was dry enough to burn.

Morton appeared twenty yards away through the gap between the tents, his silhouette limned in orange from the flickering firelight. A second later he was gone. Merritt heard the slurping sound of boots passing through the soft mud behind him as Sorenson walked the shoreline. With a crackle of dead leaves, he too disappeared into the forest, leaving Merritt alone with the roaring fire and the memories that refused to allow him a moment's peace.

The dry heat of the bonfire metamorphosed into the roasting sensation of the wicked sun above and the eternal sand below. After crossing the Dasht-i-Margi Desert, the Desert of Death, from their staging grounds in Kandahar by chopper, armed to the teeth with a fresh batch of intelligence and enough firepower to lay siege to a small country, they wait in their hiding places in the rock formations surrounding the mouth of the cave until one hour before sunrise. Upon his commanding officer's signal, they launch grenades from the MK19 through the stone maw. Muffled thumps follow, a prelude to the blinding wall of fire that blasts from the opening. The ground trembles beneath him where he kneels behind a boulder, assault rifle to his shoulder, rebreathing mask making a sound like blowing into a coffee tin. Rocks break free from the mountainside and tumble down toward them. The dust to merges with the smoke to create an impermeable haze.

And then he hears the screams, the horrible cries of pain and terror. The sobbing. The mewling of children.

The voices of his brothers whisper epithets through the earpiece in his tactical communications headset.

That's for the World Trade Towers, you sons of bitches.

I hope you all burn in hell.

Where's your Allah now, bastards?

They cover the only egress from the warren of caves until the sun rises. Several men and women, charred and burning, try to make a run for it, only to be mowed down in the crossfire, while the screams continue to drift out on the smoke, diminished in number, but amplified by pain.

Under the blood-red dawn, his commanding officer gives the order, and they hurl flashbangs into the smoke and storm through the rock orifice two-by-two. Pebbles shiver loose from the ceiling. The walls are painted black by the firestorm and the floor carpeted with charred corpses. Only those still burning cast a dim glare into the churning smoke. The rata-tat of gunfire echoes from ahead as he follows the barrel of his rifle deeper into the twisting stone maze until he enters a domed cavern. Muzzle flare draws his attention to the left, where a supine form dances beneath its glare. The cries of the injured subside under the barrage of bullets. He watches men whom he trusts with his life taking the lives of the wounded. One after another. Men and women alike, put down like curs. Through the chaos he sees crates burning against the rear wall, their contents spilled out onto the rock floor. They hadn't been filled with munitions or biological agents as they'd been led to believe, but rather with food, clothing, and containers of potable water.

He pauses in the middle of the chamber and surveys the massacre around him. The world begins to spin around him and the walls close in. There are filthy mattresses in every corner, linens burning. Bedrolls, books, clothing, a transistor radio blaring static. They hadn't wiped out an al-Qaida stronghold. They had murdered a band of refugees that must have fled from Kandahar when the American armed forces had descended upon them with weapons blazing.

To his right, he sees a young woman, her face pale, hair singed to the scalp. Her face is so badly burned that the flesh has split. Amber sludge oozes from an ulcer beneath her left eye, an intoxicating shade of blue that betrays her Northern Afghani heritage. She couldn't be more than eighteen years-old, a slip of a girl whose thin limbs resemble burnt twigs. The bleating sounds she makes...the sheer amount of pain...fear...the panic on her face when the soldier stands over her and points a rifle down at her forehead...

After that, Merritt's memory becomes as cloudy as the smoke-filled cave. Something snapps inside of him, and he only clearly recalls snippets of the following weeks. The look of surprise on his platoon-mate's face when he had turns his weapon on him.

Stumbling through the tunnels with the wailing woman in his arms. Calling for help, only to watch her slowly die while even their medic refuses to administer a single ampule of anesthetic to ease her suffering. Reliving her death in an almost catatonic state as the chopper thunders back across the desert. Blaming himself for failing her and swearing it will never happen again. Slipping away from the barracks in the middle of night, knowing they will come after him, but he can't allow them to catch him. He can never live that life again, not now that he understands the consequences. From there, he remembers running, and then nothing but infinite sand and sun, stumbling through villages that revile him for the dirty fatigues he wears, then finally the Pakistani port town of Gwādar on the Gulf of Oman, where he trades his few remaining supplies and his rifle for passage on the first available freighter, not caring its destination.

Merritt realized he was on the verge of hyperventilation and focused on slowing his breathing using the thud of his pulse inside his head as a guide. Tears squeezed from the corners of his eyes. He wiped them away and tried to think of something else, anything else. He envisioned the look of pride on his father's face when he had shipped off to Basic, and the undiluted love in his mother's eyes that was always present, but that only led to the remembrance of their cold gray features inside their caskets the day he had buried them.

He needed to get out of here, get out of his own head. This was a bad idea. He never should have come. The feeling of claustrophobia, the sensation of being smothered alive, overwhelmed him. He needed to leave this godforsaken jungle, to climb up into the sky where there were no stone walls or interminable fields of snarled trees. Only then would he be able to breathe, where the air was crisp and thin and not sweaty with humidity. His vision constricted from the periphery and he felt the panic attack swelling within him.

A cool hand settled on his shoulder and he nearly jumped out of his skin.

"Are you all right?" Sam asked. She knelt in front of him so she could clearly see his face. "I could hear you panting from all the way over there in my tent."

He nodded, but only succeeded in shaking the beading perspiration from his forehead.

"Just try to relax," she whispered. She gently stroked his cheek. Her soft blue eyes sought his gaze and held it, binding him to the moment. He placed his hand over hers and leaned slightly into it. "Everything's going to be okay."

There was genuine compassion in her eyes. No fear. No judgment.

His breathing slowed as he memorized every detail: the flecks of gold in her irises; the wily strand of bangs that curled around her eyebrow and cupped her right cheek; her slightly parted lips; the nearly unnoticeable crook right at the bridge of her nose.

She slowly removed her hand from his cheek and sat down on the mossy stump beside him.

He chuckled nervously.

"You must think I'm a complete psyche-case."

"We all have our quirks. That's what makes us human."

Her words were sensitive, her thigh against his comforting. She could easily have taken this opportunity to repay him for her earlier frustrations, but instead, she sat quietly beside him, waiting for him to speak if that was what he needed, lending quiet support.

The silence was so comfortable that he hated to break it, but some things needed to be said.

"Thank you," he whispered.

She gave his hand a reassuring squeeze. He held it a beat too long before releasing it.

"I should be the one thanking you," she said. "For what you did back there."

"For throwing you down in the bushes?"

She smiled and nudged his leg.

"For taking care of me."

"You don't need to thank me. Any guy would give his left arm for the chance to duck into the shrubs with you. Besides, it's obvious you don't need anyone taking care of you. The way you stepped into the line of fire in the village? That was downright fearless."

She leaned her head against his shoulder, a comfortable silence between them.

"Why are you still awake?" he finally asked.

"Couldn't sleep," she said, but he knew by the undertone in her voice that it was because she couldn't stop thinking about what she'd seen in the forest.

He let it drop, and together they sat by the fire under the edge of the canopy while the jungle around them slept.

The bonfire snapped and popped. The dim purple glow of lightning flared on the far horizon.

And from somewhere in the distance came the haunting *skree* of a hawk.

X

11:40 p.m.

The changing of the guards had occurred promptly at eleven o'clock. They were rotating in two hour shifts to stay sharp until they broke camp at five a.m. and struck off for the highlands under the blessings of dawn. The coming day would be physically demanding as somehow, according to their maps, they were expected to ascend roughly twenty-six hundred nearly vertical feet to reach their destination high in the Andes beneath the unmoving shroud of clouds. Rippeth was certain it would take more than a single day to surmount that task, but he wasn't about to contradict the men who signed his paycheck. After all, the sooner they were away from this lake, the better.

The stench from the clearing of death, as he had come to think of it, had somehow lodged in his sinuses. It was all he could smell, and the coppery residue lingered on his tongue. He was no stranger to death. After two tours through Iraq and an eye-opening black op in Serbia, he figured he had seen about every atrocity imaginable. Bodies blown to bits in markets and mosques, rotted carcasses barely covered in mass graves, men tortured for weeks at a time until they finally broke with what would prove to be their last breaths. Granted, the clearing had been filled with only alpaca parts, but the savagery with which they'd been slaughtered surpassed even the genocidal rampages of the Serbs. This was a different beast entirely. Men could be monsters, but they always maintained an element of predictability. Here they were dealing with the unknown, and, as such, unpredictability was inherent to the situation. The first rule of engagement was to know the enemy, and here they didn't understand a blasted thing about what might be out there in the jungle at this very moment.

Although they hadn't come right out and discussed it, he and his men were spooked. To survive under the hostile conditions of war, both declared and undeclared, a soldier had to develop a sixth sense for danger. Being caught unprepared was a mortal mistake. All of them felt it. He could see it in their eyes, in the way their nervous tendencies surfaced, and in the way they reverted to their rigid military training.

And on top of everything else, his goddamn hand was killing him. The gauze had long since soaked through and the injections of lidocaine were about as effective as the two acetaminophen he popped every four hours. Those rotten savages would pay if it was the last thing he did.

Fortunately, they had packed for every contingency. Maybe they had no idea what lurked out of sight, or what the natives might be willing to do if they found themselves cornered, but they had definitely brought enough firepower to muddle their way through any mess.

Colton had instructed them to stay out of the heavy artillery until the point it was deemed necessary. Rippeth didn't care what the man thought. As far as he was concerned, the time to break out the big guns was upon them.

He lingered near the camp, watching the tents to ensure that no shadows stirred behind the canvas. The fire had dwindled. All was silent and still as he had hoped. He waited until Webber reached the southernmost point of his circuit, an eighth of a mile into the dense forestation, before sprinting soundlessly toward the pile of supplies. His backpack was beside the wooden crate where he had left it. He unclasped the main flap and opened it. As quickly and quietly as possible, he slid back the bolts that sealed the crate and threw open the lid. The ground penetrating radar and magnetometer units were disassembled and packed in molded foam. He carefully extracted the pieces and went straight for the secret padded inserts hidden beneath, which had been machined precisely to fit the six FN-SCAR-L/Mk. 16 assault rifles, and the dozen round M67 hand grenades and AN-M14 TH3 incendiary grenade canisters.

Rippeth loaded one of each of the grenades into his backpack, and removed one of the SCARs. He placed the sensing device parts back into the crate, closed the lid, and latched it. Slinging his pack over his shoulders, he darted back out of camp with his pistol tucked under his waistband and the assault rifle across his chest in both hands. It was just small enough to fit into his rucksack for the coming day's trek if he sacrificed a few sets of clothes. As long as no one searched the crate, they would never know he had raided it.

At least not until he had to use the weapons, and at that point they'd all be thankful that he'd had the foresight to secure them.

And right now his sixth sense was telling him that he was going to need them soon.

The cry of a distant bird of prey pierced the night.

He trudged deeper into the jungle and resumed his watch. The smell of death clung to the entire area. He was going to have to swing farther away from camp if he hoped not to have to cross through that vile clearing. The stench alone was more than enough to keep him on his toes. Add to that the droning buzz of the black flies and he had to be especially vigilant to make sure he could hear even the faint snap of a twig under the ruckus. Didn't those filthy flies ever have to sleep?

Another avian shriek. This time much closer. Perhaps the raptor was circling the clearing and waiting for its opportunity to pick at the gnarled remains.

His bloody hand grew slick on the rifle's grip. He had to pause to inspect the mass of gauze, which was so thoroughly saturated that he was forced to peel it off and hurl it into the underbrush. The wound had started to scab over, but not well enough to staunch the flow of blood or hide the angled bone chips. He cursed and fumbled another roll of gauze out of his pocket, then wrapped his hand as tightly as he could bear. It didn't take long for the blood to soak through the fresh bandage.

"Goddamn savages," he grumbled.

The forest around him was so silent that even his stealthily placed footsteps made the detritus crackle far too loudly for comfort. Shadows claimed the trees and shrubs around him, and choked visibility down to a few feet to either side. A mosquito whined in his ear, but he resisted the urge to slap it until he felt the stinger poke his skin, then quietly squished it on his cheek.

A heliconia bush swayed ahead. The orange blossom, shaped like a roadrunner's head, nodded back and forth.

He felt no wind.

His finger tightened the trigger into the sweet spot. The slightest application of pressure would fire a fusillade of bullets at the rate of ten rounds per second.

The movement slowly stilled, and the flower resumed its former position, a wary bird peering out from behind the bush on a long, slender neck.

He raised the rifle into firing position and advanced in increments of inches.

A cold bead of sweat rolled down his temple from his forehead and dripped onto the stock.

Another step forward and he was directly beside the heliconia.

A low clicking sound came from the tangled vegetation to his left.

The moment he turned in that direction, he realized his mistake.

Leaves rustled and he smelled rotten flesh.

Something sharp impaled his side.

He was cleaved from his feet and pinned to the ground beneath a heavy weight.

Searing pain in his neck.

A flood of warmth over his face and chest.

Damp tearing sounds.

Darkness descended on the buzzing wings of black flies.

XI

11:58 p.m.

Tasker would have had a harder time tracking a herd of stampeding elephants for as cautious as his prey had been. Perhaps the appearance of the natives had thrown them off his scent. They had known they were being followed, but he didn't think they suspected they were being tailed by two separate factions. And now they had their hands full with the Indians, as he imagined he soon would as well. Their trackers had been trailing his men and him, too. He rarely saw them, but their presence was impossible to miss. Now, he could either wait for them to spring their trap, or he could go on the offensive. He reveled in the prospect of the latter. Only time would tell.

The expedition party's trail had led directly to the stone fortification. There had been no signs to suggest they had veered off in either direction, which could only mean one thing. They had passed through the wall and into whatever was on the other side, and they wouldn't have been allowed to do so without an escort. He didn't feel like calling out for the natives to show themselves in order to chaperone them through the city walls, so they were just going to have to go around.

His men were staggered a quarter mile apart and concealed in the jungle so they could study the fortress and the lay of the land. Based on the way the mountains rose steeply to the northwest beyond the walls, he could only assume they would be better served by taking the southernmost route around, but in this game, there was no room for assumptions.

Torches surrounded the fortress in iron chimneys built onto the tops of tall stone columns. They burned so brightly that they had to be fueled by something more than mere wood. A chemical of some kind perhaps? The fierce flames turned night to day in a fifteen-foot-wide stretch that allowed them to clearly reconnoiter the perimeter, but would expose them too soon if they attempted to approach from the jungle.

Another fifteen minutes had passed. It was time for his men to report in. They had watched the fortifications long enough. It was time to make their move.

"Northern front, all clear," McMasters whispered through his earpiece.

"No sign of movement here, either," Reubens said. He was positioned at the northwestern edge of the fortress, where the monolithic manmade wall met with the chiseled limestone mountainside. Earlier he had reported that there was no way around on that side, and none of them had been able to identify the entrance to what they assumed to be a village from the distance. The wall appeared impassable, yet somehow the others had crossed through it at the point where their tracks ended. Surely he and his men would be able to pick up their trail again wherever they exited on the other side. If they had even been allowed to leave.

Tasker waited for Jones to call in his status.

The far cry of a circling hawk broke the silence.

A minute passed.

"Jones," he whispered into his microphone.

He peeled apart the layers of static, but gleaned nothing.

Jones had been dispatched along the southern bank of the wall to the left of where Tasker now crouched behind a termite-infested log, from which an abundance of epiphytes bloomed. He had yet to miss a check-in. Something was wrong. A dozen different scenarios played through Tasker's mind, the most likely of which was that Jones had stumbled upon the natives and had been forced to bed down in radio silence. Then again, he could always have come under attack now that they were separated.

Tasker hadn't heard the chatter of gunfire, though, and no Marine could be so easily ambushed. Not without getting off at least a single shot in his defense.

"Jones," he whispered one last time. Still no reply. This wasn't good. He gave the command. "Close rank."

Tasker held perfectly still while he waited, listening for any sound to betray the approach of hostiles and watching the vine-draped stone wall for the slightest movement. Again, the only thing he heard was that same avian *skree*, farther away this time. Another bird answered from higher up in the mountains beyond the fortress.

Five more minutes ticked interminably past.

Crunching in the underbrush to his right.

Tasker spun and leveled his assault rifle at the shadow of a man as it emerged from the forest. His finger tightened on the trigger. He was a breath away from firing when McMasters's features resolved from the darkness. Reubens stepped out from the trees a moment later. Even with their night vision goggles and the infrared flashlight beams affixed to the apparatuses, they flinched when Tasker rose from beneath the drape of moss and vines.

He nodded to them, then inclined his head in the direction he had sent Jones.

They followed the face of the wall from the anonymity of the jungle until they reached the corner, then paralleled the southwestern fortification toward the point where it met with the sheer cliff that served as the western aspect of the fortress. So far there had been no sign of passage, and nothing to indicate a struggle.

He held up his fist and they paused. Minus the crackle of the detritus underfoot, he could faintly discern screams coming from somewhere ahead. Not human screams, but deeper, shriller, almost equine.

As they listened, the cries abated, and they were again swaddled in silence.

"Jones," he whispered. "State your position."

The only response was the unnerving buzz of static.

Tasker was getting angry now. If Jones had turned yellow and decided to make a break for it, he would hunt him down like a dog and teach him a lesson about desertion. The coward's death would be slow and excruciating.

He appraised the remaining men, who showed no outward signs of derision. Good.

Lowering his fist, they continued through the forest until the buzz of static intensified. Tasker lowered the volume, but the noise persevered from somewhere ahead.

Black flies. He had grown intimately familiar with their telltale noise. He would have recognized it anywhere.

The sound grew louder as they skirted a trunk the size of an overpass pylon and slipped through a thicket of spear-leafed saplings. He smelled the focus of the insects' attention and raised his rifle. Easing forward in his shooter's stance, he passed from the trees into a cluster of knee-high ferns growing in the lee of a Brazil nut tree. Moisture from the bushes soaked into his pants, still lukewarm despite the fact that it had been hours since the last rainfall. The swarm of flies swirled like snow in front of him and crawled in shades of green over the leaves and groundcover. A drop of fluid pattered his shoulder. He looked up in time to see another fall from the corner of his eye.

"Jones?" he whispered. His own voice echoed back at him from the ground to his right.

Another drop fell onto the back of his trigger hand. He brought it to his lips and dabbed it with his tongue.

Blood.

"Fan out," he whispered.

Tasker glanced from the canopy to the tree trunks and then to the shrubs as he inched forward, shoving the ferns aside with his feet so he could see the ground. The cracked lens of an infrared light was partially buried in the dirt. Two steps later, he found the remainder of Jones's helmet, turtle-shelled from a sharp impact.

"Jesus Christ," Reubens whispered.

Tasker was about to ask what the man had found when his question was answered. A broken section of skull rested at his feet, still shimmering with fresh blood. The scalp and hair were still attached, alive with crawling black bodies.

They had been separated for less than an hour and Jones had last checked in no more than twenty-five minutes ago. What could have done this in that amount of time? More importantly, what could have overwhelmed the soldier so suddenly that he hadn't had time to squeeze the trigger?

There was no doubt in his mind that Jones had been attacked by the same animals that had ripped apart the three men they had found earlier. A lone individual couldn't massacre and consume a human being so quickly. There had to be several of them out here in the jungle with them, lurking somewhere in the shadows.

He turned toward a clattering sound to his left. McMasters lifted Jones's rifle from the bushes.

The soldier pressed the barrel to his bare cheek and shook his head to confirm what Tasker already knew.

It was cold.

Tasker resumed his search. His left foot met resistance. He knelt, one eye on the forest, the other on the ground as he shoved aside a mess of wet branches. His hand closed around what felt like a sharply broken branch the thickness of the grip of a baseball bat. He evaluated it in shades of green and black. Bifid spinous processes, segments of bone interspersed with cartilaginous discs. A cervical spine. He flung it aside and stood, wiping his hands on his pants.

"God. Is that a hand?" Reubens whispered. "No amount of money is worth…this."

"Your share has already nearly doubled," Tasker said. "We're talking about several million dollars here."

Reubens didn't respond. He simply nudged the severed hand with the toe of his boot.

"You could always turn back," Tasker said. Reubens glanced up. Tasker read the look of hope on the man's face. "Sure. No hard feelings. McMasters and I would be happy to absorb your share. I just don't know if I would want to be wandering around alone in this jungle right now, do you?"

Reubens hesitated before he replied, appearing to reach a firm decision. He jut forth his chin. "No, sir."

Tasker made no attempt to hide his smug expression. He owned these men.

There was nothing they could do for Jones now.

"Let's get the hell out of here," he whispered.

"What could have done this?" McMasters asked.

"The fuck if I know," Tasker said. "But from here on out, we stay together. If anything moves, blast it to kingdom come."

Chapter Six

I

Andes Mountains, Peru
October 30th
1:09 a.m. PET

Colton awakened with a start. Hands clasped his shoulders and shook him sharply. A shadowed face loomed over his, unidentifiable. He drew his pistol from his side and shoved it into his assailant's gut.

"It's me. Sorenson," the shadow whispered. "We have a problem."

The man's Scandinavian features slowly came into focus as the lingering residue of sleep dissipated.

"What—?"

"Shh," Sorenson hissed. He tilted his head toward the open tent flaps. "Outside."

Colton slid out of his sleeping bag fully dressed, shoved his feet into his boots, and crawled out of the mosquito netting. Something must have happened. They wouldn't have roused him otherwise.

He checked his watch. 1:10 a.m. Ten minutes past the changing of the guards. A tingle passed through his abdominal viscera. Something had gone seriously wrong. The humid air was electric with tension.

With a glance back to confirm Leo was still asleep, Colton crawled out of the tent behind Sorenson. Morton and Webber stood beside the fire, whispering animatedly. The light cast shadows of worry on their faces. Where was Rippeth? Colton was still looking for the man when they joined the others. Sorenson spoke in a hushed tone.

"Rippeth's gone."

"What do you mean, 'gone'?"

"He didn't return from his patrol detail at the scheduled rendezvous time," Morton whispered. "There was no answer on his com-link, so we initiated a search of the camp. The first thing we noticed was that his backpack was gone. The second thing we discovered was this…"

Morton walked over to the pile of supplies and pointed down to the wooden crate attached to the carrying poles. A smear of blood covered the edge of the lid on the right side near the latch, where someone would have grabbed it in the process of opening it. Someone with a bleeding right hand.

"Damn it," Colton whispered. "Has anyone inventoried the contents yet?"

"All of the sensing equipment appears to be accounted for," Webber said. "However, we're missing several items from the private stock underneath."

Colton felt a sinking sensation. He raised his eyebrows to encourage Webber to continue. The man looked away when he spoke.

"One each of the fragmentary and incendiary grenades, and one of the SCARs."

"He deserted us." Colton fumed. This was entirely unacceptable. The man had been paid an inordinate amount of money in advance. Even with the remaining half due upon successful completion of their mission, it was still more than enough to live comfortably for several years.

"No," Sorenson snapped. He lowered his tone again. "Rippeth was no coward. He would have seen the expedition to the end or died trying. There's no way he would slink off in the middle of the night."

"Minus the tent you men shared, all of his personal belongings are gone, in addition to close to twenty thousand dollars worth of military-grade firepower."

"I'm telling you," Sorenson said through bared teeth, "he *did not* desert us."

Colton studied the other two men from the corner of his eye. They appeared considerably less convinced.

"Then if you're right, he can't be far from here," Colton whispered. "And there had better be a damn good reason as to why he's not here right now."

Colton forced down the images of the slaughtered jaguar and the terrified alpacas in their fully-enclosed stone pen. They held no province here. Already three men had absconded with supplies under the cover of darkness. Regardless of what Sorenson thought, he was certain that Rippeth was the fourth. But he couldn't afford a mutiny right now. The former soldiers pledged allegiance to their bank accounts, but every man had his personal loyalties, which was obvious in Sorenson's case. He was going to have to indulge them an all-out search of the surrounding jungle if he hoped to keep them on his side.

"Then we need to divide the area into quadrants," Colton whispered. "We can safely rule out the lake. Morton, you head southeast along the shoreline and work your way back into the forest. Webber, you and Sorenson strike off to the east and then split up. One of you go north, the other south. I'll follow the bank to the northwest and search the surrounding area. We meet back here in thirty minutes. Any questions?"

"Are we going to arm ourselves from the crate?" Webber asked.

"Not until it's absolutely necessary. We don't want to panic the civilians. We still need them focused to reach our goal." Colton paused to gauge their reactions. They seemed momentarily appeased by his plan. "All right then. You have your orders." He held up his wristwatch. "On my mark." The other three similarly raised their watches, and synchronized the time in unison.

Colton turned and strode through the camp and along the shoreline. He fished his communications gear out of his pocket and plugged the earpiece into his left ear. The rotten smell accosted him from the jungle to his right. He wasn't especially looking forward to revisiting the clearing filled with festering carcasses, but someone had to do it, and none of the other men had objected when he assigned it to himself. He didn't blame them in the slightest.

After another hundred yards, he ducked out of the moonlight and into the darkness beneath the canopy. He could barely see a thing, even with his penlight, which he held against the barrel of his pistol in a two-handed grip as he pressed back the shadows in slow sweeps. There was no reason to be leading with his weapon, but it provided a measure of comfort. He wasn't the kind of man prone to allowing himself to be spooked. After a decade as a SEAL, he had seen men die in just about every possible way, and he had survived with little more than cuts and contusions. Bosnia,

Chechnya, Iraq. He had done things he chose not to remember and things he would never forget. And since then, he had handled more of these private expeditions than he could count. From the Nile basin and the deserts of Africa to the polar ice caps and the thousands of feet of water beneath the Seven Seas to the smallest of uncharted islands and war-torn Third World nations. And through them all, his gut had never felt like it did now.

The jungle dictated his wending course, turning him this way and that, around massive trunks and through screens of shrubbery. Mosquitoes sang around his head in the absence of birdsong and the chatter of monkeys. Now that he truly thought about it, with the exception of the stinging cloud that escorted him through the foliage and the din of flies off to his right, there didn't seem to be any animals in the vicinity. That observation did little to settle his rising unease.

He checked his watch. Fifteen minutes had already passed. Time to start working back toward the camp.

Veering back to the south, he wound through a maze of trees and vines, ducking, climbing, crawling. The drone of flies grew louder with each step. He must be closer to the clearing than he thought, or perhaps the forest had steered him toward it. Either way, it meant that his navigational instincts were off, which unsettled him even more. As he closed in on the buzzing sound, he realized that his instincts hadn't failed him. The trees were all wrong. Even coming in from the opposite direction, he would have recognized them.

He willed his heart rate to slow, and softened his tread on the damp leaves and kindling. The darkness shifted through the branches of a ceiba tree ahead. He raised his flashlight beam toward the gaps between the leaves. Thousands of bloated flies roiled and buzzed beyond. The smell wasn't as atrocious as it had been in the clearing they had stumbled upon earlier, but it wasn't a naturally recurring scent either. It was the damp reek of the inside of something never meant to be opened, tainted by the scents of freshly chopped meat and bowels.

Colton eased through the branches and steeled himself against the sight. Arcs of black blood covered a cluster of tree trunks. Several heliconia bushes had been ripped from the disheveled ground and shredded amid tatters of clothing. He identified the rifle in the dirt first, for it was the one object not covered with insects. An FN-SCAR-L/ Mk. 16. Disarticulated remains were spread through the underbrush, seething with black flies. Even the backpack was covered with insects trying to draw blood from the fabric.

Breathing fast, he retreated from what was left of Rippeth, and hurried back toward the lake. The unobstructed shore would be the fastest route back to camp.

He pressed the transmitter button on his communications device and prepared to speak into the microphone, and then thought better of it. What would happen if he called for backup? The other men would come running, but what would be the consequences to the expedition if they found their brother-in-arms butchered in such a ghastly fashion? He had to determine how to proceed very carefully. They couldn't afford to scrap their plans now. Too much money had been advanced, too many man-hours expended. And he would not tolerate failure, especially with the potential payoff being so enormous. This one mission could provide him with enough cash to finance a luxurious retirement.

But the first order of business was saving his own skin. Lord only knew what kind of creatures could butcher a heavily-armed soldier without allowing him to squeeze off a shot. That SCAR fired six-hundred rounds per minute. A gentle tap of the trigger, just the slightest application of pressure, would have easily expelled several rounds. And he hadn't heard a single report.

He stumbled out of the trees and nearly fell into the lake before regaining his balance and sprinting through the mud toward the camp. Webber and Sorenson were already waiting beside the fire, watching him approach. Morton appeared from the far side of the tents at the same time.

Colton slowed his pace and struggled to regain his composure. He slid his pistol back under his waistband and clenched his hands into fists, willing his heart to slow. How was he going to handle this?

"Report," he said, and sat on the log they had rolled over beside the campfire.

"No sign of Rippeth," Sorenson said.

"Not a single fresh track," Webber added.

"Nothing in the jungle," Morton said. "And the path has too many sets of footprints already to tell if there was a recent set headed in the opposite direction."

Colton studied their faces. They appeared less certain that their comrade hadn't abandoned them now.

He thought of how savagely Rippeth had been torn apart. Even if he did say something, would it guarantee their safe return to Pomacochas? Rippeth had been alone, perhaps an eighth of a mile from anyone else. Whatever attacked him had chosen to isolate him in the bush rather than in the camp itself, where even more prey slept unaware. Perhaps safety was in numbers. If that was the case, then what would sharing the details change?

"I think we need to face the grim truth," Colton said. "Rippeth deserted us, and we must proceed. With or without him."

II

8:08 a.m.

The mood when Galen awakened was somber. One of the men, who no longer maintained the pretense of simple hired excavation help, had abandoned them during the night. The man with the dragon tattoo on his neck had made him uncomfortable, but he looked like the kind of man one would want to have beside him when one's life was on the line. Those that remained were grumpy and impatient. Their red eyes and the bags beneath them suggested that the previous night hadn't been remotely restful. They didn't chat amongst themselves as usual, and pressed the group harder to reach its goal, which contributed to Galen's overall sour disposition. After being awakened well before the designated hour and forced to pack at an absurd rate, the morning had started out poorly. Add the fact that he'd been denied even the comfort of a single cup of coffee filled with floating grounds, and the day was already shot.

They had passed around the far shore of the lake under the light of the moon, and witnessed the sunrise as a weak dilution of the shadows beneath the canopy as they continued to the west into the jungle. Where the bottom of the valley met the steep slope of a mountain, they had encountered a thin path that switchbacked up toward the low-lying clouds. It was barely wide enough to scale single-file, and seemed to only service whatever animals used it to reach the lake from the high country. Often it grew steep enough that they were forced to crawl, using the roots that poked out of the hillside for leverage. At those points, it took four men to haul the crate of sensing equipment.

He was amazed that so many trees could grow so densely on the nearly vertical hillside, especially where the side of the path occasionally turned into a pitfall over the treetops far below. Such moments granted stunning views of the shimmering lake way down in the valley, a small mirror set into an infinite forest of green. Even from this vantage, he could barely see the blue pinpoint of Laguna Pomacochas on the horizon and the linear depression in the trees where the river that had brought them to the foot of the Andes flowed. The fortress they had been steered through the day before was invisible from above. Even knowing where to look didn't help. It was no wonder the tribe had avoided discovery until now.

They took frequent breaks wherever the trail was wide enough to allow them to gather and pass around one of the water bladders. Conversation had been limited to heavy breathing as they acclimated to the exertion at the increasingly higher altitudes. Dahlia and Jay had seized every opportunity to capture the panoramic view since they were unable to film while they climbed. Leo and Colton had begun to consult the map more and more often, and agreed that they needed to be on the southeastern face of the peak on the other side of the one they currently ascended. Already they had encountered two tree trunks marked with Hunter Gearhardt's initials and the date he had carved them, which caused Leo to shorten their breaks and drive them ever faster.

At the end of an especially challenging section of the trail, the world fell away to the right. He stood on a sheer limestone cliff, shaded by the omnipresent ceiba trees, and finally saw what he had come here to see. A large nest constructed from broken sticks had been built onto a ledge below, from which the gnarled remains of dead, gray trees protruded. Bluish dots spotted the feather- and down-lined nest, remnants of the Andean condor eggs that had hatched there through the seasons.

Galen felt a swell of hope. If these raptors could successfully procreate in the wild, then surely there was a chance that the California condor could return to its former glory. He wondered what might happen if some of their captive-bred juveniles were to be released somewhere like this. The problem was they weren't producing hatchlings in large enough numbers to experiment with their lives. Perhaps someday...

Movement caught his eye from hundreds of feet below. Two condors, perhaps the owners of the nest, circled the jungle, easily identifiable by their black bodies and staggering wingspans, and, of course, by the white rings of feathers around their bald heads.

Galen smiled. They weren't members of the mysterious species he had come to find, but just seeing them in their natural habitat, doing what vultures do, did his heart good. Even after all of the tribulations they had endured up until now, this one sight made it worth it.

He watched them a while longer as they continued to whirl around the same section of trees before they finally dropped down into the canopy and vanished from sight. What kind of carcass awaited them? In the process of speculating, he realized he hadn't seen any animals other than the ducks far out in the center of the lake. There had been no mammalian presence. He hadn't even seen a single rodent. And the cluster of trees wasn't far from the edge of the lake, or from their campsite. Had the condors returned to the clearing where they had found all of those alpaca bones? It seemed unlikely. He had only performed a cursory inspection of the site because of the god-awful stench, but there hadn't appeared to be enough meat on any of the bones to warrant a condor's attention. And wasn't that clearing farther to the east? He shrugged. It was a question he'd be able to investigate on the return trip. Something must have died or been killed during the night. Condors weren't that picky when it came to scavenging, regardless of how old the remains might be.

The others started their upward trek once more. There was only one more thing he needed to do before he joined them. He could always catch up if he fell behind.

Galen turned back to the forest and snapped a long, slender branch off of the nearest tree. He stripped the leaves and scoured the trunk until he found what he was looking for. A crust of amber had formed over a wound in the bark. He chiseled it away until fresh sap bled through, then dabbed the end of the stick into the syrupy sludge. Once he had a suitable gob, he returned to the cliff and sprawled flat on his belly at the precipice. Holding the stick in his right hand, he extended it down toward the nest. It swung from side to side just over the haphazardly assembled wooden bowl.

Just a little farther.

He scooted closer to the edge until his entire shoulder hung over the abyss, and stretched his arm downward. The tip of the stick grazed the feathers in the nest. He retracted it just enough to confirm that several feathers were stuck to the sap. Excellent. They would make for fine comparisons to the ones he already had in his pocket. It would be a good launching point for his study into whether or not the iridescent green and brown feathers had developed as a new morph or as an evolutionary offshoot of the Andean condor.

Pleased with his own ingenuity, he pulled his arm back up. With a crack, the rock ledge broke beneath him. Fragments of andesite fell away and landed in the nest. His whole body canted to the right, toward the nothingness below.

"Oh, God."

He felt gravity pull at his body and grabbed for anything to hold onto with his left hand. More pebbles skittered out from under him and tumbled down the stone face.

His body began to slide and his stomach lurched with the inevitability of what was about to happen. He raced through the various scenarios in his mind, all of which ended with his broken body tangled in the canopy or splattered on the forest floor.

The skin on the fingertips of his left hand tore as he clawed at the smooth stone.

Galen could feel his inertia building. He was going over the ledge and there was nothing he could do about it.

He would know how it felt to be a condor in the moments of freefall before he was impaled on the branches.

"Please," he whimpered. He cried out as the right half of his chest slid over the edge. "Don't let me die."

A hand grabbed his belt, another the back of his shirt.

"Quit being so melodramatic," a voice said. With a sound tug, Galen was hauled back onto the path and away from the cliff.

Breathing hard, heart racing, Galen leapt to his feet and embraced his savior. His legs trembled so badly he could hardly stand on his own.

"That's about enough of that," Merritt said. He extricated himself from the embrace and dabbed his fingers at the back of his neck. "Ugh. What did you wipe on me?"

Galen realized he was still holding the stick. He had pressed the sappy end against the man's neck.

"I'm sorry," he said, but Merritt had already turned to follow the others. Galen called after him. "You saved my life. Thank you!"

Merritt gave a slight wave of acknowledgment over his shoulder.

Galen struck off after him, pulling the feathers from the sap as he walked. He didn't want to be left behind again. What would have happened if Merritt hadn't grabbed him when he had? The image of his rag-doll form plummeting through the sky nearly caused his knees to buckle.

Jesus Christ. He should have been dead. Merritt may have shrugged it off as no big deal, but it *was* a big deal to Galen.

He hurried back into line behind Dahlia and reached into the breast pocket of his vest with trembling fingers, withdrew one of the feathers, and compared it to one of the remiges from the condor's nest.

It didn't appear possible that they were, or had even once been, the same species.

The β-keratin fibers of the iridescent barbs were better aligned toward the center than to the outside, where they appeared slightly frayed, while those of the Andean condor feather were uniformly aligned. He blew on the greenish feather and the barbs flared subtly apart. He did the same thing to the condor feather, but the tips of the barbs remained fixed together by the barbules and barbicels. How had he not noticed this before? The feathers were nearly identical in structure and shape on a macroscopic level. If he hadn't been so excited by the prospect of finding and identifying a new species, he would have recognized it before now.

Somewhere out there was a raptor that no one had ever classified.

Only if he was right, this one couldn't fly.

III

10:50 a.m.

Over the course of the last hour, the temperature had dropped nearly ten degrees, while the humidity had steadily increased. The air grew thinner as they climbed toward the ceiling of clouds that hid the peak above. Perhaps it was only by degree, but the forest didn't appear as dense as it once had. They had only been walking for six hours now, and yet it felt as though days had passed since they broke camp.

Merritt shrugged the backpack up onto his shoulders. He was sure that it magically grew heavier with each step. He couldn't remember whose bag he carried, but the way the men struggled with the monstrous crate on the narrow, steep path, he figured it was the least he could do. Better this than being the downhill man bearing the brunt of the crate's weight.

A faint breeze penetrated the canopy as the trail wound around the northern slope of the mountain. He welcomed the cool movement of air across the skin beneath his clothes. The distant rumble of a waterfall filtered through the trees, in the upper reaches of which he could see wisps of white, a sight that set him momentarily at ease. He thought of his plane and the feeling of preparing to ascend into the thick cloud banks, where he would be flying blind, completely isolated from his worldly cares.

The birdman trailed him, scrutinizing a pair of feathers as he stumbled uphill. If the man thanked him for saving his life one more time, Merritt was going to throw him over the next cliff himself. The guy had barely been leaning over the edge, but the way he told it, he made it sound like he'd been dangling by a single fingertip. Whatever. At least the feathers kept him occupied for the time being.

Sam trudged ahead of him, eyeing everything they passed as though searching for something specific. He admired her passion, and wished that there was something in his life that mattered as much to him.

Her scent trailed on the breeze. He inhaled deeply. She smelled of mint and dragon fruit with an undercurrent of sweat. She had pulled her hair back into a ponytail, which showcased her slender neck. He imagined how it might feel to press his lips to the gentle curve under the collar of her flannel shirt...

She glanced over her shoulder and caught him staring. He offered a smile, which she returned easily enough. At least she hadn't turned around a minute ago when he'd been mesmerized by her swishing hips in those khaki shorts.

Sam faced ahead again as they wound around the northern slope. The ground fell away to the right to the point that they could have stepped from the path onto the treetops. To the left, the mountain became a vertical embankment covered in vines and lianas. The path appeared to narrow to a mere foot wide. It was hard to tell with the way the vines covered it and spilled over the edge in a cascade of flowering emerald ropes.

Colton and Leo were already scooting slowly out onto the thin ledge, testing their footing on the uneven ground while maintaining what little distance they could from the drop into the valley far below.

Sam stopped in her tracks directly ahead of him. He was about to ask if she was all right when he noticed the barely perceptible movement that had captured her interest.

The breeze ruffled the curtain of vines, behind which he saw deep shadows, not a smooth sheet of stone.

Sam eased forward and reached out with her left arm. Her hand passed through the deceptive screen. She glanced back at him with a glint in her eyes, smiled, then stepped from the path and vanished through the cascade of green.

Ahead, Leo similarly tested the invisible wall, then he and Colton ducked out of sight.

Merritt followed and crossed into muted darkness, which became complete when the vines fell back into place behind him. The sensation of claustrophobia closed around him like a fist. His heart began to pound and his breathing became labored. He couldn't bear the prospect of being underground for any length of time, and fought the surge of memories from the Afghan desert.

The thin beam of a penlight bloomed to his right. It provided too little illumination to truly gauge the size of the space beneath the rock overhang, and barely silhouetted the others.

A triangle of sunlight streamed in from behind as Galen joined them.

"I need more light," Sam snapped. Her voice positively trembled with excitement.

"This is all I have," Colton said. He flashed his beam from side to side to emphasize his point.

"Then we need to get rid of some of those vines. Who has the machete?"

"I do," Webber said as he passed into the inner sanctum.

The blade whistled through the air and struck the layers of vines with a *thuck*. The serpentine green vines fell away and slithered over the edge of the cliff. Light slanted through in their absence.

"More," Sam said.

Webber continued to whack through the screen as Sam slowly approached the rear wall of the broad cave, which was far larger than Merritt had initially suspected. It was perhaps a hundred feet long and twenty feet deep with a domed ceiling that arched a good ten feet over his head. He couldn't tell if it had been chiseled by human hands or eroded into the hillside by nature as the seas and rivers receded millions of years ago. Either way, someone had put the space to good use. As Webber welcomed more and more light into the alcove, the structures at the rear drew form. Six tall sculptures stood against the center of the back wall, nearly reaching the roof. They were all identical: four-foot-wide, appendage-less bodies painted with various designs in yellow and red ochre, supporting large, parabolic heads that must have looked like crescent moons in profile. A single thin line formed the mouths beneath sharp, triangular noses. The brows were straight and ridged, and created the impression that the statues wore headdresses low over their foreheads. Staked on short wooden posts to their heads were human skulls, their articulated jaws opened in soundless screams.

To either side of the unsettling statues, small adobe buildings had been constructed side by side against the cavern wall. They were multi-tiered, though each level was only tall enough to accommodate a man if he crouched. Their reddish walls had been painted with thick, horizontal white stripes, into which myriad shapes had been etched. Square windows lined each level, through which only darkness stared out at them. Their roofs were slanted in such a way that they reminded Merritt of Japanese pagodas. A single rectangular doorway set into the adobe to either side of the vaguely human statues serviced all of the dwellings. While they may have looked separate from the outside, apparently they were all interconnected.

Dust hung thickly in the air, stirred by the soft breeze that circulated the musty smells of age and decomposition.

They were all awed to silence.

Sam approached the strange statuary. All of the plaster figures were joined together three feet from the floor. Between the center two, what looked like a hearth had been carved into their union.

"Let me borrow your flashlight," Sam said, holding out her open palm without diverting her attention from the dark opening for a second.

Colton set the penlight in her hand and leaned over her shoulder as Sam shined it into the recess. A dull tawny glow reflected back.

Merritt eased closer and craned his neck to see around her head.

A golden skull rested on a deep shelf, situated so that it leered out at them from the shadows. It was roughly the height of a human skull, but that was where the similarities ended. It had an elongated snout filled with sharp teeth that laced together like those of a caiman, and twin ovular nostrils at the tip. The eye sockets were oblong and far too large proportionately. Fitted into each was a dusty, multi-faceted bluish-green stone that seemed to absorb the light into its core, where it radiated with what could have passed for sentience.

"What's all that stuff underneath it?" Merritt asked.

"I can't tell," Sam said. She leaned closer and blew away the coating of dust.

She coughed and recoiled as the gray cloud billowed around the skull.

"Feathers," Merritt said. He reached over Sam, withdrew one from the shelf, and held it up so he could better see. The sunlight caused it to shimmer with an emerald hue.

He turned and looked at Galen, who still held a nearly identical feather in his hand.

IV

11:18 a.m.

Dahlia leaned over Jay's shoulder and studied the odd tableau from the perspective of the camera. She had been struggling to keep up with the group. Her legs ached and her lungs burned, but her exhaustion was now forgotten as she directed her cameraman.

The spotlight affixed to the digital recorder highlighted Sam and cast her elongated shadow onto the unusual sculptures. Motes of dust swirled in the diffused beam.

"Get every inch of this place as she's talking," Dahlia whispered. "We can create a transcript of everything she says and do a voiceover in post-production."

"These statues are actually anthropomorphic wooden coffins called *purunmachus*," Sam said. "They're nearly identical to the ones at Karajia, north of the fortress at Kuelap. The Chachapoya would first mummify and bundle their dead in several layers of cloth, and set them on a short stone wall. Then they built the framework around the remains using long wooden poles. From there, they used a mixture of clay and straw to sculpt the body and the head."

"So you're saying there are corpses inside each of those?" Merritt asked.

"Yes, but not just any corpses. These were important men, likely their most decorated warriors. The *purunmachus* were constructed to look like them so that they would be honored and remembered."

"What's with the skulls staked to their foreheads?" Jay asked.

"No one is really sure. The prevailing theory is that they're the skulls of an especially reviled enemy and were displayed as trophies, or perhaps to ward off future aggression. It's a tactic they're believed to have borrowed from the Jivaro, who were notorious headhunters."

"And the golden sculpture?" Colton asked.

"Zoom in on it," Dahlia whispered to Jay, who did as she asked.

"The *purunmachus* at Karajia didn't have anything like it, so I can only speculate." Sam paused. She nibbled on her lower lip as she formulated her thoughts. "The foundation was obviously built to incorporate it, so it wasn't a later addition or an afterthought. It's the focal point of the whole display and must have been extremely important, even sacred, but its design doesn't reflect the typical Chachapoyan style. You can see from the faces on the *purunmachus* themselves that their motifs were generally more abstract, while the skull sculpture is completely realistic. And they were renowned for their textile skills, not their metallurgy, which would indicate that the idol was crafted during the years following their conquest by the Inca. Even then, it appears far beyond even their considerable skills."

"How much do you think it's worth?" Jay asked. Dahlia pinched his arm. Hard. "Ow. Jesus, Dahlia."

"It's priceless," Sam said, with a note of disdain.

"What about the other buildings?" Merritt asked. "The levels are barely high enough to crawl through. Were they built for midgets or something?"

"They're *chullpas*, burial buildings, similar to those at Revash, near the town of Santo Tomas de Quillay. They mortared stones together with mud to form the framework, then plastered over them like the *purunmachus*. They used logs lashed together with vines to create the unusual sloped roofs, and sealed them in adobe as well."

"So they're full of dead bodies, too," Merritt said.

"I'm sure. You have to understand that the Chachapoya revered their dead. Being interred in such a manner was a great honor. Not everyone who died received this kind of treatment. This is truly a sacred site, and an archeological discovery of incalculable significance. We could spend the next decade poring through these tombs and still not learn everything there is to know."

"Earlier you said that if the people in the village below us were descended from the Chachapoya, we would find their *chullpa* nearby," Leo said. "Judging by the amount of dust covering everything, it doesn't look like this one's been used anytime recently."

"True," Sam said. Her eyes glinted when she spoke. "Then I'd imagine this one belongs to an older tribe, presumably the one responsible for the headdress that Hunter discovered. Their village can't be far from here."

"Let's see what's inside those buildings," Dahlia whispered. There would be plenty of time for research when they returned to the States. What they really needed right now was something to add a little spice to their film, and she couldn't think of anything more exciting than being the first to explore a five hundred year-old tomb.

Jay rose and followed her to the rear of the chamber. She ducked through the entryway to her left and found herself in a small room framed by plastered stones. The beam on the camera cast her shadow deep into the structure, to where the darkness was marred by the almost palpable columns of wan light that slanted through the small windows. Pillars of fitted rocks supported the wooden floor above her. Egg-shaped bundles of rotting fabric lined the walls to either side of the central aisle. She could sense the presence of the corpses inside the bundles. The stench of decomposition was a physical entity crawling on her skin.

She had to stoop to keep from splitting her scalp on the low ceiling as she stepped aside and waited for Jay to pass her with the camera. The beam showcased footprints in the thick dust on the ground beyond where she had walked. They obviously weren't the first to have been in here. It was comforting to know they hadn't strayed from Hunter Gearhardt's trail.

Jay led her down the central walkway, which connected all of the structures well beyond the furthest reaches of sight. Between the smell and the confines, she was starting to feel as though she were crawling through a dry sewer.

The outer blanket of one of the bundles to her left had rotted away to reveal a second blanket underneath. From her preliminary research, she knew that these funerary bundles were created by wrapping the deceased in fetal position within several layers of fabric. Each layer contained a stuffing of objects that were both of personal importance and meant to help the dead in the afterlife. She had read about bundles filled with corn, pottery, hollowed gourds that held various grains, and different ornate textiles. The stuffing from the outer layer littered the floor at their feet.

Jay filmed the bundle a moment longer before directing the camera at the ground. The light caused a shimmer of green to pass across the mound of dusty feathers.

They pressed deeper into the dwellings, passing from one to the next through constrictive stone thresholds. There were bundles everywhere. They filled every inch of free space, shoulder-to-shoulder. It reminded her of the scene in *Aliens* when Sigourney Weaver found the chamber with all of the alien egg pods. She was just about to share her observation with Jay, whom she knew would get a major kick out of it, when she noticed that one of the corpse-filled bags had toppled into the aisle ahead. It looked like some sort of rodent had gnawed through the blankets to liberate a scattering of grains, kernels, and feathers. Through the tattered fabric, she could see a desiccated face in profile.

"Zoom in on that."

"Way ahead of you," Jay said. He brought the beam to bear on the gaunt head. The skin had taken on the consistency of parchment, the bones beneath sharply obtrusive. There was only a hollow, dark pit where the eye should have been. The lips had shrunken back from the bared, yellowed teeth, and the nose was upturned like a pig's following the dissolution of the cartilage. Thick scars bisected the cheek. She wished she could see more, but the rest of the body was still shrouded.

"There's another one over there," Dahlia said, pointing back behind them. When Jay turned with the camera, she grabbed the edge of the fabric near the face and ripped downward with a tearing sound.

"Christ, Dahlia," Jay snapped as he whirled back around. "They'll have our heads if they find out you did that."

"That's why I couldn't have it on film." She smirked. "Besides, we aren't going to fully unwrap it or anything. I just want a better look at what's inside."

"You're pushing your luck, you know."

She rested her hand on his shoulder and felt him stiffen. His affection for her was readily apparent, which made him far too easy to coerce. He was a dear friend and she hated to take advantage of his feelings, but sometimes she just couldn't help herself.

"I have luck to spare," she said. "You ought to know that by now. And what would any of them do anyway? It's not like they'd send us packing. They need us, Jay. So are you going to film this or what?"

The light again zeroed in on the corpse.

Dahlia gasped.

She didn't know what she had expected, but this was the furthest thing from it. The dead man's legs had been bent, pinned to his chest, and bound in place with a frayed rope. The left arm was jaggedly fractured mid-shaft, and the skin had curled back from the bone into a liquefied black sludge, presumably the source of the foul, gangrenous stench. The entire left half of the ribcage had been destroyed, leaving a gaping hole framed by pointed fragments of bone. The flesh that surrounded it was ruggedly torn and peeled back in leathery straps.

"That must have been one big, nasty rat," Jay said.

There was a shift in the shadows inside the broken ribcage, and, as if on cue, a gray rodent poked its whiskery face out, its eyes glowing red.

Dahlia screamed. She whirled and sprinted as fast as she could toward the entrance. Her head struck the low log ceiling repeatedly, but she hardly even felt it. All she could focus on was the distant rectangle of light.

She burst through the opening and nearly slammed into Galen, who shuffled aside just in time.

Jay emerged a few seconds later, laughing so hard that tears streaked through the dust on his cheeks.

"It's not funny," Dahlia snapped. She punched him in the arm.

"Oh, but it is, princess. It is." He raised the camera to capture the expression of terror on her dirty face.

So the rodent had surprised her. Big deal. Ha, ha.

"That was the biggest rat I've ever seen in my life. It was the size of a dog."

"You keep telling yourself that. Just wait until you see the playback," Jay said. He could barely catch his breath through the laughter. "Then you can tell me again how big it was."

Dahlia huffed and turned away. The heat of embarrassment flushed her cheeks.

Galen crouched directly in front of her before the golden skull as though praying to the obscene idol. His hand trembled as he reached out and removed a dusty feather from beneath it. He held it up and blew on it—once, then again. His gaze fell upon the shiny skull, and the color blanched from his face.

"What is it?" she asked.

He looked up at her and blinked repeatedly as though abruptly awakened from a dream.

"Not yet," he mumbled. He rose and shook his head. "Not until I'm sure."

He cast one last glance back at the skull before wrapping his arms around his chest and shuffling out of the cave and into the sunlight.

V

12:03 p.m.

Sam reluctantly allowed herself to be guided away from the ancient burial site. There would be limitless time to study and excavate the *chullpas* and *purunmachus* in the years to come. For now, the lure of the lost fortress ahead kept her moving. She could feel it out there, calling to her, drawing her with its promise of mystery. What wonders would they find inside its fortifications? Was the golden headdress really an anomaly, or were there indeed more treasures that would unlock the secrets of a culture long thought extinct? She imagined the *National Geographic* features to come, the articles she would be able to place in every industry journal, the documentary that would chronicle their expedition and bring the elusive Chachapoya to the forefront of the world of anthropology.

She hadn't been this excited since the days when she had explored the uncharted wilderness with her father as a child. His enthusiasm had been contagious, and for a long time it had more than compensated for living out of tents, isolated from the life that normal children led. She could thank him for her love of history and its misunderstood societies, for granting her glimpses of the professional adventures to come, but at the same time she felt she owed the world a debt on his behalf. He had been a good man and an even better father. It was the decisions that he had made along the way that couldn't be taken back...or forgiven. He had discovered ruins that made front page news around the globe. However, plundering the sites of their artifacts left them incomplete when the scholars arrived in his wake, like playing Scrabble without the vowels. And he had never seen anything wrong with it. To him, that was part of the job. He and Leo invested their money into finding and securing the treasures, which were the payoff for their hard work. Now, instead of those artifacts of inestimable cultural value filling displays in museums, they rested on the shelves of wealthy businessmen, or they'd been melted down and sold, or they simply sat in crates in the dusty warehouses of antiquity dealers. It fell to her to make amends, and she would start right here and now. Nothing would leave these sites without being properly logged and catalogued. This she swore.

Leo had promised her that the ruins would not be pillaged. While she had always known him to be a man of his word, she was prepared to go to war with him if he so much as thought about reneging.

Protecting the sites was an imperative, the more immediate of her concerns, but what about the descendents that had managed to remain hidden in the jungle for so long? How would they react to having the spotlight of the scientific world shined into their faces? Would that even be in their best interests? Was there a way to announce their discovery without flooding the rainforest with researchers who would insist upon poking and prodding them, and sharing the wonders of modern technology, and diseases for which they had no antibodies, and religions hell-bent on the annihilation of mankind?

They had seemed unconcerned, as though a band of strangers passing through their village was a common occurrence. Was it possible that others had stumbled upon their fortress before Hunter, and yet word had somehow never managed to leak?

Let them pass. They are dead already.

Those cryptic words echoed in her head, summoning a sudden uneasiness that had nothing to do with the dark storm clouds rolling toward the mountains from the east. Thunder rumbled in the distance. Indigo lightning strobed. Rain was a foregone conclusion. They needed to reach level ground before the storm overtook them. The already treacherous stone ledges and muddy paths would be downright lethal with a deluge racing down the slope.

They rounded the mountain and now faced west into the dense gray clouds trapped between them and the opposite peak. The valley below mocked them from out of sight with the grumble of waterfalls and the whistle of the wind across the sheer cliffs.

Somewhere out there, obscured by the clouds and shrouded by vegetation, were the crumbled remains of a vanished society, the link between the ancient dead in the traditionally accepted Chachapoya range to the south, and those still living in the jungle.

Her heart rate accelerated and her body became electric with nervous energy. She wanted nothing more than to barrel through the others and sprint ahead toward the discovery of a lifetime.

The first raindrop slapped her backpack. A moment later she felt another spatter of coldness on her shoulder. This time they were all within easy reach of their ponchos, and used the rare advance notice to don them.

"This must be just like going to Disneyland for you," Merritt said from behind her.

She couldn't help but smile.

"You have no idea."

They reached a point where the path widened and he caught up so he could walk beside her. Trees rose from the downhill side of the path to block their view of the cloud-cloaked valley and smothered the roar of the waterfalls. The timing was perfect as the rain pummeled the upper canopy, which absorbed the brunt of the storm for them.

"I don't know." He offered a lopsided grin. "I'd like to think I'm something of an expert on Disneyland."

Her smile broadened.

"So what do you think we'll find over there?" he asked, nodding to the right.

"That's half the fun. I don't really know. We could discover an amazing fortress that would make Machu Picchu pale by comparison, or we could find that whatever was once there has deteriorated and fallen to ruin in the bottom of the gorge."

"You don't really think that's the case. I can see it in your eyes. You're just downplaying your expectations. You know there's something truly astonishing hiding behind those clouds."

"I hope so. Otherwise we've come all this way for nothing."

"What will you do with all of the artifacts you find?"

It was a loaded question, she knew. He'd made no secret of how he felt about protecting the heritage of his adoptive home.

"Everything will be documented and catalogued *in situ*. Only once we've done so will I allow any relics to leave the site."

"And what will become of them from there?"

"I imagine the museum in Leymebamba will happily clear space for them." She read his next question in his eyes and answered before he could ask. "There will be no looting. You have my word on that. Like I said, we aren't grave robbers."

"What about Leo?"

"He promised that nothing would be taken, and I fully intend to hold him to it."

Merritt nodded, but he still looked troubled.

"You don't believe me?" she asked.

"No. It's not that." He paused to formulate his words. "How well do you know Leo?"

"I've known him all my life. Granted, we don't see eye-to-eye on this particular issue and haven't been on the best of terms for the last several years, but I trust him. Despite all of his glaring faults, I've never had a reason to doubt his integrity."

"But what about his motives? I mean, what exactly are we doing here?"

"We're searching for the ruins that Hunter discovered. I suppose that by doing so we're recreating his final days so that Leo can give himself a measure of closure. Hunter's death broke my heart, but I won't even pretend to understand how Leo must feel."

"I can't help but think there's more to it than that."

"How so?"

"Look at it objectively. We all know Leo's son died, but there were four other men in his party that no one seems to want to talk about. What happened to them? And no one's even mentioned why Rippeth took off in the middle of the night. He's a hard man with serious military training, not the kind of guy who tucks tail and runs when things get rough. The fact that he and the other men are even here speaks volumes about Leo's perception of the situation. Think about how much money has been invested into this expedition, and for what? Leo's a businessman. What's the return on his investment?"

"He's only human. He needs to know what happened to his son and he has the financial means to do so."

"But haven't you noticed how he and Colton have withdrawn from the rest of us? They're definitely plotting something."

"You're being paranoid."

"Am I?" He sighed. "Maybe I am, but I've got to go with my gut. Something's just not right here. There has to be another reason for this trek, and only Leo and Colton know what it is."

"I already told you they promised not to plunder the ruins. What else could there possibly be?"

"I can't put my finger on it, but I think it has something to do with the missing members of Hunter's group and the whole reason their expedition was launched in the first place."

"Leo would have told me if he had an ulterior motive," she said. "He's never been one to tiptoe around the truth, even knowing the kind of argument that might result. Believe me."

"You're certain he told you everything?"

The tone of his voice betrayed his doubt.

"Do you know something that I don't?"

He didn't immediately reply. When he finally did, he spoke in a voice so soft she wasn't sure if he had meant for her to hear.

"I know we're following a game trail, and I haven't seen any sign of the animals that could have made it."

VI

12:21 p.m.

The path narrowed and Merritt fell in behind Sam. He needed time to think. Too many things bothered him about the situation, and he was running out of time to figure them out. He felt a sense of inevitability, as though they were hurtling toward some unforeseen end. Despite what Sam said, he didn't trust Leo. Perhaps the time had come to have a little chat with Leo and Colton and see if he could determine what they were hiding.

Suddenly, he was hip-deep in the kind of problems he had sought to avoid. He had accomplished what he had set out to after leaving the Middle East. He had vanished from the face of the earth. As long as he kept his head down, the Army would never be able to find and extradite him. So why then had he stuck his neck out and risked drawing attention to himself after finding the body by the river? There hadn't even been any sort of internal debate. He had simply assumed responsibility because it had been the right thing to do. And now here he was, on an expedition he knew nothing about, miles into the untamed Peruvian wilds. The man whose son's effects he had taken to the Consulate out of the goodness of his heart had dragged him along under the threat of handing him over to the military, but had paid him handsomely to assuage his guilt. They had to be nearly fifty miles into a forest where even the animals feared to tread. The natives who had stalked them from the shadows insisted that he was dead already. And to top it all off, his feet were soaked from the blasted storm.

So why *was* he here? Why had he abandoned his life of comfortable anonymity to join this godforsaken party when he could just as easily have disappeared as he had already done once before?

Sam turned around and smiled.

And just like that, he knew.

He had known on an unconscious level since she had first hopped up into the copilot's seat in his plane and begun to annoy the heck out of him. Since he had first seen the sparkle of the starlight reflecting from her striking blue eyes as she stared past him toward the shores of Pomacochas.

"Crap," he muttered under his breath. He kicked a rotting agave fruit into the forest.

The sound of jogging footsteps and labored breathing reached him from behind. He didn't need to look back to see who approached. It was his new best friend. He rolled his eyes as Galen fell into stride beside him, wheezing heavily.

If nothing else, at least this would prove a welcomed distraction from his thoughts.

"Got a second?" Galen asked. He was huffing as though he'd sprinted up the mountain, instead of stumbling along behind them at a snail's pace.

Merritt sighed. The path through the trees lightened ahead. They were about to lose their umbrella of vegetation. From a dozen paces behind him he heard the crinkle of plastic as Jay weatherproofed his camera.

"There's something I need to show you," Galen said before Merritt could answer. The man's eyes were haunted, his expression pained. He held out two feathers and pressed one into each of Merritt's hands as they walked. "Look at those two feathers and tell me what you see."

Merritt decided to humor the birdman, and inspected the feathers. The one in his left hand was slightly longer and shimmered with green when he tilted it to the light just right. The one in his right had a slightly darker color, more black than brown.

"Other than the coloration, they're pretty much identical."

"Now blow on them."

"What?"

"Trust me, will you? Just bring them close to your mouth and blow on them."

Merritt rolled his eyes, but placated Galen, who grew more agitated by the minute. He puckered and blew on the feather in his right hand first. It shivered between his fingers, but did little else. He eyed Galen, who gestured in a rolling motion with his hands to encourage him to proceed to the other feather. With a shrug, he blew on the iridescent green plume in his left. The feathery portion attached to the quill fanned out slightly, but fell back into place when he stopped to draw another breath.

"There," Galen said. His eyes widened. "Did you see that?"

"What was I supposed to see?"

"Don't you understand? You're a pilot, for God's sake!"

This was growing old in a hurry, and farther along the path, those in the lead had pulled up the hoods of their ponchos in anticipation of stepping back out into the storm.

"Look, look, look," Galen said, snatching back the feathers and holding them where Merritt could clearly see them. "You saw how the vanes spread apart when you blew on them. If this were the wing of an airplane, would it be able to stay aloft? But the vanes on the other feather stayed together when you blew on them."

"Where are you going with this?" Merritt raised the hood of his poncho and braced himself. The path opened onto what looked like a waterfall.

"Okay. Here's a quick lesson on the anatomy of avian flight. A feather is composed of a hollow, tubular main shaft called a rachis toward the tip, and a calamus where it inserts into the follicle on the skin. Vanes branch out from the rachis to form the majority of the feather. The vanes themselves divide further into barbs, then barbules, and finally into barbicels. These barbicels serve as miniature hooks to bind the vanes together. Without them, the wind passes through the feather on the downstroke, and the bird simply can't become airborne. There are other contributing factors, obviously, like the alignment of the β-keratin fibers and the orientation of the feathers, but that's flight in a nutshell. On the other hand, flightless birds like ostriches and emus have feathers that lack the interlocking barbicels."

"So you're saying that the bird with the greenish tint to its feathers can't fly." Merritt bowed beneath the ferocity of the torrent as he stepped out of the protection of the trees and onto a sheer slope with a deadfall beside him. The path ahead veered to the right onto a jagged crest of rocks that connected this mountain with the one to the west. A series of waterfalls tumbled over the slick stone in uneven steps toward the valley floor. The air around them was hazy with spray. "What's the big deal?"

"You were the one who found Hunter Gearhardt's belongings. This is the same type of feather that he had considered important enough to pack. Only I found this one at the site where the jaguar had been slaughtered. And there were even more of them in that awful clearing with the alpaca bones. You see, they may look like the feathers of a carrion bird like a condor, which is what I initially suspected, but they're not. They belong to an avian from a different order—if not class—entirely."

"Get to the point already." Merritt had to shout to be heard over the drum roll of rain and the thunder of the waterfalls that carved a shallow valley between the peaks up in the clouds. The world had become mist and water.

"All birds of prey are capable of flight. Every single one of them. The iridescent feather has the size, shape, and structure of a raptor feather, minus the microscopic barbicels that hold the vanes together during flight. We're dealing with a carnivorous bird that can't fly."

"So what does it do, hop really fast?" Merritt smirked. "Thanks for the warning. If I see this terrifying bouncing bird of yours, I'll guard my kneecaps and toes."

"Think of ostriches and emus. They can run up to forty-five miles per hour."

"But you said this thing is the size of a condor."

"Its remige feathers are the size of a condor's. That only means that the wing size is the same. Ostriches have disproportionately small wings compared to their body size." Galen threw up his arms in frustration. "That jaguar was run down and torn apart. And those alpacas were butchered."

"You're suggesting that birds were responsible for that carnage? Flightless birds?"

Merritt shook his head and hastened his step, but Galen sped up to keep pace.

"Nearly seventy percent of the area from the Amazon basin through the Andes Mountains remains unexplored. There are hundreds of thousands of acres upon which few humans have ever tread. Who knows what could have survived through the eons out here without the intervention of mankind? Heck, there are species of plants in this jungle that date back to the Mesozoic Period."

"You've been hitting that flask of yours a little too hard, my friend."

Galen continued as if he hadn't heard.

"It all makes sense."

"No," Merritt said. "It doesn't."

"Feathers are the one thing that has remained untouched by evolution. Intact feathers have been extracted from amber dating to the Albian stage of the Cretaceous Period, and their structure is identical. We're talking about one hundred million years of mutations and adaptations, and yet in that amount of time, the feather has not changed one iota. And the Cretaceous Period was the last time that this planet knew a feathered, flightless predator."

"So you think there's a species of predatory bird that has survived out here in the jungle for millions of years without being discovered?"

"Yes. And we need to warn the others. If this species could overcome a jaguar so easily, imagine what it could do to us."

"The people in the village didn't seem overly concerned."

"What are you talking about? They live behind thirty-foot fortifications and keep their livestock inside an impregnable stone pen. Don't you remember how those alpacas screamed when we approached?"

"Tell you what," Merritt said. "Why don't you run ahead and warn the others while I hang back and have a good laugh at your expense."

"You don't believe me," Galen said. He appeared genuinely hurt. "Look around you. Where are all of the animals we saw in the forest several days ago? Where are all of the monkeys and the deer and the flocks of birds?"

Merritt's stride faltered. Galen's insinuation struck a chord with him. He'd been wondering the exact same thing.

VII

12:46 p.m.

The sound of a roaring river had just reached Colton's ears when a hand closed over his elbow and spun him around.

He drew his pistol and shoved it into his assailant's gut.

"I need to talk to you," Merritt said without even glancing at the weapon. He looked over Colton's shoulder toward Leo. "You too."

"We don't have time for this," Colton said.

"Make the time."

Colton stared down the pilot for a long moment before holstering his gun.

"Everyone take a break," he called. Then more quietly to Merritt, "You have five minutes."

He jerked his arm out of the pilot's grasp and walked away from the path until he was under the wide branches of a tree that appeared to have its entire system of roots aboveground. Leo and Merritt were standing right behind him when he turned around.

"This had better be good," he said.

Merritt stared at each of them in turn before speaking.

"What's really going on here?"

"I don't know what you're talking about," Colton said.

"You know exactly what I'm talking about. You two are hiding something. What are we going to find when we reach our destination?"

"You know everything that we do," Leo said.

"You're lying," Merritt said. "You two have increasingly distanced yourself from the rest of us over the last couple of days. You spend all of your time off on your own, talking in whispers so that none of the rest of us can hear you. You're obviously keeping something from us, and you're going to tell me what it is. Right now."

"You're in no position to make demands," Colton said. He strode up to Merritt and got right in his face. "Isn't that right, deserter?"

Merritt didn't rise to the bait.

"Why did you originally dispatch Hunter's expedition?" He was speaking to Leo, but his eyes never left Colton's. "What were you hoping to find?"

"The ruins," Leo said. "And a small fortune in artifacts, of course."

"I don't believe you."

"No one cares what you believe," Colton said.

"What about the other men from the party? Neither of you seem especially concerned about finding them. I can't remember hearing you mention them recently at all. In fact, you've never once said their names."

"They're dead. You know that as well as I do."

"Then all of this talk about rescuing them was crap?"

"We don't actually *know* that they aren't still alive," Leo interjected.

"So, if you're right and they're all dead, what the hell do you think killed them? And why are we in such a hurry to find out?"

It took all of Colton's effort to keep from breaking Merritt's jaw.

"Can't you feel it?" Merritt whispered.

"Feel what?" Colton asked.

"The silence. You served in the field. You know what I mean. The calm before the storm. Everything's too quiet. Where are all of the animals, huh? I haven't seen any since yesterday morning, so what cut this path? We're the only ones in this area of the jungle. If we were in hostile territory, you know damn well what this would feel like. An ambush."

"Your five minutes are up."

"When I find out what you're hiding, you're going to wish you had told me when you had the chance."

And with that, Merritt stepped out from under the canopy and into the rain.

"We never should have brought him," Colton said. "He's become a liability."

VIII

1:02 p.m.

Leo's heart pounded so hard it felt as though it might break through his chest. Sure, a good measure of it was due to his age and the exertion at the high altitude, but the better part of it was anticipation of what was to come. They were so close now. The stream they now crossed on a series of staggered boulders wasn't on their LandSat map; however, by extrapolating its course farther to the southwest, it appeared as a hazy indentation beside one of the sections of data loss at the edge. Somewhere on the face of the mountain that reared up into the clouds directly in front of him was the point where the satellite magnetometer indicated the presence of an enormous vein of gold ore.

Soon, God willing, he would learn the truth about his son's death.

He needed to know. The uncertainty was a cancer eating him alive from the inside out.

With each step, they drew nearer a fortune in gold, and yet all he could focus on was what it had cost him. He remembered reading the parable of Midas to a four year-old Hunter in a candlelit tent in Honduras. Never in a million years would he have thought it would prove prophetic.

Colton had been unusually quiet all morning. At first, Leo had assumed that it was the cowardly desertion of one of his men that had him in a dour mood, but they had worked together long enough for him to know better. He had never seen Colton like this. There was definitely something of a much direr nature consuming him.

He hopped from one slick rock to another. The rain bludgeoned him, attempting to drive him down into the racing stream and over the edge. Beyond the cliff to his right, he could see only clouds through the rain. The rumble of the falls echoed like a stadium filled with angry spectators shouting for blood. He slipped on the wet boulder and thrust his foot down into the cold water, but managed to scrabble back on top of it and lunge to the next.

When he reached the far bank, he doubled over, hands on his knees, and attempted to catch his breath while the others crossed the rapids. Colton paced beside him, unfazed by the effort. When Leo looked up, their eyes met momentarily before Colton averted his stare.

With a great sigh, Leo stretched his back and turned toward the jungle that covered the steep hillside to the west. A wall of greenery swallowed the thin path and reached upward into the ceiling of churning clouds.

He glanced over his shoulder at Colton.

"Walk with me."

Colton fell hesitantly into measured stride beside him as they scaled the sloppy bank and stepped under the protective canopy, out of the worst of the rain. Vines sagged across the trail and branches grabbed at them from either side, but they were able to duck and sidle their way through. Once Leo was confident they were out of earshot and that the crunching sounds of their passage would mask their words, he finally spoke.

"Give it to me straight."

Colton crashed through the underbrush behind him. He made no immediate reply.

"How long have we been working together?" Leo asked. He slowed to skirt a slender green viper dangling from a branch in imitation of a vine.

"Long time," Colton said. Leo heard the whistle of a machete and knew the snake was no more.

"Do you remember the first time? That Mayan ruin in Guatemala?"

"Of course. We hauled out enough gold, jade, and artifacts to fill the cargo hold of a Handymax bulk carrier."

"And we argued over every little logistical matter. By the time we set sail, I could have strangled you."

Colton chuckled.

"But I've never known you to hold out on me," Leo said. "Until now."

They stumbled up the steep, muddy path. A trickle of water carved a trench in the middle. Leo had to use his hands to haul himself over a snarl of shoulder-high roots. Colton dropped down on the other side behind him. Leo turned and looked him directly in the eyes.

"I'm not holding out on you," Colton finally said after a long, uncomfortable silence.

"You can't bullshit a bullshitter," Leo said. He offered a tired smile.

Colton opened his mouth as if he were about to say something, then closed it again. He sighed. Leo noticed the man's rigid posture, how his right hand never strayed far from the sidearm in the holster beneath his left arm. His gaze darted from one side of the trail to the other. Finally, he glanced back toward the empty path, and spoke in little more than a whisper.

"Rippeth didn't desert us. I found what was left of him in the forest."

Leo wished the news surprised him. Perhaps this wasn't exactly what he had expected, but with the way they had prematurely broken camp in such a hurry and Colton's intensity throughout the morning, he had suspected something serious. He braced himself for the answer to the question he had to ask.

"What do you mean, 'what was left of him'?"

"He'd been ripped apart." Colton didn't blink when he spoke. His lips remained tight over his teeth. "There was blood everywhere. All over the ferns and the trees, dripping from the leaves overhead. Broken bones were scattered around the path, still wet, flesh gone, except for patches of skin here and there."

"Are you sure it was him?"

"I recognized his backpack and rifle."

"You didn't see his face?"

"I didn't go looking for it."

"And you haven't shared this with any of the others?"

Colton's stare grew hard. Leo matched it, and within read his answer.

"Good. Not a word to anyone until we figure out what happened. This doesn't change anything. We're still several days' travel from the nearest town. Panic will only work against us." Colton nodded his agreement. "So who do you think ambushed him? The natives?"

"There's no way the natives could have inflicted that kind of damage. Whatever attacked him was some kind of animal, and there had to have been several of them. His remains were nearly identical to those of the jaguar we found. And the alpacas that had been tied to that tree. Whatever they were being fed to killed Rippeth and consumed him. Maybe an eighth of a mile from where the rest of us were asleep in our tents."

"He obviously armed himself beforehand. For Christ's sake, he had an automatic rifle and a pair of grenades."

"But he never got the chance to use them. The rifle was just laying there on the ground."

"We need to decide exactly how we intend to handle—"

Footsteps crunched on the other side of the tangle of roots. Leo fell silent.

Galen appeared down the trail, swatting at the branches in his way. His look of determination under the hood of his poncho was almost comical. Lines of water poured from the plastic. He hitched his pants when he saw them and climbed over the roots.

"We need to talk," he said as he dropped down between them. He slipped in the mud and somehow managed to catch himself before he fell.

"Now isn't the best time, Dr. Russell," Colton said.

"This can't wait."

Leo again met Colton's stare and gave a single nod. They would continue their conversation later. The portly ornithologist had his panties in a bunch. And knowing Galen, it had probably taken him several hours to work up the courage to confront them with such conviction.

"Is there a problem?" Leo asked.

"I know what killed those alpacas back by the camp," Galen blurted. "And if I'm correct, we need to head back to safety *right now*."

Leo caught Colton's glance.

Galen held up two feathers, one in each hand.

"Do you remember that golden skull back in the burial chamber?"

IX

1:08 p.m.

The Indians were growing more brazen by the minute. Unlike during the previous night, when they had remained indistinguishable from the darkness, they now openly stalked his group from the cover of the forest. Tasker saw only black streaks knifing from behind one tree to the next from the corner of his eye. Once he had glimpsed one of their painted black faces, sharpened teeth bared, for only a split-second before the man vanished again. They were on all sides of them now, and the net was closing fast.

He and his men had rounded the far side of the lake and picked up their prey's trail where it led up toward the steep mountain to the west. He had thought that once they left the fortified village behind, their escort would recede. The opposite had proven true.

Tasker slowed his pace to allow McMasters to catch up with him. They had formalized a contingency plan for the eventuality that the natives might attack. Now that the painted men were showing themselves with increasing frequency, Tasker could sense that the moment would soon be at hand.

He raised an eyebrow to McMasters, who replied to his unvoiced question in a whisper.

"At least five. Two in the jungle to the north. One, maybe two, to the south. One ahead of us on the path, and another about fifty yards back."

"Are you certain?"

"They're ghosts. For all I know, there could be a hundred."

"Suppressor?"

McMasters held up his Colt Marine Infantry Automatic Rifle. The YHM Phantom .223 Quick Detach Sound Suppressor had been affixed to the barrel. They didn't want to alert their prey. At least, not yet.

A shadow sped across the furthest extent of his peripheral vision.

Closer this time.

He glanced back at Reubens, who met his gaze and nodded his understanding.

"On my mark," Tasker said, and again took the lead.

The path ahead veered sharply to the right and vanished into the jungle. A blind bend. The perfect spot for an ambush.

Silence closed in around them. No birds called or monkeys screeched. No wind rustled through the canopy. The only sounds were the soft crunch of detritus underfoot and their hushed, controlled exhalations.

Tasker steadied his grip on the Colt IAR as he rounded the corner in the path and found himself staring straight down the barrel at a man slightly taller and wirier than him, naked were it not for the short skirt of clumpy gray wool. He was painted black from head to toe with some sort of substance that shimmered on his shoulders and pectorals, even in the deep shadows. Scars covered his body like slender leeches. The man bared his filed teeth and Tasker squeezed the trigger into the sweet spot. He felt McMasters ease into position at his right shoulder, while Reubens fell into formation behind and to his left to create a triangle with their backs to one another. The sounds of their breathing grew harsher, more rapid.

The man blocking the trail stood his ground, that wicked grin affixed to his face. Against the black, the whites of his eyes stood out like beacons.

From the corners of his vision, Tasker watched the specters that had been hiding in the jungle materialize from the foliage and close in on them with arrows notched, bows drawn. They were all similarly painted and scarred, and all showcased their sharpened teeth as they approached. He counted at least two converging on them from either side, but refused to divert his attention from the man who stood before him long enough to check their rear. He had to trust that his men would do their jobs.

Tasker locked stares with the native, whose bow still hung from his shoulder. He was obviously the leader of this pack, and the only one wearing feathers braided into his long hair.

"Eight," McMasters whispered.

The armed indians halted their advance fifteen feet from the path. If they were even remotely familiar with their weapons, there was no way they could miss from that range.

Tasker felt the butt of the rifle snugged comfortably against his shoulder. The man in his sights appeared unimpressed.

The silent standoff stretched on. Seconds became minutes, and still no one moved.

Tasker listened intently for even the slightest sound to betray the presence of any natives still hiding out of sight.

The leader remained where he was, unflinching, yet to draw his bow. His confidence bordered on arrogance.

After several more tense minutes passed, the man in front of him raised his arms slowly, turned his palms down, and mimed for them to lower their rifles.

Tasker made no reply. Neither he nor his men budged an inch.

The native made a snarling sound that could have been a word, and again motioned for them to lower their guns. He bared his teeth and narrowed his eyes.

Tasker leaned back into McMasters and Reubens, and made just enough contact to initiate the silent count.

Three.

As one, the trio of soldiers slowly lowered their rifles from their shoulders.

Two.

Tasker never looked away from the leader's eyes. He tried to read any recognition of their deception within his stare.

One.

With the IAR at his hip, Tasker pulled the trigger and a fusillade of bullets exploded from the suppressor. The native bucked as though conducting electricity. Tasker was rolling before the man even fell. A blur of movement drew his fire. An arrow shrieked past his ear and hit behind him with a *thuck* that was barely audible over the *pfoot-pfoot-pfoot* of his weapon. The native who had shot at him was thrown backward into the trees under a crimson rainbow of his own blood.

Tasker swung the barrel to the right, firing the whole time. Another black figure dove for cover. The bullets were faster. They chewed through the man's knee and sent his lower leg flopping end over end in the opposite direction.

Screams erupted from the bedlam.

Tasker launched himself forward at a crouch, and raced toward where the wailing native had fallen. An arrow sang from behind him. Its song was cut short as searing pain blossomed in his right shoulder. He whirled and fired. Bullets tore apart the shrubs and climbed up the painted man as he notched another arrow, lifting him from his feet and tossing him into the underbrush in a wash of blood.

Warmth flowed down Tasker's upper arm. He was peripherally aware of the sharp arrowhead poking out from the meat of his shoulder. The rifle grew exponentially heavier in his grasp as he staggered through the waist-high shrubs until he encountered the severed lower leg. He followed the trail of blood and matted ferns to where the man struggled to crawl deeper into the jungle.

From behind him, he heard the whispered puffs of gunfire begin to slow.

The rifle fell from his hand and clattered to the ground. Spurred by the sound behind him, the wounded man clawed at the loam, gouging his fingers into the mud to gain any sort of traction. Tasker unsheathed his knife, grabbed the man by the braid, and jerked his head back. In one swift motion, he leaned around and plunged the blade into the man's throat. A rush of blood flooded over Tasker's hand. The arterial spray painted the forest in pulsing arcs. He jerked the knife to the side and tore through the tendons and trachea, nearly decapitating the man were it not for his spine.

Tasker rose and swiped the blade on his pants before returning it to its scabbard. Turning, he found his rifle and hefted it in his left hand. His right arm hung limply at his side. Blood dripped from his fingertips and pattered on the ground.

All was quiet now.

Tasker shuffled back to the path, passing the crumpled carcass of another native before reaching the leader's remains. The man gurgled and wheezed through the foam of blood bubbling past his lips. Tasker stood over him and surveyed the area. McMasters tromped through the weeds on the far side of the path, kicking aside branches and vines. Three arrows stood at angles from his backpack, the broken shaft of another from his left thigh. He looked up and met Tasker's stare.

"All clear," he said, "but I don't think Reubens is going to make it."

Reubens was sprawled facedown in the middle of the path, arms pinned beneath him. The feathered ends of arrow shafts protruded from his backpack and shoulders like the quills of a porcupine. His rifle lay abandoned at his side.

Tasker walked closer and noticed the arrowhead poking from the side of Reubens's neck beneath his ear. He nudged the body with his toe. A rasping sound came from under the man. Tasker rolled Reubens over. The man's eyes were wide with fright, his cheeks stained with mud and tears. The broken shaft of an arrow stood from the left corner of his mouth, where it had torn away his lips. He bit down on it with a clicking sound as he tried to swallow back the blood. He looked up at Tasker like a beaten dog pleading for its master's forgiveness.

Tasker lowered his smoldering barrel to the soldier's forehead. A tendril of smoke spiraled up from the sizzling union. With a single squeeze of the trigger, he put Reubens out of his misery.

"Seven bodies," McMasters said. He reached the path, stood beside Tasker, and glanced down. "Make that eight."

One of the savages must have managed to escape.

Tasker nodded and returned to the leader of the natives, who gazed up at him through glassy eyes narrowed by agony.

The man's lips twitched and blood dribbled over his cheeks.

After several attempts, the man finally forced an epithet through the burbling blood.

"*Kuntur…*"

The muscles in his face relaxed and the last hiss of air escaped through one of the bullet wounds in his chest.

"What's that supposed to mean?" McMasters asked.

"Does it matter?" Tasker raised his boot and drove it down onto the man's face with a *crack*, then set about prying the arrow out of his deltoid muscle.

A bellow of rage and pain echoed through the still rainforest.

Chapter Seven

I

Andes Mountains, Peru
October 30th
1:16 p.m. PET

The words poured out of Galen's mouth so fast that even he could barely keep up with them. He knew how fantastic his theory sounded, but he became increasingly convinced each time it played through his head. Sam had said that the golden skull was far too precisely crafted for the Chachapoya, whose metallurgical skills were historically limited. Heck, just looking at the abstract faces of the six *purunmachus* verified their artistic style and shortcomings. The skull had been anatomically perfect, from the seating of the gold teeth in the alveolar sockets to the positioning of the orbital housings, and the irregular sutures between the cranial bones to the hollow concavities of the system of sinuses. Even the way the mandible articulated into the temporomandibular joints reflected an almost medical understanding of the skeleton. If it were simply a sculpture, then it had to be based on something the creator could physically see while he was sculpting it, but Galen didn't think it was anything as mundane as that. Then there were the feathers incapable of flight, the avian-hybrid, snake-faced deity carved into the stone walls in the village, and the immense fortifications and impregnable alpaca pen. Combined, they painted a picture that was impossible to ignore.

Something had survived in these mountains, hidden in the dense jungle, something capable of running down and butchering a jaguar, the crowned king of the Amazonian food chain.

He didn't vocalize the summation of his theory. Colton and Leo needed to reach that conclusion on their own. All he said was that it was a species of raptor, though not the modern kind that nested high on the cliff-sides and feasted upon carrion.

From the questions the men posed and the way they communicated silently in glances while he spoke, he could tell they didn't necessarily disbelieve him. But they didn't quite believe him, either.

After Galen finished, he drew a deep breath and waited for either of them to speak. The crackle of dead branches and leaves announced the approach of the rest of their party.

"Have you shared this theory with anyone else?" Colton finally asked. The hard look in his eyes and firm set of his jaw indicated that the question was heavily loaded, but for the life of him, Galen couldn't imagine why. He grew uncomfortable under the man's scrutiny, and paused to formulate his reply.

"No," he lied.

Leo nodded. "Let's just keep this between us for the time being. Even if you're right, there's no point in alarming the others just yet."

"*If* I'm right? We shouldn't even be here. Lord only knows what these creatures are capable of. Think about the alpaca bones around that tree. That could easily be us."

Colton took a step toward him and Galen instinctively cringed. Even the man's posture radiated menace.

"You *will* keep your mouth shut until given clearance to open it," Colton whispered. Voices filtered through the underbrush behind them. Colton's stare ticked toward the sound, then returned to meet his. "Do you understand?"

Galen could only nod. No threat had been uttered, but the implication hung in the air between them.

Christ. They already knew, didn't they? How long had they known, and why the hell hadn't they turned back yet, or at least warned the rest of the party?

Colton's expression softened as though controlled by the flick of a switch. He reached forward, lifted Galen's poncho, and plucked the feathers from the breast pocket of his vest.

"Thank you for sharing your concerns, Dr. Russell," Colton said. A genuine smile lit his face. What kind of man could cycle through emotions so quickly? "Believe me when I say that your safety is our primary interest, and there's absolutely nothing that would compromise our commitment to maintaining it."

Colton tucked the feathers into a pocket beneath his poncho, clapped him on the shoulder, and struck off on the path with Leo. He could hear them whispering, but couldn't decipher their words.

What just happened?

Galen was terrified. Something was out there in the jungle with them, possibly mere feet away in the underbrush, something that should never have survived this long. They had no idea exactly what they were up against. If he was right, as he firmly believed, they were dealing with a species of predator the likes of which mankind had never encountered.

His breathing grew fast and shallow, and his legs started to tremble.

Merritt scrambled down the wall of roots and hopped to the ground beside him. Galen opened his mouth to tell the pilot about his encounter. Then he remembered the expression on Colton's face and thought better of it. His mouth fell closed with the click of teeth.

Sam climbed down next, while the three remaining guards began the arduous task of scaling the wooden jungle gym with the crate of supplies. Her eyes appeared haunted as well. What had *she* seen?

The attractive director and her cameraman stood behind the men, filming their efforts. They were blissfully unaware of the danger surrounding them, as though capturing footage in a park rather than the black heart of the Amazon.

Galen turned to the forest and watched for any sign of movement. Anything. Only the insects stirred. They stayed near the tree trunks, out of the path of the raindrops.

And even though he couldn't see them, somewhere out there was a species that shouldn't exist, something capable of hunting this section of the rainforest to near extinction.

A flutter of movement drew his eye to where a large butterfly opened and closed its wings. It clung to a liana, its body the color of the bark. Folded together, its wings were nearly invisible. When it opened them, Galen recognized it as the same variety Jay had recorded in the jungle the day before: pale olive-colored background, veined to imitate scales, with twin turquoise circles on each forewing, and a design on the hindwings that simulated a sharp-toothed snarl.

Galen shuddered.

He thought of the way the walking stick insect had evolved to mimic a twig, the way the atlas moth had altered the shape and design of its wings to mimic the striking face of a snake.

The butterfly closed its wings again, breaking his trance.

They were in serious danger here.

When he turned back to the path, the others were already gone.

His heart pounded and his legs trembled.

"Wait up!" he called in a shrill voice, and sprinted up the trail after them.

II

1:48 p.m.

There were only two of them left now, but Tasker was unconcerned. This merely altered his plans and increased his stake. They were only up against eleven, maybe half of which had any military training. The remainder were civilians, who didn't pose the slightest threat. And he and McMasters maintained the element of surprise. Once their prey discovered the source of the wealth they sought, they would attack under the cover of night. With a rotating two-man patrol, it would be easy enough to isolate one set of guards and take them out, which would buy several hours to sneak into the camp and dispatch the rest while they slept unaware. The plan was perfect in its simplicity, and the risk involved was minimal at best. Assuming everything fell into place by nightfall, by this time tomorrow, their biggest problem would be how they were going to transport their fortune back out of the mountains. And that was one problem he didn't imagine he'd mind one little bit.

The only variable was the natives. Once the lone native who had eluded them returned to the village and told them about the slaughter, they would come after McMasters and him again, and this time in greater numbers. Or perhaps after witnessing the extent of the massacre, they would simply go back to minding their own damn business. Maybe on their way back out of the jungle, he and McMasters could make a detour, scale that little wall of theirs, and show them exactly what they had to fear from the outside world and the technological advancements in military weaponry.

He smiled at the thought.

The overhanging trees fell away as the path rounded a steep stone cliff. To his right, all he could see were dark thunderheads hovering over a seamless mat of green forest that stretched clear to the infinite horizon. A layer of mist clung to everything, made fuzzy by the onslaught of rain. The wind screamed along the northern face of the mountain and buffeted them with enormous droplets.

Tasker lowered his head and advanced into the storm. The path thinned until it was merely a rock ledge on the sheer slope. A mess of vines cascaded from above and covered the trail, making their footing even more tenuous. The tonal quality of the gusting wind changed. He recognized it immediately as the sound of a gale blowing across a hollow cavity in the cliffside. A moment later, he discovered a gap where the vines had been hacked away to reveal a maw of shadows.

He glanced back over his shoulder, nodded to McMasters, and stepped from the ledge into the darkness. The gray light from the outside world reached past his shoulders to silhouette the structures against the rear wall. Dust hung in the air on the aged stench of a crypt. He paused and donned his night-vision goggles, drawing contrast in shades of green. The giant humanoid sculptures reminded him of the abstract art that was all the rage, a substitute for talent and training if you asked him. The odd structures to either side were reminiscent to some degree of the conjoined townhouses in the Haight-Ashbury district of San Francisco, had they been built from mud by primitives. The site obviously wasn't of great importance, or their prey would still be here.

Something drew his eye at the base of the statuary, a recessed concavity, inside of which twin reflections sparkled. As he approached, the object took form. The reflections came from twin jewels set into some sort of bust. Not just a bust. A golden bust. He knelt before it and stroked the tacky residue of age from the smooth creation. It was some sort of idol to a long dead god; a sharp-toothed skull with gemstones for eyes, set on a bed of feathers. He carefully lifted it and appraised it. It had to weigh fifteen pounds. If that headdress had fetched a seven-figure sum, then this one piece alone could make all of their efforts worthwhile.

McMasters whistled appreciatively behind him.

Tasker set the skull back into the recess and studied the surrounding structure. He knocked against the plaster. Hollow. He turned to face McMasters.

"Tear it down."

Together they slammed the butts of their rifles repeatedly through the adobe and tore away the fractured sections. Dust billowed out and the rotten smell intensified. He had no doubt that bodies had been walled inside. If the people who had interred them were like so many other prehistoric societies, he was bound to find the most prized possessions of the dead with their remains.

By the time they were finished, the six faces lorded over a massive black ruin that swirled with dust. Debris was heaped everywhere. Inside was a platform built from rocks and wood, on top of which were several egg-shaped bundles of rotting fabric. Tasker grabbed them one by one and threw them to the ground, then scoured the shelf. He brushed aside piles of dust, plaster fragments, and feathers to reveal the coarse wood. There were no artifacts.

Unsheathing his knife, he turned his attention to the burial bundles and slashed the cloth. McMasters tore them apart behind him. The smell became unbearable. What in the world had they buried in there?

"For the love of God," McMasters groaned.

Tasker slit the final bundle and returned to where his partner hovered over the first.

"What...?" he started, but as soon as he stepped around the other man, he could clearly see the source of the foul aroma.

Tangles of dry fur, still attached to withered chunks of desiccated meat had been packed between the outer blanket and the greasy one beneath.

Tasker shoved McMasters aside and ripped through the second layer to find a stuffing of feathers.

"Where's the gold?" he growled through bared teeth.

He tore through another layer of fabric, crisp with the fluids that had long since soaked into the blanket and hardened, and jerked the frayed sides apart to expose the mummified corpse at the core.

Tasker stared down at the body for a long moment before looking over at McMasters, who had paled noticeably.

"What the hell is that?" McMasters asked, and took a stumbling step in reverse.

Tasker knelt before the carcass to study it more carefully.

There was nothing remotely human about it.

He pictured what was left of the three Peruvian guides they had found in the forest and the bloody mess that had once been

Jones. And this…thing, exploding from the rainforest in a flurry of teeth and claws.

The sooner they finished their mission the better.

III

2:34 p.m.

With the roar of the unseen falls and the clamor of the rain in the canopy, the jungle had become a cacophony of water. The steep path was now a small stream that covered their feet and turned the packed clay to mud. Ever higher they climbed, until the clouds no longer rested on the treetops, but became a part of them. Mists eddied around them, occasionally hiding even the person ahead on the trail. The temperature continued to fall. It still had to be somewhere in the upper-fifties, yet their damp clothes kept their skin stippled with goosebumps. They had to be nearing ten thousand feet in elevation, and surely the summit of the peak they now scaled couldn't be too much farther up into the clouds.

Sam's legs ached and she had lost the feeling in her toes. Her heart raced and her fingers trembled with excitement. If their assumption about the location of the ruins was correct, then it was only a matter of time before they stumbled out of the forest and into—

She walked right into Merritt's back and had to steady herself to keep from slipping. If she fell, the waterslide that was the path would send her careening down the slope.

Merritt turned and braced her by the elbow. He nearly lost his balance as well.

"Why did you stop?" She had to shout to be heard over the deluge.

He merely smiled in response and inclined his head over his right shoulder.

Holding her breath, Sam walked around him and saw Colton and Leo framed against a backdrop of rain at the terminus of the path. The trees grew sparser ahead. Creeping figs and vines tied them together and to the shrub-covered ground. Beyond she could see a sheer abutment covered with lianas and vines. It wasn't an ordinary cliff. Vertical and horizontal seams were visible through the vegetation.

It was a manmade wall.

She walked past Colton and Leo to inspect the fortification. Black stones had been chiseled to the size and shape of concrete blocks, and stacked in a staggered pattern. Most of the mortar between them had eroded away, but the lianas served to hold them in place. Some sections were so overgrown with vegetation that they appeared to have become a part of the hillside.

She ran her fingers along the smooth stones. Obsidian. Volcanic rock.

The wall extended as far as she could see to either side. Every twenty feet or so was an arched enclave barely large enough for a man to crouch inside. They reminded her of decorative sewer drains. In front of each was a column roughly five feet tall and two feet wide, composed of stacked rocks, only on top of each was a charred iron cage like a chimney. She approached one, stood on her tiptoes, and peeked inside. A sunken recess was filled with detritus, and the sides were scored with carbon. They were torches like those that surrounded the fortress in the valley below.

She could hardly contain herself. The anticipation was overwhelming. She glanced back at the others at the end of the trail. Above their heads was nothing but clouds. Her eyes met Leo's, and she felt his pain, which spawned feelings of guilt at her unbridled enthusiasm. This was presumably where Hunter had spent his last hours. He must have drowned somewhere nearby.

Sam turned away and followed the fortification toward the sound of the waterfall. The ground turned from soil to slickrock, and the forest dropped away to the right. A rugged rock slope led to a point, beyond which she could barely see the spray of a waterfall through the mist trapped against the mountainside.

She reached the end of the wall, which veered at a ninety degree angle back toward the sheer face of the peak. Here she could see the fortification more clearly. It had to be more than twenty-five feet tall, higher even than the majority of the walls at Kuelap. A large section on this northern face had fallen to ruin in a pile of broken bricks. It almost looked as though a thin stone staircase had once passed through the wall before one of the sides had collapsed down onto it. Whatever the case, it granted them access to the ruins that lay on the other side.

The rain pounded down on her, soaking her even under her poncho, but she didn't care.

She scrabbled up the steep mound of moss-blanketed stones until she reached the top of the wall, and stared down at a sight the likes of which few modern men had ever seen before. So far, all of the Chachapoyan ruins had been discovered by locals, who had thoroughly ransacked the sites, pillaging everything of value that might have helped scholars piece together the last days of this once great society. This one was different. It didn't appear as though anything had been disturbed by more than the wind and the elements since the last occupants had turned their backs on the fortress.

"What do you see?" Leo called up from below. His voice quivered with emotion.

Sam couldn't find the words to describe it. She could only shake her head. It was everything she had hoped to find and more.

She looked back at the others, who had congregated at the base of the wall. Past them she could see the rugged cut of the stone cliff beside the waterfall. With the mist, it was impossible to tell how wide or deep the chasm was. Even the eternal expanse of the jungle on the eastern foothills and plains was hidden from sight. They were alone at the top of the world, isolated by the clouds and geography. It almost felt as though they were on a different planet entirely.

The red light of Jay's camera stared up at her, along with nine pairs of anxious eyes.

She could contain her smile no longer.

"Well?" she called. "What are you waiting for?"

She turned back to the village inside the great wall, and began to pick her way down the crumbled slope toward the greatest discovery of her entire career.

IV

2:48 p.m.

Dahlia reached the pinnacle of the mound of rubble and stared down upon the ruins. They were more amazing than she had even dared to hope. She spun to face Jay, who was hot on her heels, camera in hand. The eagerness in his eyes surely matched her own. This was what they'd been waiting for. This documentary would put them on the map and they would have more work and success than they'd be able to handle.

She turned back to the task at hand. The others were already at the bottom of the pile, staring in awe at the scene before them. She needed all of this on film. This was no time to lag behind. This was when the magic happened.

"I want a panoramic view of this spread from up here, then focus down on the others where they are now. As soon as you have enough footage, haul ass down there and see if we can get a shot of their faces before they begin to explore. And stick with Sam. She's our expert. I want to see everything she sees. And make sure you're close enough to record everything she says. That information is crucial for the voiceover."

"I'm on it," he said, and took up post on the highest vantage point.

Meanwhile, she needed to stall the others to buy Jay some time to catch up. This was her moment. She'd followed patiently and stayed out of the way like a good little girl, but this was what they were paying her for. If they wanted this done right, they were going to have to do it her way.

She scrambled down the loose bricks, slipping on the mossy surfaces and catching herself on her abraded palms. The rain made the descent even more challenging, but she'd rather chance a sprained ankle than blow this opportunity.

And why did it have to be raining anyway? Sure, it added a measure of reality and ambiance, but she would have traded both for a clear blue sky.

The others appeared ready to disperse. She had to be quick.

"Wait!" She leaped from the mound and landed in the mud. Her legs buckled and she fell to her knees, tearing her jeans and the skin beneath them. She didn't even feel it. Lunging to her feet, she grabbed Leo by the arm. "This is why you brought us. If you want this properly documented, then you have to wait for Jay." She paused to catch her breath. "We enter as a group, Sam in the lead. Jay will be right at her hip with me behind him. The rest of you stay a couple steps back until I give the word."

The expression on Leo's face was one of indignation. He was obviously not a man accustomed to being told what to do. He opened his mouth to protest, but Dahlia silenced his objection in a whisper.

"You said you wanted this film to be your son's legacy. That legacy is now in my hands. If you want something half-assed with people tromping all over the ruins, then by all means, go ahead. But if you want this film to be truly special, something that will simultaneously honor your son's memory and make the viewers feel as though they're part of the expedition, then you're going to have to do this the right way. My way."

After a long pause, he acquiesced with a nod. Dahlia felt a swell of power.

She turned to Sam. "Are you ready to do this?" The way the anthropologist appeared ready to burst, Dahlia didn't need to wait for an answer. "Then on my mark, you take the lead. This is the first pass. I want you to point out and describe everything of topical importance. Save the fine details for later when we'll have plenty of time to properly document each. For now, I just want a leisurely stroll through the ruins, a cursory exploration, if you will."

"Can we do this now, or would you like to touch up my makeup first?"

Dahlia matched Sam's smirk, and with a flourish, gestured for her to lead the way.

"Stay right on top of her," Dahlia whispered to Jay, who had taken a moment to ready himself, and now advanced on Sam's left. "And don't you dare miss a thing."

"Relax, girl. This is what I was born to do."

Dahlia fell into stride behind him, so close she nearly clipped his heels with each step, and, with her heart beating as fast as a hummingbird's, prepared to make cinematic history.

V

2:57 p.m.

It was all Leo could do to keep from shouting for the others to clear out of his way and running blindly through the wreckage of the village. Somewhere inside these crumbling fortifications were the answers he required to piece together the final days of his son's life. He had to know why Hunter died, and he had to find someone to hold responsible for it. Someone needed to pay.

He followed behind Dahlia as they entered the ruins, staying close enough to Sam that he could hear her every word. His gaze darted over every minute detail. Nothing escaped his attention. He couldn't afford to miss anything.

It was apparent that they weren't entering the village from the main entrance, but rather from what appeared to be the rear. The layout reminded him of the village they had passed through in the valley, had it been struck by a hurricane and allowed to decompose over the span of centuries. Weeds and trees had grown up through the cracked cobblestone walkways, and the monstrous ceiba trees around which the buildings had been constructed had laid claim to their remains. Vines dangled from the branches, connecting the trees as completely as if woven into a web by some massive spider. Epiphytes bloomed from every surface in shades of pink and blue, and mosquitoes swarmed around the stagnant water trapped in the cups formed by the aloe-like leaves of bromeliads. Circular dwellings dominated this region, but their tall, thatch roofs had long since fallen. The rotted and broken beams that had once supported them stood from the huts at odd angles, barely visible beneath the creeping foliage that entwined the wood. Stacked stones had tumbled from the walls and were now heaped under soil and aggressive bushes. He peered through the crumbled sections and saw broken pottery and practical relics of all kinds.

"At a guess," Sam said, "I'd wager there are close to twenty of these round dwellings. If this village mirrors the modern one, as I suspect, there should be a matching number on the other side, which should place the population somewhere in the neighborhood of two hundred. That's a rough, preliminary estimate, of course."

Leo scoured the area for any sign of Hunter's passage. There had to be something here.

They wound around tree trunks, ducked under vines and branches, and climbed over termite-infested trunks. Ants so large their pincers appeared capable of stealing chunks of flesh crawled across everything. Flies buzzed from out of sight. After several excruciatingly slow minutes, during which they paused a half-dozen times for Sam to point out interesting architectural nuances, decorative friezes covered in moss, and sculpted faces on the stone half-walls that lined the path, they reached the central courtyard. Here the forest had run rampant, tearing up the paving stones and filling nearly every available inch of growing space. Flowering shrubs had shot up in the gaps between them, leaving only thin passages reminiscent of animal trails.

"We could probably date the approximate time that this fortress was abandoned by the strata in the soil," Sam said. "Or if we can find a midden heap, we could use radiocarbon dating on the top layer of refuse."

Leo recognized a similar pair of round stages to the right, all but buried beneath dirt and vegetation, which covered the gap between them where the stairs would have been. The rectangular structure behind them was masked by a façade of vines and lianas. Trees grew through the roof. Dark holes marred its face where the cubes of stone had tumbled into piles that now sprouted thorny shrubs with brilliant orange and yellow blossoms. Several of the doorways had collapsed, but two still remained open to varying degrees in the center, guarded by screens of vines.

Sam approached the main building, scurried up onto the stage in front of it, and stood before the most accessible doorway with the cameraman leaning over her shoulder. Leo climbed up behind her. He noticed that much of the foliage covering the entrance was recent growth. Thinner sprouts had emerged from bluntly severed vines, their ends coiled with still-furled leaves. Someone had recently hacked their way through. His heart ached with the realization of who must have done it.

"We're going to need light," Sam said.

Colton held out his penlight, and Leo quickly commandeered it while Jay switched on the camera's spotlight.

Sam parted the curtain of vines, climbed over the rubble, and stepped into the darkness with Jay directly behind her, his light diffusing into a weak glow that swirled with motes of dust. Leo shoved through and found himself in an antechamber that appeared to be anything but structurally sound. The stone pillars that had once supported the ceiling lay in rubble throughout the room; in their place, broad trunks had grown from cracks in the upturned floor and filled the gaps in the stone roof. There were piles of broken rock everywhere, and the back wall, which must have once featured several doorways that led deeper into the building, had partially collapsed under the weight of the buckled ceiling.

The camera's beam swept from the left side of the room to the right in a slow, steady arc, highlighting spider webs large enough to snare a grown man and pale, withered plants that somehow managed to survive in the absence of light. Water dripped from the cracks above into broad pools that had eroded into the floor and stank of rotten eggs. Roots of all kinds dangled from the ceiling like cobwebs. There was no movement of air, only the trapped heat and humidity that caused the sweat to bloom from his pores.

A mound of crumbled bricks dominated the wall to the left. They appeared to have been forged from a combination of clay and metal, which glinted as the light swept across them.

"What's that over there?" Sam asked, pointing off to the right where the wall was stained black with soot.

Jay's beam flashed across it, then focused down to a shrinking circle as he walked closer. A ring of rocks surrounded a pit in the floor filled with charcoal-colored water, fed by the rainwater dripping from a hole in the ceiling. A tangle of thick roots snaked from the roof into the stagnant pool, which hummed with mosquitoes and surely teemed with larvae. Several dented and tarnished pots rested against the wall, one much thicker and caked with black metallic residue, like a smelting pot. Beside them was what at first looked like a jumble of sticks, but upon closer inspection, there was no denying what they truly were.

Bones.

Stacks of bleached bones.

Sam crouched before the cluttered heaps and carefully removed one of the long bones from the top. It was so smooth that despite its obvious age, it appeared polished beneath the coating of dust. The shape was unmistakably human. Rounded cup for articulation into the shoulder, broad distal end that expanded into protruding epicondyles and rounded condyles. A humerus.

"This can't be right," Sam whispered.

Leo had seen enough. They had screwed around for far too long already. He whirled and shoved through the others as they entered the chamber. There had to be some sign of his son around here, and he was going to find it.

They had found Hunter's body, but what about the rest of his party? There had been no sign of them on the trail leading here. Surely that would have been the same path they used to return to civilization, which meant that they still had to be up here somewhere. Or at least what was left of them.

He couldn't shake the mental image of the way Colton had described Rippeth's remains.

An involuntary shiver rippled through him.

He turned to the right, toward where he could barely see the steep cliff that served as the fourth wall of the fortress and followed the trail through the underbrush. It became more clearly delineated with each step, suggesting frequent use. He passed more deteriorating circular huts to either side. Raindrops assaulted him in waves through the occasional breaks in the canopy. Behind him, the others called his name, but he made no reply. He was focused solely on finding any indication that Hunter's group had been here. Nothing else mattered now.

The buzzing of flies grew louder, their ordinarily lazy drone frenetic.

Ahead, the trail terminated against a stone embankment draped with vines. The last row of huts was now at his back. To either side, wending, uneven stone staircases led upward to stepped levels with flat sections designed for agriculture. He remembered the topless women tending to the crops on the hillside at the back of the fortress down in the valley. Faded designs were painted on the stone, but he couldn't decipher them thanks to the overgrowth.

The buzzing sound still came from directly in front of him.

He walked closer to the granite escarpment and determined where the noise originated. A scraggly tree grew right up against the stone, weeping with vines. He could vaguely discern an area of deep shadows past it. A cut in the mountainside. Easing around the tented roots, he saw that the vines on the stone face had been hacked away to expose a dark, triangular opening formed by a wide fissure in the rock.

The excited buzz of the flies echoed from the darkness. The stale air reeked of death.

He pointed the penlight ahead of him and followed the beam into the mountain. Fat-bodied flies swarmed in the weak light, which did little to illuminate the blackness. The air was dramatically cooler, and heavy, as though acted upon by a separate gravity. He smelled rotten meat and the timeless scent of decomposition.

Colton's voice drifted to his ears as though from miles away.

The beam faded well before it encountered any resistance. He directed it up at the ceiling. It was barely a foot above his head, but felt far lower than that in the smothering darkness. The walls, which contained pools of shadows at regular intervals, were so close that he wouldn't have been able to raise his arms out to either side. He turned the light upon the wall to his left and let out an involuntary gasp. Arched recesses had been chiseled into the stone in columns three rows high, from floor to ceiling, and extended beyond the extent of the light's reach. Vacant-eyed skulls stared back at him from the front of the rock ledges, behind which decapitated, desiccated bodies had been stuffed into the hollows. They'd been folded into fetal position and lashed into place with frayed cords. Spiders had made themselves at home within the enclaves. Webs filled every available inch of space, thick with dust and the carcasses of age-old insects. Streaks of magnetite and quartz glinted from the curved stone.

Placers.

This was what Hunter had come to find. He must have stood in this very corridor as Leo did now.

This had to be some sort of primitive ossuary. Leo remembered Sam saying that not all of the dead were deemed worthy enough for burial in the *purunmachus* or the *chullpas*. This must be where all of the others were interred, not bundled with their prized possessions, but set out on display.

He flashed the beam from one to the next. Several of the skulls were fractured or bereft of entire sections of the cranium and teeth. The bodies behind them were in sorry shape as well. Some were missing extremities, others entire segments of their thoraces, while a few were simple piles of broken, brown bones.

Corpses surrounded him, but they weren't the source of the rotten stench that pulled him deeper into the tunnel.

Colton called Leo's name. It echoed ahead of him into the infinite blackness. He was about to answer when he noticed the distinctive prints of hiking boots on the dirt floor.

His heart pounded. This was the first verifiable sign that his son's party had been here.

Leo picked up his pace and breezed past the dead with the sound of buzzing growing louder with each step. Black dots filled the cone of light and tapped at his body. The flies crawled on his skin and through his hair. He had to fan his face to keep them out of his eyes and ears. A moment later, he stumbled upon what had summoned them into the mountain.

The walls and ceiling positively crawled with flies, their shimmering green eyes reflecting his beam. He swatted at the cloud surrounding him, and pointed the light at the ground. It reflected back at him from the broken blade of a machete, beside which were tatters of fabric. Hawaiian-patterned fabric.

Leo had to pull his shirt up over his mouth and nose to combat the odor, and even then he retched several times before having to turn away.

"It looks like Hunter was the lucky one," Colton whispered from behind him.

Leo could only nod. He straightened, bit his lip, and returned his attention to the carnage.

Chunks of cartilage and muscle still clung to the exposed ribcage, and maggots wriggled through the puddle of sludge around the severed spine. An arm, stripped to the bone, save the skin on the fingers, rested against the wall. Its disarticulated twin was another ten feet farther into the tunnel. There was a foot covered with black skin and even blacker flies. The fractured remnants of the pelvis were canted against the opposite wall. And at the very edge of the light, the head lay on its side, robbed of flesh, frontal bone torn away, eye sockets seething with flies. The mandible had been yanked out of the socket and rested askew to the maxillae.

His obsession with finding the truth about his son's death had blinded him to the signs all around him. The jaguar carcass. The alpaca bones scattered at the foot of the sacrificial tree. The way Colton had described what was left of Rippeth. They were isolated in the wilderness with a threat that Hunter's party hadn't seen coming until it was too late.

"Jesus," Leo whispered. "We're all going to die here."

VI

3:05 p.m.

Merritt leaned over Sam's shoulder as she studied the mound of bones. She shuffled through the pile and lifted them out one by one, repeating the same phrase like a mantra.

"This can't be right."

"What?" he asked.

She looked up at him and blinked as though seeing him for the first time. She furrowed her brow and seemed to think for a long time before she finally spoke.

"Look at this bone here." She held up the broken shaft of the distal half of a femur. "This broad portion forms the roof of the knee joint. The edges of the condyles should be more clearly defined, and the cortex should show thin striations and grooves. This is too smooth, too perfectly rounded, almost as though it's been ground down and polished." She turned it so the broken end of the shaft faced him. "And the medullary cavity is hollow. Do you see that? There should be a crust of marrow and vessels, not a tunnel that could have been bored by a drill."

"I don't understand the significance."

"In 1964, Anasazi remains were unearthed at Polacca Wash on a Hopi reservation in Arizona. All of the bones exhibited these same kinds of fractures, and were similarly smoothed and hollowed. It's one of the great mysteries of Native American culture. The prevailing theory is that the ends of the bones are so smooth because they were boiled. Bouncing around in the water and bumping against the sides of the pot made them that way, and the shafts are hollow because the marrow was boiled and scraped out. And this puddle right here?" She gestured to the small black pool filled with putrid water. "This used to be a fire pit. You can tell by the carbon scoring on the floor and wall. There are even pots right over there. These people cooked their dead on this very spot."

"Why would they do that when they could have just buried them like all of the others?"

"Don't you get it? They cooked these bones with the meat still on them. They were *eating* their dead." She drew a deep breath and resumed in a less animated tone. "The Chachapoya weren't cannibalistic. They were primarily an agricultural society. You saw it in practice on the slopes of the fortress by the lake. They built elaborate steppes on the mountainside and filled them with soil to grow everything from agaves to maize, and were very successful doing it. And they revered their dead. You remember that cavern we found? All of the bodies were bundled with great care and placed in *chullpas* nearly as nice as the homes they lived in. They wouldn't have eaten their dead. Not unless circumstances had become desperate and they were cut off from all other sources of food."

"So what do you think happened here?"

"I don't have enough information to form a hypothesis yet, but at a guess, I'd say they were involved in some sort of lengthy standoff inside this fortress."

"You think it was the Spanish?"

"No. The conquistadors had vastly superior firepower. None of the tribes were able to hold them off for long. Even the Inca, who were known as the most ferocious warriors, were able to muster precious little resistance against the Spanish with their armor and muskets."

"What about the Inca themselves?"

"The design of the building reflects Incan design. They had already assimilated the culture."

"Then if you're right, who could they have possibly been holed up in here against?"

The question hung in the air between them for an interminable moment before Sam abruptly rose and headed for the doorway.

"I don't know, but the answer has to be around here somewhere."

Merritt climbed over the rubble and followed her out into the rain. After so long in the darkness, even the gray day was blinding. Thunder crashed overhead and rumbled down the rocky slope like an avalanche. The rain intensified in response.

His mind flashed back to the theory Galen had put forth earlier. He shook away the images that the birdman's words conjured.

Jay hustled to keep up with them, the camera jouncing in his grip. Mere minutes ago, he had been grinning from ear to ear like a kid on Christmas morning, but now a note of worry had diminished his smile and crept into the corners of his eyes. Dahlia and Galen brought up the rear, while the three remaining armed men abandoned the crate and struck off in the opposite direction toward where Merritt heard Colton calling for Leo.

"That was their palatial structure," Sam said. "Using it to defile the deceased would have been the ultimate sacrilege." She looked from side to side. "But it was also the only building with a stone roof."

"It makes sense. They wouldn't have wanted to ignite those flimsy thatch roofs directly above their heads."

"You don't get it. They could easily have made a bonfire out in the open."

"Unless they'd barricaded themselves inside that chamber."

"Exactly."

"So you're saying the stones piled in front of the entrances weren't the result of the building crumbling over time."

"I'm not saying anything. All I know is that something awful happened here, something so terrible that these people were forced to eat each other to survive."

Merritt could tell they were heading east by the sound of the waterfall to his left, toward the clearing where they had emerged on the trail from the jungle. The stone-tiled path was wider here, and accommodated trees with trunks that had to be as wide as he was tall. Huts lay in ruin to either side, overgrown by vegetation. Saplings erupted from every crack in the stone.

Sam shoved through shrubs covered with ants until she finally stopped dead in her tracks.

"What is it?" Merritt asked. He stepped to her right and followed her gaze to the ground.

A skeleton was sprawled facedown at her feet. One arm was stretched out above it, the other nowhere to be seen. Roots from the bushes had grown through the ribcage. The skull was so dirty and ravaged by age it had turned the color of brass, and the occipital bone was shattered to such an extent that he could see through to the the eye sockets on the underside. Only half of one of the legs remained attached to the cracked ilium. The rest of the parts were absent.

"He was left to rot where he fell," Sam whispered.

"How do you know it's a 'he'?" Jay asked. He rounded the remains to get a better view through the camera.

"The inlet of the pelvis is too narrow for childbirth, and the angle between the pubic bones is less than ninety degrees."

With one final glance down, Sam continued walking. Ten yards farther, she shoved aside the branches of a fern to reveal the skeletal profile of a badly fractured face. It looked like someone had taken a hammer to the temporal bone and collapsed the lateral aspect of the orbit. Both arms were stretched out above its shoulders as though it had been trying to drag itself forward, a task it had been unable to accomplish without the ends of its arms and its hands.

Sam barely paused before continuing onward. They passed what was left of several more bodies before they reached a small clearing at the edge of the fortification. The village had been built on a short, angled plateau in such a way that the outer wall was only four feet tall here, while the ground on the other side was nearly thirty feet below. Lianas and vines crawled all around their feet, scaled the bricks, and descended the face of the fortification. In their midst were a good half-dozen skeletons. These were in far worse shape than the others they had encountered on their way. They were so severely broken and disarticulated that it was impossible to tell which bones belonged to which individual. A snapped spear poked out of the underbrush, and a quiver brimming with arrows rested under a nest of ferns.

Merritt nudged one of the skulls with his toe. It rolled to the side, leaving twin rows of teeth packed into the dirt. Something glinted from the mud. He knelt to inspect it, and after a moment pried a large metal object from the ground. It was a headdress like the one he had found in Hunter's backpack. He smeared the mud away to expose the sculpted gold.

"May I?" Sam asked, relieving him of the mask before he could reply.

He walked over to the edge of the wall and stared down. The fortification was undamaged. Time had taken its toll on the smooth bricks, but none of them had been broken. Only the column that held the torch directly beneath him on the ground had toppled.

It made no sense.

"This is where the invading force breached their fortifications," he said, thinking aloud. Jay raised the camera toward him, but he pushed the lens away. "They took their stand right here, where these men fell, and there was no one left to claim their bodies. But they were so savagely attacked...I mean, their skulls were shattered and they were torn limb from limb."

He turned to face Galen, whose face had gone ashen.

"And the other bodies we found on the path leading here," Sam said, "they were all pointing in the opposite direction as though they'd been overcome as they ran."

"Like the jaguar," Galen whispered.

"They were falling back to that chamber where you discovered the boiled bones," Merritt said.

Silence hung over the clearing, marred only by the rumble of the waterfall and the whistle of the wind along the wall.

"What in the name of God happened here?" Sam whispered. The spark of excitement faded from her eyes.

"I think..." Galen started, but said no more. He closed his mouth, shook his head, and glanced at Merritt from the corner of his eye.

"What?" Sam asked.

Galen looked again at Merritt, then sighed. "Nothing."

He turned away from them and struck off on the trail. After several steps, he paused, plucked a long brown feather from a snarl of ferns, and hurried back in the direction from which they had come.

VII

3:11 p.m.

"John Kaleleiki," Leo said.

"How can you be sure?" Colton asked. He relieved Leo of the penlight and crouched to scrutinize what was left of the man.

"The Hawaiian-print shirts were his trademark. In the five years I knew him, I never saw him wear anything else." Leo's voice fell to a whisper. "He was one of the country's most respected geological engineers and a master of the martial art form Lua. And they tore him apart like tissue paper. There isn't even any blood on his machete."

Colton had noticed the same thing. Based on the patterns of spatter on the ceiling and walls, whatever killed him had attacked simultaneously from the front and the rear. The man had never stood a chance.

He raised the light from the bones and directed it deeper into the darkness.

"We need to tell the others," Leo whispered. "And we should seriously consider a plan for evacuation."

"Not until we have something concrete." Colton eased past Leo, careful not to step on Kaleleiki's carcass. The tacky blood made a crackling sound as it peeled away from the ground on the tread of his boots.

"Concrete? Tell me John wasn't killed in the exact same manner as Rippeth." He swatted the flies from his face and followed Colton. "How much more concrete can it get? There's something here in the jungle with us, something capable of slaughtering every single one of us."

"But they haven't attacked yet, have they? Let's evaluate what we know so far. This man was obviously alone when he was attacked. Rippeth had been alone as well. The rest of us haven't seen anything, have we? Safety appears to be in numbers. As long as we stay together, I don't believe they currently pose much of a threat."

"And what about Dr. Russell's theory regarding what might be out there?"

"He was no proof."

"I think what's left of John Kaleleiki would probably qualify."

Colton rounded on Leo and spoke slowly through bared teeth, making no attempt to hide his rising anger.

"You placed me in charge of this expedition because I am the very best at what I do. Do you really think panicking the others is the right decision? Next thing you know, they'll all be fleeing through the jungle, screaming the whole way. And if my assessment is correct, that's a guaranteed death sentence. What we need to do first is to gain a functional understanding of our adversary—how it thinks, how it functions, what triggers it to attack—and from there we need to plot a course of action. Only then, when everything is in place, can we make the others aware of the threat, once we're confident that we'll be able to guarantee their safety."

"And in the meantime?"

"The less anyone suspects, the better. For now, we need to determine exactly what happened here, and how to prevent it from happening again. And unless I'm mistaken, somewhere down the shaft ahead of us is the deposit of gold we came here to find."

"I don't give a rat's ass about the gold anymore," Leo whispered.

"Then it's a good thing you're paying me to be in charge," Colton said. "Because I do."

At the sound of approaching footsteps, Colton turned and shined the beam past what was left of John Kaleleiki. Sorenson raised a hand to keep the light out of his eyes. Behind the massive blonde man, Morton and Webber stepped into the weak glow. Black flies swarmed around them, but they appeared oblivious as their attention fell to the ground at their feet. The color drained from the normally red-faced Scandinavian's cheeks. He raised his piercing blue eyes to meet Colton's stare.

"Keep the others out of this tunnel," Colton said. "And see what you can do about this mess."

Sorenson looked down at the carnage, then back up at Colton. His features again became unreadable.

"I trust you have no objection to renegotiating our salaries," Sorenson said.

Colton turned to Leo and raised an eyebrow.

"Whatever," Leo said. "Anything you want."

"And as far as the contents of the crate...?" Sorenson asked.

"Equip yourselves however you see fit," Colton said, "but I don't want the others to sense that anything is amiss until we can rationalize what we're dealing with here. Understand?"

Sorenson gave a curt nod, then turned to the other men. After a brief whispered conversation, Morton and Webber headed back toward the mouth of the shaft and vanished into the darkness, leaving Sorenson to handle the untidy details.

Colton whirled and struck off deeper into the mountain. A faint aura of light bloomed behind him and he heard a chiseling sound as Sorenson set to work. The noise faded as he and Leo advanced. They now had to be close to three hundred yards into the rock crevice, and still bones filled the recesses in the ossuary walls. How many bodies had been interred here?

The ground became more coarse and uneven, and began to slope downward, imperceptibly at first, but then steeper and steeper until they descended a series of rock ledges into a large cavern. The flashlight was just strong enough to illuminate the tips of the stalactites above them. The remainder of their conical forms was shrouded in a palpable darkness that rustled restlessly. An occasional leather-winged inhabitant slashed through the shadows before disappearing once more. The walls weren't smooth, and instead showcased deep gouges and rough chisel marks, from which quartz glimmered in reflection like tiny eyes. Crumbled granite lined the base of the walls.

The air was murky with dust, through which the occasional fly circled, only to be snared by one of the dark bodies that dove from the cavern roof and vanished again as though it had never been. Based on the smell, the bats were definitely earning their keep. There was only a dull buzzing from the center of the chamber, where the thin beam highlighted first a boot, then the stump of the leg to which it had once been attached. The nubs and knots of severed tendons curled away from the bloodstained bones. All of the muscle and flesh had been stripped away, leaving a bare pelvis wearing the remnants of a black leather belt. Flies crawled on the slightly concave bones, dipping their feet in the sticky crust of bodily dissolution. There were tatters of fabric everywhere, all saturated to a deep black with blood. The ribcage was shattered, the spine acutely broken. Neither of the arms were anywhere near the shoulder joints, and what was left of the skull was a good five feet away near the far wall, where it rested against an open case of fancy picks and geologist's utensils. The entire top half of the cranium had been broken away, revealing an empty bowl where the brain and pituitary gland should have been. Dried brown skin still clung to the face beneath the eyes and across the cheekbones, but the lips and tongue were gone, leaving a frame of broken teeth frozen several inches apart in a final eternal scream.

A pistol rested on the floor near the head. Colton crossed to it and lifted it from the floor. He sniffed the barrel. Cordite. He ejected the clip of the Beretta Px4 Storm semi-automatic, and fed the remaining rounds into his palm. Seven. He ejected another from the chamber.

The man had managed to fire only two shots.

"Any idea who this might have been?" he asked.

Leo shook his head in reply.

They surveyed the jumble of belongings that surrounded the cavern. There were backpacks and boxes. A small table had been thrown together using a length of flat stone, upon which were the shattered fragments of beakers and test tubes, small bottles of chemicals that looked like eye drops, and a toppled can of Sterno. The blue sludge had oozed out into a phlegm-like puddle. Several wrappers from dehydrated rations littered the floor. A miner's helmet rested beside them, the plastic cracked like the Liberty Bell, the lens of the light a mess of frayed wires. A brownish crust lined the inside of the dome.

After a minute's search, Colton found another helmet. He switched on the light and set it on his head.

The powerful beam illuminated the better part of the chamber and startled the bats to nervous flight overhead, where they raced and collided for a long moment before resuming their inverted perches. The cavern was roughly the size of a large garage, but more ovular in shape. A sharp mat of guano covered the floor and the few stalagmites that pointed back up at the ceiling.

Both men averted their eyes from the remains.

What at first appeared to be a wall of shadows resolved into a narrow corridor as Colton neared, but it wasn't a natural formation like the crevice through which they'd entered. It was maybe twice the width of his shoulders, and he had to duck to enter. He walked at a crouch. The surfaces of the walls were uneven from being chiseled by primitive instruments. There were no wooden supports to brace the earthen ceiling as one would find in a modern mine, making it feel as though the entire weight of the mountain pressed down upon his head. The shaft stretched another thirty yards before it appeared to terminate against a solid block of granite.

Quartz glinted from the walls, which were stratified with long black streaks.

Colton smiled.

They'd found their gold.

He appreciated the width of the black veins of gold ore, which surrounded him as he walked. Lord only knew how far they extended into the mountain. His first impression was that the extraction wouldn't be nearly as difficult as he had originally estimated. The gold showed through in several spots where the vein had been tapped.

A small cave had been formed at the end of the tunnel. It was approximately the size of a half-bath, but at least it was tall enough for him to stand fully erect. Slightly to his right, a thin, angular crevice led away into the dark heart of the earth, barely large enough for a man to wriggle through. He knelt and peered inside. The sides were smooth, the level floor thick with congealed guano. It was a natural formation. Had the rest of the tunnel been widened from this narrow channel? The beam of his headlamp terminated against a bend twenty feet away.

"Hello," he called, listening as his voice echoed away into oblivion.

Based on the intonation and duration of the echo, this small tunnel led much deeper into the mountain. If this area was riddled with passages and hollows, the mining might prove challenging after all.

He started to rise again, but something caught his eye.

A subtle green shimmer.

He flattened to his stomach and reached as far as he could into the hole until his fingertips grazed something soft. After a moment of fumbling with it, he pinched it between his fingers, withdrew his arm, and held the object beneath the lamp on his forehead.

It was a feather.

VIII

3:18 p.m.

Tasker wiped the paste of sweat and dust from his brow. He had stripped to his undershirt, which was now thoroughly soaked, and his body odor probably rivaled that of the stiffs around him. They had ripped open every single mummified bundle, exposing the contents and dumping the brittle, desiccated corpses. There were enough feathers to stuff a thousand pillows and enough dry grain to sow a field the size of Texas, but outside of the hundreds of ceramic bowls he had shattered in frustration, there hadn't been a single grave good of any real value.

Where was all the gold?

He bellowed in frustration and turned to find McMasters sitting on a mound of rubble, sipping contentedly from his water bladder. The mere fact that he could be so collected under the circumstances grated on Tasker's nerves.

After what they'd found buried inside the odd sculptures, he had hoped they would discover enough treasure here to allow them to call it good and get the hell out of the jungle. Maybe the blasted pottery would have been worth something, but how many clay bowls would they have needed to sell to justify the kind of effort it would have taken to ship them downriver? Besides, right now, destroying them served as a productive way of venting his fury.

He eyed the closest of the opened bundles they had exhumed from the shelf in the base of the statuary, then quickly looked away.

Images of the three slaughtered bodies they had discovered on the trail flashed across his mind, but he chased them away, only to have a vision of Jones's bloody remains rise to the forefront. The man had been a trained soldier—a *Marine* for God's sake—and still he hadn't been able to defend himself.

Tasker ground his teeth with an audible screech and forced down the memories. He refused to allow fear to take root. It would only weaken him when now it was imperative to be strong. He allowed rage to supplant any possible feelings of doubt. They had a job to do, and they would execute their plan to perfection even if it killed them. There was nothing left for them back in Lima. There was no way they would be able to explain the deaths of Jones, Reubens, and Telford to a military tribunal. The only option now was to press on, and either they accomplished their goal and lived the rest of their lives in the lap of luxury, or died trying.

"Get up," he said. When McMasters didn't immediately snap to attention, he shouted again so loudly that it reverberated through the cavern and the valley beyond. "Get up!"

McMasters raised his cold stare to meet Tasker's and slowly screwed the cap back into place on his canteen. His eyes never left Tasker's as he returned the water to his rucksack, leisurely rose from where he sat, and walked toward his former commanding officer until their faces were only inches apart.

Tasker wanted nothing more than to grab the man by the throat, press his fingertips into the soft spots over the carotids, and rip out his trachea. He was so furious that his hands shook, forcing him to curl them into fists.

"Yes...*sir*," McMasters said, and brushed past him toward where they had shed their camouflaged jackets and rain gear.

Tasker's hand found the grip of the pistol in the holster beneath his left arm.

Not yet. He still needed the soldier's help, but once McMasters outlived his usefulness...

He reluctantly released his sidearm and followed McMasters toward the outside world. The sheeting rain filled the mouth of the cavern, the droplets whipping from side to side at the behest of the howling wind. A churning mist had settled into the valley, obscuring the view of everything but the siege of raindrops and the occasional diffuse strobe of lightning. He couldn't have asked for better weather. The storm would mask their presence and wash away their tracks. Their prey wouldn't know they were coming until it was too late. And maybe not even then.

The golden skull was sealed within one of the waterproof plastic sacks and stashed in a small alcove just inside the cave's mouth for rapid retrieval on the return trip should speed be of the essence, which he feared it would.

He donned his jacket and poncho, and smeared a liberal helping of black, grease-based paint over his face. Even the rain wouldn't be able to wash it away.

"You ready to do this?" McMasters asked.

"I was born ready."

Tasker hefted his backpack onto his shoulders and slung his assault rifle across his chest. He glanced back at the mummified face leering out of the torn bundle.

Low-set, recessed orbital sockets.

Skin the consistency of a long-dead carp's scales.

Rows of wicked teeth.

He unslung his rifle and carried it so that he could feel its weight and power in his bare hands.

Bracing himself against the storm, Tasker struck off into the gloom, mentally readying himself for the massacre to come.

IX

3:36 p.m.

Eldon Monahan sat at his antique dining room table, half a bottle of Pisco-Tabernero to his left, the broken shell of his cell phone, which he had crushed in frustration, to his right. The photographs curled as they burned in the ashtray, scattering ashes that descended like snow onto the pristine surface. He drew another long swig from the bottle and poured a touch into the ashtray to fuel the blue flames. His housekeeper had taken the rest of the day off at his request, leaving him alone with his shattered dreams and the specter of his future.

He had left his office shortly before noon, claiming to have a severe stomach ache, which hadn't required the slightest bit of embellishment. Everyone had been telling him how pale he looked all morning. He hadn't been able to focus on his work at all, nor had he been able to carry on simple conversations in passing without his thoughts reverting to the train wreck that was now his life.

It wasn't as though all hope was lost. Plenty of Senators had survived sex scandals and illegal business dealings. Many were drunks, others cheats. None of them were innocent by anyone's definition. They all owed portions of their souls to various clandestine dealings that secured the campaign contributions that had bought them their seats. Favors were owed, and were collected at the cost of the welfare of their constituency.

But what he had done was far worse, wasn't it?

He had cut a deal with the devil in the flesh. Plundering the heritage of the Peruvian people was a despicable act, but it was nothing compared to the atrocity he had implicitly authorized. He had given Tasker his blessings to follow Leonard Gearhardt's party to the source of the treasure, and then kill them all. Perhaps one could be forgiven, but there was no way the other could.

Every time he so much as blinked, he saw the piranha-chewed face of Hunter Gearhardt on that cold steel slab staring up at him with an expression of accusation.

There was only one way out of this predicament.

He watched the last picture burn until there was absolutely nothing left, then drained the bottle. His head spun and his insides burned as he shuffled toward his den. The bottle fell from his hand and clattered to the floor. The hallway canted from one side to the other, forcing him to lean against the wall for balance. He fell across the threshold into his private sanctum, crawled to the desk chair, and pulled himself up into its leather embrace.

It had been nearly two full days since Tasker had phoned. Not that he really expected the man to call again, but he had secretly hoped he would have been granted one last chance to talk the man out of what he had planned.

He supposed he didn't have the right to pray for the opportunity, especially when he'd been given so many others along the way. This was the bed he had made. The time had come to lie in it.

The headdress rested on the desk in front of him next to his best calfskin belt. He had shoved the computer onto the ground to make room. It was now nothing more than a pile of fractured components. Another object sat on the blotter, positioned perfectly for an easy right-handed grab.

He raised the headdress and held it against his forehead while he cinched the belt tightly around his head.

Tears flowed down his cheeks from beneath the golden fangs.

A mewling sound crossed his lips.

He grabbed the other object from the desk and gripped it in his fist.

A Smith & Wesson .38 Special.

Chest heaving, he pressed the barrel against the metal arch over his forehead.

He caught his reflection in the mirror on the wall across from him.

Only the bluish-green eyes of a monster looked back.

Chapter Eight

I

Andes Mountains, Peru
October 30th
3:25 p.m. PET

Galen was furious. How had he allowed them to talk him into keeping his mouth shut when all of their lives hung in the balance? They could no longer dance around the issue. The more he thought about it, the more evidence amassed, the more he became convinced that his theory was correct.

Something had survived in these mountains that had never been meant to, and it was something far more dangerous than simply an unclassified species of condor.

He needed to convince the others to forsake their quest and get the hell out of there before it was too late.

If it wasn't already.

Through the maze of trees, he saw Morton and Webber milling around an especially crooked tree. They stiffened when they noticed him coming and stood side by side across the path as though in an attempt to block it. A sheer wall of stone rose behind them to a series of terraced gardens built onto the summit. Winding staircases connected them like trails of tears down the rugged face.

It wasn't until he was upon the two men that he noticed the cut in the rock wall behind the tree, a crevice of shadows that radiated the coldness of the tomb, from which the buzzing sound originated. But right now even that was preferable to the rain that chilled him to the marrow.

The men seemed to swell in stature as he approached. Or maybe it was the fact that their pistols had been replaced by seriously intimidating assault rifles.

They knew.

"Where's Leo?" Galen asked.

"Mr. Gearhardt doesn't wish be disturbed," Webber said. "He asked that we help afford him some privacy."

"You don't understand. I need to speak with him right now." Galen veered to the right to pass them, but Webber matched his movement to bar his passage.

"As I said, Dr. Russell, Mr. Gearhardt insisted that he not be interrupted."

Galen threw up his arms in exasperation. This was maddening. He was going to have to try a different tact.

"What did you find in there?" he asked in little more than a whisper. He didn't need to see the men share an almost imperceptible glance to know he had struck a chord. "I know what's going on here. And whether Leo likes it or not, the time has come to lay all of our cards on the table. We're in serious danger here, and the sooner we face that reality and devise a plan to return to Pomacochas, the better our chances of survival."

"You're being overly dramatic," Morton said.

"Am I? Tell me then, what did you discover inside that cave?"

When neither man replied, Galen attempted to shove between them, but it was like trying to shoulder his way through a pair of redwoods. They looked through him as though he were an insignificant gnat.

"Fine," Galen said. He readjusted his poncho and slicked his wet hair back. "The moment Leo is available to talk about the prospect of living through this, you tell him to come find me."

Galen turned and stormed off. He had never felt so angry and helpless in his entire life, and, worse still, he had never been so afraid. They were beginning to comprehend the threat surrounding them, but they were hiding something at the same time. Had they made a discovery in that cave worth jeopardizing all of their lives? What could possibly justify that cost?

For not the first time, he debated gathering whoever would listen and making a run for civilization, but he knew their chances diminished in smaller groups, especially if one of the groups had all of the weapons and the skill to wield them. For now, he needed to focus on convincing everyone that their lives were in jeopardy, and the easiest way to accomplish that goal was through Leo. Galen had to find a way to reach him.

As soon as he was out of sight, he ducked off the path into the ruins. He wound around the remnants of huts that now served as planters for massive kapoks and shrubs of all kinds. The flat basalt that had been used to form the paths between buildings had been ground to gravel by time and the cruel usurpation by the forest. He stayed low, keeping the crumbled rings of the dwellings between him and where Morton and Webber guarded the mouth of the tunnel. With any luck, he would be able to use the cover to reach the abrupt hillside, then sneak along the face of the cliff and slip into the cave behind them. It was a long shot for sure, but if he somehow managed to use the broad, warped tree that concealed the cave as a screen...

The northern fortification rose into view, the crumbled section they had ascended not far to his right. Beyond, the waterfall roared through the mist, sporadically appearing in cascades of blue and white as it plummeted down the vertical rocks. Suddenly, he felt isolated from everyone else, alone in another world where even the sound of his legs thrashing through the underbrush was more than he could bear. There were blind corners and leafy barriers all around him. Anything could be lurking behind them, watching him, waiting for him to walk just a little bit closer so it could leap out of hiding and set upon him with snapping teeth and slashing claws.

He was on the verge of hyperventilation. The time had come to double back. Whether he managed to slip past the guards or not, he needed to be in the company of other people.

The wind shifted with a scream, assaulting him with raindrops from his left. He instinctively turned away as he approached the base of the cliff, and to his right, past the lip of the obsidian wall, he clearly saw the falls for the first time through the parted clouds. It wasn't a straight deadfall, but rather numerous steps that created half a dozen smaller falls, some much longer than others. A ledge crept along the stone face and terminated in a dark recess that he glimpsed only momentarily before the gust waned and allowed the mist to again coalesce.

He debated the prospect that the tunnels through the mountain might intersect somewhere underground for a nanosecond before deciding against it. The last thing he wanted was to further separate himself from the rest of the party, especially by entering a dark warren of caves where no one would think to search for him if anything happened. Instead, he headed south, staying hunched and close to the ruins. As he neared the main path, he slowed and continued at a crouch, careful to keep his tread light and silent. The crooked tree appeared through the jungle, beyond the fallen wall of one of the circular huts, which itself was nearly invisible under a wild cluster of foliage. He couldn't see either of the men, but they would have had to have been standing in the mouth of the tunnel for him to have been able to anyway.

Slowly, he advanced, gingerly placing each footfall so as not to make a single twig snap. He sorted through the patter of rainfall on the canopy and the whistle of the wind, listening for even the slightest sound to betray the location of the men. The first whisper of voices reached him when he was nearly upon the tree. He pressed aside a tangle of ferns, and craned his neck to see where Morton and Webber now stood, facing east along the trail as Sam strode toward them with the pilot and the documentary crew in tow. Webber raised a palm to signal Sam to stop, presumably so he could recite the same spiel about not disturbing Leo.

This was Galen's chance.

He dashed out from behind the cover, passed the tree, and ducked into the crevice. Not once did he so much as risk a glance back over his shoulder.

Skulls leered at him from the shelves to either side before vanishing as the darkness swallowed him whole. A coarse scraping sound echoed from ahead. After several interminable minutes of walking, during which he struggled to stave off panic and felt the smothering weight of thousands of tons of rock above his head, a faint glow blossomed in the corridor in front of him. The pale light expanded with each step. A handheld halogen lamp lay on its side, its beam directed at the wall. A dark form knelt in the center, the source of the grating noise. Details emerged as he neared. It was a man, laboring to chisel something from the earthen floor.

"You guys are supposed to be—" the silhouette started, but stopped mid-sentence when it turned in his direction.

Galen recognized Sorenson's voice, and a heartbeat later, the expression on his face.

What Galen saw on the floor in front of Sorenson caused him to gasp.

Bones.

Sorenson was clearing a festering mess of body parts into a mound that swarmed with the flies he could now clearly hear in the absence of the chiseling sound.

II

3:43 p.m.

Dahlia was positive they must have found something truly amazing inside that cavern. Why else would they have posted sentries to keep them out? It infuriated her. Here they had traveled halfway around the freaking globe to document a landmark discovery, and they wouldn't even let her commit it to film. Had Leo not been her principle financial backer, she would have shoved her way through the guards and let him have a piece of her mind. What were they going to do, shoot her? No chance of that, but worse would be the loss of funding for production and distribution, both of which were integral to the process, probably even more so than the quality, loath as she was to admit it. So for now, she would bide her time. When Leo finally saw fit to grant them entrance, she would be ready.

And there had better damn well be something absolutely mind-blowing in there.

Fortunately, Sam, who was even more perturbed than she was, didn't need to kowtow to Leo like she did. Sam had been up in arms, demanding to see what was hidden in that crevice, but had ultimately been shunned as well. The only consolation was that Sam had promised they would return in half an hour, and either they would be allowed to pass peacefully, or there was nothing on God's green earth that would stand in their way.

Dahlia respected her all the more for it. They were cut from the same cloth: ambitious, determined, indomitable. And there was no one she would rather follow through these ruins. If there was anything important out here, Sam would find it. And when she did, Dahlia would make sure Jay committed it to tape.

Sam seemed only peripherally aware of their existence as they followed, which was more than Dahlia could ever have hoped for. All of her reactions would be candid, uncensored. Even with the mounting tension, Dahlia's heart raced at the prospect of where Sam might lead them.

They headed south, the rumble of the waterfall waning behind them, toward where Sam suspected they would come upon the main entrance to the fortress. Merritt trailed behind them, his eyes distant as though lost in thought. More of those round stone huts surrounded them in various states of deterioration, overgrown by groves of ceiba trees riddled with epiphytes and vines to such a degree that it was nearly impossible to imagine that anyone had ever dwelled in them. It was frightening the amount of damage nature could inflict over the span of five hundred years. This entire fortress hadn't been demolished by an invading army, but by the gentle advance of saplings. Its former occupants were another story. What forces had annihilated them?

Dahlia peered into the living areas behind the rubble. Rounded shards of ancient pottery poked out of the soil, along with the remnants of tattered textiles, wooden and stone utensils, and the rotted roofs. The former occupants hadn't even had time to gather their belongings in their final hours. It was as though those that hadn't been slain had simply vanished into thin air. Unless there was some stockpile of bodies or a mass grave, there weren't enough remains to match the number that must have lived here. Sam's theory was that the lion's share of the population had relocated to the valley and built the fortress they had already encountered. However, that still left the most puzzling question of all.

Why?

Sam appeared hell-bent on discovering the answer. She hadn't shared any of her preliminary theories, but the way she combed through the village, she was obviously looking for something in particular. Dahlia instructed Jay to stay at Sam's shoulder. Whatever caught her eye, Jay's mandate was to capture it with his camera.

Sam slowed and stood in the crumbled threshold of one of the huts. She cocked her head as she scrutinized something inside. Dahlia had to slide to the side and stand on her tiptoes to see over the rim. There were more bones near the rear wall, though these were dramatically different from the others. They were partially buried by years of amassed dirt that had blown in through the doorway. The sharp ends of the broken bones had been smoothed by time and the elements, while the normally white calcium density had weathered to a muddy brown. But it wasn't the spider web of fractures transecting the frontal bone of the lone visible skull or the disarticulated leg that stood erect like a tombstone that held their attention. A revolver was partially concealed by the damp, rotting leaves, its owner's skeletal digit still curled around the trigger. The metal had rusted to a flaking orange.

Dahlia didn't know the first thing about firearms, but this one looked as though it had been ripped straight out of the Wild West. It had to be at least a hundred years old.

"We aren't the first to find this place," Sam whispered. She turned and resumed her trek through the ruins.

"Jesus," Merritt said. He studied the carcass for a long moment before hurrying to catch up with Sam.

"Hurry up and get a shot of that," Dahlia said.

Jay stepped into the collapsed stone ring and directed the lens first at the bones, then at the revolver. He scraped away a patch of rust with his thumbnail.

"Colt Frontier Six Shooter," he read from the inscription on the barrel. "Wait. There's more writing here." He carved away the rust below the trigger guard and zoomed in. *PNT. Sept. 12, 1870.* He turned to face her, eyes wide, face pale. The camera visibly trembled in his grasp. "I'm starting to get a really bad feeling about this."

Dahlia inwardly agreed, but refused to speak the words out loud.

"You'd better catch up with Sam," she said instead.

Jay nodded and followed the overgrown trail toward where Merritt crashed through the bushes behind Sam. After several more minutes, during which they passed another half dozen of the round structures in various states of decay, Sam stopped at the foot of what appeared to be a giant conglomeration of vegetation that reached up into the dense ceiling of leaves. The branches of the surrounding trees held it in a wooden embrace. From their boughs dangled the vines and roots that cascaded over it like a canopy over a bassinette.

Sam approached it slowly and tugged away the vegetation with a series of snapping sounds. It was definitely a manmade construct. At first it reminded Dahlia of the statues in the cave overlooking the river, but this one was made of limestone. As Sam revealed more and more of the sculpture, Dahlia realized that they were viewing it from behind and dragged Jay around to the other side by the elbow, where she could now see the outline of the southern fortification through the trees. She noticed a small break in the obsidian wall where the ground in front of it dipped out of sight. Was that the entrance to the village?

By the time she returned her attention to the statue, Merritt had helped Sam completely expose it. The contours had been dulled through the ages, and what little paint still clung to it looked more like curled flecks of lichen, but it was still easy to decipher the details.

"Quetzalcoatl?" Sam whispered. The surprise in her voice was evident. She did a double take before stepping back to appraise it as a whole. "This doesn't make sense."

"What do you mean?" Merritt asked. "It looks just like the faces that were carved into the walls in the village down in the jungle."

Dahlia scrutinized the monolith. It had to be close to fifteen feet tall, and chiseled from a single block of stone. As with the *purunmachus*, the style was more abstract than anatomic. The body was smooth and contoured, and tapered to a long, slender neck with a broad head and elongated face that reminded her of a blunted crocodile's snout, filled with triangular teeth. A crown of what at first looked like thorns adorned the crest of the cranium and the sides of the face. She stepped closer and realized that they were feathers like those sculpted onto the golden headdress. They tapered down the short forehead into a dramatic widow's peak that terminated in a point between two recessed eye sockets. A bluish-green gemstone glinted from the left orbit while the right was filled with shadows. Raindrops rolled down its form, shimmering like a serpent's scales.

"I didn't make the connection at first," Sam said, "but the similarities are undeniable. Quetzalcoatl was the Aztec god of the morning star, their creator. He had the body of a serpent and the brightly-colored plumage of a Quetzal. The Aztec civilization flourished at roughly the same time as the Chachapoya and Inca, from the fourteenth through sixteenth centuries, thousands of miles from here. They couldn't have come into contact with one another, especially this far south. And the Maya had a similar deity hundreds of years earlier. Kakulcán, the feathered serpent of the sun. While our understanding of the Chachapoya is limited thanks to a lack of archaeological evidence, we know much more about the Inca. They had a similar feathered serpent god called Viracocha, but even post-conquest, it's hard to believe that the Chachapoya would assimilate another culture's deity."

"Common threads run through all of the major religions today," Dahlia said.

"But not to this degree. Buddha doesn't have a beard and I haven't seen any renditions of Jesus with a potbelly," Sam said. She lowered her brow and stared holes through the sculpture.

"Oh God," Merritt said from somewhere behind Dahlia, who turned at the sound of his voice.

He stood twenty feet away through the maze of vegetation, nearly hidden by the overgrowth of ceibas, halfway to the point where the southern wall met with the mountainside.

"What's wrong?" Dahlia asked, shoving her way through the masses of shrubs that grew from the broken stone tiles of what once must have been a courtyard of some kind. She was nearly to Merritt when she heard a buzzing sound. It was faint at first, but grew louder with every step until it filled her ears even over the tumult of the rain and the ruckus of their passage.

She followed his gaze toward the overhanging stone cliff, beneath which she could see arched swatches of forest green and khaki. A furious black cloud roiled around them. Ebon arcs streaked the granite wall, visible even from afar. She reached Merritt's side and could now clearly see the details through a gap in the trees. Two tents had been erected under the stone ledge, and had partially collapsed onto their contents. The fabric was torn in sections, through which she could see a jumble of belongings crawling with flies and—

Dahlia caught a glimpse of a disembodied torso and had to avert her eyes, yet the image persisted. Blood-crusted ribcage knotted with the cartilage that still held the broken bones in place. Acutely fractured cervical column capped with only the base of a skull.

"What in the name of God happened here?" Merritt whispered, and struck off toward what was left of the tents.

III

4:03 p.m.

"What are we going to tell them?" Leo asked, waving away the flies swirling around his head to keep the bats from knifing from the ceiling toward his face.

"Nothing," Colton said. "We clean up this mess and no one's the wiser."

"They're going to demand to know why we posted guards to keep them from coming in here. We have to tell them something."

"You could start with the truth," a voice said from the mouth of the tunnel leading into the cavern.

Leo whirled to see Galen emerge into the pale lamplight. His face was pale and he visibly shivered. Sorenson grabbed him by the shoulder and gave him a tug in reverse.

"How did he get in here?" Colton demanded.

"Don't ask me," Sorenson said. "I was doing what you asked when all of a sudden he was just standing there."

"He *saw* what you were doing?"

"What was I supposed to do about it? One minute I'm alone, and the next thing I know, I look up, and there he is, staring right at the mess."

"There was so much blood," Galen whispered.

"It doesn't matter," Leo said. "Everyone would have found out eventually. This just accelerates our timetable. Besides, we could probably use their combined resources if we're going to figure out what happened here."

"I already told you what happened here." Galen's eyes roamed the chamber momentarily before settling on the dismembered carcass on the ground. He winced and drew the back of his hand across his mouth and nose. "Can't you see? What else could possibly have torn these men apart like this? There's no other explanation."

"All you have is wild speculation," Colton said. "Where's your proof?"

"In your goddamn hand!" Galen snapped.

Colton raised the feather he had extracted from the small tunnel at the back of the room.

"This? This is your proof? It's just a feather."

"Just a feather? Look around you. They're everywhere."

Leo lowered his gaze to the sloppy ground. He hadn't noticed at first as he'd been focused on the carnage and the thought of how much the man must have suffered during his final moments, but now that he looked closely, he could see feathers congealed in the tacky puddle of blood and fluids through the skein of flies.

"Carrion birds," Colton said. "You of all people should know that the smell of death draws them—"

"Enough," Leo whispered. He looked from one man to the other. "We need to figure out what really happened. Something slaughtered these men and killed my son—"

"You said your son drowned," Galen said. "Why would you lie about—?"

"These men were civilians," Colton interrupted. "We have four highly-trained soldiers, myself included. I cherry-picked the other three for their prowess in combat, and we have enough firepower to launch an assault on a small army."

"I trust your skill, old friend, and your judgment," Leo said, "but we need to determine what we're up against to eliminate the element of surprise. Would you not agree?"

Colton nodded slowly.

"Then we need to indulge Dr. Russell and trust his expertise—"

"Expertise? He knows nothing about—"

"Marcus," Leo said. In all the time he had known Colton, he had only used the man's first name a handful of times. "Perhaps then you would humor an old man who is ultimately not only responsible for all of our lives, but for the procurement of the millions of dollars in gold surrounding us."

"Gold?" Galen nearly shrieked. "You're willing to risk all of our lives for gold!"

Colton ignored Galen and met Leo's stare for a long moment before he finally acquiesced with a curt nod.

"But I won't entertain fantasy," Colton said, his voice firm. "When the time comes to take decisive action, my orders will not be questioned. Are we in agreement?"

"Of course. That's why I hired you. I would trust no one else with my life."

It was a small bone, but one that needed to be thrown.

Colton strode toward Galen, who raised his hand in front of his eyes to block the beam from the mining helmet, and thrust the feather toward the ornithologist.

"It's time to put your theory to the test, Dr. Russell." Galen hesitantly plucked the feather from Colton's hand, an expression of confusion on his face. "You're going to need a helmet."

"Why would I need...?"

In response, Colton turned toward the back wall and spotlighted the shadowed crevice.

"What's back there?" Galen asked, his voice cracking.

"That's what we're about to find out."

Colton stormed over to the mound of supplies, rummaged until he found another intact helmet, and held it out for Galen, who took it in his shaking hands and seated it on his head. Colton flicked the switch for him and the beam sliced through the darkness, stirring the flies and bats alike.

"What are we doing?" Galen asked.

"Just a little spelunking," Colton said, and struck off into the channel leading into the cold depths of the mountain.

Leo followed with Galen in tow. When the tunnel terminated, Colton dropped to his stomach and wriggled into the small hole where he had found the feather, his squirming form silhouetted by his bright light.

"We shouldn't go in there," Galen whispered. "Nothing good can come from it."

"Show some backbone, Dr. Russell," Leo said, and shimmied into the earthen tube behind Colton. He tried not to think about the sheer tonnage of rock overhead. After perhaps a minute, Galen's beam shoved aside the darkness behind him and illuminated the tread of Colton's boots ahead.

They rounded a smooth bend and dragged themselves by their elbows another fifteen feet before Colton's light dimmed as it reached into the vast space of whatever lay beyond. He paused at the end of the tunnel and swept his light from side to side before finally crawling out and rising to his feet.

Leo followed his example. From behind, Galen's beam cast his shadow into an oblivion of darkness.

He took a deep breath, retched, and had to clap his hand over his mouth and nose.

A different scent entirely accosted him. While it was vastly preferable to the reek of rotten meat and decomposition, it was no less unpleasant.

Colton's beam scoured the floor.

It didn't take long to isolate the source of the stench.

IV

4:14 p.m.

Merritt had seen way more than his share of corpses. Bullet wounds of all caliber, stabbings, asphyxiations. Men, women, children. He had witnessed violated bodies left in the aftermath of bombings, with appendages blasted away and skin scorched black, weeping pustulates. But none of them compared to the way the man in the tent had been so thoroughly destroyed. The sheer savagery with which this poor soul had been butchered scared him. He had seen the worst mankind had to offer, but compared to this, it came up wanting.

Arcs of blood formed a black crust on the inside of the fabric. Some of the puddles on the uneven floor had contained so much blood that the accumulated rainwater was imbued with a rust-colored tint. The condition of the body was nearly identical to the skeletal remains they had found scattered throughout the village. Perhaps the age of the other bodies lessened their visceral impact, but there was no such problem with this one.

Merritt couldn't bear to look at it any longer. He had to get out of that horrible tent, get some fresh air. Throwing aside tattered straps of nylon stiff with absorbed blood, he hurried out from under the overhang, craned his face to the sky, and allowed the rain to wash over him. The storm had intensified even in the short while he was inside the tent, but there wasn't enough water in the sky to wash the touch of death from his skin.

"This couldn't have happened much more than a few weeks ago," he said. His gorge rose, but through force of will alone he forced it back down. "What I don't get though, is why there aren't scavengers feasting on what's left. Where are the vultures and coyotes? The smell should have drawn them from miles away. There's nothing but those filthy flies."

None of the others spoke. Shock had descended upon their pale features. They had all known that four men had been lost in this valley from the previous expedition. Their hope had been to find them alive and unharmed, and simply unable to contact the outside world. No one had expected to find them like…this. Four of them. Was it possible there were more bodies, similarly slaughtered? And if so, it begged the most terrifying question of all.

Was whatever killed them in such a fashion still out there, watching them at this very moment?

His skin crawled under the scrutiny of unseen eyes. Was it a result of the paranoia spawned by his military training, or were they indeed already surrounded?

"We need to gather the others and get out of here while we still can," Merritt said, looking to each of them in turn.

Jay approached the tent and raised the camera, but Dahlia stayed his arm. There were some things never meant to be immortalized on film. Instead, he wandered toward the gap in the fortification wall, where a stone staircase descended to the forest floor. Leading with the lens, Jay reached the top of the steps and halted abruptly.

"Holy crap," he whispered, and turned away. He heaved several times over a sapling tree fern.

Merritt jogged over to where Jay wiped a strand of saliva from his chin and looked down the stairs, which were lined to either side by walls that were nearly five feet tall. Iron cages, like those that housed the torches on the pedestals encircling the fortress, topped the slanted walls of the thin trench every few feet. At the bottom, a large rectangular stone that appeared to have been carved to fit into the opening of the staircase lay cracked and covered with moss. And on the uneven steps between, Merritt saw what had caused Jay's reaction.

Another body was sprawled on the staggered rocks. Or at least what was left of it. The manner in which the man had been slain reminded Merritt of the jaguar carcass: scattered in a straight line as though torn apart while in motion. The broken legs, bereft of flesh, save the black skin on the ankles above the boots, were closer to the top, while the pelvis and torso rested a dozen steps down, ribs shattered, spine unnaturally bent and twisted. The skeletal arms pointed toward where the crushed skull rested in a puddle of muddy rainwater and hair at the bottom. Shreds of clothing had blown into the corners of the stairs with the detritus.

Only the black flies dared to disturb the unclean bones, though the rain deterred all but the most ambitious individuals.

The man had been overcome while trying to flee. He must have seen his assailant coming too late and made a break for it, but he hadn't been fast enough.

These men had never stood a chance. Merritt looked into the pallid faces of his companions. Would they?

"What the hell is capable of doing something like this?" Sam whispered.

"It's irrelevant," Merritt said. He drew a deep breath, forced aside his fear, and tapped into his training and instincts. "Right now, we need to focus on rounding up the others and getting as far from here as we can. Nothing else matters at this point."

The words of the scarred chieftain returned unbidden.

Let them pass. They are dead already.

He should have identified the danger sooner. All of the signs had been there.

Their guides out of Pomacochas had sensed the threat and abandoned them days ago. Even that hardass Rippeth had acknowledged it and slipped off during the night. Maybe if they moved fast enough they would be able to escape the fate to which the black-painted man had consigned them.

"We can't afford to waste any more time," Merritt said. He looked up into the belly of the storm and the mist that hovered in the canopy, mere feet over their heads. Somewhere above, the sun was preparing to sneak behind the sharp peak and turn day to night. He could feel it in the marrow of his bones. They didn't want to still be here when that happened. "Stay close. Move fast. Don't slow for anything."

With those final words, he turned and ran back toward the cave where they had last seen the others, listening to make sure he heard the slap of footsteps on the wet ground behind him.

V

4:28 p.m.

The stone floor was covered with mounds of fecal material. Galen immediately identified it as raptor feces by look, but certainly not by size. The older droppings had dried and crumbled, presumably the source of the cloud of dust that lingered in the cavern. There were fresh piles on top of the old, the mixture of urine and white urates still runny, the consistency of a partially fried egg, the fecal matter well-formed pellets nearly the size of a dog's.

He knelt before a heap that was perhaps a few days old. It was just dry enough that it no longer glistened with moisture. He lifted it from the rest, set it on a clear section of the ground beside him, and set to work.

"What in the world are you doing?" Leo asked.

"Exactly what it looks like," Galen said, breaking apart the feces with his fingers. "Didn't you ever dissect an owl pellet when you were in school? The point was to determine the diet of the owl. I can remember plucking out mouse bones and trying to reassemble the skeleton. Very fascinating really."

"So you're trying to figure out what it's been eating."

"And so much more." Galen's hands trembled as he sifted through the black matter. He focused solely on the project, and not on the implications of what he already knew to be true. "I could tell right away by the fecund scent that we were dealing with a carnivorous species. The smell of fresh meat processed through an avian digestive system has a distinct aroma, which is way different than the smell of digested carrion. It's like comparing the scent of an eagle's feces to that of a condor. At first glance, the feces appears to have been formed by a species of raptor. However, if you look closely, you can see several crucial distinctions. First of all, size-wise, the pellets are far larger than that of any known bird of prey. Second, the ratio of the chalky white urates to feces is totally out of proportion. Raptor species have a lower ratio than say, pigeons, but even pigeons don't evacuate such a large volume of urates in relation to the total mass."

"What are you getting at?" Colton asked. The beam on his helmet stayed in constant motion along with his eyes in lighthouse fashion. While the man remained outwardly stoic, his nerves manifested in the way he shifted from one foot to the other.

"I'm just stating what I see. We're dealing with a species that doesn't fit the mold of any modern avian. In fact, if I didn't know better, judging exclusively on the basis of the amount of urine and urates as a percentage of volume, I would suspect our subject was reptilian."

"You've already browbeaten us with your speculation, Dr. Russell. Now unless you have anything useful to add—"

Galen gasped. He could barely control his shaking hand well enough to extract his finding from the pellet. Pinching it between his fingertips, he threaded it out of the feces and held it up for the others to see.

It was a clump of thin, dark hair.

Human hair.

Colton took it from him and inspected it while Galen crumbled the remainder of the pellet and spread it out. Something hard and sharp prodded his fingertip. He picked it up and cleared off the foul coating. The base of the small object was blunt and smooth. Four thin prongs extended from the opposite side.

He reflexively dropped it and it tumbled across the granite floor.

The spotlight on his helmet fixed upon it.

"Oh my God," he whimpered.

The silver of the filling reflected the light.

It was a human tooth.

Galen scrambled to his feet and swiped his palms on his pants. If this didn't prove his theory, then nothing would. And right now he didn't even care what they thought. People had been killed here. The evidence was everywhere around them, from the remains in the ossuary and the cavern to those in the feces. The victims had been butchered and consumed, and he knew with complete certainty that there was no modern species of raptor capable of doing that.

He glanced at the fresh piles of feces. They couldn't be more than twenty-four hours old.

They needed to get out of there.

Now.

"Where are you going?" Colton snapped. "Get back here!"

Galen didn't even pause as he ran back toward the tiny tunnel that would eventually lead him back to the outside world. He dove to his belly and wriggled through as fast as he could. His head grazed the rock above, which tilted the helmet so that the beam pointed to the side and barely illuminated his way.

It had been a mistake to come here. The biggest mistake of his life.

His panicked breathing echoed in his ears and tears streamed down his cheeks. The fabric on his knees and elbows ripped. He felt the sting of cuts and abrasions, but he didn't care. If they didn't get far away from this mountain, then that small amount of bleeding would only be the beginning.

VI

4:43 p.m.

The gods were smiling on Tasker. He couldn't have asked for better luck.

A smile slashed his face as he stood at the edge of the stream, which, thanks to the ferocity of the storm, had swelled to the ranks of a full-blown river. So much water funneled down from the high country that it no longer gracefully cascaded over the edge, but fired from the top of the waterfall instead. The roar was nearly deafening. He and McMasters had barely been able to cross the strategically placed stones, which had already been claimed by the rising river. One misstep and they would have been swallowed whole and thrown into the air over the valley hundreds of feet below. Branches and debris hurtled downstream. Some lodged against the rock ledge, where they would only serve to raise the level even more, while others were launched on the flume of white spray into the nothingness over the canyon. A twenty-foot trunk sped down the rapids without encountering the slightest resistance and shot over the falls. Ten seconds later, the crack of wood shattering on the breakers reverberated through the mountains.

Until the storm abated and the level of the gorged stream dropped significantly, there would be no way of crossing it.

His smile broadened as he studied the trail in the sloppy mud that led into the steep jungle. Their prey were now effectively isolated on the peak above with no means of escape.

Everything had fallen into place more perfectly than he ever could have hoped. All that remained now was to follow the path laid out before them to their ultimate destination, loot the ruins of everything of value, and make sure that no witnesses survived. After that, it would be easy enough to float their haul down the river to where multiple millions of dollars awaited them.

Or rather, awaited him.

He glanced at McMasters, who remained blissfully ignorant. Once they neared Pomacochas with their treasure, he would have ample opportunity to end their partnership and countless places to hide the evidence.

The only loose end would be Monahan, and that little prick would be simple enough to make disappear with a single, well-placed phone call. A call he looked forward to making.

In his mind's eye, he saw an Italian villa on a hillside overlooking the tranquil blue of the Caribbean Sea.

It was only a matter of time now.

But in the interim, there was still plenty of fun to be had. They were closing in for the kill. Soon the valley would echo with the screams of the dying before silence once again descended upon this lost world.

There was only one variable for which he couldn't account, if it was even a variable at all.

He pictured the carcasses they had disinterred from the bundles buried in the statuary. A shiver rippled down his spine. He chased away the thought. Surely nothing like that could have survived this long, even so high in the unexplored Andes. Never mind the fact that the desiccated corpses couldn't have been more than several hundred years old or the fact that Jones had been mercilessly ripped apart in a manner consistent with what he would have expected. There was no problem that couldn't be solved by the assault rifle on his shoulder. He would stay vigilant, and unlike Jones, he was an excellent soldier. Nothing on this planet would be able to catch him unaware. Not even those hideous creatures from the filthy mummy wraps.

"Are you ready to do this?" McMasters asked. He shrugged his pack into place on his shoulders and clasped his Colt IAR in both hands. "If we want to be in position before nightfall, we'd better get moving."

Tasker looked to the sky. Between the low ceiling of storm clouds and the elongating shadow of the mountain peak, darkness would soon be upon them. The thrill of the endgame surged through him.

"After you," he said, gesturing to the line of sloppy tracks that led into the dense forest.

He followed his temporary partner into the jungle for the culmination of the hunt that had begun many miles and days ago.

In a matter of hours, a new river would flow, a river of blood, and a fortune in gold would be his.

Chapter Nine

I

Andes Mountains, Peru
October 30th
4:49 p.m. PET

Morton and Webber no longer stood guard over the tunnel into the cliff when they arrived. Winded, Sam slowed to a jog, while Merritt fell back behind her and stopped dead in his tracks. She was soaked to the bone, and every muscle ached from the high altitude exertion. She tried not to think about everything she had seen, but the images of the remains shoved to the forefront of her mind in grainy still-lifes reminiscent of old crime scene photographs. The memories were sterile enough to allow her to distance herself from them; however, the implications assaulted her like fresh wounds inflicted in her gray matter.

Somewhere along the trail, they had passed from the world she knew and understood, through the residua of a past she had until now only been able to imagine, into a nightmare landscape of bloodshed and death.

And even now, she couldn't help but be amazed by the sights that greeted her when she entered the dark crevice.

Jay flicked on the light mounted to his camera and directed it at the walls as they pressed deeper into the mountain. Countless recessed arches had been chiseled into the stone and filled with bones. The skulls faced her, while the rest of the jumbled skeletons had been crammed into the spaces behind them. A quick flicker of gold reflected the light.

"Did you see that?" Sam asked. "Shine your light over there again."

Jay directed the beam back into the alcove. A golden sparkle winked through the optic canal in the skull's eye socket.

"There's something inside," he said.

Sam reached through the sticky spider webs and lifted the aged skull from the centuries of accumulated dust. The occipital portion of the cranium had been cut away to create room for the object that rested on the rock shelf. It was egg-shaped and filigreed with a golden design fused to the rounded surface, a stunning piece of craftsmanship. More obsidian, she realized. The volcanic rock had been smoothed and polished, and decorated with a stylized image that depicted a man made of squares holding a sharp-toothed monster with a plume of feathers on its head at bay with a spear.

"It's an Ica stone," she gasped. Her world had suddenly tilted on its ear.

She replaced the skull over the stone and moved to the next archway. Similarly lifting the cracked skull, she exposed another stone nearly identical to the first, only the man in the design appeared to be riding the back of a dragon as it tried to snap back over his shoulder at him.

Ica stones were widely considered hoaxes, their authenticity refuted by any scholar worth his salt. They were originally discovered in a cave in the vicinity of the coastal town of Ica, Peru in the Sixties. While supposedly created by the Inca, they depicted knowledge and events beyond the scope of their limited comprehension. Everything from open heart surgery and tracheotomies to flying saucers and dinosaurs. All things that should have been well beyond their ability to conjure, even in their wildest dreams, which led to the common conclusion that they had to be fakes. Radiocarbon dating had been useless in ascertaining their age as the test could only determine the approximate era that the obsidian was formed, and not the time when the designs had been carved. And the others were merely etched, not overlaid with gold like these were.

Now here she was, staring at them in an ancient ossuary where they couldn't possibly have been planted by modern man. They weren't just decorative ornamentation either. They were death stones, renditions of something of consequence to the decedent. She moved down the row, raising cranium after cranium to uncover more stones, all of which bore representations of a man in mortal combat with the same fanged and plumed creature. Was this tunnel where their warriors were interred? A quick glance in either direction confirmed that all of the bones were roughly the same size. None of them had belonged to children. Was it possible that these depictions somehow represented their deaths?

The faint sound of buzzing brought her back to reality.

There wasn't enough time to waste any more right now. Lord only knew what was out there in the ruins, stalking them.

From ahead, she heard the distant sound of voices, made hollow by the acoustics, the words indecipherable over the drone of flies. She turned in their direction and proceeded into the darkness. The light from the camera veered to follow, casting her elongated shadow across the ground in front of—

Enormous black flies spun drowsily around her, and a smell with which she was now intimately acquainted crinkled her nose.

Her shoes made a crackling sound as she crossed the tacky floor. She noted the dark, amoeboid shape surrounding her, and then the pile of bones to her right. The sheer amount of flies crawling all over them created the impression of movement.

Jay's beam fell upon them and she had to look away. They had the same characteristics as the ones they had only just found: fractured, splintered...fresh.

"Leo!" she called, and quickened her pace, distancing herself from the carnage and the repulsive insects.

As if in answer, the voices grew louder, more animated.

By the time the buzzing waned behind her, it began anew in front of her. The ground became uneven and slanted downward, and the rocky ceiling lowered, channeling them deeper into the earth toward the now heated voices.

"Leo?"

The argument ceased at the sound of her approach. For a moment, she heard only silence beneath the relentless buzz.

"Sam?" Leo finally asked. "You shouldn't be in here."

There was something in his voice...something she had never expected to hear from him. Trepidation, uncertainty...fear.

"We need to leave this place. Right now," she said, ducking through a narrow threshold and stepping into a domed cavern. "We know what happened to Hunter's party. We found..."

Her words trailed off. It had taken several seconds to acclimate to the bright lights from the mining helmets. At first, she had seen only the five men gathered in the center of the cave and the stacks of supplies behind them, and then she noticed the body parts scattered on the ground.

That made four. All of the members of the previous expedition were now accounted for. All of them identically slaughtered. But there had originally been five of them, hadn't there?

She looked at Leo and tried to glean the truth from his eyes.

"Hunter didn't drown, did he?"

"Sam, you have to understand—"

"Did he?" she screamed.

Leo broke eye contact.

"You willingly risked all of our lives without a word of warning? Look over there. That man wasn't just killed. He was ripped apart!"

"I didn't lie to any of you. Hunter did drown. The medical examiner's report confirmed as much. The only fact that I chose to omit was that he had been stabbed in the back twice prior to immersion in the river. We had no way of knowing that we would find anything like this when we arrived."

"You should have told us," Sam snapped. Her hands shook with rage. "Now we're in the exact same situation and nobody has any clue what happened to these men, what could happen to *us*!"

"They have a right to know," Galen said. The beam on his helmet washed out his features.

"This is getting us nowhere," Colton said. "We need to formulate a plan and—"

"How's this for a plan?" Sam asked through bared teeth. "We get the hell out of here while we still can."

She whirled and stormed out of the cavern. Whether they joined her or not, she no longer cared. Her thoughts were a chaotic jumble. Her childhood friend had been stabbed and the man she had known and trusted for nearly her entire life had lied to her about it. A slideshow of horrors fueled the rising panic. The carnage all around her, from the ancient remains to the modern. The jaguar carcass in the clearing and the tree surrounded by ruined alpaca bones. The Chachapoya chief's parting words. *Let them pass. They are dead already.* And they were, weren't they?

Damn the rest of them. She was leaving this fortress right now. And either they followed her or she would have to find a way to live with their deaths on her conscience.

But at least she would still be alive.

II

5:00 p.m.

Merritt had been transported to a different place and time entirely. The moment he had stepped around that gnarled ceiba tree and faced the deep black maw in the mountain, he had frozen mid-stride. In his mind, smoke boiled out of the orifice on the cries of the wounded. The jungle around him vanished and the world became an eternity of sand. Consciously, he understood that none of this was real, that the hell before him was a product of the deep-seated guilt, shame, and horror that he had until now managed to repress, but he was helpless against the illusion. He had run half the globe away only to end up right back where he had started.

He wished his prescriptions hadn't been stolen, but even with the antipsychotic and anti-anxiety drugs on board, he knew there was still no way he would have been able to go in there. It was a physiological reaction beyond his control. His legs were leaden, his feet rooted to the earth. His hands grew cold from lack of circulation and the sensation of dizziness worsened. His chest heaved faster and faster and yet he still felt as though he couldn't breathe.

How long had the others been in there? How long had he been standing here, crippled by the irrational terror from the past? There was death all around him. The threat of the bloodshed to come lingered in the air. This was the time when they needed him most, when he needed to be sharp and focused, and he was useless even to himself as he cowered before the memories of a life long since abandoned.

With supreme effort, he forced his stilted legs to move, if only in increments of inches.

The raindrops bludgeoned him, threatening to drive him to his knees.

Voices echoed from the shaft as though from miles away. Beneath them, the buzzing sound of television static metamorphosed into rapidly approaching footsteps. A weak light blossomed from the core of the darkness. It grew larger and brighter as he watched. A silhouetted figure took form in the center, moving directly toward him. All he could clearly discern was the cape-like outline of a poncho and a pair of slender legs.

"We're leaving," Sam said, bursting from the shadows. "Now."

The sense of relief that flooded through Merritt freed his tight muscles so completely that he nearly collapsed.

Sam blew past him as Jay and Dahlia emerged from the tunnel with the birdman at their heels. Before Merritt found the strength to turn and join them, he looked back into the darkness. No one else was coming.

"Wait!" he called. His legs felt like noodles, but they strengthened with each stride away from the crevice until he was able to jog. He crashed through the underbrush and ducked around the others until he caught up with Sam at the front of the procession. They were headed north toward the rising rumble of the waterfall and the fallen section of the fortification where they had initially entered. The southern route would likely have been shorter and more direct, but he didn't blame her in the slightest for wanting to avoid the corpses.

She scrabbled down the black stone rubble, and when she reached the ground, made a beeline toward the trail that led into the jungle. What had formerly been a trickle of water was now a stream racing along the path, the mud beneath it as slick as ice. With the weight of their packs, balance was untenable, yet Sam refused to slow.

Merritt glanced back and confirmed that the rest were still following them. Jay had been forced to cradle the camera to his chest to keep from slipping, while both Dahlia and Galen were already covered in muck.

Sam squealed. He turned around to see her sliding on her backpack through the runoff. At the bend ahead, she slammed into the buttress roots of a massive tree with a resounding crack. She rolled onto her side and moaned.

Merritt slid sideways down the trail, bracing his hand on the ground for stability.

"Are you all right?" He helped her to her feet and gave her a quick once over. No visibly broken bones. No sign of blood. She rubbed her forehead where a knot was already beginning to swell.

"I'm fine," she said, brushing away his hands. "We don't have time for this."

She turned her back on him and continued down the trail.

Ahead, the rumble of running water called to them. They had to be near the stream that divided this mountain from the next. Beyond lay the sheer rock formation that contained the cavern with the *purunmachus* and the path back down to the lake where they had spent the previous night.

The sun had already begun to set and twilight claimed the forest.

It would be completely dark in under an hour. No moonlight would be able to permeate the storm clouds and mist, which now formed a haze around them as it crept to the ground from the canopy.

The path ahead would grow increasingly treacherous.

Their window of opportunity had closed.

There was no way they were getting off the mountain tonight.

III

5:13 p.m.

They had barely heard their prey coming in time to duck from the path and into the jungle. Tasker didn't enjoy being surprised, but that was exactly what had happened. From where he crouched in a cage of tented roots with ant-covered vines draped over his head, he watched them race down to the swollen stream and attempt to ford it to no avail. The dark-haired woman, Carson, had tried to hop to where the first stone lurked beneath several inches of racing water and had nearly been swept off her feet, would have were it not for a last second save by the pilot, who had dragged her to the muddy shore. She now screamed up into the raging storm in frustration and futility. The others paced the bank nervously. He could almost hear their thoughts as they contemplated the possibility of braving the rapids.

What had spooked them to flight? Had they sensed his approach? He couldn't believe that was the case. Neither he nor McMasters had done anything to warrant their suspicion. They must have encountered something that frightened them up the path ahead…but what?

Again his mind recalled the carcasses they had disentombed in the cave, but he chased the image away and focused on the task at hand.

It would be simple enough to take down their targets at the river's edge right now. Five quick shots and they could drag the bodies into the underbrush, but where were the other men in their party? Had they secured the high ground at this very moment? Were he and McMasters pinned down under unseen sights? He thought it unlikely. If that were the case, then that meant the others were using the panicked civilians as bait, and that went against their job description and any even moderately developed sense of ethics. He and McMasters needed to stick to cover for the time being. It was too soon to betray their presence. They had a solid plan in place. Straying from it would only allow variables to crop up at the least opportune moments. They had been patient thus far. It wouldn't be much longer now.

The pilot attempted to console Carson, but she swatted his hands aside, whirled away from the impasse, and stomped back toward the path.

Tasker pressed back deeper into the blind. Brown ants crawled over his face and scalp. He suppressed the sensation.

Carson sloshed up the muddy slope a mere ten feet to his left. Even over the clamor of the rain in the upper canopy, he could hear her crying. The pilot followed, trying in vain to console her, even though he appeared every bit as rattled. The pudgy academic fought to keep up, while the blonde and her cameraman trailed, visibly struggling with the treacherous footing.

Tasker caught snippets of conversation.

"…wait out the storm…"

"…try again in the morning…"

"…if we make it that long."

"…you saw the condition of the bodies…"

None of them so much as glanced in his direction.

They were distracted, which only served his purposes.

But what *had* they discovered? And where was their security contingent?

IV

5:37 p.m.

There was no way in hell that Colton was abandoning a fortune in gold now that it was firmly in his grasp. He had taken command of the situation and had his men running around making the necessary preparations. With the way the level of the river had risen even while they crossed it hours ago, he knew there was no chance the others would make it beyond the engorged banks tonight. Not with the way the rain continued to fall. They would return at any moment, but in the meantime, he and his men needed to ready themselves for the coming night. The fortress was too large and sprawling, and too thick with vegetation to easily patrol, so they needed to fortify a defensible perimeter. But against what were they defending themselves? While he had initially scoffed at Russell's nonsensical blatherings, the evidence was impossible to ignore. The broken and disarticulated skeletons everywhere. The slaughtered remains of Gearhardt's son's party. The feathers, and especially the feces containing human matter.

He couldn't fool himself into thinking that firepower was the solution. After all, Rippeth had been armed to the teeth when he had been torn apart.

How could anything like what Russell proposed have survived so long without being discovered, even this high in the unexplored cloud forest? He thought of Carson's theory, that the primitive Mesoamerican tribes had known about them and had worshipped them as gods. Unfortunately, all of those venerable civilizations— the Aztec, the Inca, the Maya—had all vanished from the face of the planet at the height of their power. Did one correlate to the other?

There was no time for speculation. There was still too much left to do, and night was already falling as the sun vanished behind the peak above them.

The first order of business had been to crack open the case and suitably arm themselves. He and his men had each slung one of the SCARs over their shoulders and grabbed a pair of both incendiary and fragmentary grenades. They now scurried around the site following his commands.

Webber had been dispatched to light fires in all of the columns surrounding the outer fortifications. While the iron cages protected the flames from the rain, they barely burned six inches tall with the limited amount of dry kindling and wood they had been able to find. Tending to them would be a full-time job.

Morton had set to work with the machete, clearing the area immediately surrounding the main stone building. If the former occupants of the village had determined that the domicile was the safest place to take refuge, then who was he to second guess them? There was no time to find a more secure location.

Sorenson was nearly finished reassembling the fallen stone barricades that had once blocked the doorways, and was preparing to move on to his next task.

Leo had managed to light the handful of torches that formed a half-circle around the stone platforms and the front half of the main dwelling between repeated attempts to raise the outside world on the satellite phone. He hadn't even been able to get a signal. Sure, the storm affected their reception, but Colton knew it was more than just that, and he was close to proving it.

The ground-penetrating radar had shown that the paving stones had been laid on a solid foundation of bedrock, as he had expected. Granted, there were varying thicknesses in the strata, but all of it was solid rock to the furthest depths of the sensing device's range. The magnetometer, however, confirmed his hypothesis.

He studied the small monitor on the magnetometer, which looked like a haphazardly assembled vacuum cleaner made of scraps of metal, as he walked in a straight line. The harness strapped to his shoulders allowed him to hold the unit suspended several inches above the ground. Different types of rocks were displayed in subtle shades of gray and black as the signal released by the magnetometer was interpreted and analyzed to determine the magnetic properties of the ground. As he had hoped, capillaries of gold extended from the main vein. Of course, there were also large deposits of quartz and especially magnetite, which composed the bulk of the stone underfoot and appeared nearly black on the monitor. And what was another name for magnetite? Lodestone. In previous centuries, its magnetic properties had been used to polarize needles to create functional compasses. The ground was positively packed with enough magnetic material to interfere with any satellite uplink.

At least now he understood why they had lost contact with Gearhardt's son's expedition. If only he could answer the question regarding how they had been caught unaware and so mercilessly butchered.

All he had to go on was that two of the men had presumably been in the process of bedding down for the night, while the other two had been overcome inside the mountain. Their attackers must have entered the cave via the tunnel from the room filled with feces, where they had killed one man and sent the other running for his life. But what did that imply? Had their assailants descended under the cover of darkness?

And how had Hunter managed to escape? Why hadn't he been similarly ripped apart?

Colton looked again to the sky. The encroaching night was advancing far more quickly than he had anticipated, as though a blanket were slowly settling over the entire region.

He returned the magnetometer to the crate and headed back toward where the others labored. The torches merely cast elongated shadows and did precious little to provide actual illumination. They were going to need more light if they were to properly secure their impromptu compound, but the forest was drenched and there was nothing combustible for miles. They had brought no fuel or—

Colton stopped dead in his tracks. The rain pattered his poncho and the grumble of thunder rolled down the hillside.

A lopsided grin spread on his face as he hurried toward the staircase leading up to the building.

"You're wasting your time," he said to Leo in passing. "The whole area's solid magnetite."

He ducked past Sorenson and through the partially barricaded threshold. He was certain he had seen what he was looking for in here.

The fluttering glow of the torch behind him made his shadow dance on the stone floor in the rectangle of orange light from the doorway. A metallic glint drew his eye to the left side of the chamber, opposite the mess of bones to his right. He approached what at first appeared to be an ancient mound of crumbling bricks, but as he neared, the metal inside of them glimmered, even in the wan glare.

He remembered the pots they had found near the fire pit. Perhaps whoever had holed up in here had used one of them to cook the dead, but the other one, the one with the carbon scoring, had been used to concoct something else entirely.

This was how the survivors before them had held the darkness at bay.

He lifted one of the jagged bricks and appreciated its weight.

Thermite.

They weren't just going to light up the night. They were going to set it on fire.

V

6:02 p.m.

One minute a murky gloaming had reigned, and the next, darkness had descended with the speed of the rain, forcing Jay to turn on the light mounted to his camera in order to see the slippery trail well enough to get a foothold on anything. They had kept up with the others for as long as they could, but he could no longer see them on the path ahead. Surely they were just around the next bend, and it was only a matter of time before he and Dahlia caught up. He was tired of falling, and drenched through and through. Somehow the mud had managed to find its way beneath his clothing, where it felt like mucus against his skin. The sludge even made it difficult for his socked feet to maintain traction inside his boots.

And then there was the fear. The images of what remained of the slain men rose to the forefront of his mind, stimulating his heart to beat faster and his breathing to grow shallow. Finding all of the ancient bones on the ground had been exhilarating, and would only enhance the documentary, but stumbling upon bloody carcasses that were only weeks old wasn't even remotely cool. Well, maybe at first. The lens did tend to sterilize everything viewed through it in the same fashion that the impact of certain atrocities was somehow lessened when watching them on television. Once he rationalized how the deaths related back to him on a personal level, the initial excitement had vanished in a nanosecond.

They were isolated from the rest of the world by forty-some miles and several days' travel. And there was something out there in the forest capable of ripping them to shreds.

A cricket chirped from somewhere off to his right. Or had it been a frog? He still couldn't tell the difference. He was a city boy at heart, and would happily give his left nut to be back in the States with a beer in one hand and a remote control in the other, living the American dream. A chorus of chirruping answered the call before immediately falling silent once again.

Jay's foot slipped. It was all he could do to hold the camera up out of the muck as he slid down the path on his chest. When his heels finally snagged on a root, he pushed himself to his feet and spat out a mouthful of filth.

"Jesus." He flung mud from his left hand and looked up just in time to see a dark shape hurtling downhill toward him. Lunging to the side, he narrowly avoided Dahlia, who careened into the underbrush behind him.

She struggled to all fours, but didn't even try to rise. Her long hair had pulled loose from her ponytail and hung in front of her face in muddy ropes. When she finally raised her head, her face brown, save the circles of white around her eyes, he noticed that she was crying.

"Hey…" He offered his hand. "We'll get through this. Don't you worry."

Dahlia was the strongest woman he had ever known. She never cracked under pressure and she was brutal in her ambition. Seeing her like this scared him. She wasn't the emotional type. He couldn't fathom anything inside of her ever snapping to the point of summoning tears. The only thing he ever imagined could break through her defenses was actual physical pain.

"I'm fine," she snapped, but she still accepted his help in returning to her feet.

Jay gasped. What he had at first thought were tears were lines of blood pouring over her eyebrows from a gash across her hairline.

"What?" She dabbed at her forehead, winced, and drew her fingertips away bloody. "Oh, great. This is absolutely perfect."

"Just a second." Jay shed his backpack and removed a tee-shirt from the main pouch. He raised it to her forehead and pressed it to the wound.

"You could have at least picked a clean one."

"Would you just hold still already?"

She rested her hand on his and held the shirt in place. Her blue eyes met his around the cloth.

"Thank you," she whispered. Her skin against his created an electric sensation that shot through his entire body. "You've always been there for me, haven't you? Every step of the way."

He could feel himself blushing and nervously retreated a step, slipping his hand out from beneath hers.

"Just keep pressure on that cut." Even his voice trembled. "We need to catch up with the others, and I don't think the path is the easiest route."

"Neither do I." She offered the bloody shirt as evidence before placing it back against the laceration. "I'll bet if we stay just to the side of the path and cut through the trees we'll find more solid footing."

"It couldn't be any worse."

"Besides, it can't be much farther to the top."

She struck off into the jungle, winding around massive trunks and using vines and branches to pull herself up the steep slope. Jay followed, shining the light over her shoulder, for all the good it did. The manly thing to do would have been to sweep her up in his arms and carry her to safety—or at least take the lead, for God's sake—but he wanted to capture as much of this moment on film as possible. She had let her guard down for just a moment, and only for him. Perhaps after all these years, his perseverance was finally about to pay off.

Twenty minutes of strenuous exertion passed before a shifting aura of light bloomed through the trees ahead.

"It's a fire," Dahlia called back to him. "It looks like they managed to light the torches."

Another few steps and Jay could see the small flames and the flickering glow on the wall beyond them. A swell of relief passed through him. He didn't think his legs had the strength to carry him much farther.

Movement drew his eye to the forest to his right, where the branches of a cluster of saplings swayed gently.

"Are you coming or what?"

He turned at the sound of her voice. She stared back over her shoulder at him, poised to step from the thicket into the clearing. Had something changed in the way she looked at him?

"Yeah," he said, spurring his aching feet toward the crest, where she waited for him at the tree line.

He panned the camera across the clearing. The entire area was awash with an amber glow from the row of torches, minus the darkened section where one of the stone columns had long ago collapsed, and the arches of shadows built into the fortifications.

"I don't know what you want to do with this," she said, proffering his shirt.

"You can keep that." He smirked. "Consider it a gift."

"You are far too generous."

A large, broad-leaved shrub shivered beside them. A handful of flies buzzed softly from beneath its protective branches.

Jay shined the beam toward the source of the motion, shoving aside shadows to reveal the slender trunk and the tangles of branches. Several black flies swirled in the light. To the left, a pair of almost milky, bluish spheres appeared behind the dripping leaves.

"It's another one of those weird butterflies," he said. "They must not be that rare out here after all."

He turned the camera toward the creature, and twin golden rings reflected the beam.

The pattern on the wings hadn't done that before. But he hadn't filmed the butterfly at night either.

Another bush shook to his right, diverting his attention.

When he looked back at the butterfly, its lower wings shifted to reveal—

They weren't wings at all.

The light reflected from interlocking rows of razor-honed teeth.

Jay barely had time to turn as vegetation was shredded and thrown into the air. A heavy object slammed into him from behind, driving him to the ground. Pain exploded between his shoulder blades and what felt like frozen spikes prodded through his muscles and between his ribs.

The camera fell from his hand and landed on its side. The beam glared blankly toward a snarl of underbrush, momentarily highlighting Dahlia's pale face. Her eyes grew wide and her mouth opened in surprise. A blur of brown and shimmering green, and she was thrown sideways beyond the light's reach.

Arcs of crimson trailed in her wake.

Something flailed at his back as more shadows raced in from the periphery. His whole body convulsed in agony. He threw back his head to scream, exposing his neck—

He heard a whistle of air and then a gurgle.

Scaled appendages flashed past.

Feathers.

Claws.

A rush of blood flooded across the mud into the camera's light as he was jerked with a crash into the bushes and the blackness waiting within them, which buzzed with the wings of flies.

Chapter Ten

I

Sam had been so focused on the tedious ascent and her own frustrations that she hadn't noticed when Dahlia and Jay fell behind. Galen had run ahead to relay the news that the river was impassable to the rest of their party in the camp. She and Merritt had already been waiting at the trailhead for more than fifteen minutes, during which they thought they'd heard a scream in the distance before it was silenced by a clap of thunder. It felt as though the entire world was crashing down around her. There was no place left to run. The aura of death hung over the mountain in a palpable cloud that promised only pain and suffering. Hunter and the rest of his party had been killed here, the most recent casualties in a chain that spanned centuries.

"The path leads straight here." Merritt nearly had to shout to be heard over the storm. "There's no way they could have gotten lost."

"We need to go back for them. What if one of them fell and is lying there in the mud, injured and in need of help?"

The expression on Merritt's face suggested he feared as much, but at the same time, she too could feel the oppressiveness of the situation, the dire inevitability of what was to come. It was an electrical sensation in the air, like the tingling potential that raised the hairs on one's arms before a lightning strike.

"I'll go back for them," Merritt said. "You find the others and try to figure out some other way to get us off this mountain."

"We can't split up. I'm staying with you."

"The hell you are. I need to know that you're safe."

The look in his eyes startled her. For the first time, all pretense of cockiness was gone and she recognized genuine fear.

She took his hand and repeated the same words, more softly this time. "I'm staying with you."

He looked down at the union of their hands and then back into her eyes.

"Then stay behind me at all times. We're going no more than half a mile. We can't afford to waste any more time if we're—"

A blinding light flared from the north. They both whirled toward where one of the torches burned so brightly it appeared as though the sun itself had been captured inside that iron cage. A shape advanced in their direction, made shadow by the brilliant glare behind it. Based on the figure's size and stature, there was only one man it could have been.

"What are you guys doing out here?" Sorenson shouted. "You should be back inside the walls with the others."

"We lost Dahlia and Jay," Sam called over the deluge.

"I'll send them along when I see them." He crumbled something in his hands and threw it onto the next torch in the series. The low flames expanded with a dazzling white light. He slid the remainder of what looked like a rusted chunk of metal through the grate. "They won't stay lost long. You can probably see these fires from space."

Sorenson smiled briefly before he lowered his brow in an expression of confusion. He turned and struck off toward the edge of the forest. As he walked, he shouldered an automatic rifle.

"Where are you going?" Sam asked.

"I thought I saw something—" Sorenson said, but the storm drowned out the rest of his words.

Raindrops the size of marbles pounded down on them with increasing force. Even the branches above no longer provided adequate protection. They were going to have to seek shelter, and soon.

Sam trailed Merritt as they followed Sorenson toward the line of shrubbery. He crouched and surveyed the shadowed jungle before returning his attention to the ground in front of him. They were nearly at his side when they caught a circular flash of reflected light. The tiny red light beside the lens on Jay's digital recorder diffused into the standing water.

Sorenson's stare never left the jungle as he lifted the video camera out of the mud.

"It's still recording," he said, passing it back to her over his shoulder. He rose and scrutinized the dense vegetation down the barrel of his rifle.

Leaves and twigs littered the area as though torn from their moorings by a tornado. The ground was choppy with a riot of footsteps. When Sorenson took his first step into the brush, the absence of his shadow revealed that the mud here was a deeper shade of black than the rest.

Sam stared at the camera. There was no denying to whom it belonged. The spotlight mounted to it was shattered and the lens cracked, and yet still it vibrated softly as the digital feed continued to record. She wanted to call for Jay, but something stopped her. There was no way he would have willingly abandoned his camera, his very lifeblood. Not unless something horrible had happened.

Sorenson's footsteps slurped and crunched on the mud and detritus.

"We should get out of here," Merritt said. "I don't like this. Something's not right here."

Leaves rustled and branches snapped as Sorenson shoved through the underbrush.

"We were just standing thirty feet from here," Sam said.

That thought chilled her. Something had happened on this spot, a mere ten yards from where they had waited at the trailhead, something awful, and they had been completely oblivious.

"Jesus Christ," Sorenson gasped. He held back the leathery leaves of a heliconia plant. The mud beneath it was gouged, and there was a trench as though something heavy had been dragged—

A hand. There was a hand on the ground, collecting rain in the palm. The fingers curled inward, minus the middle finger, which was a blunt, ragged stub. Skin muddy and torn, the wrist a collection of jagged bones and severed tendons where it had been torn from the forearm. What could have been an upper arm or a lower leg lay past it, a bloody long bone missing large chunks of muscle and flesh.

Sam clapped her hand over her mouth and turned away, only to see a large clump of blonde hair, still attached to a swatch of scalp, tangled in the branches.

"We're out of here," Merritt said. "Make no sudden movements. Slowly back away."

Sam could hear herself crying as though from miles away, but there was nothing she could do to stop it. She clung to the camera, its whirring mechanical heartbeat against her chest.

Her eyes darted from one shadow to the next. Even the gentle bowing of branches under the weight of the rain and the shifting of saplings brought the forest to life with menace. The flickering glow of the flames along the obsidian wall made her feel like there was someone behind her, but she couldn't force herself to so much as glance over her shoulder.

"As soon as we're clear of the jungle, I want you two to make a run for the collapsed section of the northern wall," Sorenson said. "I'll cover you from behind. Head for the main building at the center of the courtyard."

"What about you?" Merritt asked.

"You'd better believe I'll be right on your heels."

Merritt reached back and took Sam's free hand. She squeezed for dear life.

"You ready?" he asked. Sam couldn't summon the voice to respond. "On my mark." The tension on her arm increased. "Now!"

She spun around and sprinted toward the sheer, vine-shrouded fortification, careful not to look directly into the flames for fear of creating blind spots in her vision. Her legs churned and her feet slipped in the muck, but Merritt pulled her onward. They rounded the corner and sprinted toward the crumbled mound of stones.

Behind her, the savage light faded, allowing the darkness to again enfold them.

She risked a glance back as they ascended the rubble.

There was no sign of Sorenson.

She hadn't heard any shots fired, but she didn't find that comforting in the slightest.

II

7:00 p.m.

Leo shielded his eyes from the rain and surveyed their work. The entire front half of the structure glowed as though struck by the midday sun. Colton had just finished crumbling the edges of the thermite onto the once-diminutive flames to make them flare with blinding intensity, and had laid the bricks in the heart of the iron chambers. They had yet to determine how long the thermite would burn with such force, but surely they had more than enough stacked in the main chamber to get them through the night. At least that should buy them enough time to figure out what they were going to do next.

Once the storm abated, they would merely have to get far enough away from the mountain to escape the magnetic interference. With just a few precisely placed phone calls, Leo could have them airlifted out of there in no time. It would cost him an arm and a leg, but once he returned with the properly outfitted group and the necessary supplies, he would easily be able to recoup his loss with the sheer amount of gold under his feet. Maybe he'd have the entire mountainside napalmed first. That would take care of whatever stalked the ruins once and for all. He just hoped he would have the opportunity to see the expressions cooked onto the charred faces of the creatures that had slaughtered his son's men, and had cost him the one thing in his life that had ever truly mattered.

"What's the plan from here?" he asked Colton, who, having finished his task, strode back toward the entrance to the building.

"We bolster our defenses. Fill the gaps where the structure has crumbled over time and clear some of this godforsaken jungle. We'll run two-man patrols at the perimeter, and station another two at the lone remaining doorway. We can't trust the civilians with the weapons or our lives, so they'll be penned inside the main chamber. You too, Leo."

Leo didn't even consider arguing. He recognized his shortcomings. And, after all, this was what he was paying them for.

He turned and surveyed the courtyard. A wall of tangled trees and shadows waited at the edge of the light's reach, roughly twenty-five feet away. Morton and Webber walked uneasily through the trees, burdened by the assault of raindrops, which beat a tinny rhythm on the iron caps over the torches. Leo detected their unease in their twitchy movements, the way their rifles jerked from side to side, and the way their heads snapped toward even the slightest sound or movement.

There were no torches on the rear or to either side of the stone structure, where the forest grew right up against it. While the nearly impregnable blackness back there worried Leo, he knew there was no way anything could get through the walls without breaking through several tons of fitted rocks.

If Colton was right, and that whatever was out there hunted exclusively under the cover of darkness, then all they had to do now was survive the night. With their firepower and their defensible position, he saw it as a foregone conclusion. They weren't savages with bows and arrows after all.

A peal of thunder grumbled down from the peak.

Webber swung to his right, toward where Leo caught movement from the corner of his eye. His heart leapt into his throat as shadows raced around the side of the building.

Leo braced himself for the sound of gunfire and the resultant chaos.

"Don't shoot!" one of the shadows shouted. It thrust its hands into the air, one of which held a video camera. The whole scene was incongruous. It was Sam's voice, but Jay's video camera.

Sam stepped into the light and had to cup her free hand over her brow against the glare. Merritt was right behind her. A moment later, Sorenson burst from the forest and headed straight toward his armed companions.

"They're dead," Sam called. Her already pale features were whitewashed by the bright flames.

"Who?" Leo asked.

Merritt and Sam hurried up the overgrown staircase between the stages and stopped when they reached him. Both of them were panting as though they'd sprinted a great distance.

"Dahlia and Jay," Merritt said.

"Are you sure?"

"We discovered what was left of them in the jungle outside the fortress," Sam said.

"They'd been torn apart like the others," Merritt said. "We found Jay's camera. And it was still recording."

"Let me see it," Colton said. In all of the commotion, Leo hadn't noticed Colton walk right up behind him. Galen eased across the threshold from inside the stone domicile and stood warily at Colton's hip.

Sam held out the recorder. Colton snatched it from her and performed a cursory topical inspection before snapping out the side view screen. He tilted the camera to the light so he could clearly see the buttons and brought the small monitor to life. The screen was cracked and the image warped. Colton pressed the rewind button and twin horizontal lines of static shivered in the center. For several moments, there was no movement at all, then the blackness appeared to shake before eventually brightening to footage of the outer fortifications with dim haloes of light surrounding the evenly spaced stone columns.

None of them spoke as Colton allowed the footage to play at regular speed.

Leo held his breath.

The recorded rain sounded like someone clapping in the distance.

"You are far too generous," Dahlia's warped voice said from Colton's palm.

The image shifted to a large shrub. Flies swarmed in the halogen light, framed by the undersides of the dripping leaves. The camera struggled to focus, and then zoomed in on twin orbs that appeared as clear as stars through a mist. The pale blue spheres shifted ever so slightly, and there was a glimmer of white below them, but the screen was too cracked to discern exactly what they were viewing.

"It's another one of those weird butterflies," Jay's garbled voice said. "They must not be—"

The video shivered and Jay's words were swallowed by static.

"What did he say?" Leo asked, but by then the answer was irrelevant.

The footage resumed. Golden rings flashed behind the bluish spheres. Eyeshine. Leo recognized it immediately.

Tattered vegetation exploded toward the camera. Rows of savage teeth knifed past. The camera fell to the ground with a clatter, speeding past a blur of leaves. Or were they feathers? The image settled to a sideways view of the clearing. The top glowed with torchlight, while the bottom was filled with shrubbery. A portion of the left side of the screen was eclipsed by water. Beyond lay a field of mud.

Screams erupted from the small speaker, so loud and close to the microphone that they sounded like feedback.

A cluster of branches slapped to the ground, followed by the upper half of Dahlia's body. A skein of blood covered her face, her mouth frozen in a scream. A dark blur yanked her out of the camera's view. A wash of fluid splashed down where she'd been a second prior. The screams intensified with sheer terror before being cut short.

The steady clamor of the rain droned from the speaker.

The image remained still for several eternal moments while they watched with baited breath.

"Jesus Christ," Galen said from where he peered over Colton's shoulder.

A dark gray object appeared from the bottom of the screen with a splash of filthy water and blocked the majority of the screen. It looked like a hazy tree trunk at first, but when the lens finally rationalized the focus, it showed that the gray post had tightly knit scales. A sharp arch curled upward in front of it, then stabbed the ground several times like a scorpion's tail.

Shadows raced behind it, drawing the auto-focus in and out. Branches rustled and the audio came to life with crunching and tearing noises.

A heartbeat later, the gray object pried itself out of the muck, revealing several long digits capped with sharp nails, dripping with mud. The hooked object rose with them, attached to a stunted toe that held it elevated above the others.

"It's a claw," Galen whispered.

Several minutes passed in stunned silence before Sorenson's voice emerged from the feed and he lifted the camera from the mire.

"Oh my God," Sam said. "They hadn't been dead for more than a few minutes when we arrived."

"Those monsters were probably still there," Merritt said. "We could have walked within inches of them."

"They aren't monsters," Galen said, his voice softened by reverence and fear. "They're avians. Raptors specifically. Did you see that foot? It looked just like a condor's, only the claw on the first digit was much larger. And did you notice the extent of its arch? It could have passed for a meat hook."

Leo gasped. The Medical Examiner's voice echoed inside his head from what felt like another lifetime. *Angled entrance with inferior curvature of roughly thirty degrees. Possibly some kind of hook with a shallow arch.* He thought of his son, his baby boy, and the two stab wounds in his back. He imagined a creature cloaked in feathers made of shadow leaping onto Hunter's back and his cries of pain as he tumbled over a stone cliff and plummeted toward the waiting river.

Tears flooded from his eyes and a hideous mewling sound rose from his chest.

"It doesn't matter what it is," Colton snapped. "Right now, all of you need to get inside where we can effectively protect you. There's nothing out there that we can't kill. Especially some sort of bird."

"I didn't say bird," Galen whispered. "I said raptor."

III

7:38 p.m.

Tasker crouched on a broad branch a dozen feet up in the canopy, leaning his shoulder against the trunk. The leaves were so thick all around him that there was no way anyone could see him from below, especially now that he had rolled in mud. Saved from the brunt of the storm by the dense vegetative shield above him, it wouldn't wash away until the very last minute. By then it would be too late for his prey. Beards of moss shrouded him and vines snaked through and around the surrounding branches. He studied the ground in shades of green through the night vision goggles. He had positioned himself in such a way that if he craned his head just right, he could see the distant entrance to the domicile and the guards posted to either side of the opening, through which flames flickered. The occasional shadow crossed in front of the fire. Smoke plumed from the random holes in the earthen roof. To see any real detail, he needed to push the goggles back up onto his forehead due to the intense glow from the outer torches. What were they burning to create such bright flames anyway?

McMasters was roughly two hundred yards to the west, closer to the steep hillside, similarly hidden in the boughs of another massive kapok tree. Their watches were synchronized. In just over two hours, the siege would commence.

Their prey would never know what hit them.

The outer perimeter had been simple to breach considering there hadn't been a single guard stationed along the obsidian walls, granting them free access to half of the overgrown village, which made their initial approach far easier than Tasker could have even hoped. However, it also complicated the logistics of the final assault. The two roaming sentries would be easy to eliminate. Hell, both men had walked nearly directly beneath him twice. He could have dropped down on their heads and slit their throats without much effort. The two men flanking the entryway would prove more challenging. He and McMasters would be seen too soon if they attempted a frontal assault, so they were going to have to come around from the rear. Slipping around the sides of the building still left them too exposed for his liking, so they were going to have to scale the roof from behind. The guards would never suspect a thing, even after two quick shots through the tops of their skulls. And then there would be nothing left to do but mop up the civilians inside.

In a matter of hours, the site would be theirs to ransack as they pleased. He only wished he could account for the fly in the ointment, the lone element of unpredictability.

The thought of what had been contained in those funereal bundles made him shudder. Desiccated, scaled skin pulled tightly over a framework of thin bones, curled back from sharp, interlaced teeth. Dried feathers that crumbled with the slightest touch. Slender legs with feet like those of an ostrich, only with a hooked claw that looked strong enough to punch a hole through the hood of a truck.

He forced down the image. There was no point in chasing that line of thought. Unlike Jones, he and McMasters were prepared for this contingency.

Caressing the barrel of his rifle, he glanced at his watch.

Soon the ancient ground would again taste the blood of the dying.

IV

7:59 p.m.

The walls felt like they were closing in on him, compressing the chamber to such an extent that he could hardly breathe the stale air. A pall of smoke hung over them, but he wasn't about to let the fire wane for even a second. Its light was the only thing staving off the panic.

Merritt paced the room. He had tried to sit in the ring around the bonfire with the others, but the nervous energy had built inside him to the point that if he didn't burn off at least some of it, he was going to explode. The stone walls, the low ceiling, the smoke. All he was missing were the screams, and he would have been back in Afghanistan, in his own personal version of hell. He needed to get out of there, but where could he possibly go?

He tried to occupy his mind by checking and rechecking their preparations. The mound of thermite would last for several more days at their current rate of usage. All of the doorways leading deeper into the heart of the building had been sealed with piles of rubble. He threw a shoulder into them repeatedly to test their stability. Not once did any of them so much as budge. That left only the small gaps in the ceiling, through which the majority of the smoke fled the fire, but none of the holes were large enough to grant entrance to anything wider than the clumps of roots that dangled to the floor. Save the lone entrance, they were completely entombed.

Raindrops dripped through the roof into widening pools on the floor with a metronomic *plip...ploop...*and mosquitoes whined from the darkened corners, away from the flames.

Merritt stared at the disheveled heaps of bones and wondered if this was how the natives had felt when they barricaded themselves in here. Had they known they were going to die?

"Why didn't they leave when they had the chance?" he asked. "I mean, some of them had to have survived to build the fortress down in the valley." He gestured to the skeletal remains. "Why did these people choose to stay where they were forced to cannibalize each other, only to end up dying anyway?"

"You have to look at it in a historical context," Sam said. Until now, she had hardly said a word since being ushered into the dank, manmade cavern. "These people worshipped the creatures. Viracocha, Kakulcán, Quetzalcoatl. All of the native Mesoamerican tribes had a name for them, and revered them as the strongest and most important within their pantheon of deities. One can only speculate. Perhaps the people who died in here were some sort of sacrifice. Or maybe they feared angering the gods by abandoning them to flee to the lowland jungles. Primitive religions were based upon the natural world as much as superstition. It's possible that these people saw their deaths as an inevitable consequence of their beliefs. Or they could have offered their lives in exchange for the safe passage of their families and the security of future generations."

"Their descendents, the ones in the fortress near the lake, they knew these things would hunt us," Leo said. "That's why they allowed us to cross through their village. What did their chief say?"

"Let them pass," Sam said. And then in a whisper, "They are dead already."

"But they've figured out a way to live in peace with them," Merritt said. "Look at the sheer walls of their fortress and the surrounding torches. And the alpaca pen."

"They sacrifice the alpacas to these things. They still revere them."

"No," Galen said. "Look at it from the most simplistic biological perspective. It's a symbiotic relationship of sorts. They make sure that the raptors are fed, while the raptors protect them from the outside world."

"Like the ants in that hollow tree at the center of their courtyard," Merritt said.

"Exactly. You can't possibly think that these people have remained hidden for so long based solely on geography. They've been discovered on countless occasions. Remember the pistol in that hut from the late nineteenth century? And your son's party, Leo. They've avoided detection and possible exploitation because no one has survived long enough to betray their location. The raptors make sure of that."

"You're the expert, Dr. Russell," Leo said. "What exactly are these raptors?"

"I wish I knew for sure. All we have to go on is that they're feathered, yet incapable of flight, have scaled skin, and the lower appendages of a condor. They don't have beaks, and their teeth are crocodilian. They're nocturnal and they hunt in packs. As an ornithologist, I'm the furthest thing from an expert. I specialize in birds, specifically birds of prey."

"What are you saying?"

"These raptors are like no type I've ever encountered, and, honestly, I don't believe they're birds at all. In fact, I can only think of a few extinct species that are even remotely similar."

"Like what?" Sam asked.

"Archaeopteryx, for one, but it was much smaller and omnivorous. Possibly deinonychus or achillobator. I recently read about the discovery of fossils of a new species in Argentina called neuquenraptor, which was six feet long from snout to tail. Unfortunately, that's about the extent of my knowledge. I merely try to keep up with the evidence as it pertains to the evolution of avians for my classes."

"So you're suggesting these animals are like velociraptors?" Merritt asked.

Galen scoffed. "Fossils discovered in Mongolia suggest that velociraptors were no bigger than turkeys, but a similar concept, I suppose."

"Stop right there," Leo said. He huffed and rose from where he'd been seated beside the fire. "You're talking about dinosaurs."

"Feathered serpent gods," Sam whispered.

"What else could they possibly be?" Galen stood and paced as he composed his thoughts. "Dinosaurs are the predecessors of modern avians. Feathers are simply elaborate scales. They have the same general keratin composition and serve to maintain the body temperature of warm-blooded animals. Who's to say that something like the neuquenraptor couldn't have survived through the eons up here in total isolation from the rest of the world?"

"That's absurd," Leo snapped. "The dinosaurs were all killed by a single extinction event. An asteroid strike, or whatever the favored theory of the day might be."

"Were they? If that was the case, then how is there avian life on the planet? Everything had to evolve from something else. Man came from apes, after all. Crocodilians are nearly identical anatomically to their ancestors from tens of millions of years ago. And birds evolved from dinosaurs."

"That doesn't explain how they could have remained hidden here for millennia."

"Think about that cavern we found. They've been living underground and only coming out to hunt at night. They're the perfect nocturnal carnivore. And they even defecate where no one will find their spoor. There's no way you could track them without blindly stumbling upon them like we did."

"So if we're dealing with a species that has thrived longer than any other in recorded history, and survived an extinction event that wiped out nearly all life forms on the planet," Merritt asked, "then what are our chances of surviving *them?*"

Silence filled the chamber, broken only by the crackle of flames and the echoing patter of leaking water.

Merritt turned his back on the others and walked into the open doorway. The gentle breeze felt soothing against his face, the smell of ozone vastly preferable to that of the smoke. Where the torchlight died, the jungle was a wall of darkness.

Somewhere out there, death stalked the shadows.

And he could feel it inching closer with each passing second.

V

9:48 p.m.

Colton crept through the underbrush at the edge of the wavering light. On one side of him lay a golden wash of tangled scrub interspersed with mighty trees that cast long swatches of shadow over an obstacle course of bushes and rotting trunks, while on the other side, darkness reigned supreme. He could barely distinguish the silhouettes of the ceiba trunks from the collapsed stone ruins. The proliferation of lianas and vines made it impossible to detect the source of the movement he could sense all around him. While he couldn't see them out there, he could definitely hear them. To the untrained ear, it may have sounded like the gentle rustling of leaves at the urging of a weak breeze or the sporadic dripping of rain through the canopy and into the waiting puddles, but to Colton, it sounded as though an entire army converged upon their position, advancing in increments of inches. Even beneath the ruckus of the rain, he noticed the subtle slurping sounds of feet being pried from the muck and carefully replaced with only a slight shift of weight. He'd been doing this for far too long not to know when he was being hunted.

His finger tensed on the trigger. He was prepared to swing the barrel to his left at the first indication of the commencement of the impending assault, but he couldn't afford to tip his hand too soon. So far, as he had theorized, the predators clung to the darkness, staying well out of the light. He couldn't trust that advantage to last indefinitely. They were sizing him up, gauging what kind of threat he posed, while simultaneously assessing his weaknesses and plotting the most opportune moment to spring the trap he could feel closing around him with each step.

They were smart, which not only made them more dangerous, but unpredictable. With their sheer numbers and their familiarity with the topography, they could have slain him a hundred times over, and yet they continued to stalk him. The only explanation was that they weren't simply waiting for the perfect opportunity, they were determining the best course of action to take all of them at once.

Shift change was nearly upon him, and while he welcomed the chance to distance himself from the hunters, which he had no doubt skulked through the foliage mere feet from him, he trusted no one else with his life. Sending the other men out to the perimeter could very well mean sentencing them to their deaths, but worse was the prospect of posting himself in a stationary position at the mouth of a bottleneck with nothing more than a stone wall at his back and three-hundred sixty degrees of dark jungle surrounding him. If they were unable to hold the creatures beyond the intangible perimeter of light, then they would be forced to fall back into the inner sanctum with the civilians where there was no means of escape except through the teeth of the enemy. They would only be able to fire blindly through the opening until they either ran out of ammunition or were overwhelmed and slaughtered.

Fortunately, he still had a surprise or two up his sleeve. These creatures may have become adept at dodging arrows, and maybe even the occasional bullet, but there was no way they would be ready for what he had in store for them when worse came to worst.

Colton felt the comfortable weight of the grenades in his jacket pockets against his belly.

The hint of a smile curled the corners of his lips.

He rounded the western portion of the patch of light. The peak rose above him, stepped with gardens gone feral, all the way up into the clouds. He wondered briefly how anyone had lived here long enough to grow anything with this unknown species running rampant through the wilderness. They must have arrived and erected their village first, before their presence summoned the predators from wherever they had been previously. For them to have been worshipped by tribes as far north as Mexico, the creatures had to be nomadic. So why then had they stayed here for so long? Was it possible that the surviving Chachapoya had kept them here by feeding and protecting them?

Turning back to the east, he weaved through the foliage toward the line of blazing torches. Morton and Webber stood like statues to either side of the doorway. He felt their stares pass over him. Even from the distance, he could sense the fear radiating from them.

He ascended the muddy slope to the main entrance, wary of the darkness along the western face of the building. If only there had been more time to clear the trees away from the structure. He wished the jungle was dry enough to burn.

Webber moved away from the wall and struck off toward the forest without a word. Colton settled in behind him and watched the man tromp to the edge of the darkness, all the while expecting black shapes to explode from the underbrush.

What in the name of God were they waiting for?

VI

9:56 p.m.

Sam watched through the doorway as Morton and Webber walked across the overgrown courtyard toward the darkened trees. She felt so impotent, merely waiting for whatever was about to transpire to play out before her. The air was positively charged with foreboding. It was no longer a matter of *if* something was going to happen, but when. She looked to her right, past Merritt, to where Colton stood, his face a mask of concentration. He directed his rifle toward the trees, moving it slowly from left to right, absorbing every little detail. She was certain he could feel it too. Things were about to come to a head.

To her left, Sorenson followed Colton's lead, his posture rigid. He didn't once blink.

Merritt's hand found hers and gave a reassuring squeeze. She held it tightly, grateful for the physical contact. He had paled considerably and his hair was more unkempt than usual, but he radiated an aura of calmness that belied the situation.

"We're going to be all right, aren't we?" she whispered.

He offered a silent nod, but failed in his attempt at a smile.

She released his hand and turned back toward the fire. Uncertainty gnawed at her. There were still several questions for which she couldn't fathom the answers. She had originally dismissed them, and yet somehow they had grown more insistent.

"Why did they need so many torches?" she asked. "And why did they stockpile so much thermite? Was firelight alone not enough?"

"My best guess is the creatures are like owls," Galen said. His voice quivered when he spoke, but not nearly as badly as his hands. "Physiologically, their eyes are designed for optimal night vision, as evidenced by the eyeshine. Low levels of light are amplified by the *tapetum lucidum* so that the visual receptors accurately glean details from the darkness. Bright light overwhelms their sense of sight, overstimulating the retinas. I'd imagine that for them, the glare of the thermite is equivalent to looking directly into the sun for us."

"So the light blinds them," Merritt said.

"Definitely an oversimplification, but a functional assertion nevertheless. It doesn't technically blind them, but rather prevents them from being able to clearly see, effectively creating a massive blind spot, rather than a condition of blindness."

"Then they won't attack because of the torches," Leo said.

"I wouldn't wager my life on that. A starving owl will hunt during the day." Galen paused. "You have to understand that birds of prey hunt with more than just sight. Their senses of hearing and smell are also highly developed. Carrion birds follow the stench of rotting meat to find their meals. And while they may have acute vision, it's largely motion sensitive. That's why birds like hawks and falcons will emit shrill cries while circling a field. They can't clearly differentiate their prey from the weeds until it moves. The recognition of the bird's cry is ingrained in a rodent's DNA. It triggers the flight mechanism in their brains, and they run for cover. The raptor then sees the movement and dives toward the source, claws unfurled."

The ceiling groaned. All eyes rose in time to watch a small stream of dust and dirt cascade through a curtain of hair-like roots. They continued to stare at the stone roof for several long minutes. There was no repeat occurrence.

Something else still troubled Sam. The scars. All of the Chachapoya men were heavily scarred under the black body paint. While violence and ritualistic sacrifice were commonplace among the primitive South American tribes, self-mutilation was generally limited to piercings and tattoos. The scars had shown no identifiable patterns and almost appeared as though they had been inflicted during battle. But with no other tribe to wage war against, who could have caused such dramatic wounds? And why the head-to-toe black paint? Was there some sort of religious significance or was it a cultural sign of status? She remembered the women tending to the crops. None of them had been scarred, nor had they been painted. Only the men. What did it mean? She felt as though the answer was of great consequence, but for the life of her, she couldn't understand why.

The Chachapoya had managed to survive for hundreds of years in close proximity to these creatures. Other than sacrificing livestock to them, what were they doing to protect themselves? Hiding behind fortified walls and burning torches may have kept the village secure, but they had originally seen the painted natives at night. Knowing what lurked in the darkness, surely they wouldn't have unduly risked their lives without some way of ensuring their own safety. Was it possible that the dark paint allowed them to blend into the shadows?

She was just about to vocalize her thoughts when Merritt pressed a finger to his lips. He furrowed his brow and turned in a circle. His eyes eventually fixed upon the back wall of the chamber.

Slowly, he walked toward the row of doorways they had barricaded with fallen stones.

"What is it?" Galen asked. "Did you hear—?"

Merritt whirled and shushed him, then crept closer to the middle mound of rubble. He leaned closer and tilted his right ear to the jumble of rocks.

Sam followed and leaned over his shoulder.

She could clearly hear it now. A subdued shuffling sound. Something soft moving across stone. The faint trickle of pebbles tumbling through the pile of debris.

"Something's testing the wall from the other side," Merritt whispered directly into her ear.

This time her hand sought his.

The noises ceased, only to resume moments later behind the doorway to their right.

More dust shivered from the roof, shimmering like glitter in the firelight.

Sam turned to see Colton step in front of the outer doorway, weapon raised toward the jungle.

The muffled noises on the other side of the rubble grew louder, frantic. It sounded like something was trying to scratch its way through the stone.

A cloud of dust rained from above.

Sam squeezed Merritt's hand so hard that it hurt. He cautiously pulled her around behind him and stood between her and the lone entrance.

"Oh God," she whispered.

Leo and Galen rose from the fireside and retreated deeper into the room.

The wait was finally over.

Chapter Eleven

I

Andes Mountains, Peru
October 30th
10:00 p.m. PET

After what felt like an eternity of planning and hunting, the magic hour had finally arrived. Tasker's heartbeat reached a fluttering crescendo, which he slowed to a calm, metered rhythm. He mentally centered himself, leaned away from the trunk of the tree, and balanced on the thick branch with his feet alone in true predatory fashion. Silently, he slung the rifle back over his shoulder and unsheathed his knife. He adjusted the grip in his fist until it felt natural, like a fluid extension of his right arm through which even his blood flowed. All that remained was to wait for his prey to walk within range, and then it was all over, except for the bleeding.

He imagined McMasters poised for the kill in exactly the same stance. Whose quarry would be the first to fall? Who would deliver the first killing stroke?

Perhaps he would try to glean that information from his partner before he dispatched him as well.

Everything had gone so smoothly, so easily, that it was as if the long forgotten gods who had once lorded over this land blessed him alone, favoring him with good fortune for the hunt. Of course, sacrificing his own men might have bought him a little extra help from the ravenous deities of yore.

Ears attuned to the slightest sound beneath the thunder and the patter of rainfall, he waited patiently. He closed his eyes and attempted to become one with the jungle. Flies droned and mosquitoes hummed. The far off waterfall rumbled, a sound he could feel more than hear, as though the tree upon which he crouched were a plucked bass string.

His eyes snapped open at the first hint of footsteps on the detritus. Thus far, their prey had made little effort to mask their passage. They made enough noise to wake even the skeletal dead littering the ground. How many men had died here through the centuries? And to think that only he would ever walk away from this burial ground.

Leaves crackled and branches snapped. Soft exhalations reached him. He even heard the *shush* of pants between thighs, the tap of raindrops on a poncho.

A shadow stepped into view, farther away than he would have liked, but still well within range.

He glanced up at the front entrance of the main structure. The guards were so far away that he could barely see them, but he could tell that they hadn't raised the alarm.

Focusing on his prey, he leapt from the branch, arms extended. He swatted aside smaller branches and dodged a wide limb.

The wiry man below him stopped and looked up at the commotion. Tasker saw the pale, freckled face of a Midwestern farmboy through the fanned fingers of his left hand as he raised the blade in his right.

The man's eyes widened and his shoulders rose in a futile attempt to draw enough breath to shout a warning. He barely had time to raise his arms in his defense before Tasker's weight slammed down onto him. He palmed the man's forehead and hammered his head against the ground. Ribs cracked and bushes rustled. He pressed harder, driving his prey's skull into the mud with such force that the man had no choice but to tip up his chin.

Fatal mistake.

Tasker slashed his knife across the exposed throat. A flash of reflected silver and warmth splashed across his cheek. There was a high-pitched shriek. He clapped his hand over the man's mouth and nose, but the noise originated from the severed trachea. The voiceless scream faded to a whistle, and finally to a gurgle.

The blood no longer spattered Tasker's face and torso, but poured out onto the wet earth.

He rode out the body's final spasms until it eventually stilled under him.

Tasker removed his hand from the lower half of the man's face and rose just high enough to see over the tangle of shrubs. The two sentries still stood in the blinding light to either side of the doorway. Neither of them so much as looked in his direction.

Perfect.

He swiped the blade on his pants, returned it to its sheath, and swung the rifle around until he cradled it in his bloody hands.

There was a crashing sound from the west. A man cried out.

Damn it.

Tasker ducked and sprinted toward the source of the commotion.

"Webber?" a voice called from across the clearing. "Morton?"

McMasters had spoiled their advantage. It would only be a matter of moments before the other guards split up to investigate. One would head out into the forest, weapon at the ready, while the other would hold his post.

He heard more thrashing in the bushes. The forest was playing tricks with the acoustics. It almost sounded like the noises originated behind him.

Bursting through the thicket, he nearly slammed into McMasters, who knelt over the bloody mess of what had once been a short Hispanic man.

McMasters looked up at him. The black paint on his face glistened with the fresh application of blood, and it appeared as though a large chunk of his ear had been cut off. No. It had been bitten off, just above the conch. He held his left arm tightly against his chest, a guarding posture that suggested either a broken rib or a dislocated shoulder.

Rage boiled inside of Tasker. He wanted to lash out at McMasters, but now was not the time.

Voices echoed through the forest. It wouldn't be long before they initiated the search for their unresponsive patrolmen.

The swift death he would have granted his subordinate was no longer in the offering. For his carelessness, Tasker promised himself that he would prolong McMasters's suffering and subject him to unendurable agony.

He shoved McMasters ahead of him into a wall of saplings and around the ruins of a hut.

Speed was of the essence.

Behind him, the forest came to life with threshing sounds, as though the trees themselves were being torn apart.

II

10:06 p.m.

Colton called for his men again, but there was still no answer. How long had it been? A minute? Five?

Sorenson looked over at him expectantly, awaiting his orders. His eyes were wide with fear, yet he would do whatever was required of him.

Colton had to decide their course of action right now. He was out of time.

Shrubs rustled at the edge of sight against the jungle, bowing violently in sections. They were out there, and they no longer tried to hide their numbers. He couldn't see them, but with the way the underbrush shook, there had to be dozens of them. Either that or they were fast. Really fast.

"Morton and Webber are dead," Colton finally said.

"Don't you at least want me to try to—?"

"They're dead, soldier. Tell me you have any doubt."

Sorenson opened his mouth to object, then let it fall slowly closed. His jaw muscles bulged several times and his eyes narrowed to slits before he finally found his voice. "What are your orders?"

"Hold your post. Nothing gets past us. If anything moves, you send it right back to hell. Clear?"

"Crystal."

"What's going on?" Merritt asked from behind him.

"Can you still handle a rifle?" Colton asked.

"What happened to the other—?"

"Can you still handle a goddamn rifle or not?" Colton snapped.

"They're gone, aren't they?" Sam asked. Colton could hear the tears in the woman's voice, but he had neither the time nor the patience to coddle her.

"Get in the back of the chamber. Don't come anywhere near this doorway again until I signal that everything is safe." He reached back and shoved her into the room. "Merritt. I need to know right now if you can—"

"Where are they?" Merritt asked.

Good. He hadn't frozen up.

"In the bottom of the crate under the GPR. Arm yourself and take up position between the doorway and the others. If anything manages to get through us, you're the last line of defense. And you'd better make every shot count."

If Merritt said something else, Colton didn't hear it. He focused on the lighted patch in front of him as he swept the barrel of his rifle across the tree line and listened for any sound to betray his adversary's intent. The sheeting rain tore through the glow and pounded the already muddy ground. Torchlight reflected from the expanding puddles and lit the front halves of the tall trees, throwing blankets of shadow behind them. A flash of lightning shimmered on the wet leaves before darkness again advanced with the rumble of thunder.

III

10:12 p.m.

Tasker led McMasters around the western edge of the clearing, careful not to stray into the light. The sentries hadn't split up as he had assumed they would, but that didn't faze him in the slightest. He adjusted his plan on the fly as he always did, and in the process of doing so, was struck by a bolt of inspiration. Rather than just killing two birds with one stone, he could kill all of them every bit as easily. It wouldn't be nearly as much fun as cornering those cowering inside the stone dwelling and executing them in front of each other, but in one swift stroke, the deed would be done and they would have the ruins all to themselves.

Bushes rustled behind him and something splashed in a puddle off in the jungle to his left. Their stalkers were growing more bold by the minute. Fortunately, his masterful solution ought to serve the dual purpose of scaring them off as well.

It was the most perfect plan ever devised. Too bad there would be no one left to share in his triumph when all was said and done, and he was staring out over the Caribbean from the balcony of his private villa.

He paused when they reached the back side of the palatial structure and signaled for McMasters to do the same. Other than the clamor of the rain and the stealthy movement in the trees, he heard nothing, no sign that their ruse had been detected.

With a nod, he guided McMasters over the mounds of rubble that had nearly been reclaimed by the earth to form a rugged hillside from which trees of all shapes and sizes grew. Had he not seen it from the front, he might never have suspected that anything manmade resided under his feet. Silently, they worked their way through the overgrowth until the light from the torches blazed from beyond the next row of trees, and then lowered themselves to their bellies and scuttled toward the edge.

Tasker locked stares with McMasters and pushed himself up just high enough to peer over the precipice. While he couldn't see the guards directly underneath him from that vantage point, at least he could confirm that neither of them had wandered away from their posts far enough that they could clearly see the jungle growing on the roof above them.

He eased back to his stomach, pressed his index finger to his lips, and craned his head to listen.

Faint voices drifted up from below. He couldn't make out their words, but he didn't have to either.

He turned back to McMasters and gave a single nod.

McMasters licked his lips and rolled over onto his back. He reached into the front pocket of his jacket, removed the object as they had discussed, and turned back over again. Holding it tightly in his fist, he pulled the pin with his opposite hand.

The grenade would shred the sentries and undoubtedly collapse the entire ancient structure.

They just needed to make sure that they weren't on top of it when it fell.

Bushes shivered to Tasker's right.

They weren't alone.

McMasters shoved himself to all fours, staying as low as he could, and crawled toward the edge. With the grenade in his right hand, he leaned out over the unsuspecting men below.

Colton watched the branches across the clearing slowly tremble back into place. Again, the forest fell deathly still.

"Where are they?" Sorenson whispered. "I can't see a blasted thing."

Colton could feel them all around him. The weight of unseen eyes made his skin crawl.

The creatures were smart, too smart to blindly charge out into the light. But they weren't passively waiting out there for their prey to make the first move either. They were the hunters, and the darkness was their ally. Colton sensed them surrounding the clearing, just out of sight in the protective embrace of the shrubs and shadows.

The noose was tightening, and soon—

He felt a gentle tap on his right shoulder and leapt away from the wall before the pebble that had fallen from the lip above him even hit the ground. Twisting in midair, he raised his weapon toward the roof of the building and squeezed the trigger.

Automatic gunfire chattered.

McMasters was thrown away from the edge and into the air. Geysers of blood trailed him as he flopped backward.

Tasker watched the arm holding the grenade go limp and the hand relax. The grenade tumbled through the underbrush toward the dark side of the building.

McMasters's body formed a rainbow arch, frozen in time by the strobe of a lightning strike. Dark shapes lunged out of the shrubs and attacked him in midair with a flurry of claws and teeth. Clothes tore and skin parted. A rain of blood patterned the mud, but Tasker only felt it spatter his legs as he propelled himself diagonally to his right. He barely managed to get his legs underneath him in time to launch himself over the front corner of the structure.

Light flashed behind him. With a clap of manmade thunder, the concussive blast hurled him out over the nothingness in a fiery cloud of shrapnel.

IV

10:18 p.m.

There was a muffled *whump* behind Sam. The ground shook and knocked her to her knees. Smoke and dust blasted through the gaps in the rock barricades to either side of her, filling the room with a chalky haze. She screamed, but couldn't even hear her own voice over what sounded like a freight train bearing down on her. The stones in the ceiling cracked and debris rained down. Rocks tumbled away from the barricades and fissures raced through the support columns, one of which buckled sideways and collapsed.

The entire building was coming down.

Merritt grabbed her hand and pulled her back to her feet. The rifle in his free hand clanked against the incendiary grenades he had clipped to his hip and the spare magazine he had jammed into his pocket.

"Get out of there!" Colton shouted from the doorway. "Now!"

She glanced back at Galen and Leo. They both struggled to stand on the shaking floor.

"Come on!" she shouted, jerking Leo to his feet. He latched onto Galen's arm and dragged him away from the rear wall.

From the edges of her peripheral vision, she saw that enough of the rubble had fallen from the barricades to create dark gaps toward the top, through which clouds of dust funneled. Dark shapes twisted and thrashed in an effort to force their way through.

Something struck her shoulder from above and drove her to the ground, wrenching her hand from Merritt's. She cried out and grabbed at the searing pain. More and more of the stone ceiling cracked away and fell around her.

A shadow passed through the swirling dust, grabbed her around the torso, and hauled her to her feet.

"Hurry!" Merritt shouted directly into her ear. He half-carried, half-dragged her through the collapsing chamber and into the night air, where the dust diffused into a golden fog. She couldn't even see the forest twenty feet away.

Merritt dropped her to her hands and knees in the mud. She coughed and retched into a fern before finding the strength to stand. Her legs trembled. Or was it the earth itself?

She turned toward the building. Shadows raced in her direction through the haze. She saw the vague outline of the trees above the roofline as they fell, canting sideways and toppling on the plummeting stones. A massive expulsion of dust billowed from the jumbled ruins.

"What's happening?" she screamed.

"There's no time," Colton snapped. "We're too exposed here. We have to find a more defensible position."

"Is everyone accounted for?" Merritt asked.

"I count six," Sorenson said. "Time to move."

"Who's that over there?" Leo asked. He pointed toward where a human shape was sprawled facedown in the mire a few yards away.

"I don't know," Colton said. The *skree* of a hawk pierced the night from the jungle to their left. It was quickly answered by another on the opposite side of the destroyed ruins. "But we're not sticking around long enough to find out. He can rot for all I care."

"They want us to run," Galen whispered. "Like field mice."

"I'll take the lead. Sorenson, you cover our asses. The rest of you, keep close together and stay right behind me."

"Where are we going?" Merritt asked.

"I can only think of one place where we'll have any chance of defending ourselves."

"Jesus," Merritt whispered.

"Move out," Colton said, and struck off to the west at a jog.

Sam hurried to catch up with him. Another shrill avian cry echoed through the darkness.

She turned toward the sound.

Even through the rain and dust, she could clearly see the undergrowth rustle in the wake of something that crashed through the brush in the same direction they were headed.

V

10:22 p.m.

Leo struggled to maintain his balance on the sloppy ground as they ran through a gamut of trees and stone ruins toward the sheer face of the mountain, the indifferent goliath that ruled the village from behind the storm clouds. The horrible shrieking sounds were all around them now. To either side of the path, dark forms hurtled through the jungle, slashing through the foliage.

Colton fired sporadic bursts ahead of them, while Sorenson did the same behind. Merritt shot at the shadows surrounding them.

They were all going to die. The reality of that thought cut through the fear and panic with dread certainty. They were all going to die, and it was his fault. The blame fell squarely on his shoulders. He had lied to them from the start in order to gain their assistance. Of course, he could never have imagined the truth in his wildest dreams, but it was his deception that had damned them. He had needed to know what happened to Hunter, for he had simply been unable to accept the loss of his son. The pain had been too great, the anger a physical entity trying to claw its way out through his skin from the inside. Maybe there had been a part of him that lusted after the fortune in gold as well. It was high time he admitted it. Dedicating its extraction to his son's legacy sounded altruistic and noble, but it had always been about the money in that regard, hadn't it? He needed something tangible to hold, something of great value, since he knew he would never again hold the son that in life had always taken a back seat to his global conquests. Only after the discovery of Hunter's body did he truly realize the extent of his failure as a father. There would never be an opportunity to apologize to his son for dragging him all around the world instead of allowing him a normal childhood, to tell him how pleased he was with his accomplishments, how proud he was of the man that Hunter had become.

And it was his guilt that would ultimately be responsible for all of their deaths now.

Muzzle flare strobed the darkness, bringing every shadow to life as the jungle closed in on them from the sides.

The crooked ceiba separated from the night ahead, beyond which the cold, dark maw of the tunnel loomed. Colton couldn't possibly be leading them in there, could he? Not after what they'd seen. Two men from Hunter's group had already been slain inside, and there was that tunnel that led right into the lair of the predators. It was suicide.

"We can't go in there!" he shouted over the rain.

Colton fired a fusillade of bullets past the tree and into the corridor, where they ricocheted from the stone floor and walls with a display of sparks.

"Colton! We can't—!"

"There's no other choice!" Colton snapped, rounding on him. His eyes were wide, his skin pale. Ribbons of water drained down his haggard face. "If we stay out here, we'll all be slaughtered. At least in there we have a fighting chance."

"It's completely dark in there. They'll be all over us the moment we step inside."

"Do you want to live through this or not?"

Leo could only nod as they reached the tree and pulled up short of the mouth of the tunnel.

"Then let me do my job," Colton said. He faced the opening and fired into the pitch black until his clip ran dry, then snapped another into place. "And who said anything about not having light?"

Leo glanced back to make sure that they were all together and advanced into the mountain behind Colton, who fired a burst every few steps. The barrel flashed and bullets pinged. He bumped into Colton from behind and was about to ask why they had stopped so suddenly when he heard a snap. A blinding light flared into being. A canister stood on the ground, firing a flume of concentrated light into the air above it. Molten liquid poured down the sides and puddled around the base. An incendiary grenade.

"We have to move quickly. This won't last very long," Colton said. He kicked the canister and sent it rolling down the tunnel ahead of them. It spat flames at the wall and trailed a path of magma. "It's burning at roughly four thousand degrees, so don't let even a single drop of that stuff touch you."

The distant light created shadows in the recesses to either side where the bodies were interred. One of the skeletal corpses had fallen from its perch and lay in a heap on the ground. They stepped around it and headed deeper into the earth. The glare was already starting to wane.

This was a very bad idea. They would never leave this ossuary alive.

Skree!

The sound echoed all around them, yet there was no denying its origin.

It had come from inside the mountain.

Directly ahead of them.

VI

10:26 p.m.

Merritt balked at the entrance to the underground warren. A piercing glow radiated from inside, turning Galen and Sam to silhouettes as they ducked out of the rain and into the stone passage. Sorenson backed into him from behind with the clamor of suppressive fire.

"Get in there!" Sorenson yelled.

Merritt could only stare at the fissure in the hillside. His legs had locked up and the remainder of his body was unresponsive. Even his voice failed him at first.

"I...I can't."

"We don't have time for this."

Sorenson jabbed him in the back with the butt of his rifle and he stumbled forward, barely able to maintain his balance. The screams of the dying filled his ears, while the scent of burned flesh lingered in his sinuses. His vision grew hazy from the smoke. Even the rain no longer touched him as in his mind he was a thousand miles away in a sun-baked landscape of sand.

He knew on a fundamental level that none of this was truly happening, but that understanding made it no less real. Fear had him in its grip, and there was absolutely nothing he could do to break free.

Sorenson prodded him with the rifle again, harder this time, driving him to his knees.

"Get in there or so help me, I'll leave you right here!"

Merritt peeled his dry tongue from the roof of his mouth to reply, but no words formed.

Sorenson jerked him back to his feet by his collar and shoved him forward into the mountain. Rather than speeding up, his heartbeat slowed and a sensation of warmth spread through his body like an anesthetic, numbing his hands and feet. He was shutting down, going into shock.

"Merritt," Sam said. He felt her cold, wet hands on his cheeks before he realized that she was standing directly in front of him.

"We need to keep moving. Do you understand? We can't stay here or whatever those things are will kill us. You can do this."

Flickering light limned her outline. He could barely see her features until she brought her face within inches of his.

"You can do this," she repeated. He drew confidence from her words, and her touch brought him slowly back to the here and now. "Just look into my eyes and place one foot in front of the other."

"They're right behind me," Sorenson said. He punctuated his statement with a barrage of gunfire back into the forest. "Either you get him moving or you're both on your own."

"Then go!" Sam shouted. She turned her attention back to Merritt and softened her tone. "Just listen to my voice and look into my eyes. There are very bad things out there and we need to hurry. I want you to focus on moving your legs and following me. I'm not going to leave you."

He couldn't risk slowing her down. She needed to get as far away from him as possible. He would never be able to forgive himself if anything happened to her.

"Go on," he said. "I'll be right behind you."

"You're a terrible liar."

Sorenson fired out of the egress again at the sound of a shrill hawk's cry.

Sam lowered her palms from his face and took him by the hands. She pulled him gently at first, then more insistently. He stumbled after her, eyes locked on hers, the rifle he had slung over his neck clattering against his chest. The smoke remained, but instead of reeking of scorched skin, it smelled of harsh chemicals. The wails of the wounded faded to the sounds of breathing and shuffling footsteps. Feeling returned to his appendages with each step, and the situation resolved from the fugue. He gave Sam's hands a solid squeeze.

"Thank you," he whispered.

Her reply was drowned out by the report of gunfire, both from ahead and behind.

She released his right hand and turned so that she could drag him by his left.

The ruckus of rain metamorphosed into the drone of flies as they fled the outside world.

Merritt gripped the assault rifle in his right hand. It scared him how perfectly it still fit.

Another avian cry from behind.

Sorenson unleashed a short spat of bullets, discarded the spent clip, and snapped another home.

The glow down the tunnel ahead of Sam wavered and started to fade.

She tripped on something and fell forward. Her hand slipped out of his.

In the dying light, he saw a jumble of broken bones on the ground. Sam pinwheeled her arms for balance. Movement drew his eye to the recessed alcove in the wall to his right.

A pair of rheumy eyes set into a scaled forehead turned in his direction. A large, feathered body was crammed into the small space where the remains had once been. It unfurled its coiled body in serpentine fashion.

The incendiary grenade fizzled and died.

Blackness flooded the corridor with a *skree* that was so close Merritt could smell the rotting meat on the creature's breath.

VII

10:28 p.m.

Consciousness hit Tasker like a runaway train, bringing with it pain beyond anything he had ever experienced. His entire back side felt as though it had been fried on a griddle. He drew a sharp intake of breath and inhaled dirty water through his mouth and nose, which induced a coughing spasm that only filled his throat with blood and intensified the agony. Smoke and dust swirled around him. The rain slapped his left cheek. He tried to open his eyes, but only the left responded. The right was pressed into the ground and packed with mud. The clearing shifted in and out of focus through the small gap beneath his swollen eyelid.

He heard what sounded like an eagle's cry as it circled above him, only the sound had come from much lower to the ground, not far to his right. With the revelation of what had made the sound, the memories assaulted him.

If he didn't get the hell out of there right now, he was a dead man.

He tried to push himself up, but his arms and legs were unresponsive. Were it not for the pain, he might have suspected he'd been separated from them in the blast. He could see the back of his left hand and forearm. Both were soaked with blood. His jacket sleeve was in tatters, and wooden and metallic slivers alike stood from the exposed skin. Shrapnel. He'd been fortunate to have been wearing his backpack or his thorax would have become a pincushion. As it was, he must have broken at least one rib and punctured a lung for there to be so much blood in his mouth.

The shriek of another bird seared the night. But they weren't birds, were they? He had glimpsed them when they exploded from the bushes and attacked McMasters. Blurs of feathers and claws, the living embodiment of the desiccated remains in the bundle he had ripped open in the cliff-side tomb. They had attacked with the kind of pure savagery that he'd only witnessed in sharks during a feeding frenzy.

There would be no surviving another encounter. He needed to drag his broken body out of there right this very second.

How long had he been unconscious? Where were Gearhardt and his party? For all he knew, they could have led the creatures away from him. He drew comfort from that thought, but only for a moment.

He heard a soft splash and a slurp of mud. A shadow fell across him from out of his direct line of sight.

Tasker held his breath and listened.

Another squishing sound from behind him and to the left.

He released a stale exhalation and breathed shallowly, silently.

Something nudged his backpack, then the left side of his ribcage. And still he could only see the shadow.

More sloppy footsteps. One. Then another.

Every fiber of his being screamed for him to shove to his feet and sprint for his life, but he knew in his current weakened state that he didn't have a prayer of outrunning it.

Something nuzzled his shoulder, lifting him slightly from the muck, then dropping him back down.

He felt warm breath on his ear a split-second before a shrill cry nearly pierced his eardrum. A scream threatened to burst from his chest. He managed to contain it and remained as still as he could.

Why hadn't it attacked yet?

Pressure behind his left ear, forcing his face deeper into the mud. He could barely breathe through his left nostril and the corner of his mouth.

Two more stealthy footsteps. Closer.

A face lowered into view. Too close. Broad nostrils on an elongated snout. Scaled lips lined with interlocking rows of sharp teeth. It bumped him in the forehead with its chin.

Its breath reeked of death and decay, its scaled skin of rot and fecal matter.

It froze when another *skree* sounded from the jungle behind him.

In one swift motion, it was running. Scaled gray legs flashed past, then a long, feathered tail.

Tasker lay still, waiting for it to return.

More cries echoed through the forest, only farther away now.

He finally allowed himself to blink.
There was no sound.
No movement.
Why was he still alive?

VIII

10:32 p.m.

Sam reached back for Merritt's hand as her feet tangled in the partially-articulated mess of bones. Over her shoulder, she saw him grab for her hand too late. Beside him, movement from the wall. Something large that until that moment had held perfectly still. It turned toward Merritt with the blunted snout of a caiman and a crown of feathers that rose to erection like the spines on an iguana's back.

The light died. Darkness swallowed her as she fell to the ground and landed squarely on her shoulder.

A loud avian cry filled the tunnel.

She rolled onto her back in time to see the repeated flash of muzzle flare. In the strobing light, she witnessed snippets of chaos. A long neck, bristled with feathers, stretching out of the enclave. Mouth like a crocodile's, opening wide. Dull eyes that glinted with golden rings. Slender, curled fingers with sharp claws. It jerked in twitching motions as the bullets pounded its scaled breast.

Even over the deafening reports, she heard it scream.

The rifle's carbine whirred long after the clip ran dry.

Hissing.

Claws scrabbling against stone.

Finally, silence.

Merritt slapped another clip into the SCAR.

Sam extricated her feet from the tangle of body parts and started to cry.

"Are you all right?" Merritt asked. His voice positively trembled.

She couldn't find her voice, and nodded even though he couldn't see her. His hand found hers in the pitch black.

"Keep moving!" Sorenson shouted from the darkness. There was a thumping sound as he stumbled into the crumpled carcass on the ground. "They're right behind us!"

Another shriek echoed from the direction of the outside world.

Sorenson turned toward the sound and fired.

Merritt tugged on her hand, urging her deeper into the mountain.

Light blossomed ahead, blinding after the absolute darkness.

The tunnel framed silhouettes much farther ahead than she had expected. The floor sloped downward and became uneven. She couldn't bring herself to look to either side as they descended. The skulls of the ancient dead leered at her from the walls, but worse still would be meeting the reptilian stare of another one of those creatures.

How long had the one Merritt killed been hiding in that recess? Had it watched the others pass while waiting for the stragglers, or had it somehow slipped past them in the shadows?

The corridor ended and they stepped out into the cavern where the others had already gathered. Blazing light flumed from another incendiary grenade where it rested against the far wall. Colton and Leo wore hard hats with the spotlights turned on, while Galen paced nervously in the middle of the room.

Colton took up post at the mouth of the tunnel at the back of the cavern. The light barely penetrated the dark channel.

A distant *skree*.

The acoustics of the cavern made it impossible to pinpoint the direction from which it originated.

"I can't hold them off forever!" Sorenson yelled. He backed into the room, firing in indiscriminate bursts.

Sam looked past him into the tunnel. What little light reached into the orifice swirled with cordite smoke. The darkness beyond churned as though a living entity.

They were out there, at the limit of the fading flare's reach.

Waiting.

Nails clacked on bare stone.

The shuffling sound of bodies jostling each other in the close confines.

Muffled grunts.

The incendiary grenade fizzled and hissed. The corona of light beat a hasty retreat.

Sorenson shot again into the tunnel and something shrieked.

Merritt removed his hand from hers to steady his rifle, and pointed it past Sorenson toward where flashes of iridescent green tested the limit of the glare.

The glow dimmed, and, with a sizzle, the light extinguished.
A predatory *skree* raised the hackles on her arms.
The shadows advanced with the clamor of talons.

Chapter Twelve

I

Andes Mountains, Peru
October 30th
10:36 p.m. PET

Merritt unsnapped the canister from where he had clipped it to his belt, pulled the pin, and tossed it to his left. Gunfire echoed from directly to his right, where Sorenson shot blindly into the tunnel. Shrieks and high-pitched cries erupted from the darkness.

"I can't see a damn thing!" Sorenson shouted.

Chemical fire spouted from the incendiary grenade. The sudden influx of light stained Merritt's vision red. He raised his rifle and fired into the dark mouth of the channel. When his sight finally cleared, he unconsciously retreated a step. He was completely unprepared for what he saw.

Blood poured down the stone floor from the tunnel. Feathers filled the air. Hisses and squeals rose over the tumult of gunfire as bodies fought for position amid the carcasses of their brethren. One creature hopped up on the flank of a twitching mass of scales and feathers, lowered its head toward the ground, and released a savage *skree* from a mouth opened wide enough to swallow a bowling ball. Sharp teeth glinted, and quills stood straight up from its long neck.

They were going to be massacred inside this mountain.

"Fall back!" Colton shouted from behind him. Sam tugged at his jacket.

He stumbled away from the tunnel, firing every step of the way.

The creature hopped down from the corpse and crouched even closer to the ground. A bullet ricocheted in front of it, and in a blur of motion, feathered shapes exploded from the opening.

Sorenson bellowed and shot into their ranks, but they were already upon him. The man's battle cry turned to screams of pain. A hand grabbed Merritt by the collar and jerked him in reverse. He whirled to see Sam already running toward the smaller tunnel at the rear of the chamber, where Colton stood beside the entrance, firing back into the room while the others ducked past him into the darkness.

Merritt sprinted after them and raced into the thin crevice. The lamp affixed to Leo's helmet bounced and jittered ahead, highlighting random sections of the bare rock wall. Merritt glanced back and saw Colton spray a stream of bullets into the chamber, then duck into the corridor behind him.

Sorenson's screams were drowned out by avian cries.

"Go!" Colton shouted, shoving him deeper into the mountain. Colton's headlamp cast strange, elongated shadows from behind Merritt that made the shrinking tunnel appear to bend, twist, and turn.

Leo's weak beam grew larger and larger on the stone wall ahead of them. Merritt's heart nearly stopped at the realization that they were racing into a dead end, but then the light lowered to the floor and faded to a candle's glow.

At the end of the passage, Sam crawled through a tiny hole rimed by Leo's light. The passage couldn't have been larger than a sewer pipe. Her feet disappeared as she wriggled out of sight.

He stopped and stared at the diminutive orifice. Colton's lamp made his massive shadow dance on the wall.

"Get in there, for Christ's sake!" Colton yelled. He spun and shot into the tunnel behind him.

There were more hawk-like shrieks and the rapid clatter of talons on granite.

Merritt slid the rifle into the hole and dove in after it. He pushed it in front of him and squirmed as fast as he could through the claustrophobic tube toward the pale yellow aura ahead.

Behind him, the report of gunfire ceased, and was replaced by the scraping sound of Colton scrabbling into the tunnel.

There was no longer anyone guarding their rear.

II

10:39 p.m.

Leo fell out of the tunnel onto a crusted heap of feces and struggled to his feet. He turned his head to sweep the lamp from one side of the cavern to the other. It barely penetrated the darkness and died before reaching the far wall. This was as far as they had explored. Lord only knew what lay beyond. There was no going back, however, so their only option was to take their chances with the unknown.

He turned, grabbed Galen by the upper arm, and hauled him out of the passage. The man fell to all fours and let out a meek sob.

"Hurry!" Leo called to Sam. The moment she was within reach, he dragged her into the cavern. He removed the helmet from his head and shoved it against her chest. "Put this on and see if you can find a way out of here."

She donned it, and when she turned away, he watched the beam on the other miner's helmet slowly brighten from deep within the earthen tube as it neared.

Merritt's rifle clattered across the stone and tumbled out onto the ground. The pilot followed. Leo helped him to his feet, then returned to the hole. Now that Merritt wasn't blocking the light, he could clearly see Colton crawling toward him. Hand over hand. The lamp on his forehead swayed with the exertion, his face a wash of shadow behind the glare. He shoved his rifle ahead of him as Merritt had done.

"Get the others moving!" Colton shouted. "I can hear them right behind—"

The light grew smaller as Colton slid quickly backward.

Leo lunged inside and grabbed for Colton's hand. The two men locked wrists. He tried to gain leverage with his knees, but he wasn't fast enough.

Colton cried out as he was again jerked from behind, dragging Leo deeper into the tunnel with him. Leo felt pressure on his ankles. Someone was trying to drag him back out.

The rifle lay on the ground between his face and Colton's. He could see his old friend's mouth, bared teeth shimmering with blood.

There was another sharp tug and Colton roared in agony. Leo's arm was strained to the point that any more pressure would dislocate his shoulder. Behind him, Merritt shouted for him to hold on and pulled on his legs.

He heard the cracking sound of breaking bone, and Colton released his wrist.

"Let me go," Colton said.

Another jerk pulled Colton away, but Leo grabbed his wrist again.

"You go," Leo said, "I go."

There was a sharp *skree* from beyond Colton's prone form.

"Listen to me, damn it!" Colton snapped. Bloody spittle dotted Leo's face. Another snap of bone and Colton winced. "Let. Me. Go."

Leo groaned as he was stretched to his physical limit. It felt as though his ribs were pulling apart and his arm was about to be yanked right off. He strained to maintain his grasp.

The force working against Colton increased.

One by one, Leo's fingers started to slip.

"I'm sorry," he whispered. His eyes met Colton's through the shadows and an understanding passed between them. Blood drained from the corners of Colton's mouth. The pain contorted his features.

A loud crack of breaking bone sounded like a gunshot.

Sloppy tearing sounds.

"You have ten seconds," Colton rasped with what little voice remained.

His hand was wrenched away. Leo was helpless but to watch as Colton was dragged in the opposite direction. The light on his helmet grew smaller and smaller. A scream trailed him into the darkness.

Leo didn't stick around to watch. He grabbed Colton's rifle and frantically wiggled back out of the hole.

There was no time to waste.

The clock was ticking.

III

10:42 p.m.

The pain was beyond anything he had ever imagined. Once those jaws had clamped down on his lower leg, no amount of thrashing or jerking could free it. Teeth like hacksaws had slashed right through his skin and muscle to find purchase on bone, and ground down with almost hydraulic force. His tibia and fibula had both snapped mid-shaft. He had no idea if his foot and ankle were even still attached. A flood of blood left his body as the creature twisted and tugged, drawing him back toward the cavern where the rest of the screeching flock waited.

Even if he managed to extricate his shattered leg from its grip, he would bleed to death long before reaching help. He was a goner and he knew it. All that remained was to die. The only thing now within his control was how painful that death would be. The hell if he was going to allow himself to be dismembered like all of the others. He was going out on his terms, not theirs.

And he was going out with a bang.

The distant egress of the tunnel faded to a pinprick of dim light beyond his outstretched arms. His fingers clawed for traction on the smooth rock, yet they were unable to slow him. The skin tore from his fingertips and his nails bent backward and peeled away. The ground was slick with his blood.

It was now or never.

In one swift motion, he flopped over onto his back. The pressure on his lower leg abated as the bottom half tore away in the mouth of the predator. He screamed in agony and pawed at his jacket pocket until his hand wrapped around the smooth, round object.

Blood gushed unimpeded from his ragged stump.

The respite was brief. Jaws clamped around his opposite calf and pulled him again in reverse.

He felt the metallic ball of the grenade in his left hand and drew a measure of comfort from its awesome power. With his right hand, he pulled the pin, and cradled death to his bosom.

Consciousness fled with his lifeblood. His head felt light, detached.

The sound of the shrieking creatures grew louder by the second.

His tibia snapped with the crack of a bullwhip.

He prayed the others would make good use of the time his life afforded them, because the whole blasted mountain was about to come down on their heads.

Colton slid out of the end of the tube into a living blackness filled with avian cries.

Talons impaled his chest.

Teeth sawed into his abdomen, his groin.

He arched his back and opened his mouth for one final scream—

IV

10:44 p.m.

The ground shuddered under Sam's feet. She lost her balance and collapsed to her knees. Chunks of stone broke loose from the ceiling with the sound of thunder and crashed to the ground all around her. One rock clipped her hip and she cried out in pain. The startled bats swirled chaotically before coalescing into a single mass of whistling leather wings and swarming over her head toward the wall in front of her. Until that very moment, she had believed it to be solid. She followed their exodus through tear-blurred eyes, to where the beam on her helmet illuminated a thin fissure in the stone.

Once more, the earth trembled, and then stilled. The rumbling noise above her faded to the clatter of pebbles raining from the roof.

She rose and cried out. Her hip throbbed, but at least she could still wiggle her toes and the joint felt functional enough.

Merritt's voice materialized from the darkness and the settling dust. "Is everyone okay?"

Galen whimpered that he was, however uncertainly.

"We need to keep moving," Leo said. His voice had hardened to project a note of command. "The explosion will only buy us so much time. If there's a way out of here, we'd better find it right now."

"It's directly ahead of me," Sam said.

"Then quit screwing around and get going." She caught a glimpse of his face before she turned back toward the now silent passage. Were those tears shimmering on his cheeks?

She advanced into the crevice and focused on the diffuse beam of light. The walls were so close they rubbed against her shoulders, eliciting a constant wave of pain from her injured right. Alternately turning her head from side to side, she forced back the shadows while she navigated the rubble underfoot. They were lucky the fissure hadn't totally collapsed during the quake. Had Leo said 'explosion'? And where was Colton?

Fifteen yards later, the crack opened into a large cavern. The faint grumble of the waterfall called to her from ahead. She listened for the sounds of the bats up against the ceiling, but they must have continued past this chamber. The headlamp illuminated only a churning cloud of dust.

She hurried forward and had to clap her hand over her mouth and nose when the smell struck her. It didn't reek of feces as the last cavern had, but of the more repulsive, fresh stench of decomposition. She imagined rotting carcasses strewn across the ground in various states of consumption and decay.

The drone of flies provided an unremitting, dull buzz.

"Keep going," Leo said. He shoved her into the cavern from behind. She felt hands on her head as Leo relieved her of the helmet and donned it himself. "Lord only knows how much of a head start Colton bought us."

"Where *is* Colton?" she asked.

Leo didn't answer. Instead, he strode forward into the haze.

There was a snap and a hiss behind her, then the metallic clamor of a canister bounding across the uneven floor into the room ahead of her. Merritt's hand found hers as a fierce red glare blossomed from the incendiary grenade.

"That's my last one," he whispered, and pulled her toward it.

A shadow passed through her peripheral vision to her right. The crimson glow highlighted Galen's features and sparkled from the tears on his face. He started to jog in an attempt to catch up with Leo, who was already nearly twenty feet ahead of them.

"Hold on to my belt and stay behind me," Merritt said, releasing her hand so he could seat the rifle against his shoulder.

The ground was covered with a mat of feathers, upon which the dust accumulated like snow. She saw the hint of a ribcage to her right. Sharply broken bones stood at odd angles from the feathers, over the top of which she recognized the crowns of skulls and disarticulated skeletal remains of all kinds, human and animal alike, some fresh and glistening with blood, others older and aged to a dull brown. Something crunched under her left foot and she looked down. A thin, arched section of what looked like grayish-blue plastic had cracked beneath her weight almost like an—

"Eggshell," she whispered. She turned to her right and noticed a cupped structure composed of dry branches, leaves, and reeds.

The bowl of the nest brimmed with downy feathers and the shattered remnants of countless hatched generations.

There was a shuffling sound outside of the light's reach.

Sam stifled a scream.

They weren't alone.

Merritt stiffened at the sound and slowed his progress. He turned his rifle toward its origin.

More rustling noises from the other side of them, which slowly melted away beneath the rising rumble of the waterfall.

They had to hurry, but they could only advance so quickly. They could no longer hear the motion around them, yet still Sam could sense predatory stares upon her from beyond the diminishing glare of the incendiary grenade, which fizzled and sparkled in its death throes. A ring of feathers burned around it. The meek flames were more smoke than fire, and would only last so long.

Leo passed the canister and fired into the blackness in front of him. As the intense flare dwindled, the light on his helmet became more apparent. The pale yellow beam spotlighted the mouth of a stone tunnel.

A gust of cool air that smelled of ozone caressed Sam's face. She nearly sobbed at the realization that they had to be close to the outside world.

The sound of the waterfall grew to a roar that made the rock thrum beneath her feet. If they could just reach the river, she knew it would eventually lead them to safety. And they were so close now...

"I can see the opening!" Leo called back to them. The darkness swallowed his headlamp to weak aura. "We're right behind the waterfall. I can even see—"

An avian *skree* cut his words short.

A rush of shadows eclipsed Leo's silhouette. The helmet flew from his head and clattered against the stone wall. It winked once, then extinguished.

More shrieking, and beneath it, Leo's horrible screams.

The incendiary grenade issued a long hiss, a prelude to its demise.

Only the diminutive flames crackled from the mess of feathers.

A *skree* from ahead was answered by another to her right.

Merritt fired toward the sound and bullets pinged from bare rock.

The carbine whirred. His finger clicked on the trigger to no avail.

Out of ammunition.

His hand searched for hers and squeezed it tightly.

She knew exactly what was about to happen, and prayed it would be swift.

V

10:52 p.m.

Galen had nearly caught up with Leo, spurred by the grumble of the waterfall and the flow of fresh air, when the hawk-like scream caused him to freeze in place. He remembered seeing the mouth of the cave behind the falls and had been in the process of trying to mentally recreate the image of the thin ledge that led to it from the edge of the fortress when the creatures materialized from the darkness at a sprint and swarmed over Leo. They had leaped with outstretched legs, clawed toes raised in preparation of impaling meat, slender arms reaching. Feathers flared from their elbows in the vestiges of wings. Mouths had opened and teeth had glistened. He had turned to run back toward the cavern before Leo started to scream.

And then the darkness had swallowed him. There had been shrieks and gunfire. And now nothing but the crackle of the small flames and the buzz of flies.

They had been so close. So close…

He ran right into Merritt and sent them both sprawling to the ground. Merritt's rifle clattered away from them.

From behind him, he heard bones snap and flesh rip. The choking sounds of the creatures tossing back straps of muscle and swallowing them down into their gullets.

Merritt tried to shove out from beneath him, but Galen used all of his strength to hold the man down.

"Stay still!" he whispered directly into Merritt's face.

His mind raced with the possibilities. They would never be able run fast enough to evade the raptors. And even if they managed to get a decent head start while the creatures consumed Leo's flesh, he couldn't remember seeing anywhere to hide. The explosion had collapsed their only means of retreat, and escape meant passing directly through the flock.

He thought of the creatures' aversion to bright light. It overwhelmed their visual senses, which were enhanced by retinal reflectors that provided acute night vision by which to hunt.

They were shrouded in darkness, which gave the predators every advantage.

He remembered their shrieks, like those of a circling bird of prey, meant to flush their targets from the brush, to instill the panic that would trigger their flight instincts.

The creatures required the element of motion to hone in for the kill.

He remembered the victims all over the ground in various states of slaughter and decomposition. Unlike carrion birds, the raptors didn't eat the flesh of the dead. Did that imply a sense of smell? Taste? Or did it once again play into their necessity for movement?

Thus far, they had only attacked Galen's party one at a time, or as a pair separated from the group. Was there some sort of pack or flock mentality at work? Did they lie in wait to surround their prey and overwhelm it with superior numbers?

The jaguar had been ambushed and run down in the clearing.

The skeletal remains littered throughout the ruins suggested the same had happened to the former occupants of the fortress.

What would happen if they simply didn't run and tried to hide in plain sight?

Were these the neuquenraptors they had recently exhumed as fossils in Argentina? If so, it was speculated that dinosaurs, especially prehistoric, bipedal raptor species, relied almost exclusively on their senses of sight and hearing.

Another shrill scream from perhaps a dozen feet away in the darkness.

There was no more time.

Either they gambled that he understood the nature of the creatures, or they made a mad dash for the outside world and hoped that the monsters wouldn't be able to butcher all of them at once.

And that was a risk none of them could afford to take.

"Listen to me!" he whispered to Merritt. An avian cry echoed through the cavern. "The creatures...they can't see us if we don't move. Their vision is motion-based. They're like modern birds of prey in that sense. That's why they emit those shrill screams. To force their prey to run. Think about it! All of the remains we've encountered, from the jaguar to the humans, have indicated that

they were attacked while running or trying to seek cover. And
didn't you notice that they don't completely consume the dead?
Our only option is to lie still and pray they pass us by."

"And what if you're wrong?" Merritt whispered.

A shrill scream answered for him.

"You'll just have to trust that I know what I'm talking about."

Galen locked stares with Merritt in the dwindling firelight for
a long moment, then slowly rolled off of him. He half-expected
Merritt to immediately leap to his feet and make a break for it, but
the pilot merely stared up into the stalactite-riddled ceiling.

Another horrific screech. The sounds of cracking bones and
tearing flesh faded, leaving only the muffled grumble of the
waterfall and the drone of flies.

Galen flattened to his back and began piling the feathers from
the ground onto his legs and torso. He scattered them over his face
so that he could barely see through them and thrust his arms down
into the centuries of accumulation.

He felt insects crawling all over his skin beneath his clothing.
They started to bite almost instantaneously.

Bird mites.

Motionless, he awaited his fate.

There was one thing that he hadn't considered. Even if his
idea worked, they were still right in the middle of the raptors'
nesting chamber.

How were they supposed to get out?

VI

10:56 p.m.

Sam's eyes widened in horror as Merritt hurriedly explained Galen's plan. Were they out of their minds? She couldn't fathom the possibility that these evolutionary aberrations hunted solely with their eyes. But what were their other alternatives? She raced through them in her mind, playing out scenarios that all ended with violent and painful deaths.

Without making a conscious decision to do so, she slowly crouched beside Merritt and lay down on her back. In the weak glow, she watched Galen heap feathers over his supine form, and, with trembling hands, began to do the same. The feathers reeked of age and death, and the tiny insects that lived within them made her skin crawl.

There was a sharp cry, then another from off to her right.

Merritt's hand closed over hers under the feathers. She squeezed it for dear life.

Her heart pounded, and she was sure her chest rose and fell like a billows. She had to focus to silence her panicked breathing and slow her respirations, while she wanted nothing more than to scream.

Another *skree*.

Closer.

The feathers covering her face constricted her vision. She could see the small flames burning only five feet away. They advanced steadily outward as they consumed the feathers, producing a rich black smoke that singed her nostrils and stank of charnel. Only Merritt's eye was visible through the mound beside her. Everything else was either darkness or shadow.

A high-pitched shriek.

Mere feet away.

Every fiber of her being cried out for her to lunge to her feet and run away as fast as she could.

Soft rustling sounds above her head. More to either side.

A shadow eclipsed the glow of the fire.

Her breath caught in her throat.

A thin leg emerged from the edge of her vision. Three long scaled toes. The outer two hung limply, while the inside digit was curved upward to support a sharp, hooked claw the size of her middle finger. They flattened to the floor, save the one bearing the elevated claw, which tapped eagerly. The leg bent backward at the knee, where the slick scales gave way to feathers. Its smooth belly was covered with larger, broader scales reminiscent of those on the soft underside of an alligator, and framed to either side by a fringe of iridescent green and brown feathers. Another step, and she saw its long tail, held parallel to the ground, covered with feathers that hung downward as though parted along its spine. A twig-like arm with longer feathers, which appeared as though they had been draped from the skinny elbow like moss from a bough, reached forward a heartbeat before the creature lowered its head to the ground. Its long neck wavered from side to side in a slithering motion while its head stayed still. Snaggled teeth nestled together on the outside of the scaled lips of a blunt snout. A crown of quills grew over its cranium from a widow's peak between filmy eyes that shimmered with firelight. It had to be nearly six feet long from its finely-scaled nostrils to the tip of its tail. Its jaws snapped open nearly vertically and she glimpsed a pointed gray tongue that trilled when it released a deafening *skree*.

She pinched her eyes shut and felt spittle on her face. The thing's breath reeked of a slaughterhouse floor, of meat, red and wet...of what she recognized with a start to be Leo.

The cry ended and it nudged her head with its snout. She had to bite her lip to contain a scream.

This wasn't going to work.

She held her breath and prayed to any god that might be listening.

Feathers rustled and a toe brushed against her cheek. The raptor stood nearly directly on top of her.

A whistle of air preceded the strike. Its foot slashed at her chest. Clothing and skin ripped. She felt the sting of the wound and a trickle of blood rolling down her side from the laceration beneath her left clavicle.

It took every ounce of her concentration to keep from screaming. She squeezed Merritt's hand so hard her fingernails gouged into his skin.

The creature leaned in again and huffed a gust of foul breath onto her face that blew away most of the feathers. Its jaws snapped wide and it cried out again. A wash of saliva slapped onto her closed eyes and trailed over her cheeks, thick with chewed meat that slid through the fluid like slugs.

It recoiled and slashed at her again with its hind leg. The nails sliced through her upper arm over the biceps. Another unheralded strike, and blood flowed from her chest, just above her right breast.

The pain was more than she could bear.

More and more footsteps approached. She felt weight on her right arm before another talon clawed into her shoulder.

Merritt's hand tightened over hers. His blood spiraled around his wrist and into the union of their palms.

Another wicked slash, and pain bloomed from a gash on her right thigh.

Her thoughts turned to the extant Chachapoya in the valley below. The black-painted men whose bodies were so heavily scarred, as though they'd been attacked with straight razors. She had thought the scarring was ritualistic, but it wasn't, was it?

This was how they survived.

Another slice across her lower left leg.

Tears flowed freely from her eyes, and somehow she managed to bite back a whimper of agony.

The creatures shrieked all around them now. They appeared to be feeding upon one another, growing louder and more frantic.

Claws slashed, filling the air with a mist of blood.

She no longer prayed for escape, but for an end to the mounting pain, knowing that all she had to do to make it stop was scream.

VII

11:00 p.m.

Tasker swayed on his feet, trying to maintain his equilibrium. Every inch of his body hurt. He felt like a porcupine with the sheer amount of shrapnel standing from his back. Fractured ribs prodded at his innards, and he was certain that his left wrist was shattered. It was barely functional enough to balance the barrel of his rifle on it. So far, he had already spit out two teeth, and blood dripped through the tatter of his lower lip and over his chin.

He sloshed through the mud, out of the wash of blazing light and into the darkness that clung to the ruins.

Where the hell had they all gone? There had been dozens of the creatures surrounding that small clearing, and now there was no sign of them anywhere. Not a single shivering branch or the sound of stealthy tread. No sucking sound of footsteps in the mud or rustling from the underbrush. Only the patter of rain on the canopy and the standing water. And the occasional distant cry of a hawk.

He had felt the ground tremble and heard the muffled *whump* of an explosion inside the mountain several minutes ago. Had that taken care of the creatures for him? Was his prey now entombed under tons of rock right along with them? Did he now have the ruins all to himself? He couldn't be so naïve as to assume that was the case, but for the time being, he did appear to be completely alone. Perhaps his best option for now was to simply gather as much treasure as he could carry and get his ass out of there in case the predators returned. Granted, the nature of his injuries would limit the amount he could haul out of here, but since there was no longer anyone with whom to divide his take, he wouldn't need that much anyway. A couple more headdresses like the first in conjunction with the massive golden skull in the cave on the cliff would make him a very rich man.

Right now, the priority had to be saving his own skin, but he'd be damned if he came all this way for nothing.

Limping around trees and stumbling through shrubs and curtains of vines, he scoured the crumbled stone dwellings for the glimmer of precious metals. There were plenty of ancient utensils, potsherds, and common tattered textiles. Skeletons were strewn everywhere, partially reclaimed by the earth, left to rot where they fell. He encountered broken bows and spears, even a few rusted machetes and outdated firearms that had no business here, but thus far no—

"Gold," he whispered. A flash of lightning glinted from an arch of metal that peeked out of a mound of mud. He sloshed toward it and carefully exhumed it from the sludge. A brown skull stared back up at him, jaw unhinged, teeth broken. The man had been wearing the headdress when he was killed. The remnants of the torn leather bindings curled away from his cracked temporal bones.

It was about freaking time.

Tasker slipped out of his pack and tied the relic to one of its straps. When he shouldered it again, the treasure hung against his rear end. The added weight of a million dollars somehow made his burden seem lighter.

The thunderous sound of the waterfall grew louder as he trudged northward, inspecting the rubble of the huts for more loot. If everything fell into place, he would have enough treasure by the time he reached the fallen fortification, and he would simply be able to find the path and leave the ruins behind. Unlike the others, he was willing to take his chances with fording the rapids.

All that he had to do from there was keep himself alive long enough to reach civilization and the future of luxury that awaited him.

A rustling sound was swallowed by a peal of thunder.

He turned to his right toward the source. The trees were still. Swollen raindrops dripped from the upper canopy. He scrutinized the area for several moments, waiting for a repeat occurrence, before finally resuming his task, wary of even the slightest sound. For a second, he had allowed himself to be distracted by the gold.

The clapping sound of the rain and his slapping footsteps were too loud in his own ears.

A silhouette darted through the trees at the edge of his peripheral vision. When he turned, nothing was there. No vines jostled or branches swayed, but he was certain he had seen something.

Through the jungle and the mist, he could barely discern the black lip of the outer wall and the white spray of the waterfall beyond. He was nearing the point where he would have to make a decision. The last thing he wanted was to have to double back into the fortress. The sooner he was safely descending the mountain, the better.

His toe snagged on something under the mud and he fell to all fours. He expected to look back and see a snarl of roots, but instead, discovered something metallic with long, bent appendages shaped like feathers. With a smile, he smeared the mud from another golden headdress. A bent knee stood from the ground to the side to mark where its former owner decomposed. He tied the second headdress to his pack with the first. That was going to have to be enough. Add in the golden skull and the money from his Asian buyer, and he was looking at four million dollars minimum, several times what he would make in his lifetime in the service, and more than enough to disappear forever.

Shadows shifted on the opposite side of the path.

Again, when he focused on that section of the forest, there was no sign of anything out of the ordinary.

Time to move.

He no longer actively searched for priceless artifacts as he strode forward, sighting the jungle and the path ahead down the barrel of his rifle, finger poised on the trigger. The clip was nearly full, and he had three more in his bag.

The overgrowth abruptly ended at the obsidian wall. Only the most ambitious lianas and roots had found a way over and climbed down the sheer face of stacked rocks.

While he picked his way over the rubble, he would be uncomfortably exposed. The cloud trapped in the valley would obscure his progress to some degree, but there was no cover behind which to hide. He was going to have to move quickly and cautiously.

VIII

11:03 p.m.

The pain was excruciating. Galen felt as though he were being flayed alive. Talons struck from every conceivable angle, slashing his arms, legs, chest, and face. His skin was wet with blood, but so far most of the cuts were superficial. There was one on his thigh he suspected might be half an inch deep, and another on the top of his head where a section of the scalp had surely peeled away, yet he was still alive. And that was the only thing that mattered. As long as he didn't bleed to death first, the wounds would eventually heal. Surely the creatures would tire or lose interest soon enough.

He tried to distract his mind from the exquisite agony. They were truly an amazing species, the primitive ancestors of modern birds of prey as the evolutionary scholars believed. Feet similar to those of a vulture, with a massive hooked claw, not for tearing, but for impaling, to hold its prey still while it attacked with powerful jaws and sharp teeth. A long tail with what he assumed to be a rudimentary system of vertebrae from which retrices, the feathers that served the function of rudders in modern birds, grew to stabilize the body so it could run low to the ground. Vestigial wings with essentially useless fingers like those of a bat that appeared incapable of grasping anything with sufficient force nor strong enough to bear the disproportionately large body aloft. A combination of reptilian scales and avian feathers, which one day would supersede their less elaborate forebears. A slender, serpentine neck that offered the lateral motion of a sidewinder. The night vision and acuity of an owl. Even the way it ate intimated an avian digestive tract and gullet. They were astounding, but what surprised him most was their startling level of intelligence. No predatory birds hunted in packs, nor did they understand the potential for their prey to play possum, let alone to test them in such a vicious way that encouraged movement. Perhaps the subtle rise and fall of their chests had betrayed them, and the creatures, these neuquenraptors, weren't about to eat anything that they feared might be dying by some means other than by their teeth. It was the natural order of the wild.

His leg began to tremble with the pain. Or was he shivering because of blood loss?

He wasn't going to be able to hold out much longer. If he allowed them to continue to carve him up, it wouldn't matter if he survived this initial assault. He would be exsanguinated long before he reached medical attention.

A scream threatened to explode from his chest. It felt like each individual layer of his skin was being slowly peeled away. He was cold. He was terrified. And the torture was just too great.

His mouth opened in anticipation of the cry he could no longer contain.

Tasker had just crested the precipice of the fortification when he heard the *shush* of wet branches behind him. Whirling, gun at his shoulder, he saw a silhouette beside the wide trunk of a kapok, partially hidden by the buttress roots. He squeezed off a shot just as the shadow ducked behind the trunk. The bullet tore out a chunk of wood and sent splinters flying. Whatever was out there was faster than he was.

More rustling noises from the other side of the path. They were growing increasingly aggressive.

The time had come to put the fear of God into them.

He swung the barrel across the wall of foliage, peppering it with a barrage of bullets that shredded leaves and pounded trunks.

Hopefully, that would buy him a decent head start.

A cracking sound echoed from the outside world, drowning out the scream that erupted from Galen's lips. It wasn't thunder, but rather what sounded like a boulder breaking loose from the granite cliff above them.

The creatures around him stiffened and craned their heads toward the tunnel and the waterfall beyond.

More cracking. Louder. Faster. A rhythmic *rata-tat-tat*.

Automatic rifle fire.

Galen risked a slight tilt of his head to glance behind him. None of the creatures so much as looked in his direction. All eyes were focused away from him, toward the stone passage.

Without the slightest sound of communication, the raptors all bolted as one. Bodies collided. They snapped and kicked at each other. Long legs churned up feathers from the floor, which the scrum refreshed with new ones. They trampled the diminished flames, leaving Galen with just one final, fleeting impression of their long feathered tails before the darkness became complete once again.

Tasker had just turned to lunge down the slope of broken bricks when more movement caught his attention.

Shadows. Several of them.

Emerging from a black orifice behind the waterfall at a rapid click.

Galen held his breath and listened. All he could hear was their labored breathing. No tread on feathers. Not a single shriek.

The creatures were gone.

The relief was so great that he moaned aloud. His shoulders shook as the sobs he had held at bay for so long racked through him. He whimpered and ran his shaking palms over the tatters of his clothes and the stinging lacerations beneath them.

He tried to sit up and a warm rush of blood seeped to the surface from what felt like every inch of his body.

A hand closed around his wrist and jerked him to his feet. He cried out and stumbled forward. His legs were so weak he could barely stand and his head swam from the loss of blood.

"We have to hurry!" Merritt snapped. The pilot stared at him through the darkness with such intensity that Galen positively felt it. "We don't know how much time we have. They could return at any second." He spun Galen around and shoved him toward the exit from behind. "Run!"

Galen summoned every last iota of strength he could muster and sprinted into the darkness toward where the creatures had just vanished.

Chapter Thirteen

I

Andes Mountains, Peru
October 30th
11:09 p.m. PET

There was just enough definition to the dark silhouettes for Tasker to know he was in big trouble. Lithe bodies sprinting close to the ground. Slender necks and tails held parallel to the rock ledge. Spindly legs with absurdly long strides. He had already turned to run by the time he heard the first *skree*.

Tasker scrambled back up the slick slope of crumbled bricks, shoving with his feet and grabbing the loose stones with his hands. He risked a glance back over his shoulder. They were closing fast. Too fast. Several of them leaped down from the cliff and slipped sideways in the mud. Once they regained traction, they launched themselves along the northern wall of the fortress into the dwindling torchlight. He tried to formulate a plan on the fly. Another fifty yards and they would overcome him. His best chance was to reach one of the stone huts. He could take his stand with his back against the rounded rear wall where he could cover the lone entrance. But if they could jump high enough or somehow scale the outer walls, he was screwed.

He looked ahead again as he reached the crumbled summit, searching for the nearest ring of stones, and nearly ran straight into a man who appeared from nowhere. The rain shimmered on the black paint covering the man's scarred chest and face. A wicked smile filled with sharpened teeth. Iridescent feathers braided into long black hair, hanging from his earlobes. Two more natives materialized from the jungle behind the first.

A blur of motion. The man's arm lashed out like a striking rattler.

Tasker managed to squeeze off a single shot that grazed the native's shoulder. He registered pain in the side of his neck at the same time that warmth flooded down over his chest. The rifle fell from his grasp, freeing both of his hands to grapple with the object lodged in his throat. His mouth filled with blood, through which he could draw no breath. He sputtered and coughed as he jerked at what felt like a handle wedged against his clavicle. With a slurping sound, he yanked the object out of his flesh and collapsed to his knees. His blood dripped from a hooked talon that had been affixed to a sanded piece of wood, similar to the implement farmers used to haul baled hay.

The painted man knelt in front of him and tipped up his chin so that their eyes met. Rage and hatred radiated from the man, who snarled, grabbed fistfuls of Tasker's jacket, and lifted him back to his feet.

Avian shrieks echoed from the mountainside.

His vision began to darken as his lifeblood fled him. A cool, tingling sensation spread throughout his body. He could no longer feel his hands, which pawed at the man's slippery chest. His feet dangled uselessly several inches above the ground.

He tried to speak, to plead for mercy, but only managed a gurgle through the blood.

A *skree* pierced the confusion and understanding dawned.

The two other natives retreated into the forest and vanished, leaving only the man who held him suspended over the rubble.

Tasker read his fate in the man's eyes.

With a growl, the native shoved him backward over the crest of the hill.

For a moment, he felt weightless as he fell through the air.

And then his world became a lesson in pain.

II

11:10 p.m.

Merritt inhaled the fresh air as he slipped past Galen into the spray of water. He stepped out from behind the waterfall and eased along the rock ledge, which was barely wide enough to accommodate his feet. He leaned back against the cliff and inched sideways. The cries of the creatures reverberated through the valley from where he could see their dark forms racing up the fallen section of the northern wall. Two men stood on the precipice, holding each other close as though in an intimate embrace. A heartbeat later, one of them was flying out over the nothingness. The advancing creatures leapt toward the falling man, colliding with him in midair and tumbling down the mound of bricks in a maelstrom of slashing claws and glinting teeth. An arm flopped several feet away from the melee. The ferocity with which they tore the man apart was terrifying. He had never seen anything like it. In a matter of seconds, there would be nothing left of the carcass.

Their window of opportunity was rapidly closing. The creatures would only be distracted for so much longer, and he couldn't afford to take the chance that their primal bloodlust would be sated.

The man above the fracas looked directly at him before turning away and merging with the forest, the black paint blending into the shadows.

"Hurry!" Merritt called back to Galen and Sam, who shuffled along the ledge behind him.

Below, the water crashed onto the rocks with the sound of thunder. The mist and white spray made it impossible to tell how far down the river might be, but if they slipped, they would surely be killed on the breakers. Ahead, the creatures savaged the man's remains no more than fifty yards away from where their treacherous path let out onto flat ground. They wouldn't have a prayer of getting past the flock, nor would they be able to survive a leap into the rapids from here. There was no possible way they could scale the fortification and sneak unnoticed into the fortress, and turning around to seek refuge in the lair of the beasts was suicide. He was out of incendiary grenades and didn't have a single bullet left for the rifle he had already abandoned in the cave anyway. That left only one possible means of escape.

They were going to have to follow the edge of the high bank toward the creatures in hopes of distancing themselves far enough from the rocks to risk leaping down into the river. If they could keep from drowning, they might be able to reach the shore downstream and pull themselves onto land. If not, at least he had a pretty good idea where their bloated corpses would end up.

As soon as there was solid ground below him, he jumped down into the mud. He barely managed to stay on his feet. The impact made every cut on his skin issue fresh blood. It felt as though they had pulled even wider, but there was no time to indulge the pain. Through the fracas of feathered bodies, he could already see sections of bare white bone. The carcass was running out of flesh to hold the attention of the monsters, which threw their heads back and choked down the bloody morsels with staggering speed.

He glanced back and grabbed Sam's hand as she splashed down into the muck.

Galen fell to all fours in the mire right behind her and fought to right himself again.

"Don't let go of my hand!" Merritt said. "Whatever happens, just hold on."

He urged her forward, slipping while simultaneously helping her maintain her balance. They needed to shoot for another dozen yards and hope that would be far enough to clear the worst of the rocks.

A *skree* summoned his attention back to the congregation of blood-soaked creatures. One of them had turned in their direction. Merritt caught a flash of eyeshine before it opened its mouth and issued a horrible cry. Other sets of eyes snapped in their direction, snouts dripping with blood and clots of flesh.

They weren't going to make it.

III

11:12 p.m.

Sam's heart nearly stopped when the lead raptor shrieked once more, spurring the entire pack to motion.

It was too soon.

Merritt tugged her to the side toward where the river rumbled at the bottom of the steep embankment. She couldn't even see the water from this angle, only the hint of the far side of the trench through the mist. Was this the last thing Hunter had seen before his death too?

A glance to her right. The creatures were sprinting toward them, closing the gap far too quickly. Another ten yards and the flock would be upon them.

She pushed herself to catch up with Merritt, and together they raced to the edge.

Shrieks filled the night, drowning out all other sounds, even her scream as she and Merritt reached the cliff and leaped out into the air over the rapids. They fell through the smothering mist for an interminable second before they impacted with the water. Her body stiffened against the cold and the current dragged her deeper. She tumbled over sharp rocks that tore at her clothes and skin on the riverbed.

Her only thought was to hold on to Merritt's hand.

The pressure increased in her lungs and she opened her eyes.

All she could see was darkness.

IV

11:13 p.m.

Galen watched Sam and Merritt disappear into the cloud mere feet ahead of him. He didn't have to look back to know that the flock was right on his heels. Their cries were so close they were deafening.

Two more strides.

The splash below cleared a section of the mist. It was a fifteen-foot drop to the river, but fortunately, no sharp crests of stone broke the surface. He couldn't see the others. The river was flowing so fast that they could be half a mile away by now.

One more stride.

A shriek right behind his head.

Galen dove into the mist toward the grumbling rapids. With a deep breath, he braced for impact with the frigid water.

Bolts of searing pain in the backs of his legs.

The snap of a bear trap over his right flank.

Teeth lanced through flesh, jerking, tearing.

He cartwheeled through the air, no longer certain of which way was up.

A ribbon of blood unspooled from his side.

He opened his mouth to scream—

The force of the weight on his back knocked the wind out him when they struck the unforgiving surface of the river. It returned with a lungful of water.

Talons slashed.

Teeth ripped.

Panic preceded the jolt when he struck the rocky bottom.

V

11:14 p.m.

Merritt had surfaced a full twenty yards downstream, sputtering and gasping, and had turned back just in time to see Galen's shadow slice through the cloud behind him. And then the creature's. There had been no time to shout a warning. Legs outstretched, claws spread wide, it had struck him like an eagle snatching a leaping trout with a ferocious *skree*. Bodies intertwined, they had tumbled into the river with an enormous splash.

Several more shadows had materialized on the edge of the high bank a moment later, lowering their necks, spreading their jaws, and shrieking their indignation at their prey's escape. They had paused at the brink, then bolted after them along the muddy shore.

Sam still clung to his hand, her fingers icicles against his skin. She coughed out a flume of water and floated beside him, unable to look away from the point where Galen and the raptor had disappeared.

The rapids rose and fell, whisking them downstream amid a mess of broken branches and tangled roots. They barely managed to keep their heads above the water as they waited for Galen to resurface, praying that he would. At the mercy of the current, the bank sped past, but the silhouettes kept pace.

Their cries filled the valley.

A splash upstream and the feathered crown of a head breached the surface. Its scaled snout opened around a shriek as it floundered toward the shore, where it scrabbled against the slick slope. Rear talons dug for purchase and tiny arms clawed, but it was unable to gain any leverage. Its serpentine neck thrashed and its jaws snapped uselessly at the air. Another cry and it dropped under the waves again with a flash of feathers.

"I don't see Galen," Sam said. She coughed out another mouthful of water.

Merritt shook his head. He didn't either. The dark river made it impossible to see into the water. The churning whitecaps filled the air with spray, only to be beaten down by the siege of raindrops.

He glanced toward the ground above them. The creatures still paralleled their downstream progress.

When he looked back, he caught a glimpse of a swatch of fabric and tried to swim against the current with one arm while refusing to relinquish Sam's hand from the other. As soon as he was close enough, he grabbed the cloth and pulled it toward him. Galen floated facedown, his arms and legs limp beneath him. Merritt rolled him over and tried to hold the birdman's head above the water even as the current attempted to suck them all under.

Galen made no attempt to gasp for air.

Merritt looked to either side. The bank was too steep to drag Galen onto solid ground where he could try to resuscitate him. And even were he able, the creatures would be waiting.

Galen's eyelids were fixed partially open. In the gap under the lids, Merritt could see the blood-streaked whites and the lower crescents of the irises. Galen's mouth hung open. There was standing fluid behind his tongue.

Merritt pressed his fingertips against the side of Galen's neck.

There was no pulse.

He had to readjust his grip, and in the process felt the warmth diffusing out into the water from above Galen's hip. Following it with his fingers, he stuck his hand into a gaping wound lined by fragments of shattered ribs and filled with spongy viscera. A rope of small bowel had unfolded through the wide gash and slithered through the water behind them.

There was nothing they could do.

Galen was gone.

Merritt had been too distracted to notice the roaring sound, which grew louder and louder by the second. He didn't have to turn downriver to know what it meant.

He shoved away from Galen's corpse and pulled Sam closer.

"Hold on to me as tight as you can. Don't let go."

"What—?"

He silenced her with a kiss and wrapped his arms around her. Twisting his fists into the back of her jacket, he leaned his cheek against hers and whispered into her ear.

"Don't you dare let go."

Her arms tightened around his back.

The roar escalated to the point that he barely heard her scream right next to his ear.

Rocks prodded their feet.

The current increased.

He watched the creatures skid to an abrupt halt on a limestone overhang to his left, beyond which he could see only mist clinging to the upper canopy of the jungle.

The world fell away from under them as they plummeted through the air in a weightless cascade of water.

Galen's body fired from the top of the waterfall above them, appendages flopping lifelessly.

The raptors leaned over the edge and cried after them through fierce rows of sharp teeth.

Merritt clung to Sam with everything he had, took a deep breath, and closed his eyes.

A *skree* cut through the roar, and darkness welcomed them into the crashing waves and the waiting arms of oblivion.

Chapter Fourteen

I

Lima, Peru
*October 31*st
3:02 a.m. PET

The French balcony doors opened inward with a muffled click. Two men stepped in from the rain, soles squeaking ever so softly on the tiled floor. Dressed in black from head to toe, they became one with the darkness inside the house. Only the tan skin around their narrowed eyes was visible through the holes in their ski masks, their irises black coals.

A flash of lightning through the doors behind them glinted from the pistols they held pressed to their thighs.

Thunder grumbled as they passed through the formal living room. When it faded, there was only the timpani of raindrops on the ceramic-tiled roof.

The man was supposed to be expecting them. There should have been a light on somewhere in the house, yet even the foyer had been dark through the front windows. Of course, the man had also expected them to ring the bell, not pick the lock and sneak in through the back.

So where was he?

They passed from one room to the next. The kitchen was deserted, the pantry empty. Only the dining room showed signs of recent habitation: a broken bottle on the floor and a demolished cell phone on the table next to a glass ashtray brimming with ashes. They followed the hallway past a bathroom and a vacant guest bedroom to the open door at the end of the corridor.

The scent of cordite ushered them into a study that contained a much less pleasant aroma.

A desk chair lay toppled on its side, its occupant sprawled on the ground. The hardwood floor was sticky with a black amoeba of blood, centered around the man's head, the back of which was a ruined crater of bone fragments and singed hair. Gray matter bloomed through the hole, a sickly flower of convolutions.

Both men looked at the wall to their right, where spatters of blood and brain chunks surrounded a deep hole in the cracked plaster.

The man had saved them a good deal of effort, but he had also robbed them of the little bit of enjoyment they were ever allowed to derive from their work.

Their employer wanted the golden artifact. He was just unwilling to pay such an exorbitant cost for its acquisition. Granted, he would have easily been able to turn around and sell it for twice what he paid, but why narrow the margin if he didn't absolutely have to? Their services came at a fraction of that cost, and their employer did have a reputation to uphold after all.

Besides, the man who had approached them had been an amateur. A greedy little Anglo.

They approached the corpse. The man clearly wore the headdress. Gold glimmered under his face, and the strap he had used to hold it in place was still around the back below the self-inflicted wound. They rolled him over with gloved hands and stared down at the sad sack of flesh.

The man's mouth hung open. His pupils were fixed and dilated. Trails of dried blood coiled around his eyebrows and nose. One of his cheeks was crusted with it from lying in the puddle. And the golden headdress covering his forehead—

"Son of a bitch," the man said in Korean. "It's useless to us now."

The pounded gold was scorched and warped around the hole where the bullet had entered just underneath the inset chrysocolla eyes. There was no way they would be able to sell an ancient artifact scarred by a bullet hole. The best they could hope for now was to melt it down and sell it as bullion for next to nothing.

And considering it was covered in blood…

They had been double-crossed in the act of double-crossing, which was probably what they should have expected from the start, especially knowing that the dead man at their feet was an American politician.

Chapter Fifteen

I

Andes Mountains, Peru
October 31ˢᵗ
6:19 a.m. PET

Blackness bled into a pale red glare through her eyelids, and consciousness returned with a fit of shivers. Sam struggled to open her eyes, but barely managed a crack through which she saw glistening mud and flattened grasses. Her right arm was pinned beneath her in the muck. The current tugged at her legs. She retched and vomited a wash of vile fluids into a puddle against the side of her face and nose. Pain pierced through the fugue and she started to cry.

She pushed herself up to all fours on shaking arms, filthy strands of hair hanging over her face, and crawled out of the stream onto the bank. With a groan, she rolled over onto her rear end and propped herself up on her elbows.

The storm had finally abated. Droplets still fell from the dense canopy, glimmering with the pink light of dawn. Through the branches she could see a sliver of blue sky.

How long had she been unconscious? The last thing she remembered was going over the falls and then a sudden rush of darkness when she hit the water. How far had she traveled?

She gasped and bolted upright.

Where was Merritt?

She fought through the pain to stand, swaying as though acted upon by a ferocious gale that only she could feel.

"Merritt?" she whimpered.

She stumbled along the shoreline through waterlogged ferns and tangles of reeds. Nothing looked familiar. It could have been any section of the jungle, every section.

"Merritt!" she screamed.

Several times, she tripped and fell, but managed to rise to her feet again. She screamed her throat raw as she followed the river, peering frantically through groves of trees connected by vines and blooming with epiphytes, scouring the surface of the water for any sign of a body pinned against a rock or crumpled near the bank.

"Merritt!"

Sam crashed through a wall of shrubs and clapped her hand over her mouth.

There was a body, facedown on the muddy bank in a clump of cattails. She ran toward it, tears streaming from her eyes, and fell to her knees beside its hip.

She reached toward it, then recoiled. A sob made her whole body shudder. Gathering her courage, she slid her trembling hands under its shoulder and rolled it onto its side.

Galen stared back at her, his face a mask of mud, his mouth packed with sludge.

She jerked her hands away and he fell back onto his chest.

Rocking back, she screamed up into the sky.

"What's all the commotion about?"

She turned toward the sound of the voice. Merritt leaned against the broad trunk of a Brazil nut tree, soaked to the bone, clothes in tatters. He appeared one step shy of death.

He offered that cocky, lopsided smile.

Sam leapt up from the ground and ran to him. She threw herself into his arms so hard she nearly knocked both of them down.

"I thought you were…Galen…" she stammered.

An avian shriek from above them.

They both flinched as a dark shape swooped through the branches and alighted on the bank.

A tall bird with a broad black body and a ring of white feathers around its bald head hopped across the mud and up onto Galen's prone form. The fringe of rubbery flesh above its ivory beak jiggled.

It seemed a fitting tribute, to in death continue the work to which Galen had devoted his life.

II

9:49a.m.

They followed the river to its terminus, where it fed the placid lake upon the shore of which they had camped only the night before last. That felt like years ago now. Their trail had been easy enough to find from there. After several hours of shuffling through the oppressive jungle, the pangs of hunger had reached a level that surpassed even the sheer exhaustion, but both feared that once they stopped walking, they might never be able to start again. Already their reserves of adrenaline were running dangerously low.

The heat and humidity were insufferable, and the gashes all over their bodies attracted whining clouds of mosquitoes and black flies. Occasional cries from the birds of prey circling out of sight above the canopy were a constant reminder of what the eternal jungle thought about their odds of survival. They were nearly ready to collapse when they stumbled into a small clearing.

An alpaca stood twenty paces away, staring directly at them, contentedly chewing from side to side. Its long gray fur was tangled and knitted with briars. A rope hung from its neck, at the distant end of which a painted man walked through the knee-high ferns. He stopped, looked in their direction, and froze. Surprise registered on his face. He lowered his brow and scrutinized them as though unable to believe his eyes.

Merritt recognized him as the same man who had initially led them to the village, although this time he grazed a different animal.

The man took a hesitant step toward them, stopped, then cautiously took another. After several minutes, he finally reached them. The alpaca hovered at his side, indifferently gnawing on a tuft of grass, while the man inspected them more closely. He fingered the cuts on Merritt's arms, then looked deep into his eyes. A step to the side, and he repeated the process with Sam.

Merritt returned the favor and studied the man, whose skin was scarred under the paint in a similar manner to how Merritt imagined his soon would be. Galen had been right about how the natives had survived the creatures through the centuries. He and Sam owed the birdman their lives.

After a long pause, the native's face split into a wide grin brimming with sharpened teeth, and he squeezed each of them on the shoulder in turn. He inclined his head toward the path on the other side of the clearing, and, with a tug on the rope, led the alpaca back toward the village.

The man made a sound that Merritt could have sworn was laughter as they continued along the overgrown path behind him.

Sam still clung to his hand, though with nowhere near the same desperation she had earlier. Merritt sensed it, too. He no longer felt the aura of threat emanating from the man, as though they had passed some sort of trial in his eyes.

"Viracocha. Kakulcán. Quetzalcoatl," Sam said. "All of the ancient Mesoamerican tribes knew about these creatures and worshipped them. And the Maya and Aztec? They simply vanished from the face of the earth. Is it possible that they angered their gods, and were slaughtered? Is that how the remaining Chachapoya have managed to survive for so long in total isolation? By forging some sort of symbiotic relationship?"

A steep hill rose to their left, surrounded by a ring of stone pedestals, their torches now extinguished.

The voices of children called from ahead, shouting, giggling.

They rounded the side of the buried alpaca pen and stepped into the clearing beyond. The iron gate stood open, and dozens of tanned children ran and tumbled in the herd's midst. A young boy who'd been trying to hang from the wool under an alpaca's belly caught sight of them. He rose, pointed a finger at them, and shouted back over his shoulder to his friends. They all stopped playing to stare at Merritt and Sam before sprinting away in the opposite direction.

The man glanced back at them and smiled, obviously amused.

After ten more minutes, Merritt glimpsed the tall thatch roofs rising into the trees and saw the faint outline of the fortress walls. The low chatter of voices reached his ears, but he couldn't make out the words. Sam's hand tightened over his. The path wended around a copse of ceibas until it came within clear view of the towering fortifications.

A group of natives had gathered outside the open stone gate in anticipation of their arrival. Their voices dropped to whispers, and a nervous energy radiated from them.

The older man Merritt assumed to be the chief separated from the others and strode forward. A topless woman trailed at his hip, holding a bowl in her cupped hands. The chief spoke briefly with the alpaca herder. Both stared and gestured at the strangers, until finally their guide lowered his head and led the alpaca away from the trail.

Teeth bared, the chief stepped forward and glared at Merritt, who matched the intensity of his gaze for nearly a full minute. The chief looked him up and down, and then did the same to Sam. He probed Merritt's shredded clothing, and prodded the lacerations hard enough to draw fresh blood. His eyes again rose to meet Merritt's, and in their locked stare, an understanding passed between them. With a subtle nod, the older man turned and walked back into the crowd toward the fortress.

The woman with the bowl approached, scooped her first two fingers into its contents, and pulled out a glob of glistening black sludge. She raised her hand to Merritt's face and wiped it onto his cheek. The sting of the lacerations started to fade immediately.

The chief shouldered his way through the gathering of curious, excited, and frightened faces, toward the home they had managed to hide from the outside world for countless generations.

Sam positively beamed at the prospect of studying these people in the flesh, of living among them and learning everything she had once only been able to imagine. And that smile was more than enough to convince Merritt that there was nowhere on the planet he'd rather be than by her side.

Sam leaned closer and rested her head against his shoulder. She too recognized the gravity of what had passed between the two men, unvoiced pledges and silent promises.

The chief had entrusted them with the fate of his people. In sparing their lives, he risked possible discovery and exploitation by the outside world. In welcoming them into the fold, he had potentially damned his entire tribe.

Merritt watched the old man disappear through the gate as the woman smeared black paint all over his face. He understood all too well, and would never betray the secret of their existence.

After all, he knew how it felt to want to remain hidden.

He turned to face Sam, stared into her stunning blue eyes, and saw both those of the woman he had failed and the one he had saved. In that moment, he laid the ghost of his past to rest and welcomed a future as infinite as the most perfect blue sky.

MICHAEL McBRIDE

is the bestselling author of *Ancient Enemy*, *Bloodletting*, *Fearful Symmetry*, *Innocents Lost*, *Sunblind*, *The Coyote*, and *Vector Borne*. His novella *Snowblind* won the 2012 DarkFuse Readers Choice Award and received honorable mention in *The Best Horror of the Year*. He lives in Avalanche Territory with his wife and kids.

To explore the author's other works, please visit
www.michaelmcbride.net.

Made in the USA
Middletown, DE
16 June 2021

42417935R00246